Prais
BLACK T

"*Black Tide Son* was impossible for me to put down.
The second installment in The Winter Sea series does not disappoint,
expanding the chilly, windswept world of its predecessor with more
dangerous enemies, intrigue, and a healthy dose of magic—not to
mention a romance that had me on the edge of my seat.
I will devour every single book H.M. Long writes."
Genevieve Gornichec, author of *The Witch's Heart*

"Swashbuckling adventure, magic and a slow-burn
romance—I loved returning to this icy, watery world."
Kell Woods, author of *After the Forest*

"Intrigue and a surreal, highly imaginative magic system weave together
to form the base for a twisting plot filled with heart-pounding action and
deep-seated mysteries. Beneath the swashbuckling surface of the tale,
Long includes a thoughtful exploration of the nature of love, from fraught
familial bonds to a sweet—but fierce—romance that will make readers
swoon. Readers will be on the edge of their seats from page one."
M.J. Kuhn, author of *Among Thieves*

"*Black Tide Son* is everything I look for in a sequel; expansive lore,
amped up adventure, and fantastic characters. Thrilled
to take another voyage with this crew."
Christopher Irvin, author of *Ragged*

"A nonstop adventure packed with daring escapes and high stakes
on the high seas—and a gripping tale of betrayal and forgiveness
between brothers. *Black Tide Son* is half piratical fantasy,
half familial intrigue, and all impossible to put down."
Allison Epstein, author of *Let the Dead Bury the Dead*

Praise for
DARK WATER DAUGHTER

"A wonderful adventure! *Dark Water Daughter* swept me to the
high seas with its captivating story, rich original lore, fascinating
characters, and slow-burn romance. Immersive from start
till end, this is a hard one to put down."
Sue Lynn Tan, *Sunday Times* bestselling author of
Daughter of the Moon Goddess

"Intricately crafted, stunningly unique, and so vivid you can almost
taste the frigid air of the Winter Sea, *Dark Water Daughter* is my
favorite H.M. Long book yet."
Genevieve Gornichec, author of *The Witch's Heart*

"*Dark Water Daughter* is a unique and breath-taking slice of high seas
fantasy—H. M. Long gives us deliciously complex characters to root for
and a world full of surprises. I didn't know I needed these fantasy pirates
and their freezing ocean until they sailed into my life. Enormous fun!"
Jen Williams, award-winning author of The Winnowing Flame trilogy

"*Dark Water Daughter* is a compelling, propulsive adventure that
serves as a spectacular start to Long's new series. The vast world and
intriguing lore are complex in a way that feels effortless; it might just
be Long's best work yet. I was utterly engrossed."
M.K. Lobb, author of *Seven Faceless Saints*

"Outstanding naval fantasy; *Robin Hobb* meets
Master and Commander."
Peter McLean, author of *Priest of Bones*

Black Tide Son

H. M. Long

TITAN BOOKS

Black Tide Son
Print edition ISBN: 9781803362625
E-book edition ISBN: 9781803362632

Published by Titan Books
A division of Titan Publishing Group Ltd
144 Southwark Street, London SE1 0UP
www.titanbooks.com

First edition: July 2024
10 9 8 7 6 5 4 3 2 1

A CIP catalogue record for this title is available
from the British Library.

Printed and bound in Great Britain by CPI Group (UK) Ltd,
Croydon CR0 4YY.

For Eric: a much better brother than Benedict

Ice Shelf

Heston

Us

Kalsank

The Cape

Northern
Mereish
Isles

The Storm Wall

Aeadine

Tithe

Ghistwold

Whallum

Aeadine
Anchorage

aase

Ostchen

Mere

N

MERE—*Mere encompasses both the chief island of the Mereish peoples, south of Aeadine and east of the Cape, as well as the various other islands within their control: the Mereish North Isles and the Mereish South Isles, though rule of the latter has degraded in recent centuries and now resides primarily in the hands of pirates. The Mereish are well known for dabbling in strange magics, the secrets and traditions of which they guard with religious fervor. They possess one of the greatest naval forces upon the Winter Sea and are close allies with the Cape, leading these more peaceful neighbors into frequent war with Aeadine. See* also MEREISH, MEREISH NORTHERN ISLES, MEREISH SOUTHERN ISLES, MEREISH-CAPESH ALLIANCE.

—FROM THE WORDBOOK ALPHABETICA: A NEW
WORDBOOK OF THE AEADINES

ONE

The Demete

SAMUEL

The hush that followed the wind was portentous and thick with drifting smoke. The guns fell quiet in their cradles and the rush of water against the hull ebbed as *Hart* slowed, nosing alongside his drifting prize.

No roar of victory came from the dozens of armed men and women crowding the waist of my ship. Neither I nor their former captain had been a miser for discipline, so their mutters were low, their muskets primed but at ease. Nor did I hear defiant or vengeful cries from the pirates on our prize's deck, though they were slung about with pistols, cutlasses and machetes, and marksmen hung in their rigging. Outnumbered, outgunned and exhausted from two days' pursuit, the flag flying from their mainmast was white, crosshatched with red—not a flag of surrender, but of parley.

Their captain stood on the quarterdeck with two helmsmen, who cradled muskets and held their posts with resentment in their eyes.

She called in accented Aeadine, "I am flattered you risk so much for my head, Aead," as she came forward to lean on the rail, her voice easily carrying the dozen yards of docile waves between our ships. Her greying hair was braided, its length tied by a black silk ribbon, and she wore a felted, cocked hat with a blue overcoat faded to spruce. Her eyes were rimmed with black against the usual glare of sun off snow and ice and Winter Sea.

The pirate continued with feigned apprehension, "Bringing the Fleetbreaker's daughter into Mereish waters?" She gestured to the woman beside me, in her pale-blue calico skirts and oversized wool coat.

Mary Firth, daughter of the infamous Stormsinger known as the Fleetbreaker, had her arms crossed over her chest, but at this she raised one hand a margin and fluttered her fingers in a wave. She was tall and dark haired, her head uncovered to the wind in a way that no mother on the Winter Sea would condone.

"She knows who I am?" Mary squinted at our would-be captive, speaking quietly to me. "We may soon be notorious, Sam."

"Is that not our intention?" I murmured back. "If you wanted obscurity, you should have gone south with your mother."

Mary hid a smile and called over the water in her rounded, inland accent. "Mereish waters, you say? I see nothing but fog. Though, we've a Letter of Marque from the Usti queen and the right to be wherever we see fit."

The pirate captain snorted. "The fog that you called yourself, witch. And letters can burn. Captain, let us resolve this before we have a patrol on our heads."

"Very well. Ophalia Monna." I drew up to the quarterdeck rail and faced the other captain over the stretch of sea. Mary stayed where she was. "I am Captain Samuel Rosser of *Hart*, privateer under commission of the Usti Crown. Surrender yourself. You are taking on water, you have no Stormsinger, and falling into the hands of your countrymen will be your death. Come with me back to Hesten and you will face fair trial under the Usti for your crimes against their ships. Or we can wait here, becalmed, until a patrol sets to blowing us both out of the water."

The pirate replied, "Would you perhaps be related to a Benedict Rosser?"

There was no question in her voice. She knew who Mary was. She knew who I was. And evidently, she knew something of my brother, too.

A whisper of premonition swept over me, blurring the edges of the world—the lines of the rails and rigging, the masts and lifeless sails, the waves and Monna's fixed gaze. Then my fingers brushed the long, oval coin in my pocket, and the whisper faded. The world took on clear edges again, and I realized Mary had drawn up to my shoulder.

"Someone is coming," she murmured. "Ghisten ships."

I cursed. The fog shrouded us, but it also limited what we could see of the world around us. By natural means, at least.

"Can you delay them?" I asked, equally low.

Mary gave a nod and stepped back. I heard the smooth intake of her breath, then the first notes of a song slipped into the still air. They were low and melancholy, drawing in the hushed solemnity of the sea and returning it in sympathetic kind.

"There is a voice among the trees, that mingles with the groaning oak, that mingles with the stormy breeze..."

The wind stirred and damp air prickled across my cheeks. Monna lifted her chin, sensing the change at the same time as one of her crewmen murmured in her ear.

"We will surrender," Monna decided. "No more storms, guns or bloodshed. I will peacefully come aboard, then I will tell you how I met your twin in the belly of a Mereish frigate."

Monna sat at the small table in my cabin, fishing a pipe and pouch from her pocket. Ice rimmed each small windowpane, further obscuring our foggy view of open sea and pursuing ships beyond. It was cold; the iron-girded woodstove had been smothered for action and not yet rekindled. But at least we were out of the wind.

Distantly, I heard Mary's song above deck, accompanied by the rumble of footfalls and the piping of the bosun's whistle. Her witchwind was up and we were well on our way back to safer waters, with Monna's ship in convoy.

"I am surprised they came upon us so quickly," Monna commented as she stuffed the pipe. "But it is a time for surprises. I also did not expect you to chase me beyond Aeadine waters, yet here we are. May I?"

I nodded and the pirate leaned in to steal a taper and flame from the lantern suspended low over the table. Meanwhile, I shed my outer coat and sat across from her, leaving my cutlass and pistols in place.

Her mention of my brother itched the back of my mind, dredging up question after question. I held my tongue for now, sifting through tactics.

Monna was at least thirty years my senior, and, judging by her ease and the weathered condition of her light-brown skin, she had been at sea for longer than that. She had also evaded capture more than a dozen times and showed no sign of fear or tension—save the methodical way she puffed on her pipe, one finger tapping on the table. Dusky, rich smoke drifted up towards the hefty beams above.

"My commission is from the Usti, not Aeadine," I reminded her. "Neutral in the conflict between our peoples. I have the papers to prove it. You, a hunted brigand, are in far more danger from your people than I am."

Monna grinned around the pipe bit and relaxed in her chair. "As I said, papers may be burned, young captain. Then we have only our word to protect us: the word of pirates and privateers. And what is that worth to the mighty navies?"

"Very little," I acknowledged. "Now, you mentioned my brother."

"Yes. It is uncanny, how you two are alike. Mirror twins?"

I nodded, carefully stowing all emotion. "You saw him aboard a Mereish frigate?"

"His ship was wrecked at Eldona Island. That happens to be my winter harbor, and the locals pay well for my protection. The tides have been rather high; your brother's ship struck our hidden reef and was dashed to pieces. What was I to do but investigate? Pity the Navy came upon us, and I found myself a prisoner alongside your brother."

Concealed under the table, I unclenched my fist and stretched it across my thigh. The shock of such loss of life was an old one, dulled with familiarity, but still present. A vessel as large as Benedict's had nearly a thousand men and women aboard, many of whom I knew from my own naval days before I had resigned my commission in the face of rumors and disgrace.

"How many of his crew survived?" I asked.

"All the boats were gone," Monna replied, her tone losing a little of its uncaring mildness. She was not impassive to the deaths of fellow seafarers either, regardless of their nationality. "I cannot say what befell them. There were many dead. Some made it to shore and escaped inland, I am sure."

"Mean comfort."

She nodded, exhaling twin swirls of smoke through her nostrils.

"Was my brother given parole? Was there any mention of ransom?"

"All I know is where the ship that took him was bound. I am happy to tell you, in return for my freedom."

"If I believe you."

"Your brother spoke of a child dependent upon him, playing upon our captor's sympathies. Josephine, he called her. And he was a Magni, though I assume that is common knowledge. He compelled the guards to release us, though there was an unfortunate mix-up with the keys, and only I managed to escape."

At the last she smiled, flat and feline, and I had no doubt as to the cause of that confusion.

"In return for my freedom," the pirate repeated, "I am more than happy to tell you where your brother was headed. Perhaps you can even rescue him before the Mereish shoot him like a mad dog."

A sea of possibility spread before me, and with it, a new course. I could barter with this pirate, choose not to hand her over to the Usti as I was being paid to do, and try to save my brother. I might even succeed. But my crew expected payment, deserved it, and not every tongue could be trusted not to wag even if I paid them off myself. Furthermore, in my last report I had noted how close I was to capturing the pirate. An Usti ship likely already waited at Tithe to take her home and give me my next task.

Mary was another factor. Her contract was upheld by the Usti Crown and tied to my commission. Without it, Mary would once again be little more than a commodity in the eyes of every captain on the Winter Sea. As it was, we walked a fine line every time we were in port, every time we crossed paths with another ship.

I sat still for a long moment then smiled, small and grim and a little melancholy. "It is a pity, then, that I do not care whether my brother lives or dies. Make peace with your saints, Captain Monna. You have nothing I want."

THE MAGNI—*One of the three primary varieties of mage, Magni control the mind and actions of others through exertion of their own, greater will. Though commonly perceived as innately hostile and dangerous, use of a Magni's power need not lead to abuse or degradation. It can also be used to empower, encourage and spur a subject, to calm, alleviate pain and turn the wayward back from destructive acts.*

As in other classifications of mage, the intensity of a Magni's power varies from mage to mage. The degree of their influence will also depend on the wit and will of their intended subject, and any interventions (for good or ill) performed to enhance the Magni's power beyond natural-born ability.

—FROM A DEFINITIVE STUDY OF THE BLESSED: MAGES AND MAGECRAFT OF THE MEREISH ISLES, *TRANSLATED FROM THE MEREISH BY SAMUEL I. ROSSER*

TWO

The Other

MARY

I slipped into the silent dark of the main cabin. At the stern, a pair of windows diffused evening light, their thick panes hedged with frost. Between them was a door to a long, narrow balcony, which I could see through the foggy glass was crusted with ice and rimed with snow. The stove in its iron cradle was unlit, shedding no light or heat, and the air was painfully cold. Spring might be coming on land, but, out here on the waves, the wind still tasted of deep winter.

Samuel knelt on the floor of the cabin, stripped to his shirt. His coat and waistcoat were neatly folded over the back of a chair, lightly swaying with the roll of the ship. His hands rested on his thighs, knuckles white, and his oval coin was wedged into a crack between the boards in front of him.

He didn't rouse as I closed the door, looking straight ahead with open, unseeing eyes.

Unease wound through me. This sight was common enough— Samuel was a Sooth, a mage who could send his soul over the invisible border between our world and the Other. On the border between realms, past, present and future coexisted, gifting him visions; deeper into the Other, he could see and interact with monsters and beings found there. And he could track mages—like me and Benedict.

But Samuel was no common Sooth, and his ability to manipulate the Other was faulty. If he was too deep in to have noticed me come in, he might not be able to come back.

"Samuel," I called, loud enough to be heard, low enough not to startle.

A shiver passed over his broad shoulders. After another cold breath, steaming in the air, he twisted to look at me through deep-brown, sightless eyes.

"Can you come back to me?" I asked, still in that low, steady voice.

Samuel continued to stare for a timeless moment, his handsome face inscrutable. The sky outside the windows grew darker, the shadows in the cabin closer.

Abandoning my caution, I strode forward, reaching for the coin wedged between the boards.

He beat me to it. His cold fingers brushed my warmer ones as he pried the coin free and tucked it into his palm. His eyes cleared and he finally, truly saw me—the flesh and blood me—crouched before him.

"Was it difficult to return?" I asked.

"Only a little. It is always easier with you near."

The corner of my mouth quirked, but the expression did not last. "Did you find Benedict?"

I dreaded his answer but forced myself to ask it. To me, Benedict Rosser was little more than a villain: manipulative, remorseless and cruel. But he had not always been that way, just as Samuel had not always had to keep an ensorcelled coin in his pocket to anchor him in the human world. They had been corrupted, the pair of them.

And Benedict was Samuel's brother. His twin. His blood. His responsibility since childhood.

For Samuel's sake, I had to care whether Benedict lived or died.

"Find, no. But I sensed him." Samuel knuckled his forehead, squinting as if his head ached. He still held the coin. "He is south.

That could mean Mere, as Monna said. Or it could be the Aeadine Anchorage. He is oddly hard to see. But he is alive."

"If he's in port, there could be ghistings obscuring him," I pointed out. Any places where Otherborn beings gathered acted like veils, making it harder for Sooths to seek out their quarries. "Maybe we can learn more in Tithe."

Samuel made a sound of agreement and, slipping the coin back into his pocket, eased himself upright. He offered his hands and pulled me to my feet. For a moment we stood close—close enough for me to smell the salt and wool scent of him. Close enough to embrace or kiss.

We stepped apart, and I didn't allow myself to feel disappointment. The lines of our relationship were carefully drawn as Captain and Stormsinger—a relationship traditionally fraught with abuse. I was the first contracted Stormsinger in centuries. We had to be different, he and I, to set an example to the world.

Or so he insisted. I found myself less inclined to think of the good of all when we stood together in the privacy of his cabin with little more than notions of honor and decency between us.

Samuel moved to the chair where his outer clothing hung and I went to the stove. I added wood and kindling, lighting it with a taper as Samuel dressed behind me. I carefully did not watch him.

"What do we do?" I asked once he was dressed and the fire burned again, spreading light and skin-prickling warmth through the cold room. It lent color to Samuel's pale face and drew out threads of copper in his dark hair and short beard.

"We make for Tithe and hand her over to *Star of the Sea*, as planned." Sam came to stand next to me, adjusting his cravat. "They are likely cruising, so we will have to wait a few days. We rest and recuperate, hand off Monna's ship, and look to our next commission from the governor. If no word from Hesten has arrived to supersede it."

I eyed the stove, waiting for the flames to be hot enough to add a fresh log. "So we forget about Benedict?"

"No, no," he said, too off-handed to be casual. His coat was still open, marking his distraction. "I will make inquiries. Word of a ship like *Harbringer* wrecking, if indeed it has, will spread. And Benedict is a captain now. The Admiralty will be bound to recover him. I have always done what I could for my brother, but I will not risk your freedom and what we have made of ourselves."

I shoved one final log into the stove and closed the door, then fastened it and turned back to him. "Is there no third option?"

He seemed to remember his coat was open, his appearance as respectful, redeemed Captain Samuel Rosser incomplete. He began to work the buttons. "What are you suggesting?"

I rose, looking up the inches between us—I was tall, but so was he. "We lie to Monna. Tell her she has her deal, then give her to the Usti anyway."

My suggestion was met with an unimpressed squint from my captain. "Mary. Please."

I tempered myself. "Or, instead of letting her go, we offer her a chance to escape so that our hands remain clean."

"We would look like fools."

"Fools who know where Benedict is."

"What of our next commission? We cannot ignore it."

"Oh, we wouldn't have time to receive it. We would have to hare off after Monna, who's fleeing to Mere. And if we vanish for a week or two… well, I'm sure we can come up with a fine story."

Samuel paused at his last button and stared at me. "You are a brigand," he accused, disapproval and fondness edging his tone.

"One of us needs to be."

His expression grew heavier. "Mary, I know you hate Benedict and I appreciate that you are… trying. But all that we know right now is Monna is a desperate woman, willing to say anything to escape. And Ben is alive."

"How could she know about him if she hadn't met him?" I pressed. "She knew about Josephine."

"Monna is known for peddling secrets." Samuel fetched his hat from the table, wedging it onto his head and casting a glance out the gallery windows, where night had almost completely fallen. "We wait until Tithe. I will make my inquiries. As I said, *Star of the Sea* is not likely to be in port—we will have a few days before they claim her."

"And if not? If they seize her right away and our choice is gone?"

Samuel reached out to cup the side of my face, the barest brush of cool skin. I resisted the urge to lean into his touch, even just a little, savoring the rare contact—here, alone, in the dark. Where the crew and the world could not see.

"Then all is as it should be," he said, dropping his hand. "I cannot fight the tide."

THE GHISEAU—*A ghiseau consists of the united soul of a human and a ghisting inhabiting one body and mind. Though rarely successful, the union benefits both parties in various ways. For the spectral ghisting, they are given physical form and a root in the human world. For the human host, even those without the benefit of magecraft may be gifted with uncanny ability, long life, vitality, and insight into that Other world from which ghistings derive their life and power. Mages will be subject to a vast increase in power, as the ghisting within them acts as an open conduit between themselves and the power of the Other.*

—FROM A HISTORY OF GHISTLORE
AND THE BLESSED: THOSE BOUND TO THE SECOND
WORLD AND THE POWER THEREIN, *TRANSLATED FROM
THE MEREISH BY SAMUEL I. ROSSER*

THREE

A Tithe to the Sea

MARY

The ghisting trees of Tithe stood vigil over a quiet churchyard, where rows of graves swept down to the bay. Their leaves, unseasonably green beneath a mantle of late-winter snow, rustled as I made for the largest, oldest tree: an ash, vibrant despite the season. My boots punched through the crust, my cheeks flushed with the cold, and a coin nestled warm in my palm.

At my back, the port spread in a network of homes and yards. Women beat frozen clothes on laundry lines, children played and hens clucked. Smoke rose from chimneys and men loitered in the churned streets, gossiping.

Down towards the docks, the settlement condensed into taller, narrower buildings: warehouses, shops, inns and offices. Samuel would be there, sitting across from the port mistress with a cup of hot coffee, wheedling out the latest news and trying to learn as much as he could about Benedict.

A chorus of bells drew my gaze to the masts in the harbor, anchored beyond the reach of the ice-scaled shores. I could pick out *Hart* by feel, if not by sight. He and every other ship in harbor had a ghisting in their figureheads, each spectral creature unique and sentient—just like the ones in the trees around me now. Just like the one within me.

I laid an open palm on the trunk of the ash. Instead of raspy bark, I felt coins of every possible make and origin hammered into the wood. Some had been absorbed entirely into the tree, swallowed by time and growth, while others stood out clean and new.

I found a free sliver of bark and, taking a small hammer from an iron hook, gently tapped my own tithe into place.

Mother.

The voice came through the tree, slipping into the tips of my fingers. The answer came from me, but not from my own mind.

Child, the ghisting called Tane whispered.

"Mary Firth?" a man called.

I turned to find a man in his mid-twenties standing in the snow, bedecked with an overflowing blond beard and a thick knitted cap. His oiled brown greatcoat was open to reveal a knee-length waistcoat and loosely tied scarf, as if he'd dressed in a hurry. His eyes were blue, bright and surprised, and a grin chased the nervousness from the corners of his mouth.

I let out a short, startled laugh. "Charles! What are you doing back north?"

Charles Grant, former highwayman, fellow convicted criminal and the man who had once sold me to a Whallish crime lord, beamed at my recognition and rubbed self-consciously at his beard. "I feared you would not recognize me."

I cocked an eyebrow at him. "Well, you may look like a fisherman, but you still stand like a dandy."

He glanced down—at his back foot angled slightly out, front foot straight on—and his smile grew wry. "Olsa cannot take everything from me."

"Is she here?" I glanced behind him, startled. My heart rose. "Is *Harpy*? My mother?"

"*Harpy*, your mum and Demery are still south. I am here with the Uknaras, waiting for a ship back to Hesten. They were due for a trip home, and I was growing bored of watching Demery paint bowls of fruit." Charles's attention flicked to the ghisten ash, and I saw a note of caution in his eyes. "Have you paid your tithe?"

"Yes."

Charles offered me his elbow. "Then come, we've taken up at an inn, and I know two Usti smugglers who will be very pleased to see you."

I hesitated. Much had transpired between he and I, but a summer of recovery together had dulled those edges, and months of separation—since he had sailed for the Mereish South Isles with James Demery and my mother, Anne Firth—had nearly wiped them away. Charles had more than paid the price for his betrayals, and he had the scar at his throat to prove it: a knot of white amid the red of his cold-pinched skin, just visible between the warren of his beard and the weave of his scarf.

Reaching back to the tree, I rested the tips of my fingers on the bark for a few, gentle breaths. I heard voices, but distantly, as though my ears were covered. I saw visions—fragments of the tree's history, of Tithe's. I saw a great flood sweep up over the shoreline, all the way to the roots of this tree. I saw the digging of graves and the forging of marriages, couples joining hands in the ash's shade on a summer's day. I saw longboats with single red sails anchored in a harbor before Tithe as it had been. And, just for a moment, I saw light slip from my fingertips—a second spectral layer, sheathing my skin.

When the voices and memories ceased to flow, I turned back to Charles and slipped my arm through his. He was a little stiffer than I expected, his eyes lingering on the tree.

"Tane was giving her greetings," I explained.

A muscle in Charles's jaw visibly contracted. "I sensed as much."

I let my eyes fall to the scar on his throat again. He kept it mostly covered—recovering from a mortal wound was not a topic he wanted discussed. Our company's return from north of the Stormwall had already garnered far too much attention.

"What of you?" I tested. "Has the ghisting manifested?"

Charles cleared his throat and patted my arm with his opposite hand. "Let's speak of these things next to a warm hearth with hot wine."

I gave a soft murmur of acceptance and together we returned to Tithe and spoke of simpler things.

"Captain Demery is well established on the South Isles now," Charles explained as we circumvented manure and tried not to break our ankles in deep-wrought sleigh tracks. "He bought his title and has barely left land since autumn. But your mother is mostly at sea, with *Harpy* under her command and Old Crow serving as ghisting. They run goods between the islands. Demery paints and plays at being lord. Very dull if you ask me. Oh, I brought several letters for you—Anne expected we would run into one another sooner or later."

We paused to let a stream of schoolgirls run past, braids bouncing down the backs of their fur-trimmed capes. As weighty as the mention of my mother was, and as eager as I was for more news of Demery and *Harpy*'s crew, my mind strayed after the children. Their happiness and freedom reminded me of my own childhood in a small village between the Ghistwold and the slate hills of Aeadine. Tithe felt similar to that Wold, with its ghisten trees in the graveyard and ghisten wood built into ancient houses.

But more than that, the children made me think—just for the briefest, weakest moment—of the future and of possibilities best left unspoken.

"I did wonder if you would be Mary Rosser by now," Charles murmured, following my gaze.

I looked at him, perhaps too sharply. "I'm the first commissioned Stormsinger in hundreds of years, Charles."

"And?" He looked confused.

"If Samuel and I were to take up…" I eased my arm from his as we stopped in front of an inn, The Captain's Cut, where I could already hear busy chatter through the murky bottle-bottom windowpanes.

"Assumptions would be made. We have to set an example. Show the Winter Sea that Stormsingers should be willing allies, not traded goods."

Charles snorted. "When did you become an altruist? Ouch!"

I flicked him in the forehead and prayed the chill of the wind concealed the flush in my cheeks. I felt insulted, exposed, embarrassed and convicted in the same breath. "Is this your inn?"

Charles rubbed at his forehead, nodding. "Yes, yes. Come in."

Charles slipped into an elaborately wallpapered common room and led me past a series of tables girded by comfortable chairs. At the back, just past a blonde woman immersed in a stack of letters, sat a curtained alcove. A man and a woman were tucked within, she with one foot drawn up onto the bench, and he with a broadsheet in his overlarge hands—one of which was missing the ring and pinky fingers from the first knuckle.

"Mary!" Illya Uknara smiled broadly and exchanged his broadsheet for an ornate brass coffee pot, which he held over an empty mug. His Aeadine was heavily accented, sticky like toffee. "I have seen *Hart* offshore. Coffee?"

"Thank you." I sank down on the opposite side of the round table, smiling at the woman as I did so. "Olsa."

Olsa kept her foot on the bench, leaning forward to pat my cheek fondly. "Ms. Firth. Or is it—"

Charles not-so-subtly waved his hand to catch her attention, following the gesture with a finger across his throat and a mimed pinch of the lips. When I glared at him, he unfurled an innocent smile and waved down a serving maid. "Spiced wine, please."

The woman eyed the lot of us, eclectic as we were, then sauntered away.

Olsa crossed her arms over her chest and leaned back against

Illya. She wore belted trousers under a traditional Usti kaftan with an embroidered collar topped with fur. Her blonde hair was loosely braided back from her practical features. Illya's kaftan was open to reveal an undyed linen shirt tucked into breeches and unbuttoned at the neck, giving me a healthy glimpse of muscled, hairy chest. He wore his pale, reddish beard long and vaguely square, like Charles's. But unlike Charles, who had the pale skin of the Southern Aeadines, prone to flushing at the slightest provocation, Olsa's and Illya's mild brown skin marked them as far northern. Northern Aeadine, Mereish, and Usti all shared common ancestry, however arbitrarily wars and borders had divided the Winter Sea over the centuries.

Despite our varied origins, we were intrinsically bound together by two things: history and ghistings.

A flicker of light passed over my hand again as I reached for the coffee. Illya noted it with a secret smile and murmured, "Tane."

He, Olsa, myself and, reluctantly, Charles made contact with the wood of the tabletop—one of the only substances that ghistings could interact with in our human world. I felt a jolt of familiarity as unseen presences surged and whispered through the wood, their light hidden beneath the table. Images came with them as the ghistings that lived within us exchanged, within a few heartbeats, months of experience and information, pleasantries and reflections.

The conversation took far longer to order itself in my mind, but a few images leapt out. I saw—remembered—an expanse of water and rock and ice, blurred by blowing snow and the half-light of another sun. Shipwrecks cast across the horizon by a god's careless hand, and a sleeping forest of ghisten trees. Shards of wood stabbed into flesh by vicious hands, a fire and a black-haired man, bleeding out into a bed of moss.

Silvanus Lirr. The man who had made us. The man we had, together, killed one year and four months ago.

Olsa sat up straight and grabbed her half-empty mug of coffee. "To the death of our common enemy," she said, and we all drank—

save Charles, whose mug was empty. He looked forlornly for the serving maid and waved away Illya's offer of coffee.

"We took a Mereish pirate a few days ago," I told the three after a moment of silence. "Ophalia Monna. She claims to have seen Benedict Rosser in the hands of the Mereish Navy. Have you heard anything about that? *Harbringer* wrecking off Eldona Island?"

"Yes," Illya said immediately. He waved the broadsheet he'd been reading, topped with a heading in Usti.

"What does it say?" I asked, not wanting to distract Tane from the other ghistings by requesting a translation. Their exchange ran through the back of my mind like whispers and half-forgotten dreams—still jarring, but a sensation I was becoming more accustomed to. "My Usti is still not good."

"Bah, mine's shit too." Charles flapped a dismissive hand. "Honestly, how many words do you need to say *the*?"

Olsa gave him a quelling look.

Ignoring Charles, Illya explained: "*Harbringer* wrecked four weeks ago. The Navy tried to keep this from the public, but boats full of survivors came into many ports. Hundreds died at sea. A great tragedy."

A great tragedy indeed. I tried not to dwell on the deaths as I took another sip of coffee. It was thick, dark, and laced with honey, but the warmth failed to soothe my anxiety. Until now I could still, with effort, mark Monna's words up to desperation, a bargaining chip cobbled together from half-heard information. But no longer.

My heart ached for Samuel. He was no doubt hearing this same news from the harbor mistress as we spoke.

"Benedict Rosser is better off dead," Illya added with more regret than vengeance. "He would have killed us all if the wind had changed."

"Monna's offered us Benedict's location in exchange for her freedom."

"That would mean you breaking contract with the Usti," Charles pointed out. "And risking antagonizing the Mereish. Winter has cooled the war, but not by much."

I shrugged. "I know. Samuel won't give in, anyway."

"He intends to leave his brother to die?" Charles frowned then conjured a bright smile as his wine finally arrived. He took a sip and waited for the waitress to leave before he continued, "That doesn't seem like Sam. I mean… my brothers are a pack of lobcocks and halfwits but I would still… Well, I cannot say what I'd do for them. As of yet, none of them have had the misfortune of becoming a prisoner of war. But Sam's a better fellow than I."

"It is for the best," Illya repeated. "Better to put down a rabid dog *before* it bites you. Again."

"Is there any hope for Benedict?" I asked Olsa. "You trained Samuel to manage his corruption."

"Manage, yes. But Samuel is a Sooth," the Usti woman reminded me. She too was a Sooth, and during her mentorship with Samuel last year we had all come to appreciate the depth of her knowledge of all magecrafts and the Other. "What the Black Tide did to them as boys was a crime, but Samuel has the strength of will— and morals—to wield his power. I understand that Benedict was always self-serving and violent. And he is a Magnus. Every time he manipulates others, his conscience, his awareness of his actions, is a little more lost. He is too far gone for me to train. Perhaps the Mereish have some magics, some way of helping him. I know Samuel has wondered about that too. But it's beyond my knowing and, given the war, beyond our reach."

We were quiet for a moment. The chatter of the other patrons swelled into the lull, interspersed with the clink of utensils and the muffled thuds of footsteps upstairs. At the table nearby, the blonde woman I'd noted earlier cast Charles a lingering glance then went back to her writing. She was plain, I noticed, other than an enviable dusting of freckles.

"Well, the decision is already made, regardless," I said, picking up my mug again. "Samuel refused to bargain with Monna, and I can't see him changing his mind. But you must come to *Hart* tomorrow and breakfast with us. We can speak more, and I'm sure Samuel would be glad to see all of you. I should go now, before it grows too dark."

"Of course," Olsa said with a nod. "We will be there. I must check on my apprentice, anyways."

THE TALISMAN ENSORCELL—*Talismans and charms, imbued with various magics, have long been a practice in Mere. Created with various ingredients— their nature kept staunchly secret—and the blood of a living mage, they may grant their bearer anything from luck to premonitions to the regulation and control of a mage's power, though this field has long been a source of conflict and remains, in the opinion of this commentator, under-researched.*

The potential of such charms and their promises have naturally led to a great deal of forgery and false talismans, particularly to be found in foreign markets. It must be noted that a true Talisman Ensorcell is made through great effort and skill, and is worth far more than its weight in gold.

—FROM A DEFINITIVE STUDY OF THE BLESSED: MAGES AND MAGECRAFT OF THE MEREISH, *TRANSLATEDFROM THE MEREISH BY SAMUEL I. ROSSER*

FOUR

Hesten, Usti Chain

Ten Months Ago

SAMUEL

I tasted ash and smoke on the breeze, calling up memories and emotions that tugged my mind away from Hesten's busy streets.

Hesten's inhabitants were lively and loud under the summer sun, at the climax of the Sweet Moons. Ladies in cotton gowns with loosely veiled hair ambled by on fine mounts, old men fanned themselves with their hats in the shade and an innkeeper rolled a barrel from an archway to the common catacombs, where great slabs of winter-harvested ice kept ale and perishables fresh through the warm months. I glimpsed clothing and faces from every nation and heard a myriad of languages united under the pristine blue sky.

But the smell of smoke lingered. I squinted from under the brim of my hat to the flat-fronted, gilded buildings overhead, guided by a dreamer's rootless certainty.

I saw it: a great, charred space between rooflines. The gap was so large, so obvious, my eyes had slipped over it entirely.

My destination was gone. My shock was sudden and visceral, edged with panic. In my pocket, I clutched my coin and fought to keep my expression calm.

Still, a nearby man noticed my dismay. He had the long eyes of the Ismani, his embroidered cap at odds with the light Usti kaftan he wore. When he spoke, his Usti was unaccented.

"There was a fire, night before last." The man nodded over his pipe, languid smoke seeping from between his lips. He sat on a low windowsill, a cup of tea at his knee. "A pity. Maren was the best jeweler in this port. Very bad luck."

My stomach dropped. "Maren, the Mereish jeweler? The charm maker?"

The Ismani man tilted his head to one side, not accusatory but curious. "Yes. You are Aead?"

I gave him a smile that would have been more genuine had my skin not been crawling. "I fear you are mistaken. Pardon me."

I moved north along the canal until I sensed the Ismani no longer watching me then cut over towards the burned buildings. The crowd kept well back, though no guards enforced the boundary. The locals simply went about their business, casting me glances as I separated from the throng, stepped onto ashy cobbles—the tread of my boots oddly muffled—and approached the rubble.

Charred, skeletal timbers reached their fingers into the breach. Heat still radiated from the piles of rubble beneath and sun glinted off melted glass. Smoke eddied, thin and eerie, and the scent of burning became overpowering. Only the canals and a few stone walls had saved the entire area from destruction.

I stared at the ruin. Not long ago, families had lived here. I remembered the smell of spices and cooking food, and a Mereish jeweler who had plied me with coffee and given me three immeasurable gifts—an ensorcelled talisman, a book, and hope. Then, after our return from beyond the Stormwall, he had given me one more.

A promise.

Sadness warred with unease in my chest. Buildings burned. It happened. But…

I came a little closer to the rubble, half searching for any sign of… what? Ill intent? A body? Surely any remains would have already been salvaged.

"What are you doing? You should not be here."

I looked up to see a woman standing in the mouth of an alleyway, out of sight of the square. She wore a long, embroidered coat and no padding beneath her skirts, giving her a smooth silhouette in the Mereish style. Her hair was blonde and her skin just touched with a northern brown, freckled across the cheeks—pretty, but not distractingly so. Indeed, other than the freckles and her pale hair, there was nothing noteworthy about her. Even her age was hard to discern. A jaded twenty? A youthful thirty?

"I apologize for any intrusion. I knew a man who lived here. The jeweler, Maren." I gestured to the rubble. "Is he alive?"

The woman eyed me, sticking to the shadows of the alley. "No," she replied. Her Mereish accent—soft, gentling consonants and blurring vowels—became stronger. "Three died, including Maren."

I let out a long breath. "My deepest condolences," I said. I should not linger, not when there were people in this city—including this woman, it seemed—who had much more right to grieve than I. Besides, if Maren was gone, I needed to find a quiet place to think and come up with a new plan.

I turned to leave, touching my hat and offering what I hoped was a sympathetic look.

"Why were you looking for him?" she asked before I could step away.

"I hoped for his expertise," I hedged. I had no intention of telling this stranger the truth—that I was a broken mage looking for a cure, and Maren had been helping me.

The woman kept talking: "Well, it would be best if you forget Mr. Maren." She nodded over her shoulder, down the alley. At first all I saw was char on the brick wall, then I noticed the letters that had also been smeared there.

Against my better judgement, I stepped closer. The woman moved aside and I craned to see down the alley.

A Mereish word was painted on the pale red brick in soot and something thicker—my dreamer's sense, coiling, warned it was blood.

"It translates best to 'oathbreaker,'" the woman said, standing just two paces from me now. "But it means much more. It means to break the trust of kin. Of blood. It means to break faith and tradition. It means final, irrevocable exile. Maren was a traitor to my people, and they do not forgive such things lightly. If you knew Maren, it is best to pretend you did not."

The bitter taste of smoke was thick on my tongue now. Maren had shared Mereish secrets with me. He had promised to help me track down a Mereish healer-mage and find a cure for Ben's and my corruption.

Had that kindness—had I—contributed to his death?

The woman watched me, her eyes softened with sadness, but there was a shadow beneath them that made my fingers twitch towards the buttons of my jacket and the pistol beneath.

"I knew him very little, regardless," I told her, slipping my fingers through the buttons of my coat to rest them over my stomach, as any gentleman might. "I will intrude no longer. Again, my deepest condolences."

I hastened back to the crowd, the street and ship where Mary, I prayed, was still safe. But I glanced back as I reached the square. The woman had turned to stare at the rubble, the wind blowing the ends of her fringe into her eyes.

She did not look at me again.

THE NATURE OF GHISTEN WOOD—

Ghisten wood is harvested from a ghisten tree and possessed of that tree's vital spirit, which has grown through the boundary between worlds. Commonly used in the making of figureheads, doors and religious icons, ghisten wood is immensely valuable and highly prized by all nations of the world.

—FROM A HISTORY OF THE WINTER SEA AND THE PEOPLES THEREIN, *TRANSLATED FROM THE MEREISH BY SAMUEL I. ROSSER*

FIVE

The Woman from Hesten

SAMUEL

I stepped into the dark street outside the port mistress's high-fronted offices without feeling the cold. I hardly saw the dwindling crowds or smelled the pungent array of fish, brine and smoke. My eyes glazed over the names on the envelopes in my hands without care, noting only that none of them came from the Admiralty.

The port mistress's words, confirming Monna's assertions about *Harbringer*'s destruction, lingered in my ears. My thoughts were entrenched a hundred leagues away, in the hold of a Mereish ship where my brother languished—or the prison where he was chained, or, if my Sight had been wrong, the pit where his charred bones had been tossed.

Maybe he never made it to any of those ends. Maybe his body had been dashed to pieces on the rocks along with his crew, and his bruised, frozen flesh was long devoured by crabs.

My spirit began to drift, out from the security of my bones and into that Other realm. I ducked into the mouth of an alley, where the shadows were deep and only too happy to shield me.

I leaned against the wall and bowed my head, eyes closed, body braced as dark water began to slosh around my feet.

There. I saw Benedict's light again, dim but present. Still not dead. Not yet.

I closed my hand around the coin in my pocket. The spectral water retreated. The world sharpened once again, but for once I resented that retreat. Because here, in the human world, there was no distraction from the reality of my brother's doom.

"Captain Rosser?"

A short man peered at me from the mouth of the alley. He wore a fine blue frock coat with black cuffs and a bicorn hat—a naval captain. His demeanor was oddly amiable, even curious, with a laden satchel under one arm and a paper cone of roasted nuts in the opposite hand.

"Captain Archer." I straightened, a lifetime of etiquette moving my lips and limbs without regard for my inner turmoil. Archer was an old acquaintance from my naval days which I had, with some reluctance on his part, managed to rekindle since my part in bringing the notorious pirate Silvanus Lirr to justice. Archer captained a courier vessel, the appropriately named *Swift*, and I had no doubt the satchel under his arm was packed with correspondence to be left with the port mistress for Aeadine ships.

"Forgive me." I gave a shallow, polite nod. "I did not see you."

"Hardly saw you there in the dark myself." He waved his cone and I caught the scent of cinnamon, sugar and warm almonds. "No matter. I'm on my way to see the mistress, but you look… terrible. Nut?"

"Ah, no, thank you, Captain Archer." My eyes flicked to his bundle of letters. My lips moved of their own accord again, but this time in desperation. "Have you any word of *Harbringer*?"

Captain Archer's expression stilled momentarily, then he let out a short sigh. "Yes, yes. You've my deepest condolences."

"What happened?"

"A storm and a reef, I heard. The surviving crew reported that Captain Rosser ordered them closer to land, something to do with a few abandoned villages and locals building breakwaters in winter, strange actions. I will not dally with you—the wreck was a bloody nightmare. Did all we could to keep it from the public, but you know how these things are. The Mereish are touting it as the greatest victory of the year, never mind the ship ran aground. Not much leaks out of that country, but *this* did."

All I could see were the ships in the harbor over Archer's shoulder, and memory after memory filled my mind's eye: Ben and I at sea as boys, learning to navigate, to chart, to identify morgories and huden and read the weather in the clouds; Ben sharing a cup of spiced chocolate with me at Festus in an unidentified port, back when he still, occasionally, manifested the ability to give and share.

I cleared my throat. "But there were survivors."

Archer nodded. "To your brother's credit. His Sooth foresaw the danger in enough time for Captain Rosser to dispatch much of the crew."

That felt like a kick in the ribs. Most ships were equipped with a Sooth for just such reasons, but the notion that someone else had foreseen a danger to my brother while I had remained ignorant was not easy to swallow.

"Will the Admiralty arrange for his release?" I asked. "I believe him to be alive."

Archer shrugged one shoulder noncommittally, but I saw the truth in his grave eyes. "Even if he did survive, Mr Rosser... The Admiralty will make no allowances for him, not in the light of... his... indiscretion."

I felt the last traces of color leave my cheeks, never mind the burn of the cold. "What has he done?"

Archer cleared his throat, looking suddenly awkward. The change in his demeanor sparked a realization—he had been remarkably kind to me these past few moments. No one from my former life treated me with kindness, even if my actions with Lirr had won their respect.

"I am loath to cite rumor." He avoided my eyes. "But it has become known that you, good fellow, may have been blamed for his indiscretion with a certain lady. Again, rumors. However, they are prevalent enough that the certain lady's husband has—discreetly—marked him for disfavor. Outside of clear, indisputable evidence of his survival presented in a public way, I fear Captain Benedict Rosser is beyond aid."

The Dark Water once again lapped at my heels and I grasped the coin in my pocket. Vindication and horror warred within me, livid in the sudden, strangled stillness of my thoughts.

For all I strove to keep my expression composed, Archer must have seen something slip through.

"My very deepest condolences," he said again. He studied the street, as if searching for someone to take his place, then forced a smile. "Let me buy you a stiff drink. I'll be but a moment with the mistress?"

I broke my gaze over the harbor, blinked back an unwelcome wetness in my eyes, and shook my head. "No, no. Thank you, Captain, for your kindness and your honesty. Until next time."

"Next time." He nodded with a relieved smile and strode away.

I watched him turn the corner, against the backdrop of snowy street and many-masted harbor. No sooner was he gone than a woman passed by. She was small, the bottom third of her face hidden by a thick scarf and the upper third by a windblown sweep of blonde hair and the fur brim of her cap.

My Sooth's senses jangled. I recognized her. She wore an Aeadine coat now, double-breasted and bronze-buttoned, but there was no mistaking the Mereish woman from Hesten.

I retreated farther into the shadows. My movement snagged her attention and she glanced towards me, but evidently decided a man skulking in an alley was not someone she wanted to be caught staring at. She picked up her pace and carried on.

Curious, I waited a few heartbeats then inched to the mouth of the alley. A dark-haired man bumped into me, the cold skin of his hand brushing mine as he muttered an apology.

My attention fractured. I glanced after him then quickly searched for the woman once more.

She had vanished, and I stood alone with Archer's words drifting through my beleaguered mind.

The lady's husband has marked him for disfavor.
I fear Captain Benedict Rosser is truly beyond aid.

USTI—*The Usti are widely considered to be the most powerful nation upon the Winter Sea. Staunchly neutral in the wars between Aeadine and Mere, the Usti are mediators and peacemakers, focusing on trade and the pursuit of knowledge, though the latter may be questioned in regards to their religious pursuits. Formed from an amalgamation of peoples, various influences from across the known world can still be seen in their religion, which, at odds with the enlightened mind, continues the worship of many saints, ancestors, and even gods. See also* KALSANK, TITHE, USTI CHAIN, USTI HOLDINGS .

—FROM THE WORDBOOK ALPHABETICA: A NEW
WORDBOOK OF THE AEADINES

SIX

The Ess Noti

MARY

I found Samuel standing at the end of the dock where *Hart* was moored, staring out across the quiet harbor. He had his coat open and his hands shoved into his pockets, his attention somewhere beyond what I could see.

"Samuel," I said from a few paces away.

He glanced over his shoulder. The corners of his mouth moved as if he intended to conjure me a smile but lacked the will. "Hello."

"I heard about Benedict," I said, coming to stand just close enough that he could hear me without our voices carrying. I would tell him of Charles and the Uknaras later. "Monna was telling the truth."

"She was," he agreed, glancing over the waiting height of *Hart* to our left, then back out to sea. "I will write to the Admiralty to advise them Benedict has survived and any efforts to recover him will not be in vain."

I stepped closer, but stopped as his back stiffened. I took a second to measure my words.

"Monna was telling the truth," I repeated. The thought of the pirate, still languishing in our hold, made my stomach clench with thoughtless, irrational impulse. "Can we at least consider—"

"The Admiralty will take care of Ben. The Mereish may be our enemies, but they will offer a captain his parole," Samuel stated.

"My uncle is Admiral of the North Fleet, remember. He will not let his nephew linger in captivity."

A spark of frustration lit in me. "I don't think you believe that."

Abruptly he turned on me. "Do you want to go to Mere? Do you want to crawl into some Saint-forsaken prison to save the kind of man who would gladly abuse anyone within reach, including you? Do you want to put everything you and I have built on the line for *him*?"

I stared at him, taken aback by his outburst. Rarely was Samuel this open in the privacy of his cabin, let alone standing on the end of a dock with the water carrying our voices to the surrounding ships.

I finally replied, casting my voice lower. "If you let this opportunity go and he dies, it will torment you for the rest of your life. It will destroy you. He will destroy you, even from the grave. For him, I would risk nothing. But for you, I would do anything."

It was his turn to watch me in silence, his chest rising and falling with contained emotion. His eyes softened, yielding to me, even as he drew a deep breath and cloistered himself again.

"Leave me be, Mary," he said. "The matter is closed."

Monna squinted as I opened the door to her cramped cabin. Fatigue gave her expression a world-weary edge and she seemed resigned to her fate, tucked into a corner with chains on her wrists and ankles.

"Have the Usti arrived for my head?"

"They will soon," I said, stepping in and closing the door.

Monna's eyes flicked to the latch. "No Captain Rosser? No guards?"

I shook my head and leaned against the bulkhead, hands behind me, winter skirts heavy around my ankles. "No. He still intends to hand you over and abandon his brother."

Monna's lips tightened and I saw a shudder pass through her chest. "Do you understand what will happen to me?"

"The Usti will try you as a pirate."

"No, they will not," Monna cut back. There was real desperation in her voice, so much that I felt a tug of compassion. I'd stood on a gallows. I'd felt a noose around my neck. I knew what this woman feared.

"Fuck this. Girl, I am *seuasa*." Monna leaned forward to rest her forearms on her knees, wrists dangling. "An oathbreaker, a traitor to the Mereish Crown. I sailed too close to the shoals—I know things I should not. The Usti do not want to hang me, witch. They want my mind. They want what I know. And the Ess Noti will not allow that to happen."

"The Ess Noti?" I plucked at the unfamiliar term. Even Tane did not know how to translate it. "What does that mean?"

Monna glared at me for a moment, then spat on the deck. "If what I heard about you and your captain is true? About your days beyond the Stormwall, and what Silvanus Lirr was? You will learn about the Ess Noti *very* soon."

Foreboding prickled up my neck. "Tell me everything you know, and perhaps my gratitude will save you. I am your last hope. And unlike my captain, I am willing to bend the law to set you free."

The truth of those words struck me as I spoke them, threaded with regret and more than a little frustration. Most days, I found Samuel's preoccupation with reputation and lawfulness both vexing and endearing, but today it felt like an immeasurable burden.

Monna took a second to breathe, watching my face. "The Ess Noti are the Mereish secret-keepers. They once served Ilaad, Saint of Unspoken Words, but have since… branched out. They are a hand on the throat of any Mereish who dare to make their home in another land. The more influential and educated those travelers were before they left Mere, the higher the likelihood that the Ess Noti are watching them, ready to squeeze.

"They also hunt and kill, or capture, foreigners who have come into possession of Mereish secrets and sorceries. Tales of particularly powerful mages would certainly catch their attention. A Stormsinger who interacts with ghistings—a *ghiseau*. A Sooth who summons monsters from the Other. Close to a thousand men and women from various nations witnessed what went on north of the Stormwall during the Bountiful Moons. Rumors spread, and people take notice when pirates who should have been sentenced to die—I speak of Lirr's *ghiseau*—disappear instead."

Monna knew I was *ghiseau*. Samuel and I had known that eventually the truth would come out, but, where we had feared renewed interest in my skills from the Winter Sea's naval powers, it seemed now Samuel, myself, and likely everyone we had sailed with faced a more uncertain threat.

"I thought James Demery arranged leniency for Lirr's pirates," I said, eager to pry the focus off myself. Hanging *ghiseau* would do little more than make a public spectacle and call attention to all of us, and Demery had sought to avoid that. "Perhaps the Usti simply… disposed of them some other way."

Monna's eyes seemed to glint. "Humans have a foolish habit of disregarding anything they do not understand. The Usti did try to hang some of Lirr's *ghiseau*, and lo, when they would not die? The Usti were given evidence they could not reject. Evidence of humans and ghistings bound to one flesh. Evidence of magics unknown and untapped."

I suddenly wished I was not alone with Monna, that Samuel were here and we could untangle this web together.

"So the Usti want you for your information, and the Ess Noti want to silence you before that happens?" I clarified. "And they will… do what, to us?"

Monna spoke with dread and an undercurrent of righteous anger. "They will take you if they can, kill you if they cannot. You are *ghiseau*—your very existence is a danger to Mere's sorcerous supremacy."

"But if the Usti already know about *ghiseau*… what is the point of the Mereish still trying to keep their secrets? As you said, word spreads."

Something shifted in Monna's face, a frown that told me there was more to the tale. And she had no intention of sharing.

"The Ess Noti may already be close," she said instead. "You and I are entwined now, and that, I suspect, will be a tipping point. You and your captain are in as much danger as I am, Mary Firth."

My mind roiled. I wanted to discard everything Monna was saying, to explain it away and laugh at her, but I couldn't. She believed this. She was afraid. And even if she was the greatest actress to ever take to the waves, could Samuel and I afford to doubt her?

"Where is Ben?" I asked.

"They were taking him to prison, but he will not be there long, either. They will realize who he is, *what* he is, and the Ess Noti will come for him too."

"What is he?" I asked, testing her.

"A Black Tide Son," she replied, holding my gaze fast. "The Mereish are well aware of your people's cult and their attempts at Mereish rituals."

My skin crawled. Tane, too, was restless. She slipped from my flesh and reformed beside me—at first, a spectral mirror image of me in a woolen winter gown with modest hip pads, a shawl tucked into my bodice and my hair in a windblown braid. Then her form shifted, her face aging, her body becoming a little taller, a little harsher. A little less human.

Monna's eyes rounded but her lips remained a hard, thin line.

I reached into my pocket and pulled out the keys to Monna's manacles. I set them on the floor between us, outside her reach.

"Tell me where Ben is. Lead the Ess Noti away from us, distract them if they come," I said as my ghisting loomed and the cabin filled with indigo, Otherworldly light. "And I will set you free."

SEVEN

Hart

SAMUEL

I awoke to a soft light. Slowly my sleep-heavy mind registered the source, and I stilled.

A spectral stag stood over my hammock. His tines were huge, vanishing into the deck above, and his mane thick above powerful forelegs. His eyes of indigo sea-glass peered down into mine, and, despite their lack of soul, his stare brimmed with meaning.

He stomped and the ship shuddered.

"Awake! I'm awake," I gasped. I rolled out of the other side of the hammock and tugged my breeches from the lines, abandoning all dignity to hop my way into them. "What is it?"

The ghisting could not verbally respond—I was no *ghiseau*—but Hart abruptly shed his substance, sinking back into the wood of the ship and streaming through it towards the door then out into the passage.

I emerged into the companionway just as a small form barreled into me.

"Captain!" Ms. Poverly, the steward's girl, squeaked as I set her back on her feet. Fourteen, red-haired and narrow-faced, she instinctively touched her forehead and panted out, "We've been boarded. They're in the hold! They *were* in the hold—"

"Rouse the rest of the crew, call quarters." I pushed her aside, gently but firmly, and hastened on. "And send me Ms. Skarrow!"

Poverly bolted and I resumed my pursuit of Hart's snaking, guiding light.

The gun deck was a cacophony of shouts, jostling forms and swinging hammocks. Mr. Penn, quartermaster, shouldered his way to me.

"Two strangers, jumped out the gunport," Penn grunted. "There's a third still below, sir. He has Mary."

Ghisten light flooded the hold as I descended the ladder. Half a dozen crew already surrounded two figures at the far end: Mary and a stranger in an unremarkable grey coat, long and concealing. He had lost his cocked hat, crushed nearby, and his hair was wet in the ghisten light.

He had a long knife leveled at Mary's throat, who stood against a wall of crates, a spent pistol at her feet and her hands raised. The air stank of tar, damp, blood and gunpowder.

Rage and urgency made my blood sing and my focus narrow— Mary, the knife, the stranger. My Sooth's senses roamed, skittering the divide between worlds and sending me gouts of images, impulses, and warnings.

My eyes dropped. The stranger favored one leg, and, though the light was weak and his coat long, I could see the bottom half of his trousers were soaked with blood.

"Give me that musket," I murmured to Penn. "Is it primed?"

"Aye, sir." The quartermaster handed over his weapon and I passed him my cutlass.

"Drop the knife!" I advanced through the rows of lashed barrels and crates with the musket to my shoulder. Mr. Penn and a dozen other sailors flooded around us, hemming the stranger in. Lanterns joined Hart's spectral light and shadows cavorted about from a hundred angles.

The intruder looked at me. In his distraction Mary began to hum, low in her throat. The knife started to shake, drawing a snaking line of blood on Mary's exposed flesh. She inhaled sharply and tipped her head back, her hum faltering, her eyes snatching mine. She looked at me, prompting, demanding. Frightened.

I fired and was through the gunsmoke before it plumed, my strides eating up the deck.

The intruder moved, slashing and staggering simultaneously. Mary seized his knife and dropped it instantly, cursing and clutching a bloody hand.

She kicked it spinning down the deck. The man, barely upright, clawed after it, but, upon realizing the futility of his enterprise, turned back on Mary. He grabbed her by the skirts and hauled, trying to bring her down, to wrestle an arm around her throat.

I dove into the fray. I pulled Mary upright and smashed the butt of my musket down on the man's face at the same time as Mary recovered and stomped on one of his flailing hands. He shrieked, and a second blow from my musket silenced him.

"They came for Monna," Mary panted, staggering back into the crates. Her eyes swept the hold and she twisted, still clutching her bleeding hand at the wrist. Crimson dripped to the deck, joining a growing stain from our captive. "Tane says she escaped."

"Mr. Penn, find Monna!" I called. There was a rush of movement as my orders were obeyed, and I edged between Mary and the intruder, now flat on his back on the floor. He was barely conscious, his breaths thick, rattling things, clotted with blood.

"Who is he?" I traded my cutlass back from a helpful crewwoman. A dozen crowded around, wary, waiting for orders and led by my first officer, Mr. Keo. The rest had vanished above with Penn, and running footsteps reverberated throughout the ship.

"Mereish," Mary said at my shoulder. "Monna said they came to kill her."

"Why were you here?"

When Mary did not reply, I cast a glance over my shoulder. She met my gaze in a way I did not need my Sooth's abilities to interpret.

Whatever her reason was, she was not about to divulge it in front of the crew.

I knelt beside the stranger in a pool of spreading blood. He was plain in death, a simple, Mereish man with death-bleached skin, angry eyes and blood bubbling over his lips. The impulse to try and save him welled, and passed. He would drown in his own blood long before a surgeon could be found.

"Who are you?" I asked. "If you tell me, I will see you are given a proper burial." *Even though you threatened my Stormsinger. Even though you invaded my ship and released my prisoner.*

He tried to speak, but the effort sent him into a fit of coughing. Mary's hand tightened on my shoulder as the coughing thickened into a choke, then a garble. Then nothing, save twitching muscles.

Silence overtook the hold. Distantly I heard whispered questions, orders passed to the deck above. The ship creaked in the harbor waters. Hart's light faded and we were left with only lanternlight, the stink of blood and emptied bowels, and the gaze of the dead man.

I rose. Now that the danger had passed the urge to reach for Mary beset me, to pull her close and wrap her in my arms and make sure every inch of her was whole. I settled for pulling my handkerchief from my pocket and wrapping her hand, which she gave me silently.

"Wrap the body and bring him up on deck," I said to Keo. "I need to report this to the port authorities."

"Wait. Tell no one, yet. Ensure the crew keeps quiet," Mary interjected. "Captain Rosser, you and I need to speak first."

The first rays of dawn seeped across the sky as Mary preceded me into the cabin. No sooner had I closed the door than she turned on me, one anxious hand rubbing her collarbone. The other had been properly bandaged, though the sight of the blood already seeping through made me wish we had a proper surgeon aboard. Mary healed quickly, but not quickly enough for my liking.

"Promise not to throw me off the ship," Mary said.

I looked for traces of jest in her expression, untimely though it would have been. I found only nervous concern.

I beckoned her join me by the gallery windows, where the cool dawn light fell across us. "All right. I give you my word. What is it?"

"Last night, I went to see Monna. To try to reason with her, alone. She was terrified of being handed over to the Usti, and, when I told her that you still wouldn't agree to her proposal, she told me why."

"And?" I prompted.

"She called herself something in Mereish, an oathbreaker. She says that the Usti want her for information, not piracy, and that her own people would sooner kill her than see that happen and had likely already sent someone to kill her. Someone from a group called the Ess Noti."

"So it was these Ess Noti who boarded us?" I pressed. An inkling struck me, thick with magic. "Was there a woman among them? Blonde?"

Mary's expression was tight. "I don't know. The only one I saw clearly is the dead one. But yes, I think it was the Ess Noti. They spoke in Mereish. They moved... it was eerie, Samuel. Tane says they weren't mages but something off. I tried to use my power on the lot of them, to Quell the air in their lungs, but it only worked on that last man, briefly. In any case... before they came, I struck a deal with Monna. She told me where they took Ben in return for a chance to escape."

I held my expression carefully still. "So where is he?"

"A place called Gat, a fortress on the Mereish coast, near the town of Maase." Mary searched my eyes, anxiety leaking through her conviction. She tried to smile. "I know I betrayed you, and

I know you might hate me for it. Thus the 'please don't throw me overboard.'"

"I would never throw you overboard," I said, but my voice was harder than I intended. The name of the fortress rung in my ears, taunting and obscure. Compulsively, I clarified, "Though I would throw you overboard if the ship was burning."

Mary's smile wavered, but she seemed to take my admission as a victory and plunged on, explaining all Monna had told her.

"The Ess Noti will seek out Ben too," she finished. "That's another reason why I struck the deal. Sam, we were not delivering Monna to justice, only torture and a knife in the dark. And we needed to know what she knew, for all our sakes."

I ran a hand across my mouth, stretching my aching jaw. I could feel a headache coming on, and with it a jangling of half-formed premonitions and presentient whispers. This moment felt familiar, as if I had lived it before, and I knew, intrinsically, that everything was about to change.

"When I went down to free Monna just now, the Ess Noti came upon us," Mary went on. "But Monna did escape."

"She left you to them? After you saved her?" I was disgusted, but hardly surprised.

"Not really. Two Ess Noti went after her, and the last one… He looked at me strangely, as if he suddenly realized that he knew who I was." She gestured to her face. "He tried to take me with them. I shot him and missed. I tried to steal the air from his lungs. Then you arrived."

Betrayal. Relief. Grudging gratitude. A great, blossoming weight of emotion. I cleared my throat and focused on Mary's face again. "You should have come to me right away."

Mary's chin drifted to one side. "You would have stopped me and handed Monna over to the Usti."

Frustration hit me like a rogue wave, along with the suspicion that she was correct. If she had come to me in the middle of the night asking to release Monna, my first instinct certainly would have been to discard the Mereish pirate's revelations and say no. At least until morning.

Then the Ess Noti might have come and gone in the night, and the body in my hold might be the pirate's. Mary and I would either be dead, captured, or know nothing of the Ess Noti's interest in us and the Usti's curiosity about Mereish sorcery. And I would have nothing to lead me to my brother but a vague light on the horizon, veiled and insubstantial.

"These Ess Noti are still a threat to us," I stated.

Mary nodded. "And perhaps everyone else who came back over the Stormwall, especially the *ghiseau*."

"I knew this could not be kept quiet," I muttered, remembering our arrival back in Hesten and the warnings that the pirate James Demery had circulated among our little fleet. His intention with those warnings had been to keep the details of the Ghistwold and treasure we had found as vague as possible—guarding our own future plunders—and to keep the dual natures of the *ghiseau* private. Not all of the thousand men and women who had returned with us had even known about the *ghiseau*, confined as they were to other quarters of the battle.

But there was no silencing sailors with too much money and a hell of a story.

"What happened beyond the Stormwall—it changes everything we thought we knew about ghistings and mages," Mary added quietly. "We knew that information was dangerous, just not to this extent."

The knot in my chest began to loosen, and responsibility flooded in with a deep, even breath.

"Monna was taken from us by unknown Mereish assailants," I observed. "Our commission is unfulfilled, and their natural destination is Mere. It would be understandable for us to intercept them before they hit Mereish waters, or perhaps pursue them further south."

Mary's eyes lit, immediately catching my ruse. "That would be expected," she agreed, sounding a little breathless. "We're going, then?"

We could not see the sunrise from the windows, but the sky was light. A frozen, misty haze hung over the harbor and turned the ships to spectral webs of masts and rigging, with dark water beneath and pink-grey horizon beyond.

"Yes. But I cannot trick the crew into coming, not on a personal endeavor," I said. "We will need at least a day to resupply and reorganize. I will warn the crew that this journey is likely to take us far off course. Whoever wishes to leave, can. I will have Mr. Keo dismiss anyone we cannot wholly trust. Many of those who were with us beyond the Stormwall we can bring fully into our confidences. As to Monna's ship, I will leave it and her crew in the custody of the port mistress. That should appease the Usti for the time being."

Mary reached out to snag my hand. There was much more I wanted to say to her—needed to, once I had a chance to soothe the wound her betrayal had cut. But for now, I focused on gratitude. She was alive. We knew where Benedict was. Because of Mary, I could act. She had sullied her hands where I refused to, and she had nearly been killed for her effort.

I did not have to let my brother die.

Impulsively, I pulled her into my chest. She was stiff for a moment, startled, then relented slightly. For a time, we simply held one another, and I felt the last of my betrayal fade into a temerarious hope.

We were going to Mere. Mere, where Ben was. Mere, where the secrets to our healing might finally be found.

That feeling of impending change, of momentousness, assailed me again.

"The Ess Noti may come back," Mary pointed out, pulling away before I was ready to let go. She scratched at her throat self-consciously, came away with bloody nails, and fished a kerchief from her pocket to wipe it away.

I forced myself to watch, reliving the fear of seeing her with the intruder in the hold, the knife breaking her skin.

Mary went on, "We don't know nearly enough about them, so we should prepare for anything. Double watches. No one goes ashore alone. We… could use some more allies."

Her tone gave me pause. "Do you have someone in mind?"

She lowered the handkerchief and smiled slyly. "How about two smugglers and a highwayman?"

EIGHT

Aeadine, the Middenwold

Twenty Years Ago

SAMUEL

The forest was cold, and frosted leaves crunched beneath my feet. Snow hid in the hollows between the trees, bright patches against the patterns of grey and black and the ripple of lanternlight. Branches rattled above our heads with a dry, brittle sound.

There was no moon.

Ahead and behind us, the long line of strangers stretched, and, as we walked, they sang a familiar song, tainted by a haunting melody and their own, circular repetitions.

"When twilight is fading I pensively rove, or at the bright noontide in solitude wander, amid the dark shades of the lonely ash grove…"

My mother's hand tightened on mine and, on her other side, Benedict whispered, "Mama, where are we going?"

"Hush," was her only reply.

"We are going to the shrine," I said, because that unspoken sense of mine told me so.

The lanternlight caught my mother's smile, as gentle and fond as it had ever been. "Hush," she said again, but softer. Kinder.

The shrine was a circular little church, deep in the wold and long abandoned. It was not the church we had come for though, so the disrepair mattered little.

We came for the hollow tree that grew inside the ruins, that had punched through its rotten beams and into the free air.

"That is the ghisting tree," I whispered—again, a *Knowing*. There was only one such tree in our forest, lonely and misplaced, planted in some way I could not fathom.

My mother squeezed my hand. This time, she did not have to tell me to be quiet. The mannerisms of the strangers around us spoke louder than words. They spread into a circle with the three of us at the center, the shrine to one side, as their singing meandered off into a chanting, wordless harmony. They watched us from behind veils and beneath hoods, and every so often I caught a wolfish smile, or an expression of ecstatic bliss, or a distant glaze I recognized from my mother's own face on nights when I could not sleep and snuck into her room for comfort. One woman kept swaying, her movements becoming more insistent and uncontrolled, and her cloak parted to reveal naked skin beneath.

I looked away, as I was supposed to, and stared at my feet. My heart hammered, and the chanting made my skin crawl, prying into every corner of my mind and pushing out all else—leaving only the song and my growing fear.

The visions began. I saw myself sick and in bed, wracked with fever. Yet somehow I was also somewhere else, screaming and alone in a world of dark water. The Other.

I saw Benedict, but gangly, almost a man. He beat someone I could not see, blood between his teeth as he laughed raggedly. Joyfully.

Then he was a boy again, the vision more immediate. He looked at me across a room, tears streaming down his face, his body covered in lashes. But I could not go to him. I could not help him, because I was still in the Dark Water.

I saw my mother put a cup in my hands.

I blinked. There *was* a cup in my hands, and it was full of milk. The worlds hazed together—lapping water, shadowed woods, singing devotees of a strange ghisting.

"Drink, my love," my mother said and gave another cup to Ben. I saw the look of vacant hope in her eyes, the overflowing pride, and a love so pervasive it looked like madness.

I knew, deep in my being, that if I drank, the visions I had seen would come to pass. I knew that the second cup, the one in Benedict's hands, held something different. It would make his eyes glassy and pull his soul from his bones. Then the pain would come.

I should have stopped it. Should have tried.

But I drank, as did Ben. And when the cup was empty and the soured, wrong taste of the milk was on my tongue, I saw the ghisting himself manifest.

He was hidden in the hollow of his tree like a corpse in a coffin, with his arms crossed over his chest and an overlarge crown fallen around his throat like a noose. He did not leave the tree, did not move.

But his glow filled the clearing. And he stared directly at me.

NINE

The Red Tempest

MARY

"I am still unclear as to why I volunteered for this," Charles groused, shivering beside me as *Hart* slipped out of Tithe's sheltered harbor and into the vast, open expanse of the Winter Sea.

The waves were draped in dusky light. Clouds hung heavy in the west, mirroring the line of the sea atop a colorful slash of open sky, where the sun sank from one shroud into the next. Pale orange, pink and bronze caught the waves, illuminating a path all the way to the horizon.

"Because you couldn't stand to be left behind?"

He buried his chin deeper into the high collar of his coat, making his beard puff up. The look he cast me was dry, edged with a secret only he and I knew.

"I've learned to pay my debts," he muttered. "I still owe you. For what I did, spying for Lirr. For never telling Demery. You still haven't… have you?"

"No. Even Samuel still doesn't know," I assured him, bumping my shoulder into his. "You already paid a high price. Though I'd like to think you came with us for friendship."

He nodded, raising his eyebrows in consideration. "And adventure?"

"You don't sound sure about that."

"I fear I am not. I'm aging, Mary." Charles's tone rode the divide between jesting and seriousness, with a melancholy shadow to his eyes. "I've started to think of home and hearths, long mornings and early bedtimes, floral curtains—save me. Ah, and a woman with a sharp mind and a willingness to bear with my existential ramblings. She is critical to this scenario. Saint, I think I even want children. Is that mad?"

I laughed. "Charles, if that's the future you want, fight for it. Though you may have to do so in the South Isles, where no one is hunting you for highway robbery or piracy."

He frowned. "It was a little warm for my liking, but perhaps. What about you? Why are you going to Mere, I mean—though if you care to divulge your dreams of the future, you know I listen well." His eyes slid to mine. "I struggle to believe you would risk your life to save Benedict Rosser, after what he tried to do to you."

I squinted at the sea. The first time I'd met Samuel's brother, he had used his Magni influence to lure me into a more than compromising situation—and attempted to keep me there, against my will. Charles had interrupted us, and he'd seen how the encounter had shaken me.

"I don't know what I want my future to look like," I admitted. "Before leaving the Wold there was simply no question. I would marry, keep my own house, stay away from the wider world. I didn't know anything else, didn't realize all that was out here to see. So now my notions are… vague. Security, yes. A family, but neither of those need be on land. All I truly know is I enjoy my life and I want to *see* more." I gestured to *Hart* and, by extension, the sea. "And I care for Samuel."

"And he cares for you," Charles added with the hint of a question.

"I believe so."

That made his brows darken in disapproval. "You have been sailing together for months and months. This ship is not large, Mary. What is stopping you?"

I suddenly decided that this conversation was not one I wanted to have.

"I am going to Mere for two reasons," I said with strengthening conviction. "Firstly, because I care for Samuel, and he was going to make a choice that he would regret for the rest of his life. I could not let him do that. And, it seems, there are other forces at work that could threaten all of us."

"Ah yes, the mysterious Ess Noti," Charles mused. "And perhaps even the Usti?"

"If the Usti meant us harm, they already had us at their mercy."

"Perhaps the time was not right. Perhaps you were more useful elsewhere, for now, or your connection to Demery protected you. Or… Perhaps you are already being watched." He leaned a little nearer, dropping his voice. "Closely."

"Oh, hush," I shot back, resisting the urge to poke him in the eye. But his words gave me pause, and an ominous feeling crept up the back of my neck. "Bastard."

Charles shrugged. "I never claimed to be otherwise."

Down the deck, the bosun's whistle piped and I heard Samuel's voice from the quarterdeck, strong and carrying. It stirred my blood in more than one way—I was all too happy to be distracted.

"Ms. Firth! A north wind, if you please?"

In answer I drew in a deep breath, down to the roots of my lungs. Then I began to sing, pushing aside Charles's words and all the uncertainties surrounding us.

The closest winds came to me in a heady rush, swirling around me. These were my trained winds, the ones that always lingered nearby, tied directly to my will and the flow of my magic. They surrounded Charles and I, stirring our clothing and hair and carrying my voice out over the water.

Next came the true wind, streaming down from the sky high above and, at my command, rushing south. As I sang that wind turned colder and sailors began to support me with a chant, a rhythmic backdrop to my melody as they raised the sails. Canvas rose with a creak of lines and tackle and a ripple of heavy fabric. We tacked, and shadows eased across Charles and I and the deck beneath our feet.

The ship turned, slowly, south. Wind whipped my hair past my face as I finished my song and looked at my friend, my smile quick and my eyes alight.

"Perhaps I wasn't entirely truthful," I amended. The song had stirred me, making my blood rush faster and my worries dim. The wind did not care for distant threats—it cared only for swiftness and freedom. "Part of me is ready for a new adventure."

"Mm." Charles closed his eyes for an instant, breathing deeply with the skirt of his long coat flapping around his thighs.

When he opened his eyes again, they glistened. Just like mine.

A day south of Tithe we navigated a series of sunken islands and hidden reefs to a small, abandoned islet. The remnants of an ancient farm—little more than moss-covered stone walls and a croft with a collapsed roof—were tucked into forbidding shoulders of rock. A handful of rugged, wild goats watched us from ridges as we anchored in a small harbor and set to the work of disguising *Hart*.

The crew, a diminished complement of one hundred and fifty men and women, gathered in the close, tar, smoke and sweat stink of the gun deck.

"You and your comrades were told back in Tithe that we head into enemy waters after Ophalia Monna, who was stolen from us by Mereish intruders," Samuel said, facing down the length of the deck. The hammocks had been stowed and the crew stood around or sat on the long guns, lashed in their cradles. Sea-chests were tucked between the guns, and the deck was impeccably clean, illuminated by the open gunports and a wash of daylight. On the breeze, gulls cried.

"You, however, know the truth. We sail to the Mereish mainland to recover the captain of the late *Harbringer*, my brother Benedict Rosser. Believe me when I say that I take not one of you for granted. Thank you for staying with *Hart* during this clandestine mission. As Mr. Penn has promised, you will be well paid."

Nods and murmurs met this.

Samuel went on, "I will take no chances near the Mereish mainland, so *Hart* must be renamed, our complement disguised. We will fly Usti colors. If necessary, we will make port as Usti smugglers. Those of you who are Usti or speak that language, report to the Uknaras—Illya and Olsa—immediately." At this, Samuel gestured to the Usti couple, who stood next to me off to one side. "Everyone else, we must be about our tasks."

Before long, *Hart*'s gunports were painted blue and their edges hidden with artful paint, while new, false gunports were marked at lesser intervals. This would not hold up to close inspection, but it would not do for *Macholka*—translated to the *Leaping Stag*, from an Usti folktale—to halve *Hart*'s warship complement of forty-two guns. We were merchants and smugglers now, sly and discreet.

There was little for me to do save calm the frigid wind around the ship and ensure the painters could finish their work in relative comfort. I leaned over the stern as the Usti letters were inscribed above the gallery windows, one at a time.

Positioned as I was, I saw the sails round the island at the same time as the watchmen. The newcomer flew Mereish colors, boasted bold red sails, and, by her track, she was making for our cove.

No warning bell sounded. No watchman cried out. But the message rippled down the deck.

I looked up as Samuel appeared at my side, clear-eyed and alert. He was already wearing an Usti overcoat—broadly belted and spewing fur at every opening—along with a fur-lined hat. His hair was loose at his cheeks and his beard less kempt, but well oiled. His sun-darkened skin was naturally ambiguous, though his face leaned towards the Aeadine—his nose a little too straight for an Usti, his cheekbones a little too smooth. But he was passable.

My features were not, though that hardly mattered. Stormsingers were commodities bought and traded and stolen, and no one cared where we came from.

I thought of my contract, carefully stowed with Samuel's documents in the main cabin, and steeled myself.

"Cap'n," Ms. Skarrow called, craning out from the balcony below, spyglass in hand. Below her, the small waves of the cove chopped placidly. "Do we beat to quarters?"

"No. Finish your work as usual, though pick up the pace. Thank the Saint we already stowed the midship guns." Samuel turned. "Mr. Uknara!"

Illya topped the quarterdeck stairs, Olsa a step behind.

"You are my first officer, as we discussed. Ms. Uknara, you are my Sooth. Mr. Keo! Assemble our 'Usti' crew and get everyone else below. Mr. Penn, see our armsmen prepared, though discreetly. Mary?"

I swallowed the lump in my throat. "I'll change, but stay out of sight."

He offered me a brief, bracing smile then looked at the nervous crew. "Stay calm. Like as not she'll pay us no mind and be on her way once her water casks are full—there's little else on this island to be had. Finish your tasks. Go about your evening. Nothing is amiss."

His confidence bolstered the crew, but my stomach was still uneasy as I made my way down to my cabin and hurriedly opened a trunk. An array of garments spread out before me: Aeadine, Mereish, and Usti. I chose an overcoat from the latter, braided my hair into two braids threaded with linen, and wrapped them around my head. I topped it all with a fur-lined cap like Olsa usually wore, and my transformation from free Aeadine Stormsinger to captive of Usti smugglers was complete.

I made my way through the ship to the central hatchway of the gundeck, where a grating covered with canvas let in the barest shred of lanternlight, sound, and the occasional gust of wind to lift its edges. I wasn't the only one to shift here—Charles already loitered in the dim space, along with a dozen crewmembers and Poverly, the steward's girl.

Not one of them, spoke and Poverly put a finger over her lips at my approach. I lightened my steps and came to stand near Charles, just out of the light.

"What's happening?" I asked, so low I thought I might have to repeat myself.

"The Meres dropped anchor," Poverly returned.

"They ran up the white and gold," Mr. Penn added, sidling closer to me. His cap had slipped up on his bald scalp, forming an impish point, and the irregular shape of his ears—the tops lost to frostbite over the Stormwall—were on full display. Ten or so crewfolk loitered about him, pistols and knives discreetly shoved under their coats.

"The white and gold?" Charles repeated. "Sorry, forgot my Mereish flags."

"Meanin' peaceful intent," Poverly interjected, joining our little cluster. I'd noticed her watching Charles a little too keenly since we left Tithe, but I'd been fourteen once too, and Charles was an attractive man.

"Hush," another woman hissed.

We fell silent. Muffled voices came to us through the canvas-shrouded grating, and I recognized Samuel's rumble and cadence, though his words were obscured.

"Pov, here, child," the other woman beckoned.

Poverly complied reluctantly at first, then more quickly once the woman crouched with her hands laced into a stirrup. One of the other crewmen did the same, and together they boosted the girl up to the edge of the grating. The assembly gathered close with bated breath and straining ears.

"I can't hear them," Poverly complained. "You're being too loud."

"Oh, aye, I'll just stop breathing, then," the woman holding her up grumbled.

I retreated into the shadows and placed a bare hand on the nearest post. Everyone present knew I was *ghiseau*, but that didn't mean I intended to flaunt my condition or its benefits.

Tane's presence shivered down my fingers and into the wood as a subtle, glowing thread of spectral flesh passed up into the deck above.

Words slipped into my mind, muffled but discernable. Images came too, hedged with an odd, luminescent quality that I'd learned was how Tane always saw the world. It was something like Samuel's Sooth Sight, but subtler, more sensitive, and pervasive. He saw the signposts; she saw the feet that had trodden the path.

Charles gave me a sideways look then stepped in front of me to block the crew's view. Mr. Penn peered at us and tugged his cap back into place.

Above, Samuel stood by the rail and spoke across the water in Mereish. I didn't speak the language but Tane did, and her translation came to me a breath delayed.

"… too kind," Samuel's voice said, with a hint of deflection. "Though the hour is very late, perhaps I might extend our own hospitality to you in the morning?"

"Nonsense," came a more distant reply, masculine and flippant, distinctly Mereish. "Men such as we should not be slaves to the sun, and it's been an age since I had word from a free port. Come. Join me."

I caught my breath.

A tense silence. Tane caught the expression on Samuel's face as he looked across the water, composed but not altogether calm. The other captain was pressuring him. He knew it and let his irritation show.

Still, he inclined his head. "It would be my pleasure. We will join you presently."

THE SPRING TIDES—*Commonly and erroneously referred to as the Black Tides, given that they take place under the darkness of the moon, the two highest tides of spring are significant on numerous levels, but, for the purpose of this study, the most significant is this: their occurrence marks a thinning in the division between the human world and that of the Other, creating the ideal circumstances for various religious practices, including the amplification of mages.*

This is even more true of the real Black Tides, from whom the common name was plundered. However, these occur far more rarely and lie beyond the permissions and knowledge of this humble commentator.

—FROM A DEFINITIVE STUDY OF THE BLESSED: MAGES AND MAGECRAFT OF THE MEREISH ISLES, TRANSLATED FROM THE MEREISH BY SAMUEL I. ROSSER

TEN

Jessin Faucher

SAMUEL

The main cabin aboard Jessin Faucher's *Miaghis*—which translated rather dramatically to *The Red Tempest*—was small, considering the size of the forty-eight-gun warship. It stretched across the width of the stern, bulkheads spread with neatly spaced charts, maps and diagrams, giving more the sense of a professor's office than a captain's quarters. Books were arrayed on shelves, caged so as not to fall with the roll of the ship, and the central stove in its iron cradle kept the air warm, dry and welcoming. The scent of the fire mingled with beeswax, tobacco smoke and citrus, pleasantly overtaking the usual salt-and-damp scent of ship.

Captain Faucher directed Illya and I to a table, where his steward poured coffee from an ornate silver service. As he did, we unbuttoned our outer coats—or rather, I did while Illya carelessly tossed his over the back of his chair and squinted around the room.

"I see you enjoy your books. You're an academic?" Illya observed. He spoke in his native tongue, and it transformed him. When he spoke Aeadine his words were clipped, perfunctory and shallow. But in Usti his voice deepened and slowed, his articulation contemplative and at ease.

"Very much so," Faucher replied. He spoke in Usti as well, a common second tongue for Mereish. "Knowledge is power. Please, sit."

Illya sat, and I considered our host as the steward left.

"I was surprised to find someone else in my favorite abandoned harbor," Faucher began, pouring thick, sweetened cinnamon cream into his coffee and giving it a single stir. "Tithe may be a neutral port, but I refuse to pay for water. Some things should be free, do you not agree?"

I picked up my own coffee, leaving it black, while at my side Illya liberally dosed his with honey and plain, white cream. "Agreed."

Faucher watched me. "It is also a good place to keep one's head down for a few days."

"I suppose so," I acknowledged, tucking the hint of a conspiratorial smile around my eyes. Inwardly, my suspicion coiled. Faucher had already pegged us as smugglers, which was a success, but there was a chance he had marked our false gunports and painting efforts on his approach. Either way, it was clear we had secrets. I doubted protestations of innocence would go far, but I might be able to steer Faucher's suspicions onto safer waters.

Faucher mirrored my smile. "Tell me, what news have you?"

The three of us spoke for some time, sharing information. Faucher was naturally discreet on all matters to do with the war, our focus centering on the Usti and trade. This, thankfully, was something Illya was very familiar with.

"What is your cargo?" Faucher finally asked.

"Hesti parchment, for the most part," I said, naming the only cargo we had been able to procure on such short notice. "Bound for the printers in Port Gedden, though we will only be taking it as far as Yashm."

"The South Isles." Faucher nodded. "I envy you, sailing into summer while we ride out the Black Tides."

Even spoken in Usti, the name struck me. I felt my mask stiffen and drained my coffee to cover it. The Black Tides, when seaside settlements pulled their boats into the hills and thanked their ancestors for building their homes out of reach of the ravenous waves. A time of natural upheaval and unnatural superstitions.

A time when cults tortured young mages and made them into monsters.

If Faucher noticed my reaction, he did not comment. "Everything—save the people, I suppose—is milder down in the isles. The tides, this year in particular. The winter. Though you are still bound to sail through harsh weather. I trust you have an experienced weather mage?"

Illya snorted. "She manages, when the mood strikes her. I have never had such a stubborn witch."

"What is she?"

"Aeadine."

"Ah."

I felt a fleeting urge to defend Mary, but praising one's Stormsinger was the equivalent to shaking a pouch full of gold in the Knocks.

"A firm hand will go a long way," Faucher advised. "Hunger makes them weak, that I do not advise. But a little pain is a fine incentive."

I tried to drain my coffee a second time and found it empty. I set down my cup a little too firmly. The clatter brought both men's gazes to me.

"I wonder if I might ask a more delicate question." Faucher turned his eyes to Illya then returned them to me. "Is there any talk in Tithe of the *Godvind*?"

I forced myself to speak civilly. "I have not heard of it."

Illya also shook his head.

"She's a Mereish vessel, vanished a month ago in these very waters." Faucher nodded towards the window and the sea beyond. "The Free Channels."

"Pirates?" Illya suggested.

Faucher gave a half-hearted nod. "Perhaps, though she herself would have been no great prize. She was a passenger ship."

I caught something in his tone. "Those passengers are now missing."

Faucher nodded.

"Who are they?"

"That," Faucher refilled his cup, then mine without asking, "is a question for my betters. I do know that Usti warships left Tithe to pursue the matter. That must signal some… gravity, to the situation."

My Sooth's senses prickled. There were five Usti warships stationed in Tithe, but none of them had been in port during our brief stay. The *Star of the Sea*, the very ship we had intended to hand Monna over to, was one of them.

"I would prefer, naturally," Faucher went on, "that the Mereish be allowed to pursue their own investigation into the disappearance of our people, but the Usti were quite firm on handling the matter."

"They could be dead," Illya pointed out.

Faucher shrugged noncommittally. "I have reason to believe otherwise."

"The incident took place in the Free Channels," I mused. "The Usti are bound to keep the peace here, and neither the Mereish nor the Aeadine have jurisdiction. It is part of the Accords."

"The Accords which serve the Usti very well." Faucher's tone took on an icy edge. "I suspect the Usti will report—grudgingly, tactfully—that the Aeadine are at fault for the disappearance. And where will that leave us Mereish? With more fuel for the fire but only the word of our oppressors to ignite it."

Oppressors? I sat back in my chair, looking more directly and openly at Faucher than I had since we arrived. "You are a Separatist."

Faucher's laugh was light and sincere. "No, no, no one with half their wits would support the Separatists, at least not in mixed company." His gaze scanned between the two of us. "And our company is rather mixed, is it not? An Aeadine privateer, an Usti smuggler? A ship reeking of fresh paint and the figurehead of a stag?"

I withdrew my hands from the table and prepared to stand. In contrast, Illya leaned more heavily back in his chair, crossed his arms over his chest and stacked his feet.

"What do you want?" the big Usti asked with only a slight narrowing of the eyes.

Faucher leaned forward. "I came looking for a ship called *Hart*. I found him, it seems, but this…" The Mereish waved his finger between Illya and I. "Has given me pause. Why disguise yourselves when you have Usti papers giving you free passage? Unless your quest is unsanctioned."

"Why would you be looking for *Hart*?" I asked. Denial, again, seemed a waste of breath.

"Because I want to know why the Usti queen has hired Aeadine privateers to do her dirty laundry." Faucher sat forward, elbows on the table, legs braced wide beneath. "What are you doing? What missions does she send you on? Tell me, be honest. You and I need not be enemies."

I calculated our options. Illya and I could fight our way to the longboat, but, even if we made it, we would be open targets traversing the distance between *The Red Tempest* and *Hart*.

"First, let me remind you," I began. "You have no jurisdiction in the Free Channels, and, regardless, we have committed no crime against you. I do have a Letter of Marque from the Usti, and I am justified to use whatever means necessary to accomplish my goals."

Even if those goals are selfish? a small, aloof voice inquired.

The Mereish captain's gaze raked my face. "Sailing under false colors is a crime."

I smiled at that, wry and knowing. "True, Captain Faucher. This world, this sea, this war—it makes criminals of us all. I am bound by contracts and obligations, as are you, and too often my greatest sacrifice is my honor."

That felt a little too honest, a little too raw. But I had gambled correctly. Something passed through the other man's eyes, something like solidarity.

Resting his elbows on the table, he looked from Illya, now silent, and back to me. "I might say the same. We are the sum of our choices, and what are we to do when all those choices are evil? When the powers who govern us push us away from peace and into further violence?"

"We heed our consciences," I replied. I sat forward, mirroring him across the table.

"In this too, we agree," the other man said. "Which is why I will not apprehend you, as I have been instructed to do. Instead, I will let you go and give you this." He reached inside the breast of his coat and pulled out a stack of folded papers. "You are in a unique position in this war, Captain Rosser. I hope you will use this evidence wisely, and that perhaps—" he held up the envelopes meaningfully "—some day you might repay me in kind."

Illya stood and I accepted the papers—waxed and scrawled with Usti lettering. My heart beat too quickly and my blood felt light, bubbling through my veins. Who *was* this man and what was he after?

My Sooth's senses were silent.

DITTAMA [ditt-ah-mah]—*An Other-born creature with a form reminiscent of the Sunjani's thick-billed giant storks. They may stand over six feet tall and possess a wingspan double this length, which serves them both in the sky and underwater, as these creatures are both aerial and aquatic. Dittama are known to hunt and consume infant mages, more rarely adult ones, and are traditionally considered ill-omens in both Aeadine and Usti folklore.*

—FROM THE WORDBOOK ALPHABETICA: A NEW
WORDBOOK OF THE AEADINES

ELEVEN

Harmony and Harbingers

MARY

We parted from *The Red Tempest* without incident and continued our course, following the Free Channels close to Mereish waters until darkness fell, then veering across the line. We sounded no bells and we lit no lanterns, though we spied others on the horizon.

Either Olsa or Sam attended every watch, lending their Sooth's foresight to the task of keeping us away from prying eyes. Spring on the Winter Sea, they said, was a fortuitous time—a time of great luck or greater ill fortune. The former, thankfully, seemed to grace us.

During one of Samuel's watches, I joined Olsa in the main cabin. She sat at the central table with a lantern swinging overhead and an array of papers spread around her—the documents Faucher had given to Samuel, along with the cipher that was intended to decode them.

"How goes it?" I asked the Usti, sinking down across from her with a mug of hot tea.

The older woman frowned and picked up a page covered with indecipherable Mereish. "I am beginning to wonder if this Faucher is Yissik Ocho himself. These are encoded, and not lightly, either. I believed this here to be a key to the cipher, but I cannot unravel it. Ris cannot. Why did he think Samuel could?"

Ris was Olsa's ghisting. I saw the being's spectral flesh flutter across Olsa's hands at the sound of her name.

"Who, ah, is Yissik Ocho?" I asked.

"An old Usti god. The trickster who led St. Helga to her death in a snowstorm," the other woman clarified. "The Mereish call him Saint Yalen, Saint of Fortune."

I picked up one of the letters and tilted it towards the light. Tane, too, turned her attention to the paper, but the beautiful, sweeping letters remained as obscure as ever.

"All I have learned today—or that I have guessed—is that all of these are copied from originals," Olsa said. "Their dates, which Samuel deciphered last night, are years apart, but this paper is all new, and the writing matches Faucher's supposed key."

"So Faucher kept the originals." I laid the paper back down. "That seems natural."

The older woman let out a long breath and sat back, lacing her fingers over her breasts. "Tane, will you try?"

"She doesn't recognize the writing."

"Try, please?"

Tane slipped from my skin with my next breath and considered the papers, rounding the table in a slow, steady gait. She could not pick the pages up, linen as they were. But she stopped in front of the key, clearly displayed, and stared down. I felt her thoughts as distant whispers, a quiet wind through a forest canopy.

She lifted her sea-glass eyes to Olsa. *Did you try to read it in the Dark Water?*

Why would I do that? Her response was inaudible, channeled through Ris, but came to my mind all the same.

Tane gestured to the table. *Faucher gave them to Samuel, a Sooth. They are indecipherable, yet clearly intended to have meaning. Why not try everything?*

Faucher is no Sooth, though, I interjected. *How would he make something like that? Is it even possible to tie paper to the Dark Water? It's not wood or flesh or bone.*

Tane glanced between us, disapproving. *Both your powers come from the Other, and yet somehow you forget it pervades everything.*

Olsa stood. "Fine, we will try. Mary, join me?"

I hesitated. Tane slipped back through the wood of the table and into my bones.

"I'll only have four breaths," I reminded her. Even being *ghiseau* and bonded to a Mother Ghisting, my body was still human, and taking in too much of the Other's foreign air would begin to change me. Unlike Sam, whose physical body remained in the mortal world when he looked into the Other, mine came with me. I truly walked into that other place, and so we had begun to call it Otherwalking.

"And?" Olsa countered, unbothered. "You should practice."

"But it's dangerous. And uncomfortable," I mewed, heard how pathetic I sounded, and caught myself. "Fine, I'll come."

Olsa's smile was smug as she reached out her hand. I rarely missed my mother—I'd spent most of my life without her—but the look in Olsa's eyes and the feel of her fingers in mine reminded me painfully of her absence.

Olsa's eyes took on a distant quality. I inhaled, deep and only a little shaky, and let Tane tug me out of the human world.

The ship faded to transparency, bulkheads growing thinner and thinner until I could see an endless expanse of black waves. A chorus of lights awoke, glinting like stars at dusk.

I caught my breath. My first breath. Olsa was a specter here, clothed in forest-green light edged with grey, but I was here in my entirety, my human skin—flesh and blood—glowing a soft teal, brushed with grey.

We looked down at the table, which was transparent save for the faint remnants of ghisting influence. The papers, as I expected, were invisible.

But the ink was not. Lined with the barest light, the text remained, transposed onto the spectral wood of the tabletop.

Another breath.

"See?" Tane inquired. Her voice was sonorous here in the Dark Water, audible in a way that she never was in the human world, unless she used my mouth.

Olsa tilted her head and paced, surveying the letters with furrowed brows. Then she grinned. In the human world, her physical body must have picked up Faucher's cipher, because the lines of text rose into the air before us. The hands of her spectral body remained unmoving—one on the tabletop, one in mine.

The bizarreness of it all made my head spin. No wonder Samuel was terrified of losing his mind here.

"Look," Olsa urged.

My third breath. I looked at the floating words, Usti and Mereish in scattered rows. Then I blinked. There were more words on the page now, hidden letters that transformed the key from illegible to... something Tane comprehended, but I did not.

Movement snatched my attention up just as a malevolent orange light plunged through the deck towards us. I had just enough time to glimpse wings and a beak—a huge, thick, clattering beak—before I let out my fourth breath in a shriek and toppled back into the human world.

I landed hard on my ass, tearing my fingers from Olsa's. The older woman came back to herself half a heartbeat later, braced and calm. She cast me a high-browed look as the orange light extinguished, the Dark Water faded, the papers returned to their previous, inscrutable state on the table.

"It can't follow us back," I panted, needing her to confirm it. "Whatever that was, it can't pass through."

"No. But now we are aware that there is a dittama watching us in the Other," she observed dryly. "Nothing should have found us so quickly, and my Knowing affirms it. I think you should not Otherwalk until it moves on, at least aboard ship."

"Happily." I eased to my feet, aching and rubbing my back. "Why is it following us? I know the stories about ill omens and such, but… there must be a proper reason."

"It is hunting."

I cringed. "Hunting us?"

Olsa nodded and shuffled the papers. "So, I can read the key, though if that creature is fixated on us, this will take time. I will not be able to move in the Dark Water for long. The dittama cannot eat my spirit there, but it can harm Ris."

I dusted off my hands, forcing my lingering anxiety aside and, all too happily, shedding any responsibility for the papers and their deciphering. Whatever they said, whatever secrets they held, I did not want them on my shoulders, anyways.

"Well, then," I said, making for the door. "I'm going to bed."

TWELVE

Hesten

Nine Months Ago

SAMUEL

Warmth seeped into every part of me from the fire and close-packed humanity, the rum in my belly and Mary, her arms wrapped around my bicep, her hair spilling onto my shoulder.

The fiddler lulling the tavern into somnolence drew the last note from her instrument. The clapping was heartfelt but slow, attesting to her success.

"Captain Rosser!"

Mary quickly disentangled as a man set his tankard down on our table then proceeded to shrug off his jacket.

"Damn hot in here," the man blustered as he sank into a chair and fanned himself expansively with his hat. He was a thin, fit fellow, with flushed cheeks in a pale-skinned face—Southern Aeadine, a Whallish if I ever saw one, with the personality to match.

"Please, join us," Mary muttered sardonically.

The man scowled at her, then squinted at me. "This your Stormsinger?"

"Ms. Firth," I said, sitting straight. "This is Captain Mercer of *Fair Fortune*, who encountered some less-than-fair fortune, and has been waiting for his ship to be repaired. How long now, Captain Mercer?"

Mercer seemed put out. He sniffed and buried his face in his tankard. "Another two weeks or so. So? This your witch or just a common whore? Or both? Ow!" He jumped and spilled ale down the front of his shirt.

"Oh, my apologies! I must have kicked you!" Mary crooned, leaning over the table and helpfully taking the tankard from his hands. She promptly dropped the whole vessel into his lap.

Mercer made a gargling sound, clutching himself out of sight.

Instinct had me half out of my seat—to defend Mary, help Mercer or punch him, I was not sure. But as Mary fussed, I sat slowly back down, trying to hide a smile.

"I'm so clumsy tonight! Too much wine. Let me get you a cloth." With that Mary swept past the man and merged with the crowd.

"She did that on purpose," Mercer raged, shooting me a heated look as he finally ceased clutching himself and tried, unsuccessfully, to mop up his shirt with a handkerchief. I heard a clatter under the table as the tankard rolled away, but Mercer seemed done with it. "You should control your people."

"You suggested she was a whore," I pointed out coolly.

"She's clinging to your arm in the middle of a public house, what else is she?"

Steel crept into my spine. "A woman to whom you should show more respect."

Mercer snorted. "So she's *not* your whore?"

"She is *Hart*'s Stormsinger."

Mercer threw his sodden handkerchief on the table and gave me an irritated pout. "Tart, whore, Stormsinger—there's a difference? Both end up under your belly."

All sound in the room faded, and all I saw was Mercer's face.

Whatever he saw on mine made even his rosy Whallish complexion blanch. "No need to take offense, Rosser, we've all taken liberties with witches."

"I have not," I ground out. "I would not."

Mercer's expression stuttered into a false smile that failed to hide his disbelief or even a scrap of pity. Gathering his hat and handkerchief with a muttered curse of farewell, he got up and left the table.

Mary did not come back until he had exited the tavern entirely.

"At last." She eased back into her chair and smiled at me, warm and soft and amused. "What an awful man."

She made to slip her arm around mine again. I imagined her touch, the gentleness of it, how I wanted to bundle her into my arms and hide her from the eyes of everyone else, from men like Mercer and every atrocity on the Winter Sea.

Instead, I rose, slipping her grasp with apparent distraction, and pulled on my coat. "I need some air."

She eyed me but grabbed her jacket.

Outside, where a long summer evening graced the street with pink-orange light and the good folk of Usti traversed clean, dry cobblestones, I breathed no easier. Mary still didn't speak, and, by silent agreement, we started back towards the ship.

It was not until *Hart*'s masts came into sight, rising amid some dozen others in one of Hesten's square wet docks, that I spoke again.

"We need to be different."

Mary looked at me sideways. "What do you mean?"

"The way we were tonight, how close we were." I had pondered this the whole walk back, but I still struggled for words. "You know I care for you. I know you care for me. But Stormsingers and their captains have a… reputation."

"Mercer is an awful man," Mary cut in. "Just because he assumed—"

"He assumed I, as a captain, was abusing you, my Stormsinger," I said bluntly. "And that is what everyone else will believe as well."

Her scowl was disgusted. "And? They're wrong."

"Are they?"

Mary's expression turned aghast. "Samuel, you haven't so much as kissed me properly. I am so profoundly unsullied by you, by *anyone*, I think my virginity has actually come back."

My cheeks flamed. I looked up and down the street, relieved to see no one listening to Mary's outburst, then tugged her into the mouth of an alley.

"Oh, was that all I had to say?" Mary grinned, a mixture of bravado and nervous excitement in her eyes.

I put a fist over my mouth and held my breath, trying to corral my thoughts.

"Mary," I began. "You are the first Stormsinger in centuries to have a contract. To be her own master. I am the first captain to *hire* a Stormsinger in just as long, instead of kidnapping or buying one. We must set an example."

As I spoke, the reality of my words sank in. It was not as though I had not considered such things before, but they had seemed distant concerns. As Mary had so tactfully put it, I had not so much as kissed her. Our relationship, the warmth between us, was still too young and we too busy for anything more.

"If we are openly intimate, even if our relationship is amiable, the world will misunderstand," I said. She watched me in silence now, a dangerous quiet I knew well. "They will misinterpret us and disregard what we have achieved. What you have achieved."

"They will think less of you," she translated. She laced her arms over her chest and leaned back against the opposite alley wall, careless of the filth. "And you've just gotten your honor back. Halfway back."

I opened my mouth to protest, but a spike of guilt cut me off. "Yes," I admitted, pulling the word like a fouled tooth. "But that is only one aspect. What I have said is true, you must see it."

"I see it," she said. "I, however, do not see how our relationship robs my contract of meaning. If you want me not to touch you in public, I won't. But what you and I are to one another behind closed doors? That is no one's concern but ours. We can be whatever we want."

"I want to believe that," I said, so honest it left me feeling raw. "But that is not how the world works. Rumors. Truth. Lies. Secrets.

It always comes out. And this example we are trying to set, this security we might one day forge for Stormsingers? What you and I are could tear it down before we have even begun to build."

"People will think you a lecher," Mary added. She forced a smile, a hard expression that failed to hide how hurt she was.

"Mary, I am serious."

"So am I," she shot back. "I'll be clear, just this once, so listen to me. I joined your crew for the opportunity, yes. For the contract, yes. But I also joined because I care for you, and I am *very* curious to see where that goes. I have been engaged. I know what I want. I will not spend years dancing around your reservations, and I do not believe that you and I tangling here and there will destroy the future of all Stormsingers. So let me know when you decide that you want me more than you want shitlings like Captain Mercer to think you're better than them—because I assure you, they do not truly care."

Her words were knives, slowly pushed into my flesh, and I wanted them to stop. "Mary, be reasonable. This is not about Mercer, this—"

She ducked away and backed out into the street, smiling sweetly. "*This* is a conversation I'm no longer willing to have. Good night, Samuel."

With that, she strode away down the docks. As she went the blood roared through my ears, my control slipped, and the human world faded. Mary's form became one of grey-hedged teal light, and the Dark Water lapped around my heels, chased by errant dragonflies.

I grabbed the coin in my pocket. The human world solidified ,and I sagged back against the alley wall, still harried by the sound of lapping water and dragonfly wings.

How could I forget? How, for one night, could I let myself disregard what I was and pretend that my condition was not a critical factor in why I needed to keep Mary at arm's length?

Even if Mary and I won the respect of the world, I could not offer her a broken man. But that, at least, I had hope of rectifying.

The next day, I went to a talisman maker's shop and made my request: a cure from Mere.

It was a week before the tension between Mary and I eased. Another month before I found the charred remains of the talisman maker's shop and, in my distress, embraced her again in the privacy of my cabin, though I did not risk telling her why. A few of the knives between us were sheathed, even if a little more of my hope died the same day.

And together, we sailed on.

THIRTEEN

Smugglers and Thieves

SAMUEL

The only sounds in the night were the rush of waves up the beach and distant church bells from the small Mereish settlement of Orres. One bell came from inland, echoing between deep-carved hills, raw and ridged as if a giant had raked his fingers across the island. The other drifted down the coast from the pirate-infested town where Olsa and Illya had ventured two hours ago.

The waiting crew were quiet, perched on our longboat in the frost-laden sand, passing a pipe back and forth. Chunks of ice scattered the beach, hulks cast high by the ever-rising spring tides.

Still, the wind smelled like spring. Mary turned her face into it and inhaled reverently. I in turn drank in her expression, her dark lashes against windburned cheeks.

"Someone's coming," Grant, lingering on my other side, warned.

Mary's eyes flicked open, and all three of us looked up the beach.

Lanterns bobbed as a small party topped the rise of the bay, scattering reflections across hard-crusted snow and a treacherous, icy path. But Olsa and Illya walked with confidence, as did the stranger with them—a well-dressed man with clean-shaven cheeks and intelligent eyes.

"Captain," Olsa called in Mereish, once they were well within earshot. "We have a guest."

I went to meet them, leaving Mary and Grant where they were.

"Captain Novos," the stranger said, citing my new identity as Usti smuggler and small-time pirate. "I am Alarik Sa Vis. Welcome, and thank you for bringing such old friends back to me." At that, he cast a smile at the Uknaras.

"A pleasure to make your acquaintance," I said.

"The pleasure is mine," Sa Vis beamed. "It has been some time since I had such a unique business opportunity. Provided all is kept between us, of course."

"Of course." I nodded towards the waiting boat. "I am sure my friends passed on an invitation to come aboard?"

"They did." Sa Vis nodded and rubbed his hands together against the cold. "Lead the way, Captain."

Back aboard the ship, we settled into my cabin.

"So, what would you have from me, old friends, and new?" Sa Vis's eyes swept from Olsa to me as he pulled out a chair and sat, seeming to take up a whole side of the table with his braced arms and prominent presence.

I looked at Olsa, prompting. We had agreed it best she reveal the details of our visit, given the history she and Illya shared with Sa Vis—stories of smuggling and daring deeds she had touched on during our tense journey to the coast.

"One of our crew is imprisoned in Fort Gat," Olsa said. "We need a way into the cells. We need schedules and diagrams—anything you can give us."

Sa Vis's eyebrows halted halfway up his forehead. "You think I can help you with this? I have been trying to stay *out* of that prison for thirty-five years. Everyone in this town has."

"Then it sounds as though you'd appreciate us destroying the warden's reputation," Mary commented.

Sa Vis swiveled his head to regard her, eyebrows still high. "Now who are you?"

"The Stormsinger," she replied and tipped her wine towards him. "But do not even consider stealing me. I make a terrible captive."

I could not resist adding, "Unfortunately, she is correct."

Mary cast me a look, the smile I had hoped for nowhere to be seen.

Sa Vis's eyes narrowed, but there was amusement in them. "I would not consider it, my lady."

I said, "We are prepared to pay well for any information on the fortress you have, as well as aid getting in and out."

"I will not go near Gat, so I must decline the latter request," Sa Vis said. "It is too dangerous, and my brother died there."

"My deepest regrets."

Sa Vis puffed his chest out and patted his breast. "My heart is hard now. I can bear the pain. He died there along with two hundred other prisoners, five years ago. They blamed it on disease, a common enough cause given the conditions of that prison. But since then, they stopped filling the cells. They take only mages, and prisoners of war and politics. Nowadays, it seems the Provost's business is caging only the most powerful men and women. So..." St this, he stared at me directly, demanding an answer. "Why would your missing crewman qualify for his attentions?"

I exchanged a look with Olsa and wished, not for the first time, that I could communicate in silence as the *ghiseau* did.

"My own brother," I admitted. "A powerful Magni mage."

"Ah." Sa Vis sat back and rested one ankle on his opposite knee.

"If there are so many mages at the prison," Mary asked, leaning on her elbows on the tabletop, "do they have some way of concealing them, in the Other? Our Sooth struggled to see them."

Sa Vis started to shake his head, but paused. "Yes, I believe so. Sooths struggle to access the Other near the fort. And I have never heard of anyone breaking out, so they must have ways of controlling the mages inside."

"How?" Grant asked.

Sa Vis let out a short breath, his mouth twisted. "I do not know the details. There are rumors, of course—talismans and wards, doorways marked with symbols and carved of ghisten wood. The ghistings are guards who never sleep."

Mary watched Sa Vis, her expression sober.

Our guest went on, "I have some knowledge that will help you. How much are you willing to pay for my good council?"

Deciding on a price was not difficult. The majority of the riches we had brought back from beyond the Stormwall were safely banked in Hesten and Tithe, but *Hart*'s coffers were not light. A few Mereish treasures from bygone eras made Sa Vis's eyes ignite with want, and the rest of the evening was spent discussing the finer details of the prison's location, layout and possible avenues of entry.

Two hours later, Illya escorted Sa Vis back to shore, leaving Mary, Olsa, Grant and I in the cabin. We sat in quiet for a moment, each to our own thoughts. I added details to a sketch I had made under Sa Vis's supervision, depicting the fort from various angles, my head full of possible routes and avenues we might explore.

"Monks," Grant said, slapping his palm down on the table. "We go in as monks, offering council to the prisoners."

Olsa shook her head. "Remember there is a shrine inside the fort. They will have their own servants or monks, the order does not matter."

Grant was unfazed. "We hijack a shipment of supplies and come in as the drivers."

Olsa looked tired now. "They likely work with one company of trusted merchants. But… it is worth looking into. Put that on the list."

Pleased, Grant snatched a piece of paper and stylus from the center of the table and leaned over to steal my ink.

"I assume simply throwing a rope over the wall is out of the question," Grant observed as he wrote.

"As Sa Vis said, the walls are very well guarded."

"A good distraction can go a long way," he pointed out. "Or perhaps we can blackmail the warden? Or a guard."

"Not enough time," Mary said.

"We hold their families for ransom."

"Mr. Grant..." I rubbed at my forehead, which was beginning to ache.

"Pardon me," Grant said without a hint of remorse. "We disguise ourselves as guards."

"Still, no. None of us look Mereish enough," Olsa said.

"Sam might."

"Sam looks like Ben, one of their *prisoners*," Mary countered.

"Thus he shall be in disguise!"

I raised my voice to cut them off and lowered it as they quietened. "Whatever our plan may be, it must be quick—we can risk no more than a few days anchored near any settlement. It should involve as little contact with *anyone* as possible. And we must mitigate the risk to ourselves, the guards and the locals. We cannot cause a stir."

Quiet closed over us again.

"I have an idea." Mary's voice finally broke the quill-scratching stillness. She held up her hands, a faint glow coming into sight just above her skin.

"Going over the walls is too risky. But I could walk *through* them." Mary laced her fingers together and surveyed us. "You remember how I went into the Other to escape Lirr's fire? In body, not just in spirit like Sam and Olsa do? Otherwalking."

Grant looked aghast. "But surely... that was just one time. Is that not dangerous? Unnatural?"

Mary lifted one of her ghisting-sheathed hands. "Very little about me is natural, Charles. So, I suppose it is rather natural..."

I sat back, as if those few inches could distance me from the notion of Mary going into a prison, alone, risking her life for my twin. "What exactly are you proposing?"

"Tane and I walk through the prison walls, find Ben, and release him." Grant made a strangled sound, but Mary went on, raising her voice slightly. "I have four breaths in the Other before I must come back to the human world. That is more than enough to pass through the walls. I can explore unseen."

I stared at her across the table, wishing for a pot of coffee. "You want to go alone?"

"I would have to," Mary replied. "Though I always have Tane."

I rubbed at my temples. "You know what I mean."

"I can do it," Mary asserted.

"We can find another way," Grant put forward. "Cart drivers, I insist. Or those fellows who come to take away bodies, what are they called? The step before gravedigger. They must have dead going out here and there. We claim we are there for a body—hardly matters if there is one, we will already be inside."

"Charles, be serious," Mary said with a sigh.

"I am perfectly serious," the highwayman shot back, and began to write. "'Charles… poses… as a handsome psychopomp.'"

My headache worsened. "Poverly!" I called towards the door.

Footsteps sounded in the passage and Poverly popped her head inside. "Yessir?"

"Coffee, if you please. And tell Willoughby to prepare a light supper."

The girl bobbed her head and vanished.

"How many times have you crossed into the Dark Water since that night?" I struggled to say 'the fire'—the horror of that moment still felt far too close, the stench and the knowledge that Mary was burning alive before my eyes. It made the thought of her putting herself at risk for Benedict all the more intolerable.

"Half a dozen," she admitted. "It is very unpleasant, and a dittama tried to eat me last time. But I can do it."

"It would be dangerous," Olsa agreed. "Any creature in the Dark Water could attack you. Though the dittama following us is very unlikely to go ashore—they fixate on ships, not individuals, despite the superstitions."

"What if your breath runs out, and you are somewhere where you cannot come back through?" I asked.

"Say, the middle of a stone wall, three paces thick?" Grant helpfully provided.

"Obviously there are dangers," Mary said, growing exasperated—and, I noticed, beginning to tap a nervous finger on her opposite arm. "But this is the simplest and safest way. All I would need is a timely distraction."

"Distractions, we can manage," Olsa said. "But Benedict cannot go through walls."

"Once I have Ben, I have a Magni. He can manage the guards." Rising, Mary came around to stand beside me and spun my diagram for Olsa to see. She tapped on an anchor symbol. "Benedict and I can make our way down here to the prison's private docks. Ben can overpower the guards, then we signal, and you land. Or you can land before, if you can manage it. Then we row out to *Hart* and sail away."

I opened my mouth to critique the plan, but instead found more pieces clicking into place. "I can lay a false trail. I do look like Ben, after all. Mr. Grant and I can 'flee' in the opposite direction and ensure Mary and Benedict escape unnoticed. Then we reunite at a safe location down the coast."

Poverly reappeared with a tray and slid it onto the table before us. Perhaps it was my distraction, but I had not noticed how haggard the girl looked until she set out a tray of bread, cheeses and cured meats.

"Ms. Poverly, where is Willoughby?" I asked, glancing from the dark bags under her eyes to her thin frame, which was bordering on underfed.

"Sick in bed, sir," Poverly said, straightening and forcing her young face into a bracing smile. "Did what I could, sir."

Another weight settled on me. My own steward was sick abed, and Poverly looked well on her way to joining him. I was neglecting my crew.

"You did well, Ms. Poverly. Now go to sleep," I instructed.

She looked simultaneously relieved and distressed. "But I've duties—"

I shook my head and pointed to the door. "You are relieved. Go rest. Please."

Poverly looked from me to my finger to the door, then gave an awkward curtsy and scuttled out.

"Yes, Papa," Grant murmured, a smirk tucked into the corner of his mouth.

I ignored him. "This plan is worth considering," I stated, surveying them and trying not to let my eyes linger on Mary, imagining her creeping through the corridors of a dark prison, past rows of bars and reaching hands. "Olsa, you and Illya secure any more intelligence that you can, particularly any smugglers' coves within a manageable distance of the fort. Resupply the ship tomorrow, and keep me informed."

Olsa's nod was calm, and I might have caught a touch of pride around her eyes. Or perhaps irritation—I was growing rapidly beyond subtleties. My head still ached, and I wondered if I was coming down with whatever Willoughby and Poverly had.

I poured myself a full mug of coffee and filled my plate. We ate, and the conversation wandered away from me—Grant's alternative suggestions to Mary's plan becoming more obscure and complex. I drained my first cup of coffee and closed my eyes as the second cup steamed.

Finally, Olsa and Grant left me alone with Mary. As soon as the door closed, she rounded the table and crouched beside my chair.

"Sam?"

She looked at me with concern. I moved before I realized I had, putting a gentle palm to her cheek, fingers delving into the hair behind her ears, my thumb tracing her cheekbone. Her lips turned up in a startled smile

"Are you all right?" she asked.

"I have a devil of a headache," I admitted, distracted by the intermingling of dark blue and smoke-grey in her eyes. Short, stray wisps of hair framed her face, curling a little against winter-pale temples. "I am worried for you and am unreasonably furious with Benedict for putting us in this situation. And it has come to my attention that key members of my crew are ill, and I was not told, or did not notice."

"You have too much on your mind. But we can carry more, if you let us. Can I do anything for you?"

There was an opportunity in that question, one I was not sure she meant to give. Still, several possible answers slipped through my mind. I hastily discarded them.

"No." I pulled my hand away, cleared my throat and forced my thoughts back into line.

Mary rose, looking down at me with a gaze far more perceptive than I could handle just then. "One of these days I may seduce you, Samuel Rosser. The crew and appearances be damned."

I felt my lips twitch, but it was not a smile. "Have mercy on me a while longer."

A frown creased between her brows. For a moment she seemed unable to formulate a reply, then she cleared her throat. "Samuel, we are in Mere. Are we going to look for a healer-mage? Sa Vis may know of one."

I nodded, wishing I had thought of that myself when the man was still present. I rubbed at my forehead, reflecting how little the coffee had done for the pain.

"That is… a very good idea. Can you ask him?"

"Of course."

"Thank you."

She squeezed my shoulder and left me alone with my thoughts.

FOURTEEN

The Monastery

SAMUEL

The next day, we reached the western edge of a long peninsula that punched north from the Mereish mainland into the sea, its tip surpassing even the latitude of the Aeadine Anchorage. It was appropriately forbidding, rocky and rimed with snow and ice. The few settlements we saw seemed nearly abandoned, and there were no smaller watercraft to be seen.

I sensed Fort Gat before I saw it, a prickle of premonition that drew my gaze out and up. I called for a spyglass.

The fort sat on an outcropping high above the sea, the heights and lines of its silhouette made all the more ominous by a haze of fine snow blowing out over the tops of the surrounding cliffs. Below it, curving around to the south, lay the port town of Maase. Lights and smoke signaled an active population, but we did not intend to go anywhere near the town, or the fort, until the night of our foray.

The ship changed course under Olsa's supervision, cutting off my view behind a shoulder of coastline.

We anchored in an inlet the pirates of Orres had directed us to. It was nearly inaccessible by land, surrounded by high cliffs and sheltered from the wind. The only path out of the anchorage was a meandering, ice-laden stairway laid hundreds of years before by the monks who inhabited a nearby monastery. Thankfully for us, it had fallen out of use—likely due to the inherent danger of the climb and probable bone-cracking fall.

"Every monastery has a Cleric—a healer-mage, as you call them," Sa Vis had assured us before our departure. Mary had wisely kept the true reason for our seeking a mage quiet, and Willoughby's fever—now spread among the crew—provided a timely excuse. "They are bound to discretion. They will help your crew, no matter who you are."

That was good news, considering a quarter of *Hart*'s complement were ill and my headaches had not eased, despite the fact that tomorrow night we intended to make our play against the fortress. Still, I kept my hopes guarded. Finding a cure for Ben and I would be nothing short of a miracle. But if all I found was a cure for my crew and my own headache? I would appreciate that too.

The monastery was tucked into the hills east of the inlet. The tall, round tower, square of lodgings, and high-roofed chapel were nestled into a spiderweb of stone fences, where sheep and goats nosed beneath the snow. Garden upon garden slept underneath a blanket of white, marked by the drooping heads of dead sunflowers, the outlines of raised gardening beds, and various lattices laden with last summer's vines. Here and there monks wandered, clad in dark robes against the pale snow, and smoke rose from the chimneys of far-flung hovels in the hills.

As I strode up the long road, coat over one shoulder and steam rising from my sweating back, I reflected that the landscape looked not unlike Aeadine's midlands, where I had spent my earlier years. But those hills were rawer, nearly mountains, and in the winter the snow would make the roads impassable. These hills were gentler, more forgiving, and the sheep who eyed me through wooden gates were a soft lowland variety rather than Aeadine's rugged, crag-hopping goats.

I passed two monks on the road leading a donkey with a laden cart of hay. They both nodded but did not speak, so I did the same.

The next monk I met, though, at the open gate to the monastery proper, more than made up for their silence.

"Greetings, traveler," the old man said in Mereish, eyeing me from head to foot. He had a bloody hatchet in one hand and a headless duck in the other. A trail of blood led back across the snow and behind an outbuilding, blurred by the stumbling prints of small, webbed feet and fallen feathers.

"Hello," I said in practiced, Usti-accented Mereish.

Noticing the direction of my gaze, the man held up the limp duck and said with chagrin, "Poor soul did not realize he was already dead. How may I help you?"

As unexpected as the sight of a black-robed monk with a bloody hatchet was, I returned to my purpose. "I was hoping to visit a healer."

The monk shifted the hatchet and fowl into one hand and gestured with the other towards the main, square building. "Come with me."

I fell into step, noting the occasional drip of blood from the duck. The man's willingness to help and lack of suspicion left me feeling oddly guilty, though I intended the monastery no harm. I had not even lied about my identity—the monk had not asked my name, or where I had come from, or why an Usti stranger was wandering their desolate coast.

This seemed to be a standard practice, for when the monk knocked at a tall door with a pointed top, another monk, a woman, opened it and asked nothing but, "What do you need?" as she led me into a long, quiet ward lined with clean, empty beds. The air smelled of soap and herbs—slightly thick, though not unpleasant.

This second monk, who had a youthful look to her round, dark-skinned face, gestured for me to sit across from her at a table at one end of the ward. Still mildly shocked at being admitted so freely, I took the proffered seat.

"What ails you? Or do you come on behalf of someone else?" the monk asked. Her voice was light and had a lilt, differing from the common Mereish accents I was accustomed to.

I took a moment to collect myself. A weight lingered on my shoulders—a weight of portent and promise. I had come so far to reach this moment.

"I have two questions. The first concerns an illness many people under my care have taken."

I went on to describe the symptoms. Halfway through, the monk began to nod, and, by the end, she had begun to move about her office, gathering pouches and tinctures and asking questions.

"It is a mild imbalance," the monk said. "Very common in the spring, and anyone on this coast grows immune before adulthood— meaning adult instances are rare, and they look much different than they do in children. I cannot heal it, but these will manage the symptoms until the imbalance rights itself."

"Thank you," I said sincerely, and prayed headaches would be the first symptom to go.

"What is your second question?"

"It regards magecraft," I began, hesitated, and rephrased, remembering to keep my accent in place. "Corrupted magecraft. My brother and I were amplified as children, and I am searching for a cure."

The monk was quiet for a long moment, well past the point of discomfort. I watched her anxiously, swallowing down the age-old instinct that berated me to be silent, to deny.

"I am a Sooth," I continued. "My twin brother is a Magni. I am... unrooted, in the human world, and frequently slip into the Other, even becoming trapped there. My visions rarely come at will, and I have little control over them. I have learned to manage my condition to some extent, though I have no idea how long that will last. My brother continues to become more and more corrupted. But I once met a Mereish man who told me there may be a cure for us here."

As I spoke the monk began to slowly nod, her gaze heavy and grave. "A cure in Mere?"

I nodded, trying to quell a flutter of anxiety. Had the talisman maker been wrong?

The monk frowned thoughtfully. "I cannot heal mages. The brothers and sisters at the Oruse, however, might."

"Where is that?" I asked.

"A shrine, a little over two days southeast, four on foot." As the monk spoke she leaned back in her chair, lacing her fingers over her stomach, her expression preoccupied. "They have a High Cleric, more powerful than I."

"Is there something else?" I asked. I sensed there was something she was not saying, a warning withheld.

"Their Saint is kind to those outside their order," the woman said, waving the issue aside. "It is a place of refuge for all, even foreigners. Simply be respectful, if you go. Who in Usti would have amplified you? Your queen outlawed the practice many years ago."

"Immigrants from Aeadine did it," I said, using the lie I had prepared. But though my lips moved, my mind was mired in the conclusion that this Oruse was too far away. After rescuing Benedict, we would need to flee quickly.

The monk blew out an angry breath. "The Aeadine. Their monarchs deny the truths of magecraft, and their common folk distort it. Such willful ignorance."

I might have taken offense, but the woman hinted at something I had long suspected.

"Their monarchy *knows* and denies the truth?" I asked, leaning forward. "I assumed they must suspect, they cannot be wholly ignorant..."

"Of course they know." The monk laughed, but it was not a belittling laugh, just the laugh of a jaded, world-weary sympathetic. "But those with power must keep it, and your Saint endorsed only three branches of magecraft—the Stormsingers, the Magni, and the Sooth. Now, I am sorry I cannot help you more, traveler. But if you can, go to Oruse."

I left the monastery with a satchel full of cures and a heart like lead. Tomorrow, we would make for the prison. Tomorrow, we would try to rescue my brother.

But was he worth saving if he would forever remain a monster?

FIFTEEN

Four Breaths

MARY

Thick snowflakes clung to my lashes as I surveyed the dark bulk of the prison. It lay on the other side of another deep inlet and the town of Maase, which clustered between the ridges and scented the breeze with wisps of hearthsmoke. The tide had made a dramatic retreat that night, leaving a series of small docks clothed only in icicles from mooring ropes down to the rocky inlet floor. There were no boats to be seen, perhaps still hidden in boathouses and huts for winter repairs.

The prison was a hulking fortress with thick exterior walls roping their way across uneven cliffs. Its three main bastions had obviously been built in different eras, with the newest rectangular, whitewashed and blending with a mantle of fine snow. Only a few windows were lit, but walls were bathed in torchlight, giving everything within them a sense of separation and foreboding.

The longboat bobbed on a particularly large wave, and I grabbed the gunnel.

Perched behind me, Illya nodded towards the shore. "Well? Are you ready?"

I nodded.

The rowers turned to their oars and, hidden by snow and darkness, we made landfall below the prison, beyond the edge of town. We could not get as close to shore—not with the tide as far out as it was—but this, we'd decided, was to my advantage.

Instead of being left to scale sheer wave-battered cliffs, I set my boots on the uneven rock and frozen mud of a barren tidal shore. I pulled off my boat cloak and handed it back to Illya, revealing breeches and a practical wrapped Mereish coat, slit at the sides for ease of movement.

"Last chance to change your mind," Illya prompted.

The rowers, all crewmembers I'd come to know well, watched me with varying degrees of uncertainty.

"Your confidence is overwhelming." I gave them a smile and squinted snow-laden lashes. "Just be at the prison dock on time."

The Usti nodded, the crew saluted or whispered farewells, and the boat shoved off.

I moved quickly and quietly, clambering up an icy ladder onto the town's most distant, darkest dock. Then I found the start of a goat path and set off.

An hour later, I was hot, exhausted, and damp from melting snow. The storm had attempted to move inland halfway through my climb and now demanded a constant hum to keep it blowing. Thankfully, the snow itself muffled my song from listening ears.

It also muffled the footfalls coming towards me. It was the high click of ice-grips that finally alerted me, their tap-crunch at odds with my own careful steps.

I skittered off the path, whipping out a curl of wind to cover my tracks, and hunched behind a boulder. I stopped humming and the storm shifted, disconsolate and already turning inland again.

Three guards followed one another down the slope, muskets slung loosely across their backs. Though they didn't speak, their demeanor wasn't that of watchmen: they simply moved like tired humans, trudging home after a long night.

We can go now, Tane prodded.

I gathered myself, pushed off the cold stone, and began to hum again. The wind grudgingly returned to me, bringing a renewed veil of snow, and I continued towards the crest of the rise and the foot of the fort's surrounding walls.

Just before I reached level terrain and the section of wall we'd marked for my crossing, I slowed and transitioned into a crawl. On my belly, I peered across an open, barely sloped shoulder of rock to the base of the wall. Not far off, a snow-capped watchpost lorded over the surrounding area.

I wouldn't just need to be in the Dark Water to pass through the wall. I'd need to be in it to cross the open space too.

I swallowed tightly and focused on my breaths—too ragged after the climb, and in anticipation of my next challenge. Every part of me protested that I couldn't afford to wait, that I should run now, sprint now. At any second, someone would see me and I'd be shot or captured.

My fingers twitched, and I clenched my eyes shut. I grounded myself in frozen earth beneath my belly, melting snow beneath my hands, and cold air in my lungs.

Then, in a gap between worry and fear, I pushed off—into the open space and into the Dark Water. A ridge of opalescent black rock rippled out beneath me, swallowing the grey and white human world. My feet thudded through puddles and cascades of the Other realm's dark water, covering the rock in a constant, glistening sheath. Fae dragonflies scattered in buzzing clouds of gold and purple, and other more distant lights ignited in the gloom.

I swept the skies. No hovering, winged dittama. Just distant beings, glistening like stars in a sky with three waning moons.

Two footsteps, one breath. Three footsteps. Two breaths.

I hit the wall—or sensed I did. I could not see it here in the Other world, but a barrier of cold assaulted me.

My third inhale. The cold faded, and I carried on another pace, my entire body quavering. Fae dragonflies converged upon me, the humming swirl of their wings the only sound in the spectral realm.

Through their brilliant aura I made out other lights, reflections of Otherborn power trapped in the human world. They were blurred and dimmed, somewhere far above.

Mages.

I let out my third breath and drew my fourth. I held that last gulp of air, cheeks puffing.

We're on the other side of the wall? You're sure? I murmured to Tane. My skull rattled with a hundred horrific images—me returning to the physical world to be wholly encased in stone, or perhaps half-encased, a leg or arm or hip crushed. My blood would stain the whitewashing, and the pain would go on and on as Tane fought to keep me alive.

I am certain, Tane reassured me. *Go on*.

The dragonflies scattered as I let out my fourth breath in a long, tremulous gust. The Dark Water faded. I stood a pace inside the fortress's curtain wall, wrapped in shadow.

Another wall, a whitewashed one footed by cobblestones, brushed the tip of my nose. I let out a strangled squeak. A stray dragonfly, clinging to my clothes, took flight and whirred dazedly up into the sky.

My knees wobbled with relief and terror. I staggered backwards against the curtain wall—cold and solid and unyielding, with dormant moss clinging here and there. Touching it only made me feel worse. I pushed off and huddled between the two barriers, contemplating lying on the ground and letting the snow fall on my face for a few minutes.

Then I heard the distant church bell and knew I had to move. Eleven bells. I needed to have Ben at the docks at twelve.

An hour in this place. Just an hour. I could do that.

I rose and put a hand on the white wall of the keep. Here, hidden from sight, I could afford a small risk.

Tane slipped from my skin, glowing softly in the night, and passed through the second wall alone. I saw the world beyond through her cautious eyes. The interior was plastered, once lovingly painted in intricate designs, now faded. A raw stone floor, a room full of barrels and crates and a staircase up a natural rise in the rock to empty, sleeping kitchens.

A pace and a half. Tane slipped back into my flesh. *Let me guide us.*

I hesitated. Tane and I might share a body, and occasionally she spoke through me when she wanted non-*ghiseau* to understand her. But letting her take control of my body was something that we had only ever done in the gravest of circumstances.

Are these circumstances not grave enough for you? she asked amusedly.

Fair.

I felt a strange rush, then I was moving without conscious effort. Again, Tane pulled us into the Dark Water. Again, I rematerialized beyond the barrier, this time possessed of a deep, knowing assurance that I wouldn't end up half inside a wall or a barrel or a shelf or a door. I was still nauseous, but even that was not so intense.

Thank you, I said, and meant it.

May we continue this way? I can direct when need be. Otherwise, I will scout ahead.

Yes, please.

I started for the stair. Tane preceded me, half-manifested and serving as my spectral vanguard.

The kitchens smelled distantly of lemon and sage and grains, fermenting in huge pots on the sleeping stove. I crept on into an empty passage, past closed doors that failed to muffle the shuffles and snores of sleeping humanity—servants and off-duty guards, I guessed, as the rooms had no exterior locks.

Another passage. A stair. We stepped into the Dark Water again for four more breaths to reorient ourselves with the mass of captive magelight and then hastened across an empty hall lined with three huge tables.

Footsteps brought me up short. I grabbed the nearest door handle. Locked.

Tane?

Her light slipped through the wood, washing my face in a dangerous glow. A glimpse of the space beyond—a staircase—then she was back in my flesh. Without falter the ghisting stepped us into the Dark Water and through the door.

I rejoined the human world just as footsteps reached us. Then, to my horror, they stopped. I heard the jangle of keys. Low murmurs. A soft laugh.

Tane abruptly extinguished her traitorous light.

Fuck, I mouthed into the shadows and took off up the stairs as quietly as I could. It was tight and circular, and I'd just managed to make the second round before the door opened and voices echoed up towards me. The scuff of my boots seemed so, so loud.

I met a small landing, again with a door, teetering on the edge of panic. Even if the door was unlocked, if I lifted the twisted iron latch the sound would betray me—already the rampant thunder of my heart and the thin wheeze of my breath were too loud. Nor was there time for Tane to scout the room beyond, not when her light would give us away.

We stepped into the Dark Water, panted my four breaths, and rematerialized beyond the door. I found myself in a long, empty passageway, completely dark. The voices still approached, distorted by the stairs and barely muffled by the ancient, iron-banded door.

I hastened down the hall, chased by the too-loud echoes of my feet.

I turned a corner and came to an abrupt halt. The chamber before me was circular and small, nestled within a small tower. There was no other door—clearly for security, because this was some kind of treasury. Or armory?

I felt the presence of magic at the same time as Tane. She manifested fully, and we turned back-to-back.

Teal ghisten light flooded the space, glinting off rows of coins hanging from pegs—coins on chains. Mereish talismans. Racks of muskets and long Usti rifles were next to shelves of pistol boxes and buckets of lead shot. I counted ten sideswords lined up on a table, neatly wound with their weapons belts. Even rows of breastplates with central ridges for deflecting bullets decorated another wall—their style out of date, though the armor was obviously well-maintained, free of rust and warmed by recent oiling.

For every weapon present, the same number were missing—empty racks, empty tables. Everything save the muskets, rifles, pistols and swords felt vaguely sorcerous. Most of them, in any case. The room was so full of strange, latent power that I struggled to identify its exact sources.

My internal clock ticked meaningfully. We couldn't linger here. But nor could I simply walk away from whatever *these* were.

I quickly made up my mind. I started snatching up talismans and shoving them into my pockets. My skin tingled as I touched them, both unsettling and gratifying. I grabbed a random assortment of lead balls too, marked with different colored dots and humming with the same power I felt in the talismans. I cinched a sidesword at my waist and gathered a dagger and two pistols, the latter of which went into a brace across my chest.

Feeling much better prepared—and delightfully like an over-armed renegade—I beckoned to Tane. *Let's go.*

SIXTEEN

The Other Brother

MARY

The mages were kept upstairs, along echoing corridors and through what might once have been some lord's feasting hall. Now the tables were rough, the benches too narrow, and the colors of the tall stained-glass windows barely illuminated by the lights atop the curtain walls.

I opened yet another door, and another, Tane preceding me whenever her light had least chance of betraying us. She mapped the way ahead and slipped images into my mind as if her eyes were my own, and occasionally swept into control when we needed to duck through a door or wall in haste.

The fear that someone would happen across us—at any moment, from any shadow—harried me, and my stomach was a cramping mess. But the fluidity with which Tane and I worked was a balm. My steps were steady, and my hands did not quake.

I sensed the door to the mage cells before I saw it. It was wood and banded iron, and I could hear the voices of the guards beyond.

There's a ghisting, Tane told me.

The creature manifested before I could even contemplate hiding. Spectral light flooded the passageway and coalesced into the shape of a man—a soldier—in a conical helm and antique armor, with a breastplate similar to the ones I'd seen in the armory. His eyes were sea-glass and devoid of life.

A chill skittered down my spine. Tane slipped forward, partially manifesting between the specter and me.

Child. Tane's silent voice twisted through the air. *Do not betray me.*

Mother, the ghisten soldier's voice was distant, half-awake, but deeply deferential. *I live to serve. What do you seek?*

We seek one of the prisoners. Go back to your rest, child.

The ghisten man tilted his head to one side and surveyed me through Tane. For an instant, I was sure his eyes would fill with malice and he would raise the alarm.

Of course, Mother of mine, he said and faded back into the wood.

Well that was convenient, I murmured to Tane. *Thank you.*

Indeed, she replied, sounding pleased with herself.

We crept forward, and, carefully, I laid one hand on the wooden door. The ghisting within allowed Tane to peer through, and I glimpsed a guard chamber with four guards, one reading while three played dice.

I took a breath to calm myself. I had known tonight would test the extent of my abilities, but there was one I had truly hoped not to use. Quelling.

I recalled quiet afternoons with my mother on the coast of Usti, in a croft punctuated by tiny beams of light, in view of a crashing sea. Over and over, I had driven the air from the little house until dead, smothered mice and insects had fallen from the thatch, and I had refused to continue.

But I knew how to do it now. How to turn closed rooms into coffins and coax the air from an enemy's lungs. To force others into unconsciousness. Or kill.

Tane brushed across my mind, a quiet consolation, a reminder of why I was here, and I rallied. I began to sing lightly and softly, funneling my intention into the space beneath the door and the slim crack around the frame, where light seeped out.

At first, all I heard was my own voice. The ghisting in the wood shifted, and Tane soothed him in words I did not register. In the guard room, I heard a brief swell of conversation, followed by the clatter of a chair. The candlelight dimmed and went out. I heard a scramble then a series of thumps.

I counted a few seconds of perfect quiet, save for the barrage of blood in my skull. I only needed the guards unconscious. Too long, and they would die. Too short, and I would find myself in a well of trouble.

I waited one more breath. When the quiet was so complete that my ears rang and I could bear the tension no longer, I eased the door open. Immediately my song wavered. Lack of air would not kill me, not with Tane in my bones, but I needed it to sing.

Air rushed back into the chamber from the hall, cool and sweet and smelling faintly of cheap tallow candles and smoking wicks.

Two of the guards had fallen over. Another had slumped onto the table, skewing their game of cards and dice, and appeared to be slipping slowly to the ground. The last guard was curled up on the stone like a child, a limp hand on her chest.

All were still breathing. Relieved, I focused on the other side of the room, where another door lay. This one was wholly iron and marked with runes, and the frame was rounded in a way that reminded me of the coin talismans in my pocket. It also had the same feeling as them—magic. Other.

My eyes fell to the lock, massive and intimidating, and I turned back to the guards. "Keys. Keys. Pardon me, sir."

I began to pat the guards down. Sure enough, I found two sets of keys, both nearly identical. The pressure of magic, and the size and intricacy of the key, told me which one I was looking for.

I slipped it into the lock of the round iron door. The feel of power shifted, and I sensed the ghisting from the hallway door manifest, watching the procedure with glassy-eyed indifference.

Boots planted, I put all my weight into hauling the door open. As soon as it parted from the wall a fresh sense hit me—one of power and brooding anger, and the impulse to run. But that impulse did not come from me.

Magni power.

I stepped into a circular chamber. A huge brazier burned in the center, chasing back the cold just enough to make it livable, and ten cells spread like the petals of a flower. Several were empty. The others contained one prisoner, each in various stages of waking or staring or ignoring me with eerie detachment.

The exception was the cell to the left of the door. This one contained two women.

One lingered against the bars, fingers wrapped around cool iron. I saw with horror that her eyes were little more than pits of scarred tissue. A Stormsinger's gag restrained her jaw and mouth, and the nails of her fingers were torn to the quick. She couldn't speak. Couldn't see. But one finger tapped against the bars—a familiar, Aeadine rhythm. A children's song.

The fox is in the bushes, my memory whispered. *The wolf is in the wood.*

Behind her, the other woman began to hum along from beneath her own muffling mask, swaying back and forth. She too had been blinded. The air in the cell began to eddy, just a fraction. Enough to make the flames in the brazier flutter and my skin prickle with gooseflesh.

The deer is in the meadow, but John is in the well.

Blinded eyes. That was a hallmark of the Black Tide, the same cult that had tortured Benedict into madness and shattered Samuel's connection to the human world. This fruitless cruelty—was this what would have happened to me, if the cult had caught wind of me? If my parents hadn't protected me so thoroughly?

Compassion welled, so painful and raw that I forgot to breathe. What horror it must have been, for Sam to be a child, to be handed over to such monsters by his own mother. For Benedict.

John is in the well, Mama, John is in the well. The hen is in her roost, Mama, but John is in the well.

The urge to silence the Stormsingers rose up in me and then was overcome by a desperate need to cross the room.

Another impulse came, then another and another—from every direction. I stood transfixed, feeling like I were being pulled apart at the seams. More faces appeared at the bars of the cells and figures moved, hidden in the darkness. Hollow, hungry eyes came into focus. Desperate eyes. Emotionless, glassy eyes.

Eyes of deep, earthen brown, staring at me from a pale, bearded face. My instincts immediately recognized him as Samuel, but my mind—and Tane—knew otherwise.

Benedict.

I advanced on his cell, moving with a slow, inexorable pace. He watched me come, at first in disbelief, then with intense scrutiny. All the threads of power besetting me cut away, save one. Benedict's magic overrode them all. It felt like freedom, so I did not fight back.

The last time I'd seen Benedict he had been impeccable in his lieutenant's uniform, clean-shaven, clear-eyed and hateful. Now his beard grew wild and his skin was sallow, his powerful frame reduced by hunger. But his eyes were the same. Sharp. Arresting.

"Benedict," I greeted.

His hand shot out. I flinched back too late and was hauled forward, right into the bars. Cold iron pressed into my chest as he held me close, his fingers gouging through my heavy clothing and into my skin.

"How are you here?" he rasped, his eyes darting around my face, over my shoulder, to the door and back. "*Are* you here? Did they catch you? Where is my brother?"

"Let go of me," I hissed. "I'm here to rescue you."

"You?" He barked a laugh, so close I smelled the foulness of his breath and felt a splatter of spittle. He seemed scattered, nearly manic. "How?"

"Yes, me," I bit back, pulling the keys from my pocket and holding them up for him to see. "Which key is it?"

He immediately let me go. "That one." He pointed to a medium-sized iron key with a long stem. "Where is my brother?"

"Pretending to be you and staging a false breakout at the southern gate," I replied, rubbing at my collar where he'd grabbed me. The lock tumbled and the door whined open.

"Woman!" another prisoner whined. "Take me with you!"

"My apologies, gentlefolk." Benedict vanished into the dark and returned with a worn cocked hat, which he popped onto his head as he stepped through the opening. Without permission, he reached for one of my weapons belts and unfastened it with quick fingers. I bit back a protest—he was already done. He relaced it around his own hips and checked the sidesword in its sheath.

Evidently satisfied, he went on, "This is a personal rescue only, I'm afraid."

Protests exploded and a wave of impulses assaulted me—*come, keys*, the urge to claw my own face to the bone. Even prepared as I was, the magnitude of the onslaught staggered me. Compassion and pity and rage and terror battered at my defenses, piercing me like shrapnel.

Benedict grabbed my wrist, his skin clammy with cold sweat and rough with dirt. Every other voice silenced, again leaving only his influence—a low thrum, a distant quiver in my guts. One magic restraining another.

I swallowed my bile and took a ragged breath. "Should we release them?" I managed, low enough that I hoped only Benedict would hear.

"No," he said firmly, releasing my wrist but maintaining his sheltering power. He breathed, low and deep, his focus on those around us. Their voices died one by one, and I heard a muffled, straining sob.

"Most of them are imprisoned for an actual reason, rather than just being foreigners," he explained. "Feel no pity for them. Where do we go now? What is your plan?"

I wasn't sure I believed him, but chose to regardless. "This way."

Only one face made me look back as we slipped out into the room of unconscious guards and Benedict pulled the door closed. The Stormsinger at the bars, still tracking me over her mask with scars for eyes. Still tapping, though more slowly now.

The fox is in the bushes. The wolf is in the wood.

I soved the door closed as Benedict began to strip one of the guards of his coat and weapons belt. As he donned them, I crossed to the main door, looking through Tane's eyes at the hallway beyond.

Somewhere distant, I heard an alarm bell begin to clang. Benedict looked up, his new guard's coat at odds with his soiled, battered, cocked hat. He set to priming one of my stolen pistols.

"That bell is probably for Sam," I reassured him. "It's part of the plan. He'll lead the chase into the town and west into the hills, then meet up with us."

"I see." The Magni joined me in the doorway and adjusted his commandeered weapons belt, now heavy with additional provisions. "I assume we are going the other way, then?"

"Yes. With me." I started off down the stair, following Tane's guidance. We slunk and darted, ran and paused our way through the maze of the prison, avoiding the great hall and slipping past the doors to the common cells.

"Illya will be waiting with a boat at the prison docks," I murmured as we paused in a shadowed alcove, Tane rejoining my frame at the same time. Her light extinguished, and shadows swept over us.

A guard sprinted past, oblivious. Benedict's eyes were distant, and I suspected the guard's distraction was not entirely natural.

My companion's focus sharped on me once the guard was out of sight. "Illya Uknara?"

I nodded and stuck my head back out into the passageway—right into the sight of six guards and an armed, raging gentleman.

"Stop!" a voice roared.

I jerked back into the alcove.

Ben cocked his pistol. "That's the Provost. I take a shot, you run." He'd barely finished speaking before he stepped out into the hallway. "Run!"

His pistol cracked. Gunsmoke plumed. And we ran.

SEVENTEEN

The Great Chase

SAMUEL

"This is going rather well," Grant panted, pinned next to me along the alley wall. The shouts of guards echoed up the street behind us, interspersed with cries of locals, who hung out windows and doors at the commotion.

I labored for breath as guards thundered past in a stream of heavy coats and glistening muskets. "Too well."

It had been simple, baiting the trap. A rope thrown over the prison's curtain wall, which had been discovered almost instantly. Grant and I had initiated an obvious flight from the foot of said rope, down the road and into the town as the guard bell began to ring. We had sprinted past staring villagers, both Grant and I slathered with dirt and wearing our worst clothes, shivering in the night. We looked like escaped criminals. To the good people of Maase and the guards who poured out of the prison at our backs, we *were* escaped criminals. And to the guards who heard my description, I was none other than Benedict Rosser, escaped Aead Magni.

"Right," Grant said when the guards had passed. He peeled off the wall and nodded back to the street. "Shall we?"

"There!" a woman's voice cried from above. I just had time to glimpse a pointing finger and a vindictive, pale face leaning out of a second-story window before the coordinating cries of the guards rounded back on our position.

I bolted, jerking Grant after me with a fistful of stinking coat.

"Wrong way! Sam, wrong way!" he protested, then the street behind us was full of guards, and he revisited his priorities. He took the lead in a wholehearted sprint as I skirted a slick patch of ice and jumped a pile of frozen horse droppings.

We burst out onto a new street to find it blessedly clear, lined with stone buildings shuttered and barred against the night. The exposed beams between their carefully stacked stones were richly painted with Mereish psalms and their roofs layered with snow. Only a cat watched us from under a nearby cart, tail twitching, whiskers caked with white as if she had just been rooting about in the snow.

"Right, now south? Shit!" Grant's sprint abruptly turned into a slide. Ice coated a steep descent to the harbor, unbothered by the layers of sand and sawdust the locals had half-heartedly thrown down.

I lunged, trying to grab hold of the highwayman again, but he was gone—skidding down the road with all the grace of a drunken colt. And I went sliding right on behind him.

When the road spewed us out onto the docks, neither of us were on our feet. I slid into a pile of ice and lay there for a stunned moment, breathing raggedly and praying I had broken no bones. Then I pried my eyes open and squinted into the shadows.

Ridges of jumbled ice coated the quay, but they were not the only thing. Debris was thick among them—including a dishevelled Grant, staggering to his feet. Mud, pieces of wood, tattered ropes and broken crates were interspersed by other, more unrecognizable refuse. Even in the cold I could smell a mix of brine and rotting things, human and animal shit, and just a hint of mold.

The docks had been flooded, all this left behind when the waters receded—though the lap of encroaching dark waves warned the tide was already waxing and would soon bring another host of ice and refuse.

I looked around more carefully. Judging by the mess and the fact that the nearby buildings looked wholly abandoned, the locals had simply withdrawn from this part of the town, yielding it to the rise and fall of the sea. Sa Vis had mentioned unexpectedly high tides, but *this* high? High enough for coast-dwelling Mereish in a well-established town to simply withdraw from the docks that supported them?

My curiosity swelled and passed, chased away by distant shouts. I stumbled upright and pointed Grant south along the quay.

A few tense minutes later we slunk out of town, wrapped in a pale, snowy gloom. Grant was scraped and bloodied, as was I, and there were no more quips or jesting. We trudged on, leaving a trail of staggering footprints and blood-speckled snow.

At a small shrine in the hills, just past a sprawl of farms, Grant and I met two shadows. They stepped out from behind a shelter with a high roof and a statue within, surrounded by drifts and sad, dried flowers. The monument sat next to a swift-flowing river, half-iced, and two horses stamped impatiently in its lee.

"Captain," said *Hart*'s Ms. Fitz, doffing her hat. Her eyes rounded at the state of us. "Are you all right?"

"As well as can be expected. Where is our gear?"

She pointed to a bundle just inside the shrine. "There. The other trails are already laid. We'll be off now and back aboard *Hart*?"

"Yes, thanks the both of you." I gave a grateful nod. I could see the evidence of her and her companion's hard work all around us— myriad trails coming and going into the forest, to the river, and farther up the road. The snow that could so easily have betrayed us now concealed us in a maze of footprints. "Give Mr. Keo and the Uknaras my regards. We will see you in two days."

"Aye, sir. Good luck, sir."

Grant and I ducked into the shrine and opened our bundles of clothing. Working quickly, we scrubbed dirt and blood from our faces with snow, hissing at the cold, and put on black robes along with cloaks and knitted caps under heavy hoods. I combed my beard back into line and proceeded to stuff our former, stinking rags high in a pine tree.

Then we rode. We headed up into the hills along a track I had carefully mapped, past the sleeping quiet of the monastery, where a few high windows glistened warm in the chill, crisp night. Distantly, over the rolling hills and down the valleys, I thought I heard more horses, perhaps a shout or two. But by the time our pursuers sorted through the tracks we were far, far away.

EIGHTEEN

Blood Ties

MARY

Benedict dodged one way, I the other. Three guards and the Provost bolted after Benedict while the last two charged me.

Here. Tane pulled me around a corner and down a flight of stairs.

Where did Ben go? My reply was more image and nerves than words.

I'll find him. Go right, then left. Through the door.

Tane left me, ghisten light vanishing into the shadows and the thunder of running footsteps. I felt naked, though a tether of ghisten flesh remained between us—thinning with each passing moment.

"Stop!" a guard roared.

The stairs ended. I darted right but instantly stopped, flattening myself to the wall. I began to whisper under my breath, subtle notes turning into a melody that barely reached the ear but it stole the air from the hallway as surely as punch to the lungs. It would not work as well, not here in a space without doors, but even if I could disorient the guards—

One barreled around the corner, cudgel in hand. I stuck out my foot and he fell hard, his cudgel clattering away. I seized it and backed away, making for full, clean air before I lost the breath to sing.

The first guard, gasping like a fish out of water, fumbled to his knees. The second—a middle-aged man, cold-eyed and moustached—stumbled to a halt behind him, registered what was happening, and leveled a musket at me.

A bullet tore through the air beside my head, and the crack of the shot was deafening in the enclosed space. I barely twisted away, breath gone, song disrupted. Air rushed back into the hallway and Moustache charged.

I ran, cobbling together fresh notes, but my pursuer was too close, my control shaken. I crashed into another door, pulling the keys from my pocket as I went and shoving in the first one.

It didn't work. The second. No luck.

My hands were trembling so hard I nearly dropped the whole ring.

Tane, I need you! I can't find the key!

I'm coming.

The third key jiggled uselessly in the lock as Moustache charged around the corner so fast he nearly hit the opposite wall of the passageway. Pushing off with a growl, he lunged for me with his sidesword drawn.

I could feel Tane rushing back to me, our tether winding back on its spool, but the guard was four paces away now. Three.

I spun, pulling out the stolen dagger and ducking into a lunge just as the soldier came into range. I caught his sword with my blade as I sidestepped and grabbed his wrist with my other hand, wrenching hard. His sword dropped with a clatter.

His elbow struck me right in the head. I managed a stumbling lunge as I fell and he caught me gracelessly—a child tackling a runaway goat. We toppled to the floor, I flailing and cursing, he slapping my hands away.

Somewhere in the chaos my head took a second hit. My vision blurred, and when it cleared again the guard was pinning me to the wall—one hand on my throat, the other on the wrist of my dagger hand. My pistol was on the floor, kicked out of range.

He shouted something in Mereish, but with no Tane to translate, I couldn't understand. No Tane. Without Tane, I was vulnerable.

Without Tane, I could die. Then she would cease to exist, and—

The guard's hands closed tighter, cutting off my breath and crushing my wrist until my fingers felt as though they would rupture with trapped blood. My grip shuddered open and the dagger clattered to the floor.

The guard's eyes grew suddenly wide. He tilted his head to one side like a startled hound, but whatever he heard was beyond me. His hands began to tremble and his gaze turned inwards.

A surge of courage hit me, so fierce and vivid that I no longer felt the hand loosening on my throat or the cold stone grating against my back.

The guard stared at me, his face a muddle of confusion and distraction. I smashed my forehead into his nose, and he reeled with a shrieking gargle.

Before I could go after him, a shadow stepped between us—a large, masculine shadow stinking of sweat and dirt and worse.

Benedict threw a punch. The guard's head rebounded off the wall with a solid crack, and he crumpled like a sail without wind.

Benedict watched him fall while I staggered away and stooped to pick up my dagger. This proved to be unwise. My head swam, and the next thing I knew, I'd sat down hard on my backside and Benedict was staring down at me in wrathful disapproval.

"How are we supposed to get out, Mary?" he demanded, not bothering to ask if I was all right. "Tell me you have a better plan than this."

I bit off a colorful retort, centered around his ingratitude, and instead pointed to the locked door. At the same time Tane reappeared from the wall, a half-formed gust of sapphire mist, and we reunited.

My dizziness and aches began to abate, though they didn't fade entirely. I fumbled for my dagger and sheathed it, then snatched up my pistol and patted at the wall for a handhold.

"Where are the keys?" Benedict hauled me upright, his grasp debatably more painful than my head, then began to search my pockets.

"Already in the door, you ungrateful prick." I fended him off and pointed to where the ring dangled in the lock. He immediately abandoned me, stepping over the unconscious guard and beginning to try keys.

I crowded in as he worked.

"Back away. I will not leave you behind," he growled without looking at me. The keys jingled, obnoxiously merry in the tense stillness.

Back on the floor, the guard twitched and moaned.

"I wouldn't put it past you," I returned, one eye on the keys, one on the guard.

He scoffed. "I just saved you. Where do you think your courage came from?"

"I know," I admitted. "Though I didn't know your power was good for anything other than murder and seduction."

A key turned in the lock with a satisfying *clunk*. He shoved the door open and pocketed the keys. "Then you know very little."

I inched past him warily. As soon as I was through Tane slipped out, heading for the far reaches of her tether to check the path ahead. That left me aching and weak, but my knees held, and I was grateful when Benedict fell in at my back—where he couldn't see my sweating, pain-pale face.

We met no one else on our flight. Cellars packed with goods began to appear, and, at last, I smelled salt and brine and lantern oil.

Light bloomed as we entered an underground docking area, brimming with crates and barrels and rope-fastened bundles. A large archway of stone led to the sea, tall enough for a short mast to pass under at low tide—though it was waxing now—and it provided a murky glimpse of the sea beyond.

I stumbled to a halt, looking to Tane at the same time as Benedict looked at me.

"No boat?" the Magni asked.

No boat, no Illya. I spied the body of a guard down the way and signs of a struggle, but there was no one alive now.

"They were here, but they didn't wait." I darted onto the empty dock, boots clattering on the icy stone of the quay. I looked at the sea entrance, shrinking with the rising tide. "But we can't be so late! The tide is coming in faster than we expected but it's still not… He should be here. Why would he leave?"

Benedict looked around, taking in every inch of the man-made cavern. His expression was dangerously flat. "There's nothing else. Not even a skiff."

I stared at the water and the ice on the rocks. Readying myself, I slipped my fingers up to pull my pistol from its brace. It might be wet and useless if we followed my new plan, but even a water-choked pistol was better than none.

"I can swim out. Can you?"

"I'd rather drown than go back to a cell."

As ready as I was, the cold water left me clinging to a mooring post, gasping and trying not to let my muscles seize. Luckily my toes touched the bottom, and I didn't go under as the initial shock passed.

Shivering in nothing but his breeches, Benedict watched me from above with a critical eye. He held our bundle of clothing, belongings and two muskets—all tightly wrapped in plentiful oil cloth—on his shoulder. As I slowly stopped gasping, he handed it down to me.

I held the bundle as he lowered himself into the water.

"Bloody fucking Saint," he rattled, nostrils flared and every muscle taut—which, as thin as he was now, were already prominent beneath bruised, sore-scattered flesh. He stifled the rest of his complaints and took the bundle back from me. "I'm ready."

I heard the lie in his voice but let my legs float up and began to swim.

Each stroke felt like an eternity. Each little wave that rocked me found a portion of skin not yet numbed and the shock of the cold went through me again. But by the time we splashed out into the open air, Tane's preserving warmth had come. I moved more quickly, eyeing the cliffs for a path or staircase.

We swam and swam, buffeted by salty waves, and, with each moment that passed, Benedict fell farther behind.

"Let me take it," I said, treading water. I nodded to the bundle as another wave jostled Benedict.

"No," was all he said.

An eternity later, I sighted what appeared to be a path lancing up the steep embankment. I made for it, glancing out to sea as I went. There were no shadows on the waves or lanterns to mark a ship: nothing but silver-crested water under the half-moon, cliffs draped with snow and ice and the single path—which looked more like a happenstance of ridges and flat rocks than any intentional way.

I clambered onto the ice-caked shore first, and finally Benedict let me take the bundle as he clawed up after me. He moved like a lizard in spring and still shivered, but every child of the Winter Sea knew that was better than the alternative.

He looked too much like Sam in that moment, and it was too easy to think of his brother, with his lingering eyes and the way his arms enfolded me in rare moments of intimacy. *Hart* was nowhere to be seen, and our plans already in disarray. Had Sam been captured? Had Illya and Charles?

I shook myself and opened our bundle. I passed Benedict his stinking shirt then the coat and scarf stolen from the dead guard. He did not look grateful for my help, but I attributed the grinding of his teeth to the cold rather than my patient distribution of clothing.

While his goosefleshed skin disappeared under dry wool and buttons, I threw a short Mereish cape around my shoulders and pulled up the hood.

"Your clothes are still soaked," Benedict pointed out—a statement of fact, not concern.

"They will just freeze. The cold won't kill me."

He strapped on his weapons belt—still holding the sword I'd stolen from the armory—and adjusted it, checking his pouch of ammunition.

"Maybe I should have let Lirr infect me," he commented, and I noticed his fingers were still shaking, white with cold. We needed to get him somewhere warm. Quickly.

"That's nothing to jest about," I returned tartly.

Unrepentant, Benedict passed me a musket and threw the oilskin over his shoulders like a second cloak. "No, it's not."

I bit the inside of my lip to stop myself from speaking again, tasting salt. Though the source of his corruption had been different, it was all too easy to draw lines between Lirr and Ben. The image of Benedict possessed by a ghisting, nearly immortal and funneling unpredictable power from the Other, chilled me more than any waves.

When we capped the rise, we looked back down the coast. The hulk of the fortress was distant now, its lights little more than pricks in the night. There were no sounds save the wind across the hard crust of the snow and the crash of the waves on the shore below. The musket was cold beneath my hands, and I wished for mittens.

"What now?" Benedict asked through chattering teeth.

"We find somewhere to shelter and light a fire, rest, then head east. Hopefully Olsa and *Hart* will be waiting for us."

Benedict surveyed the land to the east, all bare cliff and smooth snow. "Then we had better start," he said, took one step, and collapsed into the snow.

NINETEEN

Ismoathe Port, Aeadine

Five Years Ago

SAMUEL

There were only six letters in the stack, but they weighed heavy in my hands. Each one bore my name in a smooth, precise script, and, even after months sitting in my private rooms in Ismoathe, they smelled distantly of roses.

I turned the top letter over and stared at the seal. Unbroken. Pristine white wax. No family mark, just a thumbprint.

Without bothering to shrug off my snow-caked coat, I strode to the fireplace—lit by servants as soon as *Reliance* had dropped anchor in Ismoathe harbor—and made to throw the letters in.

My fingers tightened with a protesting crinkle of thick linen paper and refused to open. Memories assailed me instead, twined in the thin scent of rosewater perfume. Alice Irving, young and sweet, watching me across the garden of her husband's—my captain's—estate. Ms. Irving standing listless beside her husband as he berated a midshipman over a minor breach of etiquette at table. Ms. Irving clutching my hand as I helped her ascend a staircase.

"Sam, where is your razor… What are you burning?" Benedict appeared at my side—my twin and mirror in every way, from our faces to statures and lieutenants' frock coats: knee-length, dark blue, and cuffed with black.

I shoved the letters into my pocket. "I just needed more light."

Benedict glanced around the chamber. It was well-appointed but plain, with a curtained bed, an array of rugs, a desk and a bookshelf. Each book sat perfectly aligned, each rug squared to the walls and furniture. My sea trunk still sat by the door, unopened next to my shoes and hat.

"It *is* dingy in here." Benedict started towards the curtained window, leaving a trail of snowmelt on the rugs.

"Shoes," I snapped.

Benedict glanced down then back up at me with arched brows. "Yes, sir," he drawled, tugging an imaginary forelock and kicking off his shoes. Stocking-footed, he padded the rest of the way to the window and opened the curtains.

My rooms might not have been lavish, but they had a fine view. On the top floor of a boarding house at the edge of Ismoathe's cluttered docks, my window afforded an impressive outlook of both the public harbor, packed with trade ships of every size, and the naval docks. There in the dusky, lavender light, the tall masts of *Reliance* were shadowed by the sprawling fortress that housed the Admiralty, barracks, and the academy where both Benedict and I had begun our careers.

Benedict squinted over the vista, any talk of burning apparently forgotten. I took off my coat, hanging it on a rack in the corner— the pocket with the letters towards the wall—and went back to my desk. There were other missives and correspondences there, neatly organized by sender. The landlady was discreet, but the thought of her stacking Alice's letters in this way, sniffing them, pondering what love-affair I had gotten myself entangled in…

I rubbed at tight muscles in my neck with one hand and picked up a letter from an old shipmate with the other.

"Is she pretty?"

I twisted to see Benedict at the coat rack. I had not heard him leave the window, but I was used to his power and manipulations, and it failed to shock me.

The sight of Alice's letters in his hands, however, did. I bolted for him, nearly tripping over the desk chair. "Put those down! Ben. Ben!"

"My God." Benedict danced away, holding the letter out of my reach, broken seal dangling from his hand. "Who is she? When did you meet? Again, is she pretty? Never mind, your taste has always been a bit off. Perhaps I should just read—"

I lunged. My fingers caught paper and in the tussle the letter tore, the others fluttering to the floor like damning feathers.

Benedict immediately snatched another up and darted across the room, leaping onto the bed and crowding into the corner. Torn between gathering the fallen letters and pursuing him, I let out a frustrated growl.

A maid passed by the open door to the hallway and stared in at us, wide-eyed, before scuttling away.

I kicked the door shut with a distracted apology and advanced on my brother.

"'*Samuel*'," Benedict began to read, raising his voice to imitate female tones. "'*I have thought to write to you a dozen times, yet still I struggle to put my feelings into words. Though we have met but twice now, your kindness, your dignity, and your gentle words have awoken an affection in me that I cannot deny.*' Damn, you do make an impression with women. How do you do it?"

"I listen to them," I snapped, trying to snatch the letter away again.

Benedict snorted and twisted to face the wall, presenting me his back as I scrabbled. "'*Given the delicacy of my situation, I fear that, upon reading these words, your good opinion of me and my virtues will, rightly, waver. But—*'"

I grabbed Benedict by the legs and jerked. He hit the bed with a squawk and a *thunk*, but still managed to kick me in the chest. Winded and sprawled on the floor, I clasped my chest and reached for a chair. Benedict, already on his feet, moved the chair neatly out of reach and kept reading as he backed away.

"'*My husband is...*' Husband?" Benedict's voice faded, and his eyes dropped to the bottom of the letter, just as I finally tore it from his grasp. "Alice I.? Irving?"

"I have done nothing," I snapped. I tried to fold the letter, then realized the ridiculousness of that and crumpled it instead. "I was kind to her. That is all. She became infatuated."

"With you?" Benedict gaped at me, stuck half-way between delight and mortification. "Samuel, Charles Irving was our captain. He secured your posting to *Reliance*."

"Which is why," I grated out, "I have not returned a single message or gone anywhere near her since these began." I held up the letter, crushing it further and blocking out an insidious tug of regret. Or was it pity? The two blended where Alice was concerned.

"How long?" Benedict sounded suddenly sober, but there was still a light behind his eyes I did not trust, a keenness I had learned to be wary of long ago.

"A year. I opened the first one." I put the back of one hand to my forehead, letter still crumpled between my fingers. "The rest... I told the landlady to burn them, but she has got it into her head that I need to marry and move out. So she keeps delivering them."

"Then burn them yourself," Benedict said.

I hesitated.

Benedict's eyes lit with realization. "You have not decided whether to reject her."

The truth of his accusation made my cheeks burn. I stormed across the room to the fireplace, passing a long mirror as I did. My flushed face—our face—flashed back at me.

Without hesitation, I threw the crumpled letter into the flames and stooped to snatch up another, forgotten on the now-skewed rugs. They both began to blacken and crisp, fine lines of flame racing up the expensive paper. White wax melted, dripping into the coals.

I turned back to Benedict to find he had retrieved another fallen letter and opened it.

"Give me that."

"Sam." Benedict sidled sideways, fingering the paper. "I have never met Ms. Irving, but by all accounts she is beautiful. Very beautiful. And according to these letters, very willing. Are you—"

"Give that to me." I stalked after him.

"What if you just—"

"Give it to me!"

"Easy there, easy." Benedict finally handed over the letter.

I returned to the fire to burn it, gathering others as I went, and did not look at Ben again until he opened the door.

"Well, brother," he said, slapping the frame on his way out. "Do make wise choices and make Uncle proud. Saint knows I will not."

TWENTY

Mereish Magics

SAMUEL

G rant and I moved quickly along the eastern road. It was elevated and windy, and only a few sleigh tracks marred the fresh snow. To the west I could just discern the coastline in the gloom, where the blanket of bright snow ended and the land dropped away. The ceaseless drone of waves on shore and wind in the crags had long since faded from my awareness, my cheeks burning with the cold and my hands stiff on the reins.

Leaning forward, I slipped my fingers beneath the horse's mane and tried to leech off the animal's heat. We had taken our mounts to a gallop not long before, and the mare's flanks still steamed in the chill. She flicked her ears but kept plodding. I turned my touch to an affectionate scratch.

"Do you have a name?" I murmured to her. "What shall I call you?"

The mare plodded on and I sat back, a presentient unease sweeping across my shoulders.

"Grant," I called, reining in.

Grant twisted in his saddle with a squeak of leather and rustle of heavy clothes. Seeing I had stopped, he immediately brought his grey-speckled gelding to a halt. He watched me with a keen readiness I had learned to value early on in my career. Whatever else he was, Grant was useful in a tight spot.

I sat straight in the saddle and divided my awareness between the road and the Dark Water. The snow beneath our horses briefly shifted to water, silvered black and lapping, and Other lights sparked across the sleeping Mereish countryside.

Grant took on a greyish haze, marking him as non-mage *ghiseau*. Farther off, in a forest cloaking the southern hills, a cluster of yellow sparks marked implings on the hunt. I noted those with caution and turned my gaze to the coast, looking for the lights that would identify Olsa or Illya, the pale blue of *Hart*, Ben's rust-red, and the grey-edged teal of Mary.

A cluster of lights moved out on the sea, distant enough to blur together but near enough for me to sense another grey haze. Olsa and Illya were aboard *Hart*, but they were still west, and farther out to sea than expected. They were also not alone. Other ghisting-possessed ships punctuated the sea around them. I had no way of knowing just what kind of vessels those ships were, but, if they had driven *Hart* off course, they were unlikely to be allies. Had he been captured? Was he about to be?

I swept my gaze down the coast and marked a grey-hedged teal. Mary—I knew her light like no other. The grey was stronger tonight, as Tane attempted to hide the red burn of Benedict from enemy Sooths.

"*Hart* has been delayed," I conveyed to Grant, not bothering to keep the grimness from my voice. I pointed towards the red and teal lights. "Mary and Benedict are alone and close, in that direction."

Grant loosened his saber, drawing and slipping it back home to ensure the cold had not stiffened it. Then, hips at ease in the saddle and reins draped across the saddle horn, he set to priming a pistol.

I primed my own musket. Then I nudged my mare into a cantering lead, and we made for Mary's light.

A farmhouse soon parted from the gloom. It was low and made of stone, every corner rounded and every eave and peak decorated with intricate wooden knotwork. It lay in a distinct U-shape with its open side inland, away from the sea wind. One side of the U consisted of the barn, the other the kitchens, and the center the living quarters.

A massive, shaggy dog met us at the gate without so much as a huff of displeasure, and I offered the creature a hand to sniff as we led our horses into the yard.

"Eerie," Grant commented. He stood beside his placid horse, pistol in one hand and cutlass in the other. He eyed the sliding door of the barn and the kitchen stoop, where sealed pots nestled in the cold and a little awning had been built against the chimney foot. The dog, still unbothered by our intrusion, retreated to the awning and lay down on a pile of sackcloth.

"Benedict is here," I explained, eyeing the main door of the house. The small windows to either side wore heavy shutters, painted in quaint, bright patterns, but light flickered as one moved.

"Mary?" I called, just loud enough to be heard.

No answer came, and the shutter closed. All my fears about leaving Mary alone with Benedict resurfaced, more potent than ever.

I rested my musket loosely on my shoulder and, leaving the horses, approached the door.

It opened before I reached for the handle, and there stood Mary. She wore petticoats and a man's shirt with a blanket for a shawl, and her hair was in disarray.

My breath left me in a relieved, misty rush. Mary squeaked as I bundled her into my arms, musket clattering and my face buried in her cool, damp hair.

"I'm not dead," she assured me, her voice muffled by my shoulder. "*You're* not dead!"

Not nearly ready to let her go, I let a fraction of my tension ebb away.

"Yes, I am quite fine out here in the cold," Grant called, overloud, from the steps behind me. "Should I see to the horses, or will we be fleeing right away?"

"Hail," Benedict's voice called from farther inside the single, large common space. He sat in a large, quilt-smothered chair next to the hearth, forearms wearily braced on his knees. He looked out of place in the homey chamber, a battered criminal wrapped in a worn quilt of faded jewel tones, with a brimming basket of knitting beside him. "The house is asleep. Yes, everyone is alive, Sam. Do not look at me like that, I have no energy for your castigations."

My relief at seeing Mary was pure and warm, but the sight of Benedict brought a host of more complex feelings. Even cloaked in the blanket I could see he was thinner, his beard wiry and unkempt, his hair wild and his eyes haunted, shadowed. His cheeks were windburned and the rest of his skin unnaturally pale.

"Right, I'll see to the horses, then," Grant muttered. "Glad you are still among the living, Mary."

"I'm glad to see you too," Mary called after him. "Charles! Charlie!"

"Then where's my dramatic embrace?" Grant shouted back, sounding not altogether joking. "And never call me Charlie! I had a friend with a dog named Charlie, and he got run over by a cart."

I cleared my throat pointedly. "Thank you, Mr. Grant."

Grant's response was concealed in the clatter of hooves, and I shifted inside so we could close the door. My urge to go to Benedict was strong, but I took one more moment to look at Mary. I snagged one of her hands, feeling the lingering chill in her skin. She squeezed my fingers in return, and for that brief second we took rest in one another, all reservations forgotten.

Then I saw the bruising on her throat and a swelling at her hairline. I pulled away quickly, remembering how tightly I had embraced her.

"What happened? Did I hurt you?"

"I'm fine," Mary assured me, her voice steady. "I had an... encounter with a guard."

"She threw up three times," Benedict cut in. "She is concussed."

My heart staggered. "Mary."

"Tane has me," Mary reassured us both. "I feel much better."

"Concussed," Benedict repeated, ignoring us.

"Sit." I urged her towards the divan. Mary gave me a flat-lipped, wan look, but sat. I eased down beside her, battling the urge not to fuss.

Ben surveyed us, his haggard eyes bland with fatigue. "Your boat did not come."

"They were chased out to sea," I returned, crooking my legs to fit the narrow space between the divan and a low table overladen with books, a pipe on a stand, a jar of tobacco and various children's toys. The sight of the latter made me look at Ben more closely. "The family is unharmed?"

Mary, evidently deciding she had sat for long enough, rose and moved over to a rack next to the hearth, where the rest of their clothing was hung. The bare stone beneath it was puddled with water, and the clothing sopping wet. I smelled the stink of salt-watered wool and realized the two had been in the sea.

"Mary, please rest—" I started.

She shot me a look that made me bite back my words, her patience clearly waning.

Benedict leaned his head back onto an embroidered cushion and closed his eyes. "These bumpkins will never even know we were here."

"They're well," Mary affirmed, crouching to mop up the dripping puddle with a rag, then squeezing it into a bucket. She moved slowly, I noted, but seemed steady. "I checked."

Benedict eyed her with resentment.

"You swam from the prison?" I asked.

"Yes. Who's gone after *Hart*?" Mary returned to the divan and sat with a leg tucked up under her petticoats, careless as a child.

I pried my eyes from a length of exposed calf and a delicate bare foot. "I haven't a clue, but they were ghisten ships."

"Every ship on the waves is ghisten at this time of year," Benedict pointed out. "But I doubt anything short of warships would hold back the Uknaras. We should proceed as if they have been captured and find another way back to Aeadine."

Mary's head shot up. "We will not!"

I rubbed my forehead, feeling the beginnings of a new headache coming on. "They may be able to shake them or talk their way out or escape. We will have to keep our heads low and bide our time until something changes. I will keep watch in the Other."

"Well, we help no one by staying here," Mary stated. "We should keep moving."

I nodded. "Discreetly."

Benedict's expression swung towards irate. "And if they're captured? What are we supposed to do? Rescue *them*?"

A thick silence fell, riddled with unspoken truths and possibilities, most of them grim. Benedict's expression was an angry kind of disgust and Mary's the tight, distant stare she often took on when she was struggling not to be afraid. As for myself, I sat back and stared at the wall as I tried and failed to find any hope in my heart.

The door opened and Grant blew in, followed by the shaggy dog. It made right for Mary, who made a startled sound as the creature lay across her lap with a heavy sigh. Mary wasn't a small woman, but the hound enveloped her.

I found a damp dog's hindquarters on my leg, and a tail thumped against my chest. The thumping increased in tempo as I scratched its spine.

"He's wet," Grant warned.

"I can see… *feel* that." I sighed, but could not suppress a smile as Mary ruffled the dog's ears and leaned down to kiss its head.

"I don't mind one bit," she said.

"We have to find another way out of Mere," Ben pushed.

"We had planned to wait for Olsa at that cove. I vote we head there first and entertain more dire options later," Grant said, stomping snow from his boots, kicking them off and going to crouch beside the hearth in rumpled stockings. "Is there anything to drink?"

Mary nodded to the teapot on the table, her hands now occupied with scratching the dog.

"How far from the prison are we?" Mary glanced at Benedict. "We can't have gotten far. I practically had to carry him."

My brother made a disgruntled sound. "You were terrible at it. You also vomited on me."

"An hour's ride," I supplied. "If we leave a few hours before dawn, we can still reach the cove under the cover of darkness. I agree with Mr. Grant—we should go there first on the chance Olsa will still make the rendezvous. Will you be all right to travel?" I directed the question at Benedict but glanced at Mary to include her.

"Oh, I'll be quite all right after a few hours of sleep," Grant replied, tea in one hand and leaning down to plump the cushioning of the divan, right next to me, with the other. "This will do."

"Can we afford to sleep?" Mary glanced at Ben. "Can you keep control of the farmers?"

"I can maintain my control when I sleep," Benedict replied. "Instinct is enough."

"That's unsettling," Grant commented. "What if you dream? Do your instincts not… change?"

Benedict closed his eyes. "I do not dream."

"Never?" Mary clarified.

"Never," Ben affirmed. "Now if you three would be so kind as to shut up, I feel as though I have been in prison for weeks, then dragged through the Winter Sea and hauled through the snow for an hour by an ill-tempered hag."

"I could have left you there," Mary pointed out.

"You could never do that."

"Because you'd compel me?"

"No." Benedict gave a huffing laugh, low in his chest, and cracked an eye to look at me. "Because I look too much like Sam."

∞

"Samuel?"

I cracked open bleary eyes to find Mary easing an unfinished tea from my loose fingers.

The others were asleep, Ben in his chair, and Grant on the other side of the divan, his legs hanging over the armrest and his head cushioned on a pillow next to my leg. I had slid down into a slump and my neck ached.

Mary set my cup on the table. "I need to show you something."

My body was loath to move, but my curiosity won out— particularly when Mary extended her hand out to me, fingers waiting to be held. She had a heavy satchel under her other arm.

I slipped my hand into hers and allowed her to lead me down a corridor to a warm kitchen. The fire was banked, bread rising in covered bowls, and the air smelled of woodsmoke, herbs, char and yeast.

We did not speak again until she set the satchel down on a workspace with a weighty clunk. "I stole this from the prison."

I cleared my throat. Mary had a habit of theft, but, given the greater crime of freeing Ben and my own recent exploits, I hardly had a leg to stand on.

She opened the satchel. Inside was a muddle of lead shot dotted with colored paint and Mereish talismans on sturdy chains.

A familiar Knowing swept over me, and one brush at the Dark Water told me that each of these items had a signature there—a soft, muddied glow. Some were edged with Magni red, others Stormsinger teal, and still others a Sooth's forest green. The lead balls were the same, their glow matching the color of dots of paint, though their base glow was an unsettling orange, close to the shade that usually hung about dittama, huden, and similar Otherborn beasts. That orange, twined with reds, greens and teals, looked sickly.

I reached for a talisman with a green glow and slowly took it up. My senses shuddered—I felt as though a pillow had been dragged over my ears, rasping and muffling. The Dark Water vanished along with the glows of the various items.

"This acts like my coin," I mused and set it back down on the worktop. My sense of the Other promptly returned. "Did you look at these in the Dark Water?"

Mary shook her head. "No, but Tane and I sensed something off about them."

"So you stole them."

She shrugged. "It felt like the right thing to do."

I looked at the Sooth talisman for another long moment then picked it back up again. "Mary, can you please step into the Other while I'm holding this? Tell me what you see."

She visibly hesitated, but relented after a moment of thought. "All right."

I closed my hand around the new talisman. The world around me remained solid, and, between one blink and the next, Mary disappeared.

I counted my own breaths, timing her absence. One. Two. Three. Four.

Mary reappeared, looking a little nauseous. She raked in a deep breath and braced on the worktop.

"I couldn't see anything," she said once she had reacclimatized.

I drew my brows together. "But you were in the Dark Water. You saw nothing there? No lights?"

She shook her head. "I saw everything but you."

I stared down at the coin in my hand, my mind whirling. Then, abruptly, I held it out to her. "Will you please hold this?"

Mary slowly accepted the talisman. I slipped into the Dark Water— as easy as breathing, now the talisman was away from my skin.

Mary's usual glow, her and Tane's eternal reflection in the Dark Water, was nowhere to be seen.

I slipped back into the human world. "Mary, this suppresses a Sooth's abilities *both ways*."

Her lips parted in shock. "That means we can hide in the Other. All of us. There has to be…" She sifted through her gleanings and came up with another talisman identical to the one on the table. Her face fell. "We only have two."

I nodded, simultaneously intrigued and unsettled. If the Mereish had magecraft this advanced, what did it mean for the war? How long had they possessed it?

"You and Ben should wear them," I said practically. "There is no chance any Sooth from the prison touched Grant or I. Besides, if I wear that, I cannot use my abilities and we may miss a timely warning."

She nodded slowly. She surveyed the rest of the talismans, her thoughts clearly at silent war. "Also… If these new talismans work like your coin, they could make you worse."

"They may," I admitted.

"Ben and I take them, then. Now, what about these?" Mary reached for another talisman, this one embossed with a woman's face, eyes closed. The moment she wrapped her fingers fully around it, she stilled, and her eyes flew wide. I instinctively peered into the Dark Water. I could still see her, and the coin was teal, matching Mary's own glow.

Mary choked and dropped the coin. "I couldn't sing," she whispered, fear creeping into her eyes. "But what use is that? Why would the guards wear that?"

I held out a hand and she relinquished the Stormsinger talisman.

"Try to sing now. Direct your winds against me."

Mary lowered her chin and let out a slow breath. Then she sang a few, wordless notes.

The air in the room moved, rustling her skirts and whooshing up the chimney. But it did not touch me. I was protected, alone in an eddy of calm.

"The Mereish have talismans to protect themselves from mages," Mary breathed. "How is that possible? How could we not know? Our peoples have been at war for centuries. If they had this kind of knowledge, surely we would *know*."

I rubbed at my throat, stretching my jaw in the vain hope that it would ease the resurging pain in my head. "It must be a recent discovery. Or they have hidden it very, very well."

"Another secret the Ess Noti would kill for?" Mary murmured, her eyes scanning the rest of the satchel's contents. She reached for one of the lead balls marked with a blue splotch of paint. She closed her fingers around it and opened her lips.

Her voice came out, but the air in the room did not stir, and the soothing wash I usually felt when she sang did not come.

When Mary's eyes met mine, the horror in her gaze was matched by the dread in mine.

"It's not just the coins," she whispered. "If I was shot with one of these, when we were under attack… I'd lose my power."

"Until it was taken out," I theorized.

Together, we stared down at the table. But I hardly saw its contents anymore. I saw possibilities and futures, a shift in the balance of power on the Winter Sea. If the Mereish could nullify our mages, if they could hide theirs in the Other… it was an advantage too massive to contemplate.

"We have to tell someone," Mary murmured, lifting her dread-filled eyes back up to mine. "We have to get back to *Hart*."

TWENTY-ONE

The Highwayman
and the Hounds

MARY

I awoke to the smell of bread and a warm back against mine. I lay facing the smoldering fire across a thick, old carpet and smooth stone floor, a cushion embroidered with Mereish patterns beneath my head. Beyond the shutters and the murky glass of the windows, I saw nothing but darkness. It wasn't yet dawn.

I turned my head, expecting to find the shaggy dog lying behind me. Instead I found Sam, his face turned away and buried in another cushion. Even separated by layers of clothing and blankets as we were, his closeness made my thoughts scatter. Instinct told me to roll over, to slip my arm around his chest and bury my face in his back. It urged me to do far more than that.

But a sick feeling lingered in my stomach. As the haze of sleep and the consolation of Samuel's closeness faded, I remembered our situation in all its hopeless complexity.

Us, hunted. The Mereish in possession of staggering new magecraft. *Hart* waylaid and us trapped in our enemy's heartland.

Tane, how are we going to survive this?

Her answer was a wordless nudge of consolation, but she made no platitudes.

I sat up sharply as a door opened and a sizzling filled the air. A woman bustled in, her eyes dim and her hands holding a cast-iron pan with a wad of cloth. She set it on the dining table, where an oil lamp already burned. She left without casting us so much as a glance.

I looked to Benedict. He was still in his chair, his eyes open and his shirt unfastened to reveal a new Sooth talisman hanging against his own bruised skin. Its twin was warm against my own chest, hidden under my clothes.

The Magni's emotionless, weary gaze dropped to me. "She won't remember us," he promised, his voice overloud in the still house. "She thinks she's dreaming. Go back to sleep; I will wake you all when breakfast is ready."

I'd known the strength of Benedict's influence before, but to see it used in such a way was a new kind of unsettling.

The urge to dig into the satchel and pull out a Magni talisman assailed me. We had yet to test it, but it seemed natural that they would protect against Ben's influence.

I wanted that protection. But until we knew more about the items and their magics, Sam and I had agreed it was best to only use what we absolutely needed.

"Are you… controlling that woman? Like a puppet?" I hissed.

"I am not controlling her. The sleeping mind is much more susceptible to impulses—it does half my work for me. I simply convinced her that she should cook a meal before returning to bed, to sleep late and wake with no memory of what she has done."

"Benedict—"

"Mary?" Samuel sat up, pushing stray hair from his eyes in bleary, sudden concern. His gaze swept from me to Ben and then to the table. The iron pan wasn't alone; there were two loaves of fresh bread, a steaming pot of coffee, and various platters whose contents I couldn't see.

I thought Sam would scold Ben, but he didn't. He just rubbed the sleep from his eyes and pushed upright, wincing and rubbing his back.

A few minutes later, I plodded to the outhouse in the snow-bright, violet gloom just before dawn. I dressed in my clothes from the prison, now dry and partially clean, if stained with salt at the hems. Then we ate, watching the eerie, distracted Mereish woman trail back towards the bedrooms, her expression still blank, her cheeks flushed from laboring over the stove.

"They'll talk," I murmured to Sam as we ate next to one another. "There will be food gone and things amiss. Ben needs to take clothes. I can call up a snowstorm to cover our tracks but…"

"We left a thorough trail in the opposite direction," Sam reassured me. "Hopefully no one will think much of a disoriented farm wife this far our way, and Tane did well to hide Ben in the Other."

"Whether or not they can track us, it changes little," Benedict interrupted and drained his mug of coffee. He still looked a mess, but his eyes were as sharp as ever. "The farmers will not remember our stay, and we need to leave."

He was right—we had no choice—but my skin still crawled as Charles and Samuel led our horses out of the courtyard. The dog, back under his warm awning, watched us dolefully and paid no mind when the gate clattered shut.

Samuel led his horse up next to me and held the stirrup in place while I mounted. Ignoring aching muscles, I arranged my coat as Sam climbed up behind me. His arms slipped around my waist, taking the reins, and I resisted the urge to snuggle back into the press of his chest and thighs.

"Are you comfortable?" he asked in my ear.

"Passably," I replied.

"Don't get handsy," Charles warned Benedict as the other man climbed up behind him and sat on a thick blanket behind the saddle.

In answer, Benedict put a firm hand through the back of Charles's belt and tugged him back an inch. Charles, startled, glanced at Sam for support.

"Never fear," Benedict told Charles, adjusting his cloak with his free hand. "If I had an eye for men, you would already know."

"Is that a compliment?" Charles asked as both he and Sam nudged the horses into movement and we started for the road. He unfurled a crooked grin and glanced slyly back at Ben. "It is!"

Benedict, to my surprise, laughed. It was a genuine sound, hedged with relief, and when I looked over he'd turned his face into the wind. "If that consoles you."

I began to sing as we left the farm. The winds came to me curiously, flowing in from every direction and whispering what they held—snow, sea-salt, ice, warmth. I began luring snow in from the southwest, and, as the farmhouse passed from sight, the storm arrived. A flurry battered us until, breathless and bright-eyed with the chill, I convinced it to come to rest. Flakes ceased to drive and instead fell thickly then, layering the road behind us and filling in our tracks.

As my song faded Samuel made a warm, soft noise in his chest, and I looked up at him.

"It never fails to surprise me, when you sing," he murmured, his eyes distant on the road ahead and the soft, thick snow. "I'm here, wholly. With you."

I tentatively clasped his hand where it held the reins, forearm resting heavy on my thigh. There was a tension to the moment, an expectation of more to be said. I waited, willing him to speak.

"I am sorry," he said, low and only for me. "For holding back from you. Once we are safe… can we speak?"

"Of course."

He cleared his throat and changed topics. "We should let the snow clear in a quarter hour or so. We may be hidden, but we also cannot see or hear, and that unsettles me."

Soon after, I began to sing again and the snow ceased to follow us. We left the storm behind, chased by fading flurries into open farmland and the growing light of dawn. The sun warmed the eastern horizon, pushing back the bruised twilight and diffusing in our misty breaths—beautiful, crisp and clean in the way that only snowy mornings could be. But I felt growing tension in Samuel's arm at my waist.

At first, I feared I was the cause. But when I twisted to look into his eyes, his gaze was towards the sea.

"They're still not at the meeting place?" I guessed. The forest inland to the south took on more shape and definition, and up ahead I saw the smoke and pricks of light that marked more farmhouses nestled among snowy hills. "Olsa isn't coming."

"She is not," Samuel affirmed. "*Hart* is moving east, but in convoy with the other ships. I... I have no doubt he has been captured now."

"What is east?" Charles asked. "Where are they going?"

"Ostchen," Ben said. "The naval port. It would be the natural place to take any captured ship."

Samuel's arm retreated from my waist, and I realized he was adjusting his weapons—loosening his cutlass in its scabbard with a rasp of frozen steel.

I unfastened clasps of the saddlebags so we could reach our pistols quickly. "Is someone coming?"

A dog began to bark. It came distantly, back up the road—too close to be the shaggy dog at the farmhouse. It was also not alone. A howl joined it, then another.

"Fuck," Benedict growled. Charles had slowed his horse, and we came alongside to confer. "How could those dogs be tracking us? I was in the water long enough to kill me."

"Regardless. *Always* assume the dogs are after you," Charles said with grave conviction. "If Olsa is not coming, we need to take to the forest."

"Now," Benedict added, reaching for the reins.

Charles elbowed him back and gathered the reins himself, directing the horse off the road. Samuel followed without a word.

I looked back the way we'd come. The sun slipped up over the eastern horizon, casting our shadows over the mottled line of our tracks. My thoughts slowed, clotted with fear, and, for a few breaths, I gave it rein.

I imagined hounds tearing through the snow, harrying us into the trees. I imagined the riders that would come behind them, muskets sparking and pluming. I imagined a bullet in Samuel's back. Hands, dragging me back to the prison, to the cell with the other Stormsingers, gagged and helpless. Chains fastening me to the mast of a Mereish warship.

I began to sing. The snow returned quickly, remembering the song I'd sung it a short time ago. A flurry of thick, fat flakes melted on my cheeks and swept us silently into the pines.

When the trees surrounded us, I changed my melody. I sent the snow driving ahead of us at a blistering, nearly horizontal angle, carrying away our scents. My trained winds, however, kept us in a bubble of calm, full of the clink of tack and the crunch of snow beneath the horses' hooves.

"There's a monastery called Oruse, two days' ride from here. One, now," Samuel said, raising his voice just enough to be heard. "They are bound to shelter anyone, even foreigners and criminals."

"Are they also bound not to betray them?" Benedict asked, his eyes haunted for one vulnerable moment.

"I've hidden in my share of monasteries," Charles put in. "Aeadine, given. But they were not prone to betrayal. Half the monks were hiding from sullied pasts."

"I'd prefer to ride right for Ostchen," I said, surprising myself with how true it was. The prospect of staying another minute on Mereish soil chilled me, and the weight of unbelonging was oppressive. "We can find *Hart* and get out to sea."

"Because reclaiming your ship will be entirely straightforward," Benedict said with false congeniality.

Dogs bayed in the distance, muffled and distorted through the snow. We were all quiet for a moment, listening to them echo and fade through the trees.

Charles was as serious as I'd ever seen him. He flicked his gaze between us. "I can lose them, if you trust me."

"We have no choice," Ben pointed out.

I nodded and felt, more than saw, Sam do the same.

"Then follow my lead and do as I say." Charles nudged his mount into movement and we set off after him.

TWENTY-TWO

Blood Upon the Snow

SAMUEL

Hooves rippled. Dogs bayed. Mary and I huddled close in the saddle, following Grant's lead down a track of ice-crusted mud and dusted snow. With every thunder of my heart, I resisted the urge to shout to Grant, to question him and drive our mounts to a gallop. The road was too uneven, slick with ice and scattered with fallen branches, not to mention our horses were already fatigued.

Grant threw out an arm and we diverted, clustering on the bank of a swift creek. Ice rimmed the shores but a recent thaw had opened the center, where water glistened in the filtered forest light.

"Take the saddlebags," Grant instructed. He helped Benedict dismount and lean against a tree. "Ben, give me your shirt."

"Pardon me?" Benedict squinted at him, the question disorienting him.

Mary and I dismounted, and I pulled off the saddle bags.

"For the dogs. Give it to me." Grant drew his pistol and primed it, sparing my brother half a glance. "Mary, get into the river and sing up the thickest snow you can. Start walking, that way."

He pointed downstream.

Shivering, Ben pulled his shirt over his head and passed it to Grant. The top half of his pale stomach fluttered above his breeches and belt. He wore layers of bruises, better seen in the daylight.

Mary held out her hands to me. "Give me some of those."

I laid the lighter saddlebags over her shoulder and watched as she picked her way across the ice. It cracked beneath her feet, but she kept upright and, gasping at the cold, grinned stiffly back at me.

"Brisk," she commented and began to slosh downstream. She hummed as she went, picking up notes of a simple tune.

Dogs continued to bay, jarring with her song. Closer now. The wind picked up, ghosting across my cheeks, thick with the scent of snow and frozen forest.

A whirl of fresh snow swept Mary up in a ripple of clothes and hair, then she vanished from sight.

I squinted through snow-laden lashes at Ben. "Ready to move?"

My brother finished buttoning his coat over his bare chest and held out an impatient arm. "Help me."

I put an arm under his shoulder. We descended into the creek with a splash and a round of muffled curses, only half of which came from Ben. The water was shockingly cold, and my bones hurt from my toes to my clenched jaw.

"Say goodbye," Grant called. That was all the warning we got before he slapped the flank of my anxious mare. Both horses cantered away up the road, tack jingling and hooves thundering. I glimpsed Ben's soiled shirt fluttering from one saddle, then they too disappeared into the snow.

"How many times have you done this?" I asked Grant as he joined us in the water, wincing and muttering. We started off after Mary, I supporting Ben while Grant watched our backs.

The former highwayman shrugged. "Four or five. Though I've never had a Stormsinger to cover my tracks, and I prefer to weigh the horses down with something. Hopefully the snow will disguise the trail enough. They'll likely scout the creek after us regardless, but the hounds will go after the horses."

"If I remember correctly," Benedict said through gritted teeth. "You met Mary in prison?"

"I was only caught once," Grant scoffed. "And I escaped."

"Thanks to Mary." Despite the situation—or maybe because of it—the flash of resentment I felt at Grant's casual mention of the incident caught me by surprise. "Whereupon you sold her."

Grant fell silent, cowed. In that quiet Mary's voice came to us in eerie gusts and snatches.

"Desperation makes fools of us all," the highwayman muttered.

A plodding, wind-harried silence overtook us. Our pursuers drew ever closer, my Sooth's senses prickling, teasing the hair on the back of my neck. I looked back, edging into the Dark Water, and noted magelights off in the forest.

I caught Grant's eye. "They are still closing. One Sooth, one Magni."

"That we can see," Ben interjected. "There may be more with talismans."

Grant surveyed our surroundings. We had entered a thick stand of cedars, dark leaves and fraying trunks girded with white. "We should make a stand. This is as good a place as any."

We made for the bank.

"Can you shoot?" I asked Ben as he slouched into the shelter of a thick, divided trunk.

He unshouldered his musket and set to priming it, despite a perceptible shiver in his fingers. He drove the ramrod down in two sharp passes. "I can, but I would prefer not to waste that shot Mary stole. I would prefer they killed one another."

He spoke with the practicality of a butcher at his bench.

Grant met my gaze, and I saw in his face the same look I had seen in the eyes of my uncle, my aunt, Mary, and countless others when they were reminded of the depths of Ben's power.

"Try to leave one of them alive—an officer, if there is one," Grant suggested. "Samuel, will you find Mary?"

Ben nodded and looked to his priming.

He and Grant fell into position, and I slipped up the bank, moving quickly away from the uneven creek bed. The wind and snow whipped past me in a steady stream, but my feet had long numbed, and I felt no cold beneath my thick coat. There was only heat, sweat, and the unyielding threat of danger.

Mary came into sight, harried by nearly horizontal snow.

"We shall make a stand," I called, just loud enough to carry. "They have a Sooth and a Magni, at the least."

She took my proffered hand and splashed onto shore then followed me back towards Grant and Benedict. I spied my brother on the far side of the creek, rifle nestled in the crook of a branch. Grant crouched beside him, pistol in one hand and cutlass in the other.

Mary dropped the saddlebags on our side of the water and reached into her pocket, producing a few lead balls. She plucked out two—one marked with a red splotch of paint, one green. "I have extras to give the Admiralty. But there is only one for a Sooth. I think it is worth using."

She held up the ball in question. I paused, simultaneously grateful for and saddened by her pragmatism. I plucked the green shot from her hand, bare and cool, and pinched with cold. My connection to the Other immediately faltered, then recovered as the ball disappeared into my musket's barrel.

Mary's own fingers closed on the red shot, and she readied her pistol.

After an interminable time, six figures emerged from the snow— three on each bank. They crept soundlessly, even with the wind at their backs, and my esteem for Mereish soldiers rose a grudging notch. For soldiers they were: they wore the pale grey of Mereish infantry rather than the brown of the prison guards.

The Other tugged at me, and I let it swell. Daylight fled and gloom rose as the creek overflowed its banks and transformed into the Dark Water. Mary and Ben were both hidden, their talismans intact, but a small woman was surrounded by a deep, forest green. Their Sooth. The Magni was across the creek, on Mary's and my side.

"The Magni is that older man—grey hair, short beard," I murmured to Mary. "The Sooth that short woman, on Benedict's side."

She nodded, already seeking out her target. I did the same, tracking the other Sooth on the opposite bank. She was small, the kind of woman one might mistake for a child in a crowd, but there was nothing childlike about the cool set of her lips. She slipped through the trees, her gaze flicking from my location to Benedict's sheltering tree. She might not be able to see Ben in the Other like she could me, but she had certainly sensed his presence.

Benedict met my gaze across the water, through the veil of snow. His expression was cool, but I saw a twitch beneath it, a readiness for violence that bordered on hunger. It was a face he had worn a hundred times before. On any other day, this was the moment when I should intervene, talk him down, seek to separate him from circumstances where the full brunt of his corruption might be unleashed.

But I did not. Instead, I dropped my chin in the barest nod, and he inclined his in return.

The soldiers all halted in their tracks. I saw the terror and confusion in their eyes for an instant, then Benedict had them completely in his thrall. Their expressions glazed.

Only the mages broke free. The Sooth dove for cover while the Magni, not ten paces from Mary and I, stepped neatly behind a tree.

What happened next came in rapid sequence, nearly too quick to follow. Benedict's musket rang out. A soldier's head snapped back in a spray of blood, brain and skull, and the rest of her crumpled. One of her comrades screamed—a fractured, masculine wail that made my stomach flip. That cry cut off with another shot as one of the grieving man's own comrades, on Mary's and my bank, turned to shoot him in the throat. Arterial blood burst, scattering across the white of the snow.

His cries turned to a gargle, and Ben allowed him to collapse into the water with a splash and crack of ice.

In the same breath, the Sooth rose up from behind a hulking, many-trunked cedar and shot Benedict. My brother spasmed back into the snow, roaring in frustration and clutching at… his chest? No, his upper arm.

Grant shoved in front of my brother and shot at the Sooth, but she was already gone.

The enemies on our side of the creek broke out of Ben's thrall and scattered for shelter. Mary crouched lower beside me, still as a rabbit in the brush, and I sighted the Sooth down the length of my barrel.

"Shoot her," Mary hissed.

The other mage vanished behind a tree and did not come out again. "No clean shot," I grunted.

My voice sounded louder than I intended. Silence had fallen around us, a thick hush that clawed at my nerves and compounded my aching head as each party waited for the other to act. In the creek, the soldier who had been shot in the throat ceased to bleed, and the last tendrils of red dispersed in the bubbling current.

I glimpsed Ben exchanging rapid whispers with Grant. Ben pulled a knife and shoved it into the other man's hand, jerking his coat from his wounded arm. Grant looked ill, and I guessed what was happening: Ben wanted him to cut the Magni-suppressing shot from his arm.

"Tane wants to use the trees." Mary's voice was low and soft, carried between us on a tamed scrap of wind. "We can force the Mereish out of hiding."

"They will know you are *ghiseau*," I countered, though my mind already leapt to the possibilities.

"They already may." Mary shifted into a crouch. "Besides, they won't be telling anyone else. Am I doing this?"

"Do it."

She pressed her bare, free hand into the bark of the tree and closed her eyes.

A new voice cut through the forest.

"We have twelve more soldiers on their way," a female voice called in Usti. The Sooth, her small frame well hidden behind her tree. "This is your opportunity to surrender. Three of you are mages. Two of you are *ghiseau*. Your lives have value, and I do not want to kill you."

None of us were foolish enough to reply. Mary remained eerily still, a faint glow manifesting where she touched the tree.

On our side of the river, a different tree shuddered. A male voice cried out and a musket immediately cracked, tearing my focus from the hidden Sooth.

One of the hidden soldiers toppled into sight, scrabbling at his chest and gasping. Grant meanwhile ducked back under cover, gunsmoke dispersing above him. Benedict could barely be seen beside him, tucked into the tree and clutching an arm soaked in blood. I could not tell if Grant had been successful in removing the shot.

The entire forest began to shudder, then to sway and creak. Branches broke and toppled into the snow with muffled *whumps*, while the ground began to ripple with coiling roots.

The Sooth twitched into sight. I fired. She fell.

My victory was short-lived. I had barely felt the musket kick before Mary darted out of shelter and sprinted through the snow and falling branches—directly towards our enemies.

The Magni man rose, facing her down. I had no time to reload; Mary, steadily advancing through the snow, leveled her pistol and fired.

The Magni jerked and dropped his musket, but not before the muzzle flashed.

A shot slammed into a tree branch right in front of Mary's head— a branch that had not been there an instant before. The branch exploded and ghisten light flared.

Not a single shard touched Mary. She was already behind another tree, breathing in quick, measured breaths.

The mages were down. There was only one soldier left.

An agonized shout broke the stillness. Across the river, Ben rose to his feet. His arm was still sheathed in blood, his coat hanging off him and shoulder exposed.

But I felt his power billow out once again. The last soldier stepped out from behind the tree, her arms raised, every inch of her trembling as she pointed her own pistol under her chin.

More blood splattered across the snow.

In the stillness that followed, Mary's eyes found mine. I saw relief in her face, along with an odd closedness—an echo of shock and a shadow of turmoil.

I went to her, but something in her posture warned me not to pull her into my arms. Instead, I extended a hand, and she took it. Her touch wavered, fingers trembling, but, as I tightened my grip, they stilled.

"Ready?" I asked.

She ducked her chin.

The four of us regrouped around the Mereish Sooth. She sat against a tree, bleeding profusely from a wound to the chest. I had been aiming for her arm and felt a rumble of regret. Whether or not that wound was fatal would entirely depend on how far behind her comrades were.

It also destroyed the possibility of recovering our single Sooth shot without killing her outright, and the thought of sifting around in the open chest of a still-warm corpse was not one I entertained.

"How are you tracking us?" I asked.

The Sooth clutched her chest, her face sheeted with pain and her eyes battling to stay open.

"She's in too much pain, it's useless," Mary said. She looked more frantic than ever. "We need to move."

Ben crouched before the Sooth, and she cried out, though he had not touched her.

"How are you tracking us?" Ben asked. Using his good hand, he pulled the Sooth talisman from beneath his shirt. "Does this not work?"

"The Ess Noti," she rasped. Her eyes were so wide with panic I half feared they would rupture. "Tracking *him*."

"How?" Mary demanded, turning on me. "When did a Mereish Sooth touch you?"

I shook my head, more unsettled than I cared to show.

"How are they following me?" I repeated to our prisoner.

The Sooth shook her head in a compulsive shudder and every muscle in her body flared taut. "I don't know!"

"Then who is it and where are they?"

"Enisca Alamay. Magni. And Inis Hae, the Summoner," she rattled, her voice weakening. In her compulsion to speak, Ben was not allowing her to breathe. "Coming. Close."

Summoner. A Sooth Adjacent, like me. As to Enisca—that was a woman's name.

A piece clicked together in my mind, backed by my sorcery. "Is Enisca Alamay blonde?"

The Sooth stared at me in blank desperation, tears streaming down her face and blood leaking from the corner of her mouth. The sound of her breaths was becoming thicker.

"Are they with the other soldiers you spoke of?" Ben pressed.

"No." The word was almost inaudible, the tension in the dying mage difficult to watch.

"Ben," I snapped. "Be gentler."

My brother muttered something under his breath, but he stepped back. The other Sooth sagged as if a hand had dropped from her throat.

"We need to leave," Mary said, her voice far calmer than her expression. She stared back downriver. "We're losing any lead we had."

Grant nodded reluctantly. "Agreed. But... should we leave her? Alive?"

The Sooth's legs contorted as she tried to push herself farther away, but there was nowhere to go. "Yes, there is no reason to kill me! Just… leave me as I am. Please. They already know who you are. They will follow you everywhere you go. They find us. That's what they do."

"Us?" I repeated.

Her eyes swiveled to me, now filled with haunted desperation.

"Us," she affirmed in a whisper. "Mages. Mereish or Aeadine, there is little difference."

My skin crawled. "What else do you know?"

"Nothing." Her voice was a whimper now, Ben squeezing each word from her. "I'm given orders. I execute them."

"And I am leaving now," Grant said, grabbing his and Ben's muskets and giving us all a flat smile. He caught Mary's gaze and raised his brows.

She took a step backwards, away from Ben and I, then went to retrieve the saddlebags from where we had dumped them in the snow.

Mary's departure was like a dash of cold water. I took Ben's arm—his good one, as the other was limp and soaked with blood. "They are right. We cannot afford to waste time, and you are already injured."

Ben remained, looking down at the helpless Sooth. "She shot me," he pointed out, his voice cold again. "I want to kill her."

"And I shot her. Let us *go*."

I thought Ben would not comply, but he did. Together, the four of us set off, leaving behind the carnage—the soldiers and the mages, some dead, some clinging to life.

"I am going somewhere warm after this," my brother told me, scrubbing blood from his face as we trudged into the forest. "The Mereish South Isles. I hear it hardly snows."

I felt myself smile, but there was no emotion to it. "Maybe I will come with you."

THE SAINTS—*Before any intelligent discussion of the Saints may be attempted, we must first differentiate the Saints of Mere from those observed by the world at large. We do not speak of the powerless, logic-bound Saint of the Aeadine, who serves as little more than a sword of conquest and subjugation. We do not speak of the Saints (and gods) of the Usti, whose venerated beings are so numerous and chaotic as to render one another obsolete.*

No, here we will speak of the true Saints, those who live but do not breathe, who watch over us from beyond and before the veil, who rise above their lesser cousins and will guide Mere into ever greater prosperity, understanding, and devotion.

—FROM A DEFINITIVE STUDY OF THE BLESSED: MAGES
AND MAGECRAFT OF THE MEREISH ISLES, *TRANSLATED
FROM THE MEREISH BY SAMUEL I. ROSSER*

TWENTY-THREE

The Sacred Servants of Adalia Day: Divine Daughter of Unbroken Light

MARY

By the time I approached the gate of Oruse, I hadn't eaten or slept since the farmhouse. Charles's encouragement to look extra pathetic proved unnecessary, as the old woman at the gate took one look at my stumbling frame, opened the door, and ushered me in with wide, compassionate eyes.

"My friends," I said in Usti, pointing back down the road. "They're hurt."

So it was that the four of us—our weapons and the items stolen from the prison stashed in the forest—were welcomed by the Sacred Servants of Adalia Day, Divine Daughter of Unbroken Light. The monastery was sprawling but modest, with a central chapel, a two-storied dormitory and several other buildings connected by covered walkways. Nearly everything was built of wood, including the encircling wall, which was perhaps ten feet tall and crowned with snow.

The shrine itself—the proper 'Oruse,' as the monk explained— was nowhere to be seen. But Tane had a sense of something, some whisper of power, and it made the hair on the back of my neck prickle with awareness.

"Sam." I caught Samuel's sleeve as we were ushered through a courtyard, where staring novices in grey robes labored with shovels and ice scrapers. "Do you feel that? What can you see?"

He slowed, taking in the courtyard with a glance that, while discreet, held the detached quality of a Sooth.

"There are other mages here, and a great deal of ghisten wood," he returned in a low voice. Ahead, our guide opened a door and led us into a long, echoing hallway where monks stood aside with bowed heads. "They are difficult to differentiate in the Other."

"Like as not, these monks are more afraid of us recognizing them than the other way around," Charles interjected, misinterpreting our conversation. "Did you see the scars on that woman's face? Powder burns, likely from a rifle backfiring. Folks at a monastery this remote are not here to be found."

I resisted the urge to glance back at the old monk in question. I caught Samuel's gaze instead, silently promising to pick up our conversation at a later time, and kept walking.

"They still might betray us," Benedict muttered. He skulked behind Samuel, his arm in a makeshift sling. I had no idea how he was still upright. "I assume we are worth some kind of reward."

"I should hope so," Charles scoffed.

"We won't give them the chance to turn us in," I said. Up ahead, our guide opened a door on silent hinges and waved us through. "We get help and leave."

The room beyond proved to be an infirmary. An ebony-skinned man in a dark-grey robe approached at the same time as novices converged from all sides, and he and Samuel began to speak in Mereish. I sensed Tane listening, so I let my own attention wander.

The infirmary was quiet and warm, scented distantly with lemon and sage and clean sheets. The shelter, the quiet rumble of Samuel's voice and the presence of my three companions—even Benedict— lulled me, and I found my head bobbing.

The relief was short-lived. My body, realizing it was no longer in imminent danger of freezing to death, began to make a hundred lesser miseries known. I needed to piss. I needed to sit down. I needed a bath—a very hot one, with lots of soap. I needed cloth and herbs to make suppositories, because, Saint pity me, I had a fresh ache in my lower stomach that refused to abate. And I was starving, of course—I wanted food, roasted venison with potatoes and cream sauce and too many carrots, with cinnamon cakes for dessert, and thick, hot cardamon coffee.

I was contemplating how many potatoes I could eat when a female novice took my arm.

"Come with me," she said in Usti. I was apprehensive at being separated, but the novice's hand was firm. She added in a gentler tone, "You are safe here."

Safe. The word was enticing, her tone so gentle. I wanted to forget Tane's unrest, I wanted to believe the novice, but it wasn't until I caught Sam's gaze that I did. His smile was reassuring, and he gave a subtle nod.

I allowed the other woman to lead me away. We passed through a door and into another chamber, where another female novice waited.

I stripped at their direction, handing over my torn and soiled clothes, and submitted to having my scratches and bruises examined. The sister who had brought me quietened at the sight of my throat and exchanged a look with her companion, a brown-skinned woman of small stature who I recognized as southern Sunjani.

"If they did this, we can protect you," the Usti-speaker said.

I blinked at her, too tired to understand. "This?"

The novice exchanged another look with her companion. "Did your companions hurt you?" There were more questions in her eyes, sharp and hard-edged, but she did not ask them. "Are you with them willingly?"

"No! I mean no, it wasn't them," I hastened to add. "I trust them."

The novice didn't look entirely convinced, but the matter was dropped. My injuries pronounced superficial, I was given a robe and escorted to a small, private room where a bath steamed. Both unsettled and relieved, I glanced from the door to the wooden tub, the hand pump and the hearth. More water was already set to boil, and the steamy warmth of the chamber was exquisite.

Exhausted tears prickled at my eyes. I let out a half-relieved, half-pained sigh, and submerged myself in the water.

Tane slipped from my skin and came to stand over the tub. *I will keep watch.* She didn't wait for affirmation—she already knew I agreed—before she glided away through the wall. Her voice still drifted through my mind though, unaffected by the distance. *And see what else I can sense. There is something here, something beyond mages and harvested ghisten wood.*

Something bad?

I cannot say yet. Perhaps not. Rest, Mary.

A strange absence settled over me. Now I was truly alone, with only the thinnest thread of ghisten flesh to connect me to Tane.

I released the sides of the tub, letting the water close over my face. It stung on my cold-burned cheeks but the silence—interspersed only by the distant slosh of water and the rhythm of my own heart—soothed me.

I surfaced when my lungs began to burn and set to scrubbing. My mind wandered, freed by heat and comfort and Tane's steady vigil. Memories presented themselves, drifting and muted. The prison guard grabbing me by the throat. Benedict collapsing on shore. Samuel staring at me in the doorway of the farmhouse.

The Mereish Magni I'd shot appeared in my mind, clearer than any of the other memories. His power had been so pitiful compared to Benedict's. I had hardly felt it in the moment before I pulled the trigger and he crumpled into the snow.

I had dealt violence before. I was—quietly, darkly, in a hidden part of my soul—sure I'd even killed, though I'd never watched the life drain from my enemy's eyes. I had given my tithe of sleepless nights to that reality.

Now, perhaps, I would tithe more. The Magni mage was probably dead by my hand. I hadn't shot the Sooth—or the other soldiers—but I felt just a responsible for her death. She had looked at all four of us with such fear, riddled with Benedict's magic. I had felt her terror, watery and maddening.

But as I rinsed my hair and dried myself with a towel, it was not the memory of that fear, nor even the probable deaths of the Mereish that perturbed me most.

It was my apathy towards them.

TWENTY-FOUR

The High Cleric

SAMUEL

M r. Scieran, High Cleric, had a deep, rumbling voice that reminded me of dark-paneled studies, strong whiskey and pipesmoke. His accent was calculated and rounded, and his eyes were so green they were nearly black.

"Two *ghiseau*, one of which is a Stormsinger, and two amplified mages appear from the forest and beg shelter," he had observed, holding my gaze across his desk at the back of the infirmary.

I was too tired to be startled by his insight. "How do you know?"

"The Saint."

"She speaks to you?"

"In a way." His reply was not cold, but his tone made it clear that I would receive no more clarity on that front.

"You are a High Cleric," I observed, and he nodded. "Clearly, you know my brother and I were amplified, though imperfectly. Can you help us?"

The healer laced his long, fine fingers together on the top of the desk. "I am bound by my vows to protect and help anyone within these gates."

A knot of tension inside me loosened a fraction. "For that you have my utmost gratitude. But I meant in terms of our corruption."

Scieran's brows drew together. "Corruption?"

I searched for another Mereish word and came up short. "The

Black Tide Cult attempted to amplify my brother and me. It worked, but… we were left broken too."

The other man sat straighter in his chair, a new caution coming into his eyes. "Then you were not amplified by the Ess Noti."

The name hit me like a fist. "No. Aeadine immigrants to Usti, Black Tide cultists, stole my brother and I and performed their rituals. The Ess Noti amplify mages?"

"You know *of* the Ess Noti but not what they do? What are you doing in Mere, Sooth?"

I thought quickly. Telling him anything closer to the truth was a risk, but would I ever find anyone with more answers than he had?

"My brother—my twin, you see there—was captured, and we came from Usti to rescue him. But not all went to plan and, yes, we are fleeing. Fleeing from soldiers and the Ess Noti. But we barely understand who they are."

"Was your brother taken to Maase?"

I hesitated, then nodded.

Scieran's expression darkened, though I sensed his ire was not directed towards me. "You must have moved quickly to get to him before the Ess Noti. They and that prison are intimately connected. In any case… You should not linger here. I may be bound to protect you, but that does not mean I can. Leave tomorrow."

My relief evaporated. "We will. I would not willingly bring danger to you. But if you could tell me all you know about the Ess Noti, I would be grateful. And if you could heal my brother and I of our corruption, I would be eternally indebted."

The last sentence felt bizarre on my tongue: too simple, too straightforward for the magnitude of what it meant.

"I cannot heal you." Scieran destroyed my hope of a future with a gentle, low voice. "But the Ess Noti could."

I felt the color leave my face. My eyes strayed to the door Mary had gone through, images of a future with her—of belonging and intimacy, of family—flickering from existence as quickly as they formed. In their place came the helplessness of the Dark Water, where my mind would eventually become trapped, and the enduring reality of our positions in the world.

"Then we are doomed," I said, my voice hollow and far more resigned than I felt.

"Ostchen is the heart of Mereish power and, naturally, the Ess Noti," Scieran said, still gentle. "If you were to pursue a cure, you would need to go there, to them. Though how you could do so while maintaining your freedom? I cannot say."

Another redirection, another vague hope. I felt no encouragement this time, only a dull, rootless certainty that continuing to pursue a cure would be the death of us.

"As to who the Ess Noti are, that I can tell you." Scieran drew a deep breath, seeming to shed the grimness of our previous topic. "A hundred years ago they were like us, servants to a saint—Saint Ilaad. But their zeal—and the offer of greater power—carried them too far. Now they terrorize any Mereish overseas. They hunt foreign spies and mages on Mereish soil and, I have heard, have begun to do so across the Winter Sea. They cannot hope to keep Mereish secrets from the world for much longer, but still they try. In the last year, their efforts have become even more… militant."

"Do you know why? What changed?"

Besides three ships crossing the Stormwall with bellies full of treasure and hundreds of new ghiseau *spreading across the world.*

Scieran shook his head. "I do not know. Powerful secular figures have begun to affiliate themselves with the Ess Noti, though. A shift was inevitable."

"Who?"

He shrugged. "Rich and powerful people. Politicians. Distant relations of the royal family."

That seemed to be all the detail he could give. "May I ask how you know all this?" I asked. "You are Capesh?"

"Yes." Scieran's smile was wan. He rapped his knuckles on the desk. "Sequestered in a monastery far from home, like many of my companions."

"You are a captive?"

"I would be if I tried to leave Mere," he said. "I was forcefully recruited from the Capesh Navy. My homeland, as I'm sure you know, has no Ghistwold. We rely on Mere to equip our ships, and as such… we are bound to one another. I served the Mereish Navy as a Cleric for twenty years, and this is my retirement. It is not a bad life."

I sat back in my chair, reflecting on his words. "If you tried to leave, the Ess Noti would hunt you down."

The other man nodded. "Now that you understand the circumstances, let me tell you again. You should leave tomorrow. Leave my monastery, and Mere."

"I intend to," I muttered, rubbing my forehead against a fresh headache—the cure from the previous monastery had either failed me, or I was simply doomed to have an aching head from here on out.

To have found safety, even for a short time, and know it was so brief? It left me close to breaking, not just for myself, but for my companions: for Ben, his arm in danger of festering, and Mary, so exhausted I feared she would not wake up this morning. Even Grant, who had complained little, despite finding himself plunged into the worst of circumstances.

I needed more answers. Quickly. "How connected are the Ess Noti with the Mereish Military? We encountered soldiers on the road, with mages."

"Officially, Ess Noti and the military—the army, the navy, the royal battalions—are not connected. But in practice, they are hopelessly entwined," Scieran said. "The Ess Noti has power only over mages. But given how much power the mages possess over others, whether by rank or value… the Ess Noti's grasp on everyone is tight."

"Do Mereish mages have reason to fear the Ess Noti?" I asked, recalling the terror in the Mereish Sooth's eyes. "What would they have done with my brother after they claimed him?"

The High Cleric looked past me, down the infirmary hall. "I only know rumors. They amplify mages regularly—that is well known, as is their success. They are always refining their methods, studying, pursuing new knowledge. I think, perhaps, we can both imagine what that might entail."

A sick feeling began to clench, low in my stomach. The Dark Water brushed at my ankles, and with a dreamer's rootless certainty I saw two images. One was Ben, locked in a chamber of stone, chained and haunted, his arms covered with scars and bleeding wounds. The second was of the talismans and lead balls Mary had stolen.

Talismans, I knew, were made with the blood of mages.

"Do the Ess Noti also pursue new technologies?" I asked, though I already sensed the answer. "Adjacent to magecraft. Talismans and the like."

Scieran shook his head. "That, I do not know. It has been years since I was in contact with the outside world, and I do not make a habit of interrogating fugitives who pass through my gates." He raised an amused brow. "Unless they are Aeadine, pretending to be Usti, and are, at most, days ahead of their pursuers."

My smile was brittle. "Understood. We will leave tomorrow."

"Thank you."

TWENTY-FIVE

Four Moons

MARY

I expected to reunite with the men as soon as I'd finished my bath and dressed, but instead I was met by the Sunjani novice and led into an underground passageway.

Nerves, settled by the bath, prickled back to life.

"Where are we going?" I asked in Mereish, supplied by Tane.

The Sunjani blinked at my change of language. "Your Mereish is very good." Her own was pleasantly accented, with the light vowels and soft stops of her native tongue. "My name is Nitha."

"I'm Mer," I said, using an Usti form of Mary.

I was aware that my facial structure was staunchly Aeadine, with the broad cheekbones, small mouth and nose common to the midlands, but the chances of her recognizing that were slim, and the Usti ancestry I claimed was notoriously mixed.

"Where are we going?" I repeated, hoping to distract her.

"I am taking you to the Oruse. Our shrine." Nitha turned her attention back to the tunnel ahead. It wasn't as dank as I expected, the floor and walls dry and brightly lit with oil lamps on silvered iron hooks. "You must pay your respects."

Hidden in my bones, Tane stirred. *Whatever I sensed lies this way. Mary, it feels like another ghisting.*

Samuel said there was ghisten wood here.

I do not speak of doors and lintels. This ghisting has not been harvested.

But we are nowhere near a Ghistwold.

Precisely.

Curiosity deepening, I asked, "Have my companions already paid their respects?"

"Your friend with the pale hair will join us soon."

"Not the others?"

Nitha wasn't a terrible liar, but there was evasiveness in her eyes as she said, "They were not summoned. You will see them at table, regardless."

Perplexed and more than a little wary, I fell silent.

The tunnel was long enough for me to recognize we must have left the monastery grounds. We reached another set of stairs that broadened as they rose, each rock-hewn step worn with age and smooth in the lanternlight. We passed several monks in low, smiling conversation and two novices with empty baskets and scuttling feet. They all nodded to us, but kept their eyes from my face.

"Why won't they look at me?" I asked. Surely not *everyone* at the monastery was in hiding and would act the same way.

"The Saint summoned you but has not seen you yet," my guide said.

The beginnings of suspicion began to trickle between Tane and myself.

"No one else should see me before this Saint?" I clarified.

"Yes."

"But you may?"

She smiled. "It is not a rule—just a courtesy. This way."

At the top of the stairs my guide turned right, moving swiftly. Natural light touched the slate floor beneath our slippers, filtered through tall, narrow windows as we passed down a short hallway. At its end, an ancient, almost entirely circular archway of alternating yellow, blue and white stone opened into a vaulted, also circular chamber.

I'd been in places of worship before, from my village's small chapel with its singular, gold-leafed icon of the Aeadine Saint in his scarlet crown to Hesten's gargantuan cathedral, its floor set with as many tombstones as tiles. This place had the same sense of gravity and reverence, but... more. Every inch of stone, wood, plaster, gold, ivory, anything in the space that might be carved was, and everything that could not be was painted with intricate Mereish psalms and patterns.

I shared Tane's sense of a presence now, a similar feeling to when I stood next to *Hart*'s figurehead or we encountered another ghisten ship at sea, but more elusive. There was another ghisting in this room. But where? In the carvings? In the door, as a guardian?

As in an Aeadine chapel, I expected a saint's statue to be central to the chamber, properly pious and surrounded by offerings. But here I saw only a carved wooden pillar, graced by a beam of sunlight from a small, circular window.

I fixed my eyes on the pillar.

"The walls show the life of Saint Adalia," my guide said, moving to the center of the chamber. Rows of cushions covered the floor in apparently random lines, but when I followed Nitha's gaze, I realized they were positioned to face different sections of the carvings.

The nearest façade was carved of nearly black wood. Inlaid with pieces of opal, it depicted a woman crowned in beams of light, holding out her hands to rows and rows of kneeling onlookers. Her left hand cradled a small sun, its light illuminating half her body. The other half was cast in shadows, highlighted by a gentler, silver illumination from a full moon cradled in her right hand. The moon, I noticed, she held higher than the sun—one at her breast, one at her hip.

Facing Adalia, behind rows of carved, kneeling supplicants, were two robed figures. One was male, one ambiguous. Both mirrored the Saint with golden sunlight on half their bodies and silver moonlight and shadows on the other. The main differences, I saw, were in the positioning of their hands and the phases of the moons. One held the sun higher than the moon, while the final figure held them even. One moon was a sickle, the other a nearly invisible orb of obsidian.

"They represent the three suns and three moons of the Other," Nitha murmured. She seemed pleased that the motif had stolen my focus and directed me on to the next section of the story. The three figures appeared again, their hands—the sun and the moon—held at new levels. "They balance the tides and in the spring summon the Black Tides."

The pillar in the center of the room still drew Tane's attention, but my human eyes fell on the final motif, where all three figures stood waist-deep in dark water. Their hands were held evenly here, the suns draped in cloth, and three perfect obsidian moons set in a row. Behind them, a fourth obsidian moon hung, bathing them all in shadow.

"What is this?" I asked.

"The true Black Tide," Nitha explained. She began to move towards the central pillar, and something in her posture told me to follow. "When the dark of the Other's moons aligns with that in our world. Four new moons, two Black Tides—the first greater than any natural tide has a right to be, and the second surpassing even that. It happens every few centuries. We are fortunate to live to see one."

I startled. "We will see one? When?"

"This spring."

A new rush of questions clustered on my tongue, but they stalled as we rounded the central pillar and my sense of the ghisting flooded back.

There, carved into the other side, was a woman. Adalia Day. She was tucked into the wood as if it were water, every angle fluid and smooth and so utterly lifelike that I feared my mind played tricks on me. She clasped her arms loosely at her chest, cradling the sun and the moon to her skin like precious, breakable things. Her head was bent to one side, hair draped to her ankles, her eyes closed, and her body clothed in just the hint of a spidersilk gown.

As I stared, a ghisting unfolded from the wood. The perfect image of her carving, her statue, her host.

Adalia Day was no simple icon, no rendering of a distant, long-lived woman.

She was a ghisting.

TWENTY-SIX

Mother, Daughter, Saint

MARY

"Ah, Mary—Mer—there you—" Charles halted as he rounded the pillar. He was clad in a robe now and was nearly unrecognizable with a clean-shaven face and damp, combed hair.

Behind him, another novice—presumably his guide—fell back and knelt with Nitha on a cushion facing the ghisting.

Adalia Day turned to regard Charles. The sun and the moon were gone from her long-fingered, delicate hands.

Child, she addressed him, then her eyes drifted to me. *Sister.*

Tane manifested. I felt a moment of fluttering panic, my secret revealed to the novices and anyone else who might enter the shrine, but Tane had no such hesitation. She approached Adalia.

Both ghistings turned to look at Charles, as if expecting his ghisting to join them.

Charles retreated. "I'm not—I am not like her," he said aloud, waving a hand to me. To make matters worse, he spoke in Aeadine. "Mary, am I imagining this? Their saint is a ghisting? An actual ghisting, like the old Aead…"

I widened my eyes, silencing him with my stare.

Charles realized what language he'd spoken and clenched his jaw shut.

Tane spoke to Adalia, ignoring Charles. *The child still sleeps within him.*

Adalia nodded slowly and reached for Tane. Tane reached out in turn, their fingers brushing, and I was hit with a sudden deluge of information.

I saw a glistening sun, three moons spinning into shadow, a century of supplicants passing through this chamber. I felt instincts and impulses not my own, feelings and inclinations that came not from me but from Adalia—her purposes, her intents, her concerns and her demands.

The influx was overwhelming, but I caught Adalia's most immediate, pressing intentions.

Charles.

I started towards the highwayman, mouth open to warn him, hands already reaching to shepherd him from the room. Tane flowed after me, her form losing its solidity in the haste of her intercession.

But Adalia moved between one blink and the next. Charles's back hit the wall, framed by depictions of worshipping monks in a winter forest.

Adalia took his face in her hands and breathed on his lips.

Behind us, Nitha and the other novice raised their heads and stared.

I saw the ghisting within Charles shudder in a surge of indigo light. It flickered over his skin like lanternlight on oil, then peeled away.

Adalia took a new, secondary figure by the hands and pulled them away from Charles. The ghisting mirrored Charles in a vaguer, more blurry aspect, bound to the highwayman by dozens of spectral threads. Its face had only the suggestion of features, but it reflected Charles in shape and intention.

For a few breaths, the new ghisting's form held. Then it became smoke, drifting around the petrified highwayman.

"Mary," Charles croaked.

Tane and I merged as I shoved between my friend and the ghisten saint. The smoke of Charles's ghisting seeped over me like rain, and goosebumps flared across my entire body.

You had no right, Tane and I spoke as one, our indignation one. If I felt fear, it was distant—I thought only of Charles.

He has no right to join the ghiseau, Adalia countered. *The least we can do is let the child breathe.*

There is a reason the binding did not work.

When a limb breaks, do humans not set it? Adalia's sea-glass eyes held mine.

I felt a hand on my shoulder and looked back. Charles had found his footing again. His ghisting had vanished, though I saw wisps of indigo-grey in the whites of his haunted eyes.

Apparently satisfied with her meddling, Adalia Day retreated. Wisps of her flesh trailed back towards the pillar—her tree, I understood now, the information sifting up from the deluge of images I'd received when she and Tane touched. They had carved her tree into the very heart of the shrine, its branches in the roof and its roots beneath the floor. Then they had built their lives, their religion, around it.

You are welcome to shelter here, my children, Adalia said benevolently. *So long as you heed me and do no harm to my children.*

I felt Tane balk. She was a Mother Ghisting. Adalia was not—I knew that innately, even aside from the fact that the forest around the monastery was entirely mundane. In the hierarchy of ghistings, Tane was the superior, but it seemed that centuries of worship had led Adalia to believe herself outside that framework.

We needed shelter, though, and, if Adalia's condescension granted us that, we had to take it. For now.

Will your servants betray us? I asked in the unspoken speech of ghistings.

Adalia's expression was one of gentle amusement as she slipped back into her tree. *Never. There are no countries, no peoples, no external loyalties here. There is only me and mine. Respect me and the outside world will never find you.*

My head was too full, and my blood was still up over Charles's violation. But I forced myself to incline my head, just slightly, in respect. Then I took Charles's hand and guided him towards the door.

"It's in my head." Charles's breath was a rasp, and his shoulder wavered into mine. I slipped an arm around his back and supported him as I'd done a dozen times after nights of drinking.

Nitha and the other novice rose and followed us.

"Let's get you some place quiet," I soothed, pulling one of his arms across my shoulders and patting him gently. "All will be well."

"It's awake." Charles's voice faded out on the last word, then rasped back to life as he added, "I'm not alone in my head."

OTHERBORN—*A broad term referring to all creatures born from that Other plane, including ghistings, morgories, dittama, huden, implings, and their ilk. Mages are often referred to as Otherborn, though this is not strictly true. While a mage's power is sourced in the Other and they are born with an innate connection to that place, they themselves remain as human as their non-mage counterparts. See also:* BEASTS, OTHER.

—FROM THE WORDBOOK ALPHABETICA: A NEW
WORDBOOK OF THE AEADINES

TWENTY-SEVEN

Aeadine, the Middenwold

Twenty Years Ago

SAMUEL

The Midden Ghist continued to stare from his coffin-like trunk as the Black Tide cultists danced and the taste of sour milk lingered on my tongue. He stared as the world began to diminish, the Black Tide worshippers dimming, the wind ceasing, sound muffling. The trees began to transform, shifting from the oak and pine and poplar of the Middenwold to a rawer, darker variety—trees without leaves or needles, trees with their roots in the sky.

Water began to seep up from the ground, flooding the forest floor like spring melt. It ran cool about my ankles, dark and full of stars. No, not stars. Full of the reflection of the thousands of dragonflies that lifted from the knotted root canopy and took flight around me.

I was in the Dark Water, a place I had rarely ventured unaccompanied since my training as a Sooth began the previous year.

I was alone now. Ben's light lingered at my side, but it was vague and distant, his body outlined in the red of his Magni power and his awareness still in the human world. The Midden Ghist was not truly here either, just a memory etched upon my vision. He had no tree here, no roots that pried through the divide between worlds and knotted in the Other's dark sky.

I knew, intrinsically, that this region of the Other was not his home.

I blinked, and his staring eyes finally faded. A little more of my connection to the human world went with him, and I felt the brush of a strange wind on my cheeks, saw the light of three sliver-thin moons peering at me through the canopy.

My eyes began to burn with tears, my blood bubbling with disoriented terror. My hand reached out instinctually, desperate for touch, for consolation. Not for my mother, but for Benedict.

My hand passed through his arm like vapor, and I recoiled. That turned into full retreat as Ben's signature in the Other flickered and began to fade. As little as I knew, I knew that was not right. He was a mage. No, I should not be able to touch him, but he should always be visible here, visible to *me*.

I glanced back at where the Midden Ghist had been in the human world. I saw only other trees, other ghistings not yet connected with my realm, some of whom had begun to materialize and study me. Their light danced across the surface of the water, interrupting the pulsing, punctuated darts of the fireflies as they took on forms.

But their forms here were not like the ones ghistings in the human world would take. There, they were men or women, wolves or serpents. Here, they were distorted imitations of Otherborn beasts—creatures of claws and tentacles, skewed proportions and far, far too many eyes.

I turned and fled.

TWENTY-EIGHT

Sanctuary

SAMUEL

I lay in my cot that night with a full belly, a warm blanket, and the sound of Ben's gentle breaths drifting across the small chamber we had been given. He looked younger, not simply because of the dim light or the fact that we had both shaved and bathed. There was a vulnerability to him that reminded me of countless childhood nights, sharing a room just like this.

From beyond the door, I heard the echo of a soft, gentle singing. Night prayers. The Mereish the Servants of Adalia Day sung in was old and complex, but I picked out phrases. It was a song to the moon, to the forest. To the ghisting that was their saint.

When I closed my eyes, the sound shifted—merging with another, simpler song sung by a long stream of robed strangers on the night my mother, in her madness, had destroyed Ben and I.

A chill swept up my arms, raising gooseflesh, and I rolled onto my side. Mary was right not to trust this place or the ghisting Adalia Day—my Sooth's senses affirmed it. Still, I could not regret coming here, not with all our wounds tended, a warm bed, and all that I had learned from Scieran.

Someone approached our door. A touch at my Sight told me it was Mary, and my thoughts promptly dissipated. Was something wrong? Did she need me?

Was there another reason for her to visit in the dead of night? Against my better judgement, the tension in my body shifted into an entirely different variety. But after a moment's hesitation, her footsteps moved on, softer than before.

"Are you going to stop her?" Ben prompted from the other side of the room. "Or must I?"

I was already halfway to my feet. "Sleep."

"Gladly."

I slipped out into the hallway and closed the door softly at my back. Night prayers still drifted though the hush, haunting and beautiful. Mary was already out of sight, but I caught the soft tread of her feet around a corner and followed.

"Mary!" My hissed word caught her just as she started down a set of stairs. "Where are you going?"

She looked back at me, and I recoiled. Her eyes—her human, natural eyes—were sheathed in a ghisten glow, opaque as sea-glass.

"Tane?" I asked.

Mary's lips twitched into a flat line and something of her human self resurfaced. "Yes. Adalia has summoned us again." With that, Tane seemed to take control once more. She nodded for me to follow her and disappeared down the stairs.

Unease, perpetually close to the surface now, coiled. I lowered my chin and hastened to catch up, but, even when I hovered at her shoulder, she ignored me. I wanted to grab her, to stop her, but Tane was not to be trifled with.

Instead, I whispered, "Do you have Mary's permission to do this?"

"We are one and the same." Tane spoke through Mary's mouth. Her voice was Mary's too, though it bellied into the woman's lowest register, rich and deep and feminine.

"Then why can I only see you in her eyes?" I asked coldly.

Tane glanced back at me then, those sea-glass eyes taking me in with a clinical detachment. "Because we share this body.

And there are some matters that should stay between ghistings. Which is why you may accompany me now but will let me enter the Oruse alone."

We had already reached the end of the passage, with its broad steps and flickering sconces. There was not a single acolyte or Servant in sight.

"Wait here," Tane instructed. She mounted the remaining steps and turned right, vanishing through a circular archway.

I followed more slowly and lingered outside the door, taking in all I could see of the shrine—its carvings and gilding, softly illuminated by candle and ghisten light. I saw the trail of Mary's robes swish around the far side of the gilded room's central pillar, then silence fell.

I stood vigil for long, painstaking minutes, until I heard footsteps in the tunnel, distant but echoing, and glanced around for a place to hide. I could go into the shrine—but Tane had forbidden that, and I had other options.

I darted across the mouth of the stairs and went the other direction. The corridor split, and I ducked down one way while the footsteps ascended the stairs. They approached, driving me farther down the passage and away from Mary.

I plastered myself into a window alcove, layered with glass that did little to keep out the cold, and held my breath.

The steps went down another passage. I listened to them fade, counting them and judging the distance until a familiar, presentient whisper stole through my mind.

I stepped out of the alcove and turned. There, at the end of my passageway, was a door. Curiosity assailed me—half a child's curiosity, half an uncanny need. There was something of the Other behind that door.

I quickly returned to the main passage and glanced at the shrine. Mary was still there, her robe visible, and did not appear to be in any distress.

Returning to the mysterious door, I cracked it open. A dragonfly lantern hung from the center of a domed ceiling, illuminating a small, octagonal room. It might have reminded me of an observatory if the roof had not lacked any hatches or openings.

In the center of the chamber was a massive looking glass. It was directed up at the ceiling, and golden light from the lantern ran down a smooth, polished surface of faintly glowing ghisten wood.

"It is an observatory."

I spun to see Mary, Tane still shining from her eyes. She watched me with an odd posture—her arms loose, a bit too far out from her sides, her head cocked. It was eerie and unnatural, and I longed for Mary to wake up.

"To observe what?" I asked, speaking just as quietly as she had.

Tane's eyes trailed over the spyglass. Coming forward, she pushed my hand from the door latch and pulled it shut with a soft tap of wood. "The Dark Water—its suns and moons and stars."

Questions rushed forward, but she spoke before I could. "All that is irrelevant right now, Captain Rosser. We need to leave. Now."

Moments later, we were striding back down the tunnel.

"What is happening?" I pressed. "Mary! Tane? Answer me. Is Adalia banishing us?"

"Adalia is arrogant and reaches beyond her place," Tane returned. "But she is not our greatest concern. There are soldiers at the gates."

We re-entered the cells to the sound of hammering fists and low, hurried voices echoing off the wooden walls and floors. A monk shoved between Tane and I, pulling up his cowl as he went, while others streaked by in varying directions.

I saw Mary stagger as someone shouldered past her. I reached out to steady her, then sheltered her against the wall as two more monks hurried past, heading into the tunnel and out of sight.

Tane trickled from Mary's eyes, and Mary blinked wholly awake. I started to step back, conscious of every place our bodies touched, even as my mind calculated our next steps. Get Ben and Grant. Get out of the monastery.

Mary looked as though she might be ill. She clasped my upper arms, keeping me in place as more and more monks ran past. "Give... Give me a moment. Tane has never been in control for that long while I was awake. The soldiers are looking for us, Sam. Adalia... her roots spread everywhere here. *Everywhere*. There is nothing she doesn't see. And she blames us for this."

"Does she intend to hand us over?" I pressed.

Mary shook her head helplessly, her face and lips inordinately pale. "She gave her word to protect us. But I don't trust her. She was so angry."

"There you are." A breathless Grant shoved in next to us, Ben on his heels. Grant looked harrowed, while Ben looked so dour that even the panicking Servants of Adalia Day began to give us a wider berth. "Mary, are you well?"

"I may throw up," she warned.

"Let's do that outside, shall we?" Grant patted her perfunctorily on the back. "Time to flee?"

"Past time," Ben grumbled.

I nodded. "If we are separated, meet where we left our gear and weapons."

A bellow overrode the shuffling chaos of the hall. "To the courtyard! Everyone is to convene in the courtyard, now!"

A final few monks fled into the tunnel or rocketed down side passageways, then the soldiers were there. Rifles glinted, boots tramped. Mary inched behind us, towards the tunnel, and grabbed Grant's robe to pull him with her—or hold herself up, it was hard to tell.

A rifle leveled at us.

"You four, to the courtyard," a soldier snapped.

Ben shot the man a glare so full of sorcery, even I felt it. The soldier wavered, then ground his teeth and shoved the mouth of the musket into Ben's chest.

"Try that again, Magni," he hissed. Four more soldiers saw the confrontation and gathered in, all armed. "We are prepared for your kind."

In the background, someone dragged a shrieking, bloodied monk out of a cell and shoved her into a line of her shuffling fellows.

"Well, this is looking worse and worse," I heard Grant murmur behind me.

"Move!" another soldier yelled at us.

Prodded by muskets, we joined the flow of devotees. Footsteps, pleading and frustrated voices jarred against the walls, growing louder and louder as we reached the entry hall. Too many bodies were crammed into the tight space. Tall, narrow windows with murky glass panes filtered dashes of torchlight from the courtyard outside—more soldiers—and open doors spilled wafts of cold, biting air.

Mary shoved in front of me, and I pulled her into my chest, protecting her as much as I could from the jostling of the crowd.

Her breath ghosted across the side of my face as she leaned back to whisper in my ear. "Ben and Charles. They're gone."

I glanced around. We were being herded like sheep, dozens of faces and bodies pressed close, but none of them belonged to my brother or the highwayman.

I touched the Other. Lights sprang up—in the crowd around us, in the courtyard beyond. Ben was nowhere to be seen, hidden by his talisman, but I glimpsed Grant's subtle indigo-grey somewhere behind us in the crowd.

I quietly translated this to Mary.

"Is Ben abandoning us?" she asked, her voice more defeated than accusatory.

A sick feeling twisted in my chest, but: "He knows his chances are best with us."

"What happens when they're not?" Mary's back bumped into my chest as the movement of the crowd slowed. Cold air from the open exterior door blew over our heads. "He couldn't control the soldiers; they have talismans. Does that mean they're Ess Noti? What if we are captured and he's not?"

"I have no answers, Mary."

The jostling of the crowd increased and we were squeezed out into the courtyard. Soldiers sifted through the Servants, directing men and women into different groups on the trampled snow.

"I'll meet you in the forest," Mary hissed. She sounded calm, but her hand clenched mine too tightly.

I held hers just as firmly, valiant promises drying up on my tongue. If I tried to fight the soldiers and keep us together, I would call attention to us and likely end up getting both of us bloodied.

"In the forest," I affirmed lowly, but could not manage to let go of her hand.

"You, here, now." A soldier grabbed my arm and hauled me across the yard. I nearly slipped in the snow, and Mary was torn away. The soldier snorted something derogatory then shoved me into the knot of male monks.

Mary was prodded into a knot of shivering women, both monks and novices.

"Stand in a line and pull back your hoods!" a Mereish officer shouted.

No one moved. A frigid breeze threaded through the yard, rustling the leafless branches of occasional trees and biting my cheeks. Mary watched me briefly then looked down, pulling her hood deeper and easing back into the press of women. I lost sight of her.

Soldiers elbowed into the crowd, grabbing women and lifting their heads with rough hands and musket muzzles. A figure I thought was Mary edged backwards, ducking behind older, more stoic monks and keeping her head down.

A soldier seized her by the robe and spun her around.

I lunged out of line. Soldiers shouted and swarmed. The cold mouth of a pistol pressed into my forehead, and I went still.

I saw the monk and soldier again a moment later when he forced her back into line. Her cowl was gone, red hair escaping at the temples from carefully wrapped braids. Not Mary.

"Him."

A Mereish officer took stance in front of me. He looked vaguely familiar, with sun-narrowed eyes, smooth black curls tamed into a queue, and light skin with the slight hint of brown.

The officer snapped to his men in Mereish, sending more of them scattering off across the grounds, then gave his full attention to me. As soon as our eyes locked, I knew him for what he was. Another Sooth.

Furthermore, I recognized him. He had bumped into me on the docks in Tithe, right after I had glimpsed Enisca Alamay.

"Where are your companions?" the man asked.

I gave him a flat, cold stare. "You are Inis Hae."

His eyes narrowed for a breath, then he shrugged. "I am. Now, where are your companions?"

Shouts erupted, and I glimpsed a blur of horses and men near the gates. The horses were wild, the men panicked, their eyes wide with feral, unconstrained terror. Ben or some other Magni had found an outlet for their sorcery.

Hae, too, glanced in their direction. In that briefest of openings I ducked to the side, snatched his pistol, and smashed the butt down towards his forehead. He deflected with preternatural swiftness, but I was already running.

Wind blasted through the crowd, throwing back hoods, tearing away hats and snapping clothing like flags. A Stormsinger's voice rose, then another, and another, chanting and harmonizing and building off one another in a twisted version of a midnight prayer.

Mary's voice was not among them.

I ducked reaching hands and exhaled half my consciousness into the Other. The Dark Water swelled around my ankles, lights pricked into view and I marked the Mereish mages. There were two Magni, desperately trying to calm the horses and ensorcelled soldiers. Then the bright, Sooth beacon of Inis Hae.

I caught a flash of teal. A nun fled past me, her body shrouded in Stormsinger's light. But there was no grey in her aura, and her face was older—in her fifties. Other Stormsingers shifted at the edges of my vision, but they, too, lacked Mary's signature blend of mage and ghisting. She must still be wearing her talisman.

I could not see Benedict directly, but his power burned in the Other—close, then far, near Hae's light and then passing me by. Magni force laced out like flames, wrapping around soldiers and horses and Servants alike. The Servants broke from their lines, and the chaos in the courtyard became complete.

Someone caught my arm. The human world resumed its solid forms and snow-blurred lines as Ben hauled me behind a hedge. He had commandeered a staff—now streaked with blood—though his other arm was still in its sling.

"Where are Mary and Grant?" I panted.

"Grant's already on the road south, took four horses. He will fetch our weapons and gear," Benedict replied, craning to keep watch behind us then motioning me to move. We edged into the shelter a cloister. "You lost Mary?"

As if in answer to his question, Mereish voices cut the night in sharp, coordinating shouts. I could not catch all their words over the chaos, but I heard a warning cry of, "*Ghiseau!*"

Figures scattered from our path as Ben and I rounded the hall, the chapel, and passed through the gardens. The snow was a chaos of footprints, but I needed no trail. I knew where Mary was now. I could hear her screaming and swearing.

We rounded the kitchens just as a soldier wrestled Mary to the ground. Another soldier fought a Stormsinger's mask over Mary's mouth, momentarily drowning her shouts. She struck him on the head, a fist to the temple, but the soldier holding her down flipped her over and ground her face into the snow.

I lunged, but three more enemies leveled muskets into our path. Ben struck one. I raised my pistol in return, and time slowed.

I pulled the trigger. The shot took a soldier square in the chest, and I swung the butt of my weapon into the face of the man next to him. They both toppled. A third swerved past me and, on impulse, I reached out and grabbed the glistening Magni talisman at his throat. The talisman broke free, and Ben began to laugh.

The soldier screamed as he drove his sword through his own stomach. Still smiling, Benedict strode around him, surveying Mary's remaining assailants.

The one with the mask froze, turning his eyes slowly up. He was clearly fighting Benedict's influence, but not well enough—either he did not have a talisman, or not all of them were created equal. He spasmed, falling back, and Mary shook the mask loose.

She screamed a single note, thick with rage. Tatters of wind raced away from her, and the last guard spasmed, gasping without sound. When I grabbed his hair and jerked him off her, he toppled with blood-shot eyes and a terror-stricken face.

Mary rolled over, face scraped raw and covered with mud and snow, tears and blood. She coughed and raised both arms, one hand reaching for me, the other for Ben. Together, we pulled her to her feet.

"What did you do?" Ben asked, glancing at the blood-shot man before he grabbed a fallen pistol and set to reloading it, grimacing as he utilized his bad arm.

"Told the air to leave his lungs," she managed, blinking back tears and stooping to grab the sword of a dead soldier. She rubbed her face with a sleeve and pointed towards the main building—and a side door standing open. Figures flitted through the night, but the chaos was ebbing. It left us in a fragment of stillness, but it would not last long.

"We can try to escape through the Oruse," she said. "It's outside the walls."

"Will Adalia let us past?" I asked.

"I will manage her," Tane's lower voice replied.

Ben shrugged and tossed a musket to me. "Then lead the way, witch."

TWENTY-NINE

The Dark Observatory

MARY

The halls of the monastery were eerily silent, save for a cluster of soldiers, who appeared to be running from something rather than after it. We crushed into a side passageway as they streaked past, then descended into the tunnel to the Oruse.

I led the way, though it took all my will to focus. Tane was the only thing keeping me on my feet between pain and a head full of the taste, the *feel*, of Quelling the air in the soldier's lungs. But as we reached the stairs Tane began to glow, separating from my body and preceding us up the stairs.

I immediately stumbled, the injuries I'd taken from the soldiers suddenly manifesting in a dozen ways. I managed to snag Samuel's arm before I fell, but my stolen sword hit the stairs and clattered back down into the tunnel.

"Tane!" Samuel braced me and shouted after the ghisting—half rebuke, half question.

She ignored him, standing at the top of the stairs and peering into Adalia's shrine, her chin thrust forward like a hound catching a scent. I had just enough time to resent her neglect, then fear its cause, before Adalia Day stalked from the chamber with a spear in hand. Aside from the shaft, the head of the spear was wooden too, hardened and polished, and reflected her own ghisten glow.

She cast one look between Tane and me, her gaze flickering to the gently glowing tether of ghisten flesh between us. Then she hurled the spear at Tane.

Tane buckled around the projectile, her ethereal flesh dissembling into a churning mass of smoke. The spear clattered across the floor, but the damage was done. I buckled too, an explosion of pain rippling through my chest and out to the crown of my skull, the tips of my fingers and toes.

You brought them here. Adalia's words were only audible to Tane and I, but they still reverberated in my ears, in my bones, chased by the agony of Tane's spectral wound.

Sam's arm cinched, holding me up. He shouted something, presumably to Benedict, since the Magni appeared at our sides a second later with my sword in his good hand.

I had no choice but to go with them, stumbling to the far side of the stairs.

You gave your word to shelter us! Tane shot back. She was moving now, sweeping backwards in a form that was half herself, half smoke.

Adalia scoffed, her face transforming into a ghastly smile. She was still lovely, still poised and regal in her gossamer robe, but her features hardened into jagged, wrathful lines. *I protect my own, and you have risked them all.*

"Mary, can we risk leaving her?" Samuel asked me.

"Of course we fucking leave her," Benedict snapped.

"If Tane and I are separated, she can be killed," I snapped back. I found my footing, watching over Samuel's shoulder as ghisten light swelled. It filled his face with shadows, half-turned as he was, and I saw the prompt in his eyes.

He had no idea what to do. Ghistings were my world, not his.

We all startled as Tane seized Adalia's spear from the tiled floor and lunged at the supposed Saint, stabbing and sweeping with speed and ferocity.

As she moved, even as Adalia shattered the wooden beam above her head and armed herself with long shards of wood like daggers, Tane's voice came to me.

Run. Through the observatory. There is another way out.

What about you?

I am right behind you. Go!

"Through the observatory," I said to Samuel. I grabbed my sword from Benedict, who glared and took up his pistol again. I held out my other hand for Samuel. He took it, warm and tight, and we hastened up the stairs. "She'll follow."

Adalia's head snapped up and dust began to fall from the ceiling. The structure around us trembled.

Roots erupted from the floor. I darted aside as a thick tendril lanced towards my ankle, coiling like a snake.

Benedict was not so quick. He elected to stomp on a reaching root and succeeded only in making his leg more accessible. The root wrapped around his calf, and he smashed it unsuccessfully with his pistol butt. Samuel, meanwhile, was driven away by a rush of smaller roots.

"Move!" I raised my sword. Ben froze, more in shock than capitulation, and I hacked down at the tendril. It did not yield, too fresh and green and strong.

Benedict cursed and tried to take the sword from me, but I elbowed him aside and hacked again and again. Samuel intercepted another root trying to claw my robes and pinned yet another to the floor with his musket butt.

The root holding Benedict finally yielded, but more rose up. Three lunged directly for my hand and wrapped around my sword—I let go rather than see my fingers snapped. More roots peeled out of the walls, reaching for the three of us as we stumbled on down the passage, around a corner, and into sight of the observatory door.

Now weaponless, I glanced back, watching the tether between Tane and I thin more and more, its glow fading until it was little more than a thread.

Tane!

Ghisten light swelled. The thread thickened, and Tane burst around the corner. She lunged back into my bones as Samuel led us through the observatory's already yawning doorway.

No roots reached for us here, though a rumble persisted in the ground beneath our feet.

What did you do to Adalia? I hissed to Tane.

I should have burned her from her tree, was Tane's only response.

We glanced around an octagonal room dominated by its huge spyglass on a stand. I ignored walls covered with star charts and diagrams, noting a dragonfly lantern on an iron hook. I ran over, my body steady again thanks to Tane's support, and took it.

Its golden light washed around us as Samuel passed through another door on the far side of the chamber and down a sloping passageway. A curve, a drop, and we faced another iron-banded barrier.

Samuel shoved, and the door swung outward a few inches before it jammed. Others had clearly fled this way before, the passageway scattered with snow and forest debris, but roots had attempted to close it again.

Samuel pushed a second time. Dry leaves rustled and rained through the gap, accompanied by a rush of cold, fresh air and the groan of straining roots.

I glanced back down the passage, sure at any second the tunnel would explode with knotted branches and clawing roots. The floor rumbled again, and dust rained from the ceiling.

"Sam?" I prompted, backing closer to the door.

Ben craned to see. "Push harder!"

"I am," Samuel gritted out. I heard a crunch of ice-hardened snow and the snap of a branch, but the barrier remained in place. "Stand back, both of you."

I shuffled away and Ben skulked, an expression of quiet disgust on his face. At first I thought it was directed towards Samuel or the door, then I saw the way he shifted his bad arm and glanced back down the passageway. His eyes were pained and haunted beneath his perpetual glaze of anger.

Pity tugged at me.

Samuel slammed into the door with a crack, a moan, and a fresh rain of deadfall. The door relinquished another few inches, and he finally squeezed through. I made to go after him, but Ben beat me to it. He elbowed me aside and pushed through the gap.

I swallowed my irritation and followed into the cool of the night. "We need to find Charles."

"I see a road," Ben called from a pace away. His half-shadowed form moved and, carelessly, let go of a pine branch. It immediately smacked me in the face.

I let out a garbled curse and just resisted the urge to throw the lantern at him. My nerves were beyond frayed now, the pain of Adalia's attack on Tane lingered in my bones, and the stab of a thousand needles on my rapidly cooling skin made my eyes water.

"Watch out," he said belatedly.

"I am not your enemy," I shot back, still grasping the lantern like a weapon. With effort I took hold of myself and held up the dragonfly-filled glass. "We can't risk this light, not out here."

Sam nodded and I unlatched the lantern's small door. The dragonflies flew free, swirling around us in eddies of gold. They converged on Samuel for a breath, and, despite the tension of the night, I was not impassive to the eerie awe of that scene— Samuel in his dark monk's robe, framed by pine boughs and girded with snow, surrounded by a swirl of tiny, Otherborn creatures. The Sooth's expression was stalwart, with a quiet fatigue and determination.

Then the dragonflies streamed away into the trees, darkness resumed its hold, and Sam and I joined Ben on the road. We set off at a jog, or as much of one as our injuries and the rutted, crusty snow afforded.

What felt like an eternity later—minutes riddled with tension and straining ears, and an unsettling lack of sound drifting from the monastery—we found Charles. He had already retrieved our stashed weapons and readied a stolen quartet of horses, which we dispersed to.

"Sam, will they be tracking us in the Other?" Charles asked, setting his musket across his knees as he pulled up his collar and tugged down his sleeves against the cold. Dawn was breaking, and a morose twilight spilled through the trees behind him, throwing his haggard face into partial silhouette. "Enough other monks have fled that our trail will be hard to find, at least with a natural eye."

Samuel shook his head. "Yes. Inis Hae was there, the Sooth the mage at the creek mentioned. We came into contact in Tithe, and it is him that has been tracking me all along."

"I may have killed him," Ben stated. "I certainly tried."

That failed to console me, not least because of Ben's callousness towards his actions. Still, I couldn't help but envy the simple, uncomplicated way he accepted his violence.

Images of the soldiers flickered through my head again, accompanied by flashes of terror, satisfaction, and anger so deep, so fierce, I'd been blind with it.

Charles nudged his horse into movement. "If Hae has your scent, you should wear Mary's talisman. I know there are risks to you using Sooth talismans too much, but—"

"Either way, he can track us. Our best chance is to claim what lead we can." Samuel glanced at his brother. "Though I hope you did kill him."

My horse came up alongside Charles, and we exchanged a look of veiled uncertainty. Then, knowing my part to play, I began to hum. I drew the winds to me gently, tasting them. The varied possibilities of spring were all within reach, and I saw what they could be.

A storm of deadly ice.

Sam went on, "I have lost sight of *Hart*. The last I saw of him, he was still being escorted east, presumably to Ostchen."

The gathering winds scudded around me, sensing my distress. I snatched at them again, singing low words now—a child's lullaby, the only thing my exhausted mind could produce.

Tane felt my hopelessness. *We will escape Mere*, she told me, the familiarity of her speech an ineffective balm.

"How could you lose the ship? I thought only ghistings could affect your sight," Charles asked.

"Any concentration of Otherborn creatures will," Samuel hedged.

"Including a fleet of ghisten ships," Ben said, the word like a stone dropped down a long, dark well. "Like the Mereish Fleet. In Ostchen."

"All roads lead there," Samuel concluded ominously. He twisted in the saddle to survey us. "I cannot abandon *Hart* and the crew, and the Uknaras. Besides, if I struggle to see into Ostchen, Hae will too. It will be simple for us to disappear in a city full of mages and ghistings. Would you all agree?"

His question was weary, irritated, with a hint of beseeching. I knew that tone. He was driven towards his duty as *Hart*'s captain but hated to risk us.

"*Hart* is as much of a home as I have," I said, infusing my words with the courage I wanted to feel. My winds blew steady now, strengthening and turning around us in an ever-widening churn. They smelled of rain and snow and power. "I'm with you."

Charles shrugged. He looked more than a little intimidated, too tired for bravado. "All right," he agreed.

The wind tossed Ben's tangled, blood-sticky hair into his eyes as he stared into the dawn and grunted, "Fine."

IMPLING—*An Otherborn creature with a ghastly appearance, resembling the blending of a human fetus and a malnourished canine. They are small, rarely larger than the infants they appear to be, and are possessed of a profoundly malevolent and devious nature, as well as a fierce hunger for living flesh. They are also one of the few Otherborn creatures who can pass through the barrier between the worlds at will, making them both common and deadly, and a common fixture of folklore across the Winter Sea.*

—FROM THE WORDBOOK ALPHABETICA: A NEW
WORDBOOK OF THE AEADINES

THIRTY

Floodwaters Rise

MARY

Muted morning light crept into the road, filtering through the storm that blanketed the forest in our wake, chasing our horses' hooves with the crackling shush of freezing rain. As the storm grew so did my fatigue, until finally the rain slipped my control and overtook us.

For hours we rode as the snow turned to ice, and the cold worked into the marrow of our bones. I could hardly breathe for my streaming nose, let alone coerce my sore throat into another song. Tane, who I might have leaned upon for support, was uncommonly quiet, recovering from Adalia's attack.

Just when I was sure I would topple from my horse, slide into a gully and sleep my final sleep, we began to see signs of a town— literal, helpful signs that pointed us towards what roughly translated to Riverbank, combined with a thinner, tended forest, a few houses tucked among the trees, and the remains of a dead chicken in the snow.

A few minutes later, the forest ended and the town materialized. It looked morose in the rain, its layers of grey cloud and sodden brown wood made worse by a frozen fog rising from the snow and miles of flooded farms. Every fence post, every tree branch, was lined with glistening ice.

There was no light in the settlement, no signs of life. No glowing windows or smoking chimneys. There was not even a wayward goat to stare at us or a dog to bark from the closest farms. The town was a tomb and the farms surrounding it drowned and hushed, save for the patter of the rain, rush of the river, and distant creak of overburdened timbers.

A fresh chill crept up my spine. I glanced back into the forest, sure the town was an ill omen.

"Sam," I murmured. "Can you see if we're alone?"

Samuel nodded, rain dripping from his hood, and sat back in his saddle. Benedict, Charles and I all watched as his eyes became distant and then cleared once more.

"There is an impling in the woods, some distance away. No mages or beasts."

I opened my mouth to point out that that did not mean there were no soldiers or mages with Sooth talismans, but he continued speaking.

"But the Other is darker than usual." Samuel indicated the sleeping town. "The first Black Tide, it seems, is close."

"A week away," Tane said through my lips.

"That is the coastline," Benedict added, his gaze cast north. I squinted, just able to make out a low shore of snow drifts and black rocks. The sea was both a churning blur and an encroaching tide, swelling upriver and turning the entire waterway into an ice-choked monstrosity. It had overflowed its banks as far as we could see in either direction, forcing its way up into the town and turning the surrounding fields into sheets of ice for miles, smeared with snow fog.

"The locals must have been warned," Charles observed. "Pity. Though an abandoned town should still provide some decent pillaging, if we could reach it without drowning."

Benedict perked up at that, but, upon contemplation, made a discontented noise. "We should go back and spend the night at one of the houses in the forest. We will not be getting anywhere near that settlement, let alone finding somewhere dry to sleep and stow the horses."

I couldn't bear the thought of repeating that experience of Benedict puppeteering the woman at the farm. The houses we had passed had still been inhabited. "There must be another way in, some road not flooded."

"The bridges are what concerns me most," Samuel said. From our vantage, I could see that the bridges that connected the eastern and western banks were shattered or submerged, the former little more than stone markers on either shore and the latter beset by mounds of ice and debris.

Samuel sat straighter in his saddle with a creak of cold leather. "I see one intact, to the south. If we are still a week out from the full tide, the water will only continue to rise. By tomorrow morning that bridge may be gone too, and our road to Ostchen blocked."

"So, we cross now," Charles summarized, sounding dubious.

The bridge was too far away to see clearly, but its dark shape appeared whole, if barely above the rush of the glutted river.

"The east bank does look drier," I admitted. "I would feel better with a river between us and anyone following us."

The men descended into debate. I adjusted my hold on my reins, glancing again at the forest track behind us. Snow fog had spread across it, too, as the day drew to a close, playing tricks with my eyes. Was that a pine bough swaying under a weight of snow or a soldier with a musket?

Benedict's voice cut through my pondering. "Meet me in Ostchen when you have made up your minds."

He abruptly spurred his horse down the churned road then off into one of the flooded fields. The sound of cracking ice and sloshing water drifted to us, loud in the twilight hush, but the water was no deeper than the horse's fetlocks.

Sam let out a long breath and gathered his reins, while Charles promptly followed Benedict across the flooded fields. I nudged my horse after him, grateful to leave the forest and its shadows behind.

"What are you thinking about?" I asked Samuel as we guided our mounts carefully down the road.

"I am wondering if Ben was worth saving," he said, just loud enough for me to hear. "Worth putting you through this."

I sat back in my saddle as our horses descended into the field. Icy water splashed up onto the hem of my robe, adding to an already substantial rime of ice and mud.

"I chose to come with you," I reminded him. "You can't think like this, not now—"

"I can and must." He seemed to catch himself and grimaced. Beneath him, his horse dutifully picked her way through the ice, seemingly resigned to the discomfort. "I am sorry, Mary. I am tired and overburdened."

His honesty cut me to the bone. I leaned over the gap between our horses and snagged his hand, holding it tightly. He gripped mine back, and for a moment we were quiet, our breaths steaming in the chill.

Ahead, Benedict and Charles closed on the bridge. Their forms were growing harder to see, the Winter Sea's rapid dusk cloaking the already gloomy landscape.

"If the healer-mage at the Oruse didn't have a cure, where can we look next?" I asked, releasing his hand as my horse navigated a deeper section and I swayed in the saddle.

"Nowhere." The word was like a closing door, firm and final. "We must put that behind us. We make for Ostchen. Reclaim *Hart*. And then sail for safe waters. That is all that matters."

The shadows that were Ben and Charles had reached the bridge, or as near as they could with the deeper floodwaters. On a quiet day their voices might have reached us, but the rush of the water and the sweep of the wind tore them away.

I fought the urge to look back at the trees again.

"Surely there will be healer-mages in Ostchen," I said. "There is still hope."

"Hope will only endanger us. We focus on finding our ship and crew and escaping with our lives," he countered, a fresh hardness in his voice that warned me he was finished with the conversation. Abruptly, he twisted in his saddle. "Someone is following us."

I turned just in time to see a flash in the gloom. The crack of a musket reverberated at the same moment, echoing and overloud, yet distorted by the rain and fog.

My horse startled and reared. I hit the frigid water an instant later, rolling, twisting away from a cacophony of pounding hooves. Dirty water filled my mouth and ears, ice scratched at my face, then I found my hands and knees.

I tried to stagger upright, but my sodden robes dragged me back down. I tore at my belt, loosing it with shaking fingers, and snapped one of the hidden ties that bound the garment closed. Distantly, I was aware that my horse had bolted—one set of splashing, pounding hooves fading while a dozen others closed.

"Mary!" Samuel's boots landed beside me. I could hardly make him out, but his voice, his presence, that I knew.

His bigger hands grabbed at my sodden robe, snapping the last ties. He pulled the soaked garment off my shoulders, took my hands, and I lunged upright.

His horse, too, must have fled. But the splash and pound of hooves still came to us, ever closer—not at a gallop now, but a more inexorable pace. Another musket cracked in the night, and I heard a voice shout some command.

"Fuck," Samuel hissed, one arm around me, the whites of his eyes pale in the darkness as he stared back. "Hae is with them."

"Not dead, then," I wheezed.

"Mary!" Charles's voice shouted up ahead.

I grabbed Samuel by the robes and urged him forward. One of my legs nearly buckled, numbed by my fall and the cold, but we steadied one another as we raced towards Charles's voice.

A shadow peeled from the twilight—a man on horseback, robed and looming, coming not from the forest but the river.

Benedict reined in as he passed us and turned about, placing his horse between us and our oncoming pursuers. He lifted his chin and exhaled a long breath of steam, closing his eyes.

Another musket cracked, followed by a scream of shock and pain. Then another shot, and another.

Our pursuers were shooting one another.

"Ben!" Samuel yelled. "Enough!"

Benedict wheeled his horse about but remained between us and our pursuers.

A light bloomed up ahead and took the shape of another mounted man, horse prancing nervously. Charles, lit with ghisten light and looking none too comforted by it.

"You are making yourself a fine target!" Benedict scolded as we closed in.

"I cannot make him stop!" the highwayman returned. A musket ball cracked off the wood of the bridge, just behind him, and he ducked.

Ben left us all behind, urging his horse onto the hefty wooden bridge, he and his mount shedding water as they went. "Then move!"

Charles followed the Magni, Samuel and I mere paces behind now. His ghisten light just illuminated the boiling river beneath, where chunks of ice thudded into the supports and the water frothed, dirty and hungry. Even the thick icicles that coated the low rails trembled.

A creaking, lamenting moan sounded as a fresh clot of ice began to build up.

"Stop!" a Mereish voice ripped through the night, so close I stifled a shriek.

Samuel and I lunged onto the bridge, slipping and sliding but somehow managing to stay upright.

Another moan and the whole bridge swayed. Tane prickled across my skin and launched into the wood of the structure, igniting it in the same way that Hart did when he strengthened his ship.

The bridge creaked dangerously, and the thud of hooves sounded behind us.

Samuel and I burst off the structure, passing Benedict and Charles and carrying on for a few paces until I realized Tane had not followed. I spied her light still riddling the wood of the bridge. I felt her strain, felt her intent, and retreated another step.

"Keep back!" I warned.

A great crack and a groan split the night, then the bridge began to move—not crumbling, not buckling, but shifting entirely. One end swung north while the other slid down the bank to the south, and the whole thing spun off into the center of the current.

Mereish soldiers screamed. A horse toppled into the current, and one woman made a wild leap for the eastern shore, only to land short and be immediately swallowed by the crush of ice. The rest toppled to the wood or seized the rails, holding on as the bridge became a tottering, sinking ship.

Tane swirled after me in a cloud of ghisten smoke and leapt back into my skin.

I realized I had the back of one cold-swollen hand clamped over my mouth to stop myself from crying out and shakingly lowered it. Drowning in a river of ice was no kind way to go. But they couldn't cross. We had escaped. We were safe—

Muzzles flashed from the opposite shore. All of them went wide or struck the ground short, but it was enough to banish us farther into the deepening night.

"Time to go." Charles leaned down to offer me one arm and an empty stirrup. Ghisten light still gilded his skin, though much paler than before.

I seized his hand and mounted behind him. Samuel joined Ben, and the four of us left the drowning bridge behind.

I glanced back once, as light flared on the western shore. A lantern had been unveiled, packed full of golden dragonflies, and the face of a man watched us go with an intensity that chilled me deeper than frigid water and sodden clothes.

"Is that him?" I asked Samuel, voice just loud enough to carry. "Inis Hae?"

His only response was a silent nod.

THIRTY-ONE

The Martyr

SAMUEL

Midnight found us wading into the yard of an inn up the coast, situated just above the submerged homes of a small fishing hamlet on an island of snowpack and ice. The courtyard lay under two feet of water, but the inn itself was raised on a stone foundation and appeared dry, as did the stables.

I leaned close to Benedict—we had been forced to dismount and lead the horses some time ago, exhausted as they were.

"Do not harm anyone here," I warned. "We are monks on the road; they have no reason to be suspicious until *you* give them one."

His glare was palpable in the gloom.

A shutter opened, and a light bloomed from an upper window.

"Monks!" an elderly woman's voice observed in Mereish, complete with a rural lilt I had never heard before. "Wait you there, pious folk, and I'll have you warm and dry. See to your horses, there's hay in the loft."

The shutter closed and the light vanished, leaving us back in the damp cold and dripping shadows of the spring night.

"See?" Mary whispered. "No reason to be suspicious."

"I will see to the horses." I looked at Ben. "Come with me?"

Ben looked ready to protest, but something in my voice must have caught his attention. It caught Mary's too, as the inn door opened and light spilled into the courtyard once more, illuminating her cold-burned cheeks, dry lips and deep blue eyes, nearly back in the night.

The innwife ushered Grant and Mary inside, and Ben and I led the exhausted horses into the hay-scented shelter of the stables.

A glow seeped from a closed lantern. Ben drew back the hatch, and a mixture of gold and purple dragonflies lit five stalls, along with an assortment of racks and tools. I immediately went to work, removing the saddles and scanning the shelves for brushes and picks.

"How did you know about the Oruse?" Benedict asked, sitting on a stool.

"You could help," I pointed out, beginning to brush down Grant's horse.

"I have one good arm. Answer the question."

"That arm still works."

"Samuel."

"When I visited the other monastery, looking for a cure for the crew's fever. Their mage mentioned it."

Ben eyed me coolly. "That is all? I know you spoke with that Cleric about the Black Tide Cult. Why? Why would a healer care about our magecraft?"

How had he overheard Scieran and I? I drew the brush across the horse's sweaty, damp flank. It hardly mattered. He knew more than I had wanted, and now he and I were on a precipice.

I held his gaze, measuring him and the possible outcomes of this conversation, as well as the proximity of several pitchforks and other implements that could easily be turned into weapons—even one-handed as Ben was.

I ignored the warning drum of my pulse and spoke the truth. "I asked if there was a way to cure my corruption."

"Why would you need a cure?" he asked, voice still cold, still flat. "The Uknara woman trained you to manage."

I gave a half-shake of my head. "Manage, yes. But I still struggle to access visions at will—or at least, the *right* visions—and I will still end my life mad and young, unable to tell one world from another. Olsa bought me time. A decade or two. That's all."

Benedict's expression did not change. "Does Mary know?"

"Yes."

"About this 'cure'?"

"Yes."

My brother sat forward, resting one elbow on his knee. "Why did you not tell me?"

His interest—and the fact that he was not raging at me—kindled a spark of hope. "Because you have no interest in the wellbeing of anyone but yourself."

"That is untrue."

I waited for him to elaborate, but he did not. I went on as if he had not spoken and moved to brush down Benedict's beleaguered horse. The creature nuzzled me tiredly, and I scratched between his ears.

"It hardly matters," I said. "The High Cleric could not help me."

"Surely there are Clerics more powerful than a monk in the forest." Ben huffed a laugh, harsh and too loud. "What of the Navy's? The king's? The bedamned Ess Noti? They seem to have their fingers in every bit of magery. I cannot believe—"

"Stop," the word cut out of me. To have Ben of all people poking holes in my decisions? I could not stand for it. "Stop, Ben. There is no cure."

"I do not believe you," he retorted. "You have that expression on your face, that fucking martyr's glower. You are trying to find a way to suffer for the good of everyone around you, which means there *is* a cure, but it is too dangerous to go after. Be selfish for once, Sam. Tell me the truth."

I snorted in disgust, more offended than I could admit. "One of us has to think of others."

"Tell me the truth."

My resolve weakened, and it was a testimony to the depth of my fatigue that I did not immediately mark that shift as Magni power.

Benedict watched me, his eyes… not softer, but more open than I had seen in years.

"There is a cure, and it may be in Ostchen," I admitted, looking through him now, brush paused. "But it is with the Ess Noti and therefore out of reach. Even if we *could* learn it, you would have to be healed too. Or your corruption would eventually unravel me again."

"I will not give up my power," Ben stated, whatever else he thought hidden behind his eyes.

"You might retain it," I said, holding my brother's gaze. "What the Black Tide did is a poor imitation of Mereish practices. Perhaps they can… not undo what the Black Tide did, but correct it."

"'Perhaps,'" Ben repeated tonelessly. "This is why you have not had her."

I raised my brows, taken aback by the sudden shift in topic. "Pardon me?"

Benedict smiled, small and pitying. "Mary." He slid into a leer and pronounced each of his next words with singular intention. "You. Are. A. Fool. Once more, you have a woman on offer at this very moment, and you will not have her because of your worthless scruples."

His words shoved under my skin like splinters. I stepped away from the horses and faced him, every slam of my pulse in my suddenly aching skull threatening to shatter my self-control.

"Ben," I said lowly. "Every time you use your power, you lose more of yourself. You lose the potential of goodness. You forget more of what it is like to be human, to feel and love and care. My corruption will drive me mad and set me adrift in the Dark Water. But yours will make you into a monster. Lirr was a shadow compared to what you will become."

At my mention of 'goodness' a snarl had tightened Benedict's lips, but now he grinned, vicious and unforgiving. "Have you considered that is what I want?"

Gooseflesh rose on my arms and neck. "What if a day comes," I asked very slowly, "when you are so far gone, so lost, that I am the one you hurt? Kill? Torture? What if you see your daughter on the street—in whose veins runs your own blood—and she is nothing but meat and bones in your eyes?"

That struck a chord. Benedict's lips pinned shut, his nostrils flaring, and his gaze locked to mine. I felt his power ripple across the room, bringing with it feelings of terror and remorse and *run, run, run*. The horses shifted, tossing their heads and tugging on their tethers.

I weathered it.

Ben did not speak again, and that, I knew, was as much of an answer as I would get. He had heard me. There was nothing more I could do.

"Saint, I am starving," he said abruptly, standing up and striding out the door. "I am off to find some food."

I bit back a protest. The ache in my head had transformed into hammering, and I closed my eyes, fingers pressed to my temples.

I had grown so used to sloshing through floodwaters in sodden boots that when the Dark Water began to swell around my ankles, I hardly noticed. The Other condensed, overwhelming what little senses I had left beyond pain. A few lights flickered—Grant's subtle indigo-grey in the inn, a creature with an orange glow somewhere off in the night. Mary's and Ben's were still hidden, but I felt no consolation.

The billowing light of another Sooth burned on the horizon. His light was forest green edged with purple, bruised and battered. And his focus was wholly, exclusively, on me.

Inis Hae.

I fumbled a hand into my pocket. The coin was not there. Had I lost in in our flight? Had it fallen on the floor?

Panic threatened to smother me, raging free before Olsa's training surged. I began to separate my mind, edging part of myself back into the human world and slowly, tediously, drawing the rest back on a fragile thread.

I came back to myself, crouched with my back to one of the stables' squared posts. My headache had dulled but was still there, aching and warning. Warning me that, in the Other, Hae was watching.

My fingers finally touched the coin, crammed low in a forgotten pocket. As soon as I nestled it into the warmth of my palm, the headache ebbed and my sense of Hae faded.

But only dread came in its place.

By the time I finished grooming, feeding and watering the horses, an extensive meal was being laid out in the inn's common room. Mary, Grant and Ben were nowhere to be seen, but the innwife directed me to a bathing room—already damp and showing signs of use—and pressed a banyan and a men's long shirt into my arms.

"Get warm and dry, then come and eat," she instructed with maternal firmness, then left me be.

By the time I finished and returned to the common room, my companions were already there, the air full of the scent of thick, hot meat pie, bread and a fruity wine spiced with cardamom, drowning out the perpetual damp and nip of the cold.

Mary smiled at me across the table, her skin pinked with warmth and cleanliness instead of chill. Her hair was in a drying knot, and she wore a Mereish wrapped gown of modest colors.

I smiled back, hiding my raw nerves. I almost told her about Hae's connection to my headaches right then, but the contentedness in her eyes stopped me.

Just an hour. She deserved an hour of peace. We all did. Hae, if my senses were to be trusted, was still trapped on the other side of the river. We had time.

I self-consciously ran my thumb across my opposite forearm, where I had pinned my Mereish coin to my skin with a handkerchief, hidden under my sleeve. While it remained there my connection to the Other remained smothered, my head did not ache so fiercely, and, I prayed, the other Sooth could not actively track me. My coin was not the same as Mary's and Ben's, but it was all we had.

Such constant use would, however, corrupt me all the faster.

Mary's smile dimmed, and she shot me a lingering glance, but either she marked my expression as harmless or she granted me my silence.

"Eat," the innwife said as she made for the door. "I'm for my bed, pious children."

Ben smirked slightly at the name. He and Grant wore clothes as eclectic as Mary and I did, but they were clean and dry and he seemed unbothered.

Mary stole a bread roll and ate it while she shook out her hair beside the fire, then claimed the chair beside Grant, who had filled our cups. Tane, for her part, slipped to the window to keep watch. To my surprise, the indigo-grey light of Grant's ghisting, in the form of a mangy hound—very much like the one we had seen back at the farmhouse—separated from the highwayman and joined her, sitting patiently at her side.

Grant watched him with a proprietary kind of distrust.

Beneath the table, Mary's sock-clad foot wedged between my calves. This time my smile was genuine.

"This is wonderful," she said, reaching for her cup. "Thank you for seeing to the horses. Are you all right?"

"I am very well," I placated.

"How long can we stay here?" Grant inquired, still watching his manifest ghisting. It had taken the form of an overlarge crab now, and was crawling inexorably up the wall.

"Until dawn," I said.

"Well, then," Grant rallied and looked to his plate, "let us make the most of it."

Over the course of the meal, some of my tension ebbed, soothed by Mary's apparent contentedness and her sock-clad feet, leeching warmth off my legs. Grant carried the conversation, speaking of everything save our situation. Benedict seemed content just to eat, occasionally staring between us but otherwise keeping to himself.

"They have a proper summer there, you know, in the Mereish South Isles," Grant said, though every child of the Winter Sea knew of the fabled southern climate. He was into his third cup of wine and showed uncommon restraint in taking this one slowly. "A full six months without snow, can you imagine that? No fear of your face freezing off your skull. No being snow-stayed with your mother's second cousin in Jurry because even the sleigh coaches cannot manage the drifts."

"Very specific," Mary commented, using bread to mop gravy from her plate.

"It happened not once, not twice, but three times," Grant said with an air of conspiracy, leaning forward. The light of the oil lamp on the table gave his blond beard, newly growing in, a reddish glow. "Have I mentioned I hate Jurry? Parties and perfume shops, and pastries so sweet one needs a gallon of coffee to wash them down."

"As much as I enjoy pastries," Mary said, "perhaps it is best I never made it there."

Discreetly, I tried to gauge whether this turn in conversation was one she wanted to take. Mary's first venture away from home had been to Jurry, but her coach had been attacked on the road by highwaymen and she had been set adrift in the world. It was the first step that brought her to Whallum and into my path. It was also a topic Mary steadfastly avoided, and she had only shared the account with me once.

Mary caught my eye. She must have seen my concern, because her expression softened into a wry smile, and she gave a nearly imperceptible nod.

"I am quite sure it was the Tumblers who took your coach," Grant continued tactlessly. He swished his wine in its red-glazed clay cup. "I do keep my ear to the ground when it comes to these things, if the opportunity arises. They are a foul lot, Saint knows it. I know it. Did I tell you about the time they robbed *me*? I suffered theft *and* unnecessary depontication. My wig was ruined."

"Indeed," I said with finality. "Speaking of wigs. We need new clothes, disguises, before we reach Ostchen. We should search the next village."

"You mean steal?" Ben clarified.

The word riled me, as did his voice and the memory of all that had passed between us in the stables. "Yes. Our situation, I fear, has grown worse."

Mary lowered her fork, and Grant pried his eyes from his ghisting, who now hung from the ceiling over the table in the form of a misshapen spider.

"Inis Hae is tracking me, as we suspected. My headaches are connected. I believe they come when he is actively in the Other, seeking me out. My coin should thwart him for the time being, but I do not know how complete that protection is," I said, issuing these truths calmly and steadily. "This must be our last night of rest."

THIRTY-TWO

Never Again

MARY

I caught Samuel's arm. We were in the close warmth of the inn's kitchens, lit by the dying embers of the hearth and a jar with a single dragonfly, gold and pulsing softly at his rest. The remnants of our dinner had been stowed and Benedict and Charles already retired to their rooms, leaving Samuel and I in more solitude than we had had since leaving *Hart*.

"You should take this," I said, pressing my Sooth talisman into his hand. "If Hae is so fixated on you."

Samuel shook his head and pulled up one sleeve, showing me a kerchief bound around his arm. "My own talisman will suffice."

"But it makes you more ill," I pointed out. "Isn't it better to take a chance on this one? Surely the Ess Noti wouldn't make talismans that corrupted their mages."

He hesitated, his eyes dropping from my fingers to my lips. If he intended to reply, no words came.

I wanted to press him, to put the talisman around his neck myself. But instead, the impulse to kiss him beset me, and, in that moment, there was no history, no barriers to hold me back—just the warmth of wine in my stomach and the relief of warm shelter.

I saw the kiss play out in my mind, each subtle movement as I leaned up and pressed my mouth to his, the warmth of our breaths and the taste of wine. The heady rush of heat, burning away the memory of the cold and the very real threat of our pursuers.

Awareness spread over him, his chin lowering, shoulders leveling, his reserve transforming into focus. But his back remained straight. He did not bend down. He did not allow me in.

"If I take that, you will be the one being tracked," he pointed out. "I could not rest, knowing that. My own will not work on you."

I stepped back, disappointed and worried all at once. "You could not rest, but you will not kiss me?"

He pushed my hand, with my talisman, back into my chest. It brought him even closer.

"I do want to kiss you," he said. "But now is hardly the time."

"Then the time will never come." I put the talisman back over my head. "You make me feel unwanted, Samuel Rosser."

I stepped around him and left the kitchen, climbing the short set of stone stairs back into the darkened common room.

His voice came from close on my heels. "Mary, never think I do not want you. We have… you know my reasons for holding back."

I *tsk*ed, irritated. We reached the stairs to the upper floor, and I lowered my voice to a whisper. There was a tremor inside me, the exhaustion and emotions of days of flight, cold and discomfort colliding with his nearness and his unwillingness to yield.

"Yes," I snapped. "I must remain chaste for the good of all Stormsingers."

His voice as quiet as mine: "That would be unfair."

I turned to face him from the first step of the stairs. I wished I could read his thoughts, but the light from the stoked fire only cast his face in deeper shadow.

"Once we are safely back at sea, you and I… we must talk."

Disappointment clawed at me, only thickened by the hope that tried to surge up behind it.

I started to climb the stairs again, turning my back to him. "Good night, Samuel."

I was at the top of the stairs before his response drifted up to me: "Good night, Mary."

⁓

We left the inn just after dawn. The innwife had refused payment from such 'pious children,' instead loading us with more food and drink for the road. She chattered with Charles as Sam and I readied the horses and Benedict stood at the mouth of the yard, looking out across the flooded roads and the abandoned hamlet to the white-foamed sea.

The rain had stopped but the sky remained clouded, and the flooded, empty land was no less unsettling in the light of day. The discomfort of sodden boots and socks still rankled me, though at least our clothes were dry and the floodwaters low enough not to soak our hems when we took turns walking. The men had returned to their robes, and I wore a gifted, wrapped winter dress from the innwife, with a short cloak and a fur hat that I very much appreciated.

There was a warm wind from the south, stirring more mist from the snow and ice. We took turns riding the horses, and I bore perpetual goosebumps on my skin, wondering if, just then, Mereish soldiers were crossing the river or Inis Hae stalked the Other, waiting for our lights to appear.

Once, we passed a sleigh, stuck in the mud-thick snow and stripped of all valuables. Another time we saw people at a distance, but they avoided us as readily as we avoided them. One hamlet we passed had managed to evade most of the flooding but was watched over by a line of hard-looking men and women, while the next contained little more than a scattering of forgotten chickens and the body of a horse with a visibly broken leg, its slit throat yawning and its wounds crusted with pinkish ice.

I leaned forward to stroke the neck of my mount and forced myself to focus on the road ahead.

As dusk came on we neared another small settlement, sprung up close to a smooth length of shoreline. Only half-flooded but wholly abandoned, we agreed it was as good a place as any to take a few hours' much needed rest, though we dared not linger for the whole night.

"We should divide to search for provisions," I said as we tied the horses in the shelter of a lean-to and appraised the house we had selected. It was a small, croft-like affair of wood and stone with white-painted sides and Mereish psalms depicted beneath its thick, sheltering thatch eaves. Its yard was scattered with icy puddles but otherwise unspoiled. Whoever had lived here evidently anticipated higher waters to come or had chosen to follow their neighbors inland for other reasons.

The men agreed, and before long Samuel and I split off in one direction, Charles and Benedict in another. We combed the eerie streets as dusk thickened and the mist turned towards a fog, creeping in on the still-warm southern breeze. Everywhere, eaves dripped and floodwater clutched at our boots and the hems of our garments.

"If this weather keeps up, we may see grass before we reach Ostchen," I commented, turning my face to the wind and relishing its gentleness. I knew it would not last—these first thaws of spring rarely did—but I would take any encouragement I could find. "Grass and endless mud."

Samuel made his way towards a closed door, the water lapping a foot up its sturdy façade. "I never thought I would look forward to mud."

"Our feet may even rot off more slowly," I pointed out brightly, earning a true, crooked grin as he shouldered open the door and we entered the interior. The expression transformed him, lifting away days of exhaustion and strain, and reminding me of simpler, easier days—days in Hesten markets, or in the warmth of his cabin, reading and mending and passing the hours in familiar mundanities.

Days separated only by the distance propriety and his corruption forced between us.

I watched him move through the shadows, the long lines of him, the reach of one broad hand to push open a shutter and allow in a vestige of thin light.

An ache awoke in my chest that had nothing to do with fatigue.

Tane, evidently deciding it was time for a distraction, manifested across my skin. Illumination flooded the house, revealing that the bottom floor was a living space and storeroom, with stairs to a second story. Eager to be out of the water, I made for the stairs as Samuel sloshed behind me.

The upper floor consisted of two cramped sleeping chambers, both with large beds. One obviously belonged to children, scattered with abandoned toys, its window left carelessly open. The other belonged to the parents of this eerie home, inhabited by a wardrobe with sparse clothing, an empty clothes press, and sun-stain marks on the floor where chests had once sat at the foot of the bed. No linens remained on the mattress, and the wardrobe had been ransacked, but there remained enough for me to rifle through.

Samuel moved to the window as I threw a collection of worn, stained and unmended clothes onto the lumpy straw-and-canvas mattress.

"I can see why these were left behind," I muttered, thumbing a hole the size of my fist in the bottom of a sock. "And that whoever lived here disliked mending."

Samuel didn't reply. He was staring out the window, up at the sky, and I realized there was light on his face—not firelight, not Tane's light. Moonlight.

I drew up next to him, the unfortunate sock still in one hand. The sky had begun to clear. There in its dark embrace I saw a sickle moon perched amid wisps of thin cloud. And beyond it, another moon. And another.

Four moons, all at nearly the same degree of darkness and light. All sickles. All within days of one another, in their turning.

"How am I seeing this?" I whispered, speaking to Tane and Samuel at once. "Those are the Other's moons."

Samuel shook his head. He had drawn closer to me, his chest brushing my shoulder. "I… I have no answers."

"The division between worlds is at its thinnest during the Black Tides." Tane's subdued voice came from my lips. "That is what we are seeing."

Unsettled, I inched back into Samuel, resting partially against his chest. He wrapped his arms around me, and together we watched the moons until the clouds covered them again, and darkness retook the settlement.

We spoke little as we finished scouring the house, filling a crate with provisions. Samuel carried it to the next house, then the next, and then we made our way back to the cottage we had selected for our shelter.

I glanced at the horses nibbling at buckets of grain. Inside the house, a fire burned in the hearth and there were numerous new crates and bags scattered about. Charles and Benedict had apparently been and gone, for there was no sign of them now.

Sam stopped. I turned to see him slowly setting his own crate on a table, then he closed the door at our backs.

"Should we go find…" My voice faded as he took the bundle from my arms, set it aside and reached for my hands. He took them, his skin cool and rough.

"What you said, at the inn, about making you feel unwanted. I cannot forget it. Mary, that is the last thing I want you to feel." He gave me each word clearly and gently. There was a rawness to him, perhaps something awoken by the sight of the moons in the sky and the reality of the changes taking place around us. But there was more—a steadiness, a decisiveness, and a need.

"I am going to kiss you now," he said. "Are you opposed?"

"I'm… no, no, not opposed," I tried to reply, but my words were lost in a soft gasp as his mouth closed over mine.

His kisses were gentle but insistent, hungry but measured, and it was all I could do to breathe between brushes and touches and the skim of his tongue. His hand slipped around the back of my head, large and warm. Soon the other came up to meet it, cradling my head and grazing my cheeks, my jaw, the curve of my ears.

"I'm dizzy," I finally managed to whisper.

"Do you want me to stop?"

"No."

"Then I will hold you up." His arm slipped around my waist, pressing my hips into his, and the world receded for another few moments—now just a haze of warmth and want and need, of his touch and his closeness.

"Do you believe that I want you, now?" Sam's voice wheedled through my stupor, just as I was beginning to contemplate shedding my gown and dragging him to the floor.

His lips retreated, and he rested his forehead against mine as he waited for an answer.

"Yes." My reply was so soft, I almost didn't hear it myself. "I've no doubt."

The door clattered open.

"Skirts up, trousers down, that's the next step," Benedict advised, a satchel over one shoulder. He no longer wore his robes but had found breeches and a heavy, wrapped Mereish coat with a broad belt. He'd also lined his eyes darkly with black paint as Mereish sailors did, and his hair was mussed.

I stiffened. Something had shifted in Ben, and it was more than the shedding of monk's garments and the dulling of fatigue. He was more intense, more self-satisfied, the malign threat of him closer to the surface. I felt it at the same time as Sam, whose touch became more protective than amorous.

Ben smirked, slipping past us and depositing a small barrel of water on the table. "Should I take Grant for a drink? Give you two some privacy?"

"Drinks? Where?" Charles came through the door behind him, noted Sam and I entangled, and unfurled a slow, knowing grin. He nudged Benedict. "We should, ah, yes, go find drinks."

Sam stepped away from me. The interruption and his brother's words had clearly jarred him. "No one should go out again. We need to sort all this and sleep while we can. Mr. Grant, Mary, you're welcome to sleep first."

The last thing I wanted to do was rest, my body still heated with need, but fatigue was there too. "I feel like it's dangerous to leave you two alone," I said, looking between the twins.

"There is no 'alone' in a place like this." Benedict threw out an arm to encompass the room, then reached into a crate. I saw a knife glint and he stabbed it down, lifting it a second later with a small wheel of cheese impaled on the blade. "Cheese?"

Charles glanced between all of us, then joined Benedict with his hand outstretched. The tension dissipated, and Samuel stepped back from me as Benedict began to carve portions of hard, pale cheese.

"I am sorry," Samuel murmured.

"Sorry you kissed me?" I whispered back, though I knew that wasn't the case. I simply wanted him to speak plainly.

"No, for the interruption." He looked back down at me. Despite the shadows and Benedict's presence, the smile on his face was true and his eyes intent in a way that made my belly heat all over again. "Not for kissing you. Never again."

THIRTY-THREE

Rosser House, Aeadine

Twenty Years Ago

SAMUEL

I awoke with a coin in my hand and a scream in my throat. I registered figures shifting around me in the dancing light of a fire—leaning, reaching, conversing in tense, hushed tones. They were hunched and grotesque, distorted by shadows, and so close. Too close.

I let the scream loose.

"Samuel, my dear boy, stop. Stop! Listen to my voice." A large, warm hand cupped the side of my face and pressed me into the damp softness of a sweat-soaked pillow. "It is only Uncle John. Your aunt is here too. You are safe."

I choked on a sob and pinned my eyes closed, anchoring myself to his hand, his voice. I wished his was my father's voice but had long grown accustomed to that disappointment.

"Where is Ben?" I whispered. "Is Papa back? Where... where is my mother?"

"Your mother has been taken away for her own safety. She is not herself, Samuel. Open your eyes, let me see you."

I complied and found my uncle's face, illuminated not by fire but by the steady warmth of an oil lamp on a table beside my bed. My bed, in my own room.

My uncle smiled. His smile was a dependable thing, kind but brief, always the bridge between other expressions.

"Now," he said, turning graver. "Ben is here too. He woke up a little before you and is in the kitchen eating. Your father, Samuel, is dead."

I stared up at him, his familiar face losing its consolation with every thinning breath I took.

"John! Now is not the time!" my aunt hissed, shoving at her husband and going to her knees beside my bed, trying to take my hand.

I pulled it away and shifted back, staring at the pair of them. My father, dead? That could not be. He was one of Her Majesty's finest officers, a hero, rarely seen but as fixed in my world as the sun or seasons.

"There is no good time to tell a child their father has died," my uncle countered, rising to stand over the pair of us but keeping his gaze on me. "And Saint knows the boy's mother put it off too long, poor mad creature. Your father died at sea six months ago, a good, honorable death defending Aeadine. I will take you to his memorial in Ismoathe as soon as you are well. They have put a fine plaque in the cathedral."

His words dripped through my mind like oil, smearing at the slightest touch. "Ben," I croaked.

My aunt stood and offered me her hands, which I finally accepted. "Come, I'll take you to him. Carefully, now."

A handful of minutes later, I stood in the doorway of the back kitchen. The flagstones were warm beneath my stockinged feet, and the fire was high, the ovens built into the enormous fireplace radiating a dozen good smells. The sky outside the single window was bright and clear, at odds with the ache in my chest.

"Sam." Ben looked up from where he sat too close to the fire, the edge of the blanket he wore like a cloak inches from the neatly raked coals. His face was bruised, and one foot, also too close to the coals, was wrapped in bandages.

*Tsk*ing, our aunt bustled forward and reached for Ben. "I'll help you up now, Ben, and move your chair. You will be singed, my love."

"No," Ben replied. He did not move. He did not even look at her. Instead, his eyes moved from me, back to the flames.

It was not his wounds that made me stare, nor the realization that they were well into healing and that I must have been lost in the Dark Water for quite some time. It was the emptiness in his eyes as he said that singular, "No," and his total disregard for my aunt—not simply as a fussing adult, but as a human altogether.

"Ben?" I asked tentatively.

I noticed that behind him, on the kitchen's heavy table, several of the cook's habitually decorous platters of food lay scattered. They looked as though a feral dog had been at them.

"Did they tell you Father is dead?" Ben asked, not a scrap of regret in his voice. "And Mother went mad. So now we will go to the Naval Academy and learn how to sink ships and cut apart pirates. I think I will enjoy that."

SAMUEL

Eventually, after days of arduous travel, we reached Ostchen. The port city, home of the king's summer palace and the heart of the Mereish Navy, poured over the low mountains at the hilt of a deep bay in three distinct layers.

The ancient heart of this sprawling settlement was marked out by narrow, layered roofs, and tall stone buildings crammed shoulder to shoulder and racing one another towards the sky. This was surrounded by a thick wall, which divided the ancient from the simply old. Remnants of a secondary wall then divided old from new, and there the main body of the city rambled down to the shore of the water and a complex network of docks, locks, and seemingly isolated villages on stilts and lofty, irregular rocky islets. I saw masts of at least a hundred ships, and longed for *Hart* as I never had before. Was he there, now, within sight? Surely I would know.

Or perhaps I would not, with my Sight stifled. I felt blind.

"What is *that*?" Mary breathed. We had just dismounted and now stood at the top a long, switchbacking road down into the city. Black sheep dusted with white snow watched us over a mossy wall, and the scent of warm manure permeated the air.

Other travelers passed us by in clattering streams—carts and sleighs, riders and people on foot. Most headed into the city, and only the sleighs seemed to be heading out.

None paid us any mind. We were simply road-worn pilgrims and not worth more than a nod.

Following the line of Mary's pointing finger, I saw a huge cathedral with four spires, tucked into the city just before the docks. It perched above the sprawl, within the city but not part of it, and faced north down the length of the bay to the distant, fog-shrouded sea.

"The Cathedral of the Four Faces, which I understand to be the points of the compass," Grant replied.

We all glanced at him.

"How would you know that?" Ben asked.

Grant tapped the side of his head, smiling a humorless smile. His horse idled behind him, lipping at the first green flush of grass at the foot of the wall lining the road. "The beastie knows things, ostensibly. Adalia told him a great deal, though he seems to understand little of it."

"Understanding will come with time," Mary soothed, though something about her cadence had shifted, and I sensed Tane in her words.

Turning my focus back to the city, I marked how, beyond its limits to the east, west, and south, farms and rocky pastures for goats, sheep and rugged cattle occupied the heights of the low mountains. There were few trees—all was open and exposed, and ill-suited to an overland escape, if the need arose.

North along the bay, just on the edge of the fog bank and below the walls of a lording, star-shaped fort, several ships-of-the-line were anchored, including a massive second-rater with uncommon red sails furled and likely a hundred guns stowed behind her black-painted gunports.

"That is a fine ship," Ben commented covetously.

"And the bay must be deep," I added, studying her. "Deep and large enough for the bulk of the Mereish Fleet. So where is it? They cannot all be cruising."

"In that fog, I presume." Ben's gaze swept into the miasma. "Which inclines me to believe either the Mereish coast possesses some very tactful fog in the spring, or the fleet is intentionally concealed."

"Why conceal your fleet from your own people?" I muttered.

"Spies?" Mary stepped in closer, her cheeks flushed with cool sea air and her gaze distracted. Backed by the grey sky and the stony hills, she looked lovely in a raw, wild kind of way.

"Regardless, we have no idea how many ships are in that fog," I said to the company. "*Hart* may be among them, or he may be at the city dock. If I entered the Other, I might be able to sense something of him and the Uknaras, but Hae may be able to sight me or at least sense what direction we have gone."

"A last resort, then," Grant observed. "We follow the plan. Sell the horses, put our ears to the ground and search for *Hart* the traditional way."

"We could search for a High Cleric, too." Ben sent me a lingering look as he mounted again. He offered his hand to Grant. "Ride with me. Those two need to talk."

Grant handed over his reins with a shrug and took Ben's arm, mounting behind the saddle. Ben immediately set off, leaving his suggestion hanging in the air.

"Talk about what? Does he know about the healing?" Mary inquired quietly.

"Yes," I said, mounting up and freeing a stirrup for her. "But he is not willing. And there is no possibility of finding the cure now, regardless."

Mary swung up and settled behind me, closer than Grant had been to Ben. Her arms laced around my middle, her welcome warmth seeping through me.

"So you keep telling us," she said resignedly. "Let's move along, before those two get us into trouble."

Sprawling farms soon became networks of houses and shops, which ran all the way up to the outer wall. The stone barrier's watchtowers were clad with brightly painted shutters, and laundry criss-crossed the street to the neighboring newer buildings— wood with shingles or thatch roofs and lovingly decorated façades. Children played and splashed through puddles, carts rumbled and adults milled about, shopping and chatting and going about their labors.

We found a livestock market before long, where Ben and Grant went about selling the horses and tack for a mildly exorbitant sum. We divided the money as discreetly as possible and embarked on our next task: finding our way through the hellish press of the city to the city docks.

"You visiting? If you're looking for an inn, you won't find one tonight," a hawker told us an hour later as we sheltered in the mouth of an alley. The gangly young man had a crate of broadsheets at his feet and sold them for small, tin dette coins to passersby. "Not with the tides and the refugees."

A parade of red-cloaked monks forced their way down the center of the street, chanting and leading a gilded palanquin. Briefly, the crowd grew so loud that even the hawker was drowned out.

He scowled at the commotion and bent, riffling down through his crate of papers. He pulled an older, crumpled one out and held out the opposite hand, palm up. "You'll want this," he said, directly in my ear.

I pulled back but handed him a dette in exchange for the paper and rejoined my companions in the relative privacy of the alley, which here meant we were alone except for three whores, wrapped in blankets and smoking pipes on a balcony several stories above, and a sleeping drunk under a pile of equally somnolent dogs.

I smoothed the creases from the paper and held it up so we could read together. I heard Mary murmuring the words under her breath, and Ben gave up almost immediately. He leaned against the wall, lacing his arms over his chest and looking up at the whores. One eyed him dispassionately, one smiled falsely, and the last came over to lean on the balcony rail and stare down at him in wordless assessment. Ben stared right back.

"'*Soon we will see the second-highest Black Tide of the last centuries, surpassed only by next month's. The lower city has already been evacuated, and upper Ostchen now hosts many thousands of refugees from coastal villages,*'" Grant read, seemingly for Benedict's benefit.

Mary contemplated the broadsheet. "The Aeadine know how difficult this spring will be, right? All our coastal villages and ports will be prepared? Tithe?"

I shook my head. "They will not be prepared for it to be *this* high. Ostchen is bursting because even the Mereish villages are not equipped, and they knew it was coming."

"Good thing we do not intend to stay long," Ben muttered. He and the whore still watched one another, though he spoke low enough only we could hear his Aeadine.

"Did that word come from Adalia Day?" Grant asked. "Or is this all common knowledge in Mere?"

"If the Oruse had an observatory, others will too," Mary said. "Like the Ess Noti."

"Yes, I have no doubt the Ess Noti were well aware," I affirmed. Every thought of the organization grated my nerves, not only because of their threat and the coin still bound tight to my skin.

A cure was closer than ever. And for the sake of all of us—Mary, Grant, Ben, *Hart*, the Uknaras—I had to ignore it. Perhaps if we had to stay the night, I might slip away, but—the risk was so high. No.

No.

I continued, "It does not change our immediate needs. We must find *Hart*."

Ben squinted at me. At the same time, the whores grew bored and vanished from the balcony above. "Just go into the Other, Sam."

"There is no need to risk that. Yet," Mary interjected. "We've all eyes in our skulls, and there cannot be so many ships around the city. I say we split up—Samuel and Charles, Ben and I. We search and set a place and time to reunite."

We all looked at one another: Ben impassive, Grant startled, and I off-footed. Despite all we had endured together, I doubted Mary would volunteer to partner with Ben without reason.

She, evidentially, read my thoughts. "You twins are too notable together and Benedict—" she added with the ghost of a grin "—is a terrible influence on Charles."

Grant scoffed. "Well I am a marvelous influence on him."

"*And*," Mary added, becoming more serious, "I have Tane. I can Otherwalk, though I can't track as well as you. And if all else fails, Sam, we can look into the Other. So each pair will have similar advantages."

Ben studied Mary for a moment, passably curious now, then nodded. "We can meet in front of the cathedral we saw from the hill, the one with the four spires. Midnight bells?"

I glanced up at the sun, only to find it completely hidden in the crush of roofs, spires, chimney caps and laundry lines.

We still had a few hours before nightfall. Eight hours, then, to search for *Hart*. Eight hours separated from Mary, knowing she was alone with Ben. I did not like it, but I saw the wisdom in it, and I doubted Ben would outright harm the Stormsinger this far into their acquaintance.

I nodded. "Grant and I will go out to the naval docks and see what we can through that fog. Mary, Ben, search the public ones. We will see you at midnight."

THIRTY-FIVE

The Ess Noti

MARY

"I presume we are doing something my brother would not approve of," Benedict observed as we were swallowed by the crowd. He was shockingly close, the buttons of his coat a breath from my shoulder. "Are we seeking out the Ess Noti?"

"Yes," I affirmed. My instinct was to speak low, but the market was so loud that was both impossible and irrelevant. "Sam will not save himself, so we must try. Will you help me?"

The Magni shrugged and nudged me aside—none too gently— as a large man with a huge, slathering hound barged through. We were not the only ones to move, and for an instant a swath of open cobbles remained. I could see to the gates to the city proper, the second-oldest tier. Beyond its stretch of wood and slate tiles, the stone ramparts of the Old City rose—the heart of Ostchen, summer seat of the monarchy and headquarters for every power in Mere.

Including the Ess Noti.

Like a sigh, the crowd overflowed back into the space and the press resumed. I imagined the forest for an instant, the scent of earth and the feeling of blessed loneliness among the trees. I took a calming breath, caught a whiff of a passerby's pungent odor, and gagged.

"Whatever cure the Ess Noti have, I will not use it," Benedict warned as we started off again towards the gate.

"I don't expect—" I was cut off as we were forced to weave through the line for a vendor selling spiced, roast meats, and my stomach clenched in hunger.

Ben and I met up again on the other side and he passed me one of two skewers of meat.

"Did you just steal these?" I asked, startled and grudgingly impressed.

"Do you care?"

I stared at the skewer, thick with savory scents of fat and pepper and other spices. Hesitation fled, and I took a bite. Flavor burst over my tongue, and I resisted the urge to make an undignified, happy sound.

"Fine, don't use the cure," I said. Whether or not Benedict wanted to use it now, Sam needed help. Perhaps Ben could be convinced—or forced—at a later date. "We find the Ess Noti's headquarters and see what we can see, steal what we can steal."

Ben eyed me askance. "That is your plan?"

"Yes," I said stolidly. I snagged his sleeve and tugged him behind me as a stream of shrieking children passed. "Tane and I will go in alone, if need be."

"You intend to Otherwalk into the Ess Noti."

I shrugged, pretending to be far more nonchalant than I felt. "I walked into a prison to save you, and you were quite the task. Little more than dead weight for half the escape, I might add. Why shouldn't I be able to walk into the Ess Noti and steal a book or two?"

Ben considered me archly. "Dead weight? I remember saving your life."

"I saved yours at least twice."

"You have no idea what you are looking for or where to find it."

"I'll start in the infirmary. Tane can read Mereish and we move through walls. I have a good chance."

He simply grunted at that, though I was still left with the feeling I had lost the argument.

The gate to the inner city was open and unguarded. Beyond, humanity condensed even further. Inns and taverns crammed in beside tenements, constructed of both wood and stone and occasionally slate. There were more sailors, men and women alike marked out by their short coats, broad gaits, and black-rimmed eyes.

The gates to the Old City, however, were not so welcoming. The ancient walls were thick and high, and, beyond them, the towers and roof of official-looking stone buildings loomed. There were many gates, each one named in Mereish and leading, presumably, to various compounds. All were closed, guarded, or both.

No children played here. No one loitered, chatting in a brief wash of sunshine in the wide, circular road that surrounded the Old City, or lingered around the statues that graced its circumference. I saw a couple try to sit together on the edge of a fountain, only to be barked away by two passing soldiers.

We took a second to breathe as Ben finished eating a large, flat pastry that had appeared from nowhere and brushed off his hands.

I stared at one particularly grand spire, capped with a shrieking dittama weathervane.

"This may be harder than I expected," I murmured.

"Nonsense," Ben scoffed. Two soldiers strode past us, a man and a woman, and his chin drifted to one side. "Follow me."

I had made a mistake. That became quite clear to me as Ben and I saluted our way through the closest gate and entered the Old City, dressed in slightly mussed soldiers' uniforms.

In my mind, this endeavor had been simple: stay hidden in the crowds as we weaved through the streets until Tane noticed something that would identify the Ess Noti's headquarters, since I doubted there would be a sign.

But there were no crowds on these streets, no common folk with common concerns to conceal ourselves among. Almost everyone was a soldier, though their armament varied and their uniforms were diverse, from plum to grey to dark yellow. Some stood guard. Some patrolled. Some hastened on errands. Servants and clerks formed the remainder of the population, moving efficiently with their heads down. Lastly, we spied well-dressed men and women of ambiguous affiliation.

This way, Tane whispered in the quiet of my mind.

I nodded Benedict down a sidestreet and into an even denser region. The streets, alleys, stairs and bridges became positively labyrinthine, and we were forced to wait in line to pass over a narrow canal that stank like a flooded cellar.

Then, rising amid the towers, I spied a dome of stone in varying colors and patterns. Through Tane I felt a stir—the presence of other ghistings and a sense of the Other itself.

Down the street, a large but otherwise unremarkable set of double doors stood unguarded.

"We've found it," I murmured to Ben. "That must be the Ess Noti."

We situated ourselves in one of the many alleyways, and I took a few moments to calm my nerves, eyeing the walls and doors of the building I intended to enter. My nervous hands, fidgeting with my uniform, quickly discovered the woman I'd stolen it from had a fondness for sweets, which I grudgingly shared with Ben. I paced. He stood stolidly, less emotive than the walls all around us, but accepted a sweet and began to suck on it distractedly.

At last, Ben prompted, "Are you ready?"

I paused, a sweet lodged in my cheek. "Yes. Wait for me as long as you can. If all else fails, we reunite at the cathedral."

"Which cathedral?" a female voice asked.

"The one with—" I began to reply thoughtlessly, my tongue overridden by a wave of Magni magic.

A blonde woman strode towards us, dressed in fine but practical Mereish clothing. A man came behind her, dressed much the same and leveling a pistol as he did.

I had barely registered the pistol when, calm as doldrums under a clear sky, Inis Hae fired.

Benedict staggered. I stepped in front of him and threw out my hands defensively—why, I wasn't sure, my valiance spawned from shock and stupidity—only to see the woman level her own pistol. I saw the flash of a muzzle, a puff of gunsmoke against a backdrop of ancient stone.

The musket ball punched into my flesh—my thigh, I thought, though the pain was not immediate. The separation I felt from my magic was. Between one breath and the next I felt my winds depart, eddying away in confusion. Dizzy and panicked, I tried to find a note to hum, to wet my lips to whistle.

No music came. No magic pried through that barrier.

"Tane," I croaked aloud, the word compulsive, unintentional.

Her presence surged, soothing and strong. I had her, at least.

The blonde woman—Enisca Alamay, I supposed—approached. Hae came behind her, blocking Ben and I in the alleyway. I tried to retreat, to at least stand beside Ben as we faced our capture. But my leg would not move. He inched closer, his shadow falling onto the cobblestones beside my sagging one.

I looked back at him, pleading in my eyes. "Do something."

He dug his fingers into the bleeding hole in his already injured shoulder. Blood gushed, his lips peeled back in a snarl of pain. The image alone was so grotesque, so horrifying, I tasted bile on my tongue.

"Stop," the blonde woman demanded. It took me a breath to realize she was not speaking to Ben or me but to a dozen soldiers converging upon us. "Stay back."

"Lay down your arms and come forward," Hae said, reloading his pistol with efficiency. His expression was controlled, but he tracked Ben's movements with an eagle's focus. "Now."

Ben let out a cracking, whining roar. A lead ball hit the cobblestones and rolled into a divot, languid with blood and sounding far heavier than it should have.

Ben's power flared, and chaos erupted. Soldiers staggered in, creating a barrier between us and the Mereish mages before attacking them directly.

Hae dodged with preternatural speed—as if he knew where each shot would pass and each hand would grab. Enisca Alamay vanished into the chaos.

Ben grabbed my arm and shoved me forward. "Run!"

I toppled, hitting the stones hard. Pain did come then, so thick and blinding that I retched.

"I can't," I panted. It felt like a ridiculous thing to say—of course I could run. It was just a bullet, a little ball of lead. I hadn't *lost* my leg. It was still there, only with a little hole.

I felt Ben's hand on my arm again. He tried to pull me to my feet and only succeeded in nearly dislocating my shoulder.

"If you escape, find me aboard *Hart*," he said, then dropped me like spoiled fish.

The next hand that touched me was Enisca's, gently tilting up my face. Magic came with her searching gaze, calming and settling me and easing my pain. Hae was gone. And where Ben's shadow had hovered over me, there was nothing but the rising walls and bands of clear blue sky.

"Carry her," the woman said, casting her voice over her shoulder even as she scrutinized my face. "The rest of you, make haste to support Mr. Hae. Keep me informed."

∽

In the end, I was grateful I had been shot—in a pain-giddy, disconnected kind of way. Instead of being immediately imprisoned or tortured, I was brought right to the very person I had been seeking: a High Cleric of the Ess Noti.

The downside, of course, was that I had actually been shot and was in a great deal of pain, as Tane's innate ability to mitigate my wounds seemed stifled by the ensorcelled lead ball. Once the ball was removed from my thigh—a procedure I thankfully passed out for—my magic returned to me in a heady rush, but my jaw was locked in a Stormsinger's gag. I was now manacled to a narrow cot in a pool of murky sunlight, filtering through high, narrow windows. The place smelled of camphor and lemon and lye, with something chalky and dry behind it.

My restraints ensured that, as Enisca Alamay and the High Cleric conferred, I could not even begin to ask tactful questions or sneak glimpses at notes or assess the rows of books on the walls of the High Cleric's office, which I could see through an open door.

I realized just how idiotic my hope had been. And as much as I wanted to blame my stupidity on Benedict's influence, I couldn't excuse myself.

My desperation to help Samuel had made me a fool.

Tane, thankfully, was listening to Enisca and the Cleric, gathering information that eventually sifted into my bleary mind.

"Please keep the witch here as long as possible. Once she is in the cells, she will be out of my reach. For now, I must speak to Faucher directly," Enisca said. Her back was to us, and my vision was still unclear, but Tane could see her tension. "Tell him I will be waiting in his office, and summon a page to direct me there."

Faucher? I grasped at the name. Jessin Faucher was here and was some kind of official?

"That would be inappropriate," the High Cleric said. Their voice was light and their features pretty and androgynous. Their slight body was hidden in a long, belted robe of jade, and their age was hard to discern—much like Enisca's. They added something else in a lower voice, which I could not catch.

Who is Enisca, giving a High Cleric orders? I asked Tane, but she had no insight.

Enisca reached out of sight, and I heard a bell ring. Within a few moments a servant knocked at the door of the ward—empty other than myself—and presented himself with a bow.

"You may be waiting some time. Faucher will not return for at least half an hour," the High Cleric warned. I thought I caught a deeper meaning to their words, a layer that I couldn't quite identify. It was in their eyes too, cautioning and insightful.

Enisca cast them a lingering glance, and I saw her hand reach out, just at the bottom of my view, and clasp the Cleric's. Then they parted, and Enisca and the servant were gone and I was alone with the High Cleric.

I heard the rustle of papers and the closing of a drawer, then the clink of tea being poured.

Tane, can we escape through the Other? Out of these restraints? I was wearing little, I noticed with a horrible, twisting feeling of violation—just my stolen, thigh-length shirt, rumpled around my hips. It would be hard to evade notice dressed like that, but surely it was better than being here, at the mercy of the Ess Noti, while Ben was on the run and soldiers hunted for Sam and Charles at every cathedral in the city.

Perhaps. But you still need to be able to walk.

How soon, then?

My next conscious understanding was that someone was very, very close. I pried open my eyes, realizing I must have passed out, and saw a man standing over me.

Inis Hae.

I jerked against my restraints. Hae showed no sign of shock, but he did straighten and look back at an older man who I was sure I had never seen before, and yet was equally sure I recognized.

"Mary Firth of the *Hart*, I am Adamus Faucher," the older man said, watching me down the long nose he shared with Captain

Jessin Faucher of *The Red Tempest*, who I devised must be his son or nephew. "I am the head of the Ess Noti, and I will be your primary caretaker in the coming days. This is Inis Hae, whom I understand you have led on a great chase."

I stared up at the two, feeling obscenely vulnerable in my cursory clothing. The mask was tight, and my nose felt clogged with unacknowledged tears.

"Hmm. This can come off," Faucher Senior said to Hae and gestured at my mask. Something swung from his hand—a thick, iron bracelet. "This will suffice. Enisca was foolish not to use it immediately. Where *is* that woman?"

"Lord Faucher." The light voice of the High Cleric drifted across the hall. "What an honor. Can I assist you?"

The two began to speak as Hae clamped the bracelet—the manacle—tight around my wrist. It had no keyhole, no obvious mechanism, and as soon as it was fixed I felt my magic die once more.

Dread assailed me. Did the manacle only suppress Stormsinging? The Ess Noti knew I was *ghiseau*, perhaps even that Tane was a Mother Ghisting. Would they have taken precautions against Otherwalking, or was that a skill only Tane and I had unraveled?

I raked in fresh air as the gag came off. A hundred questions hit the back of my teeth, and I barely stopped myself from asking them. What could I say without condemning myself or my friends?

And if Hae was here, had he lost or captured Ben, Sam and Charles?

"Where is the man I was with?" I asked, deciding that mentioning Ben could do no further harm.

A hand immediately covered my mouth. Hae, casually pressing my skull into the bed and squishing my cheeks grotesquely.

"Are you sure you wish to speak with her now, sir?" Hae asked. His hand tasted like sweat and metal and gunpowder. "Cleric, perhaps you could make her more amenable?"

I bit him. He jerked away and stared from me to his hand, aghast. Sadly, it was not bleeding.

The Cleric looked from Faucher to me, to Hae and his hand, which he was shaking vigorously. "Amenable?"

Hae's expression darkened, but it was Faucher who spoke: "Enisca was here, so where is she now?"

The High Cleric said, "A page escorted her to your office. She insisted on being able to speak with you personally."

"She is alone in my office?"

"Yes, sir."

Something passed through Faucher's expression, and his posture shifted, as if he were already halfway to the door. "It seems I am required elsewhere. Mr. Hae, please escort Ms. Firth to one of the apartments and ensure she remains there."

Hae went stiff. "Surely someone else could—"

"I trust no one else," Faucher cut him off. "Ensure she is secured."

Hae's jaw tightened. "My skills would be much more useful pursuing the Rosser twins."

Sam and Ben were still free? Relief enveloped me. But where did that leave Charles?

"We have their ship and their witch," Faucher broke in, heading for the door now. "Do not let her leave your sight."

Hae swallowed his indignance until his superior left the room, then descended into muttering curses. He began to unfasten my restraints, and my heart—already worn to tatters—began to hammer again. Did I dare try to Otherwalk? Right out those windows and… where? I had no idea how high up we were.

We have their ship and their witch.

I looked back to Hae. By the sounds of things, he knew where *Hart* was. Could I trick him into telling me? Or simply distract him? If he was here, watching me, he was not in the Other tracking Sam.

I could use this.

The Cleric considered Hae coldly. "You are aware that she is badly injured. She cannot walk. Or do you intend to carry her?"

"She's *ghiseau*," he replied, tossing the last strap and grabbing my arm to haul me upright. "She will manage."

I gasped in pain and punched him, but he easily deflected the blow and grabbed me by the hair.

The Cleric watched with clear disapproval. "Where will you take her?"

"The apartments."

"I am aware of that. Which one?"

I lost track of their exchange as Hae dragged me upright, and, as soon as weight settled on my leg, my world cracked into blackness. I blinked back an instant later, still wavering on my feet, with Hae on one side of me and the Cleric on the other.

The Cleric eased away, searched my eyes for a moment, then nodded to Hae, who prodded me towards the door.

The realization that I might not see the Cleric again made me desperate.

"Can you heal a corrupted mage?" I asked, throwing aside all caution. "Please! Can you?"

Hae shoved my head forward with a brutal, open palm.

The Cleric's expression twitched in disapproval, but they gave a subtle nod.

Hae shoved me through the door of the infirmary and slammed it behind us, then prodded me into motion. "No more talking. No more questions."

"Questions *are* talking," I pointed out, and received another shove for my trouble. I grabbed the wall and barely kept my feet.

Mary, Tane warned.

Where I had expected tight, dark corridors and locked doors, the passageways of the Ess Noti were blessedly broad and frequently interrupted by archways to brightly lit chambers. Clean air flowed from cracked upper windows, cool and fresh with spring. Some

chambers were empty, halls lined with books and cabinets and cases
of astonishingly clear glass, behind which various treasures or weapons
loomed. One chamber held human skeletons, all wired together
in semblance of life and interspersed with desks where figures
labored over ink and ledgers. Another room, small and circular,
held a singular statue of stone—a figure with his arms crossed over
his chest as if he lay in a coffin, and a crown about his throat like a
noose. A memorial, perhaps? Still another chamber held the skeleton
of some Otherborn beast, like the spidery squid Sam had once
summoned from the Other.

Rather than a den of secrecy, the halls of the Ess Noti were open
and unreserved. This was a powerful display of control, knowledge,
and confidence, here in the seat of their power.

Soon, however, the windows grew less frequen,t and several
doors were closed. One I saw through for a short time, held open
by a page who froze and ducked her head at the sight of Hae. I saw
a man with impossibly tired eyes, workng in a leather apron. He
straightened slowly from a stone table laden with a tiny forge, rows
of vials and bowls full of pellets of various metals that shone in the
light from the window. A wall of tiny drawers was to one side, and
bowls of coins—talismans—lay on the table.

A talisman maker. The back of my neck prickled, then Hae
prodded me on and the stranger was left behind.

CONCERNING SUMMONERS—*One of the most fascinating types of Adjacent Mages, Summoners possess a Sooth's insight into the Other and a natural allure to creatures of that realm, along with the ability to control and influence such beasts. Some speculate this is the effect of Magni magic in the bloodline of the Sooth, others that the skill remains separate from Magni magic and is a breed entirely its own, if similar in application.*

Regardless, a Summoner's ability to compel, tame, and even train Otherborn creatures has broad and exciting applications, and is of immense value to the Mereish people.

—FROM A DEFINITIVE STUDY OF THE BLESSED: MAGES AND MAGECRAFT OF THE MEREISH ISLES, *TRANSLATED FROM THE MEREISH BY SAMUEL I. ROSSER*

THIRTY-SIX

The Implings

SAMUEL

Mist prickled across my skin as Grant and I crested the low mountains beyond the fort and, hopping a wall, picked our way down to the sea. We moved casually, speaking here and there and generally maintaining the appearance of friends escaping the city on a warm spring evening.

The fog, however, undercut our façade. It shielded anything not within half a dozen paces, encapsulating us in our own, small world of last season's crushed grass and melting snow—the latter adding its own gentle mist to the greater miasma.

The hulking rise of the fort briefly came and went. Shaggy cattle watched us pass with squinty, furtive eyes, and once I swore I heard a child laugh.

Then the ground gave way in a crumble of sodden, half-thawed earth. I flung out an arm to stop Grant, who made a startled sound and slipped on muddy snow. His legs struck mine, and the two of us hit the ground in a graceless tumble.

I froze, fully expecting us to slide off the mountain in a deluge of earth and rock and clots of grass. But the ground was solid other than a gentle rustle of falling dirt.

"Damn." Grimacing, I smeared mud from my cheek and started to rise, staring over the cliff we had nearly wandered off.

"Wait!" Grant grabbed my arm, his eyes round as coins. We held our breaths, not daring even to breathe until the silence, the press of mist, began to ring in my ears.

A sound came from the fog. A thud. A brush. The shifting of feet.

I slipped a hand slowly inside my mud-smeared coat. Grant did the same, crouched low and ready to spring.

The fog swirled, and a great, hulking mass appeared. My mind transformed it into a hundred, twisted shapes—Otherborn beasts come to tear us limb from limb. I would have to remove my coin to fight them, then Hae would come, and all would be lost.

The mist abated, and a shaggy, long-horned cow considered us sedately.

I rasped out a breath, half laughing, half winded. "Saint."

"It may be premature to give thanks," Grant muttered, pushing himself upright. At his feet, his ghisting had manifested in its mangy-dog form, glowing a faint, dark indigo.

I followed the creature's gaze back to the cow. There, perched atop the cow's enormous, broad head, was an impling. The unholy mingling of an infant and a starved dog, it rode upon the beast's neck and held its horns, all the while watching us over its mount's windblown fur. It was naked, bones sticking out against pale, nearly necrotic flesh and contrasted by chubby, round belly and cheeks.

Had I been in the Other, or even attuned to it, the impling would have shone orange. But here, wholly in the human world, its glow was barely discernable. The last burn of a setting sun.

"Sam," Grant said, very low. "Now might be a good time to risk taking off that talisman."

"Hae will find us," I reminded him, equally low. My voice did not quaver, but my guts were watery. Could I take command of the impling without my contact to the Other? Or would my status as a Sooth be wholly irrelevant as it sliced our throats to ribbons and pried our eyes from our skulls?

Back atop the cow, the impling began to crawl forward, kneeling on the creature's head, its vaguely humanoid skull cocked to one side. The cow itself did not move, unperturbed.

"Either he finds us alive today or a cowherd finds our bodies tomorrow," Grant gritted out.

The impling leapt into the grass and began to crawl towards us. Grant pulled a knife. I reached for my sleeve, and the cow lowed in sudden distress.

Movement revealed a new source of subtle orange advancing from the left, more from the right. A dozen implings, crawling towards us like hungry, four-limbed spiders.

Grant's ghisting began to flit in front of us, a decidedly un-canine pattern to his steps. One of the implings shied away from him, but the others came on, crowding us back to the edge of the cliff.

I tore the handkerchief from my forearm, shoved it and the coin into my pocket, and dropped into the Other. I reeled at the suddenness of the shift, but my instincts were already in action, gathering my power and infusing it into my voice.

"Stop."

The implings, blazing orange reflections here in their natural home, paused. One was so close to Grant it might have reached out to claw his ankle with its long, thin claws.

"Back up."

Half the implings retreated. The others wavered, but one—the one who had ridden upon the cow—advanced another pointed step.

It met my gaze, its eyes pits of ochre matte sea-glass, and as it tilted its head I saw something about its throat. Tight. Bronze. Not a decoration.

A collar.

Impossible, one part of my mind declared.

Undeniable, the other concluded.

"Someone else is… controlling them," I murmured to Grant. I could feel my lips move in the human world, though my other senses were wholly occupied. I risked a glance at the horizon, searching for the other Sooth's dark-green mark. But Ostchen and the sea behind us were endless hazes of lights, all jumbled together and obscuring one another.

Dividing my mind as Olsa had taught me, I began to subconsciously search for *Hart*, Olsa, and Illya. I could not waste a single moment here.

Immediately the implings all surged forward. Grant made a strangled sound and our shoulders bumped together.

"Sam!" Grant protested.

I clapped the full force of my focus onto the implings. Some froze again. The remainder fully fled.

"Go back to your forests. Abandon your master," I told the last creatures, though I looked at the one with the collar. "I will try to take that off you, if you permit."

More implings trickled away, until only three remained. Two lingered nearby, clustering, waiting for the collared one.

It crawled forward and stood on its too-thin legs, distended stomach sagging.

Slowly, I crouched to meet it. The longer I was in the Other the more natural my movements felt, the easier it was to breath and sense and *see*. I felt gentle tugs in various directions, like sparrows plucking at my clothing. Visions and Knowings slipped closer, like penitents wringing their hands.

The impling approached until it was within arm's reach.

"Turn around," I said.

The creature sneered at me, revealing densely packed lines of teeth. *Four* densely packed lines of teeth, to be precise.

"Or leave," I told it. I felt calmer now, and my patience waned. "I will give you no other choice."

With a silent shriek, the little monster lunged. I shied back, throwing up a hand just in time to stop its claws from my face. Flesh parted. Skin and fabric tore.

My power billowed out. The creature fled, and I staggered back into my body to an assault of senses—cold and condensation, the sight of snow and mist and the first brush of green. Blood running down my arm, though no pain came yet. Grant's round eyes and his ghisting, swirling around us in a panic of sudden, avian wings.

Then, as if dragged by an invisible hook, I crashed back into the Other. I spun, searching for lights. Grant. His ghisting. Fleeing implings. One, lingering, hovering, clacking its long nails together in obvious distress.

A murky green light growing in the distance. A tug, no longer gentle. A fishhook around my ribs.

Inis Hae was not only tracking me. He was summoning me.

"The coin," I croaked. "Mr. Grant. Charles!"

I felt no fumbling in my pocket, just the coin when Grant pressed it into my hand. I awoke as if from fever, in flickering fits and starts and flashes of vision.

I braced on my knees and retched. Nothing came up, which left me feeling infinitely worse, and I was grateful for Grant's hand on my shoulder. One of my forearms felt hot, and when I squinted at it, I saw blood. So much blood.

"If you are finished," the highwayman said slowly. "There is one more impling."

I squinted through a tangled curtain of hair. One final creature, small and young, squatted on a patch of snow. It wrung its fingers, like I'd seen it doing in the Other.

"You can leave," I grunted to the little monster, though with the coin on my skin once again, my power over it should have been nullified.

I was not sure it was, however. I still felt nauseous and dizzy, trapped just on the edge of my own skin with the Other hovering close. Grant's ghisten light and the impling's innate glow seemed too strong in this human world, and a blur refused to leave the very edges of my vision.

The impling retreated a step, but seemed incapable of leaving.

An idea came to me, impulsive. "Wait. Go find the ship with the figurehead of a Hart. Then come find me again."

The creature shuddered, then launched itself past us—over the edge of the cliff and into the impenetrable fog. There was no splash, no screech, no distant impact. The creature simply vanished, and I was left unsure whether it remained in our world at all.

Perhaps it would obey. Perhaps it would not.

With its departure, the pain came stronger. I held up my arm to check the locations of the wounds—would it not be fitting if the monster had slit my wrists and I bled out here within moments?

Grant took the arm before I could get a good look and began to bind it tightly. In my free hand I clenched the coin tighter, though my awareness of the Other still did not fade. The visions that had clamored for attention before now strained—seeking a crack in my barriers.

For there truly was a crack now, one I could not close, no matter how hard the talisman dug into my skin.

"You need stitches," the highwayman said.

"We must be discreet," I warned him.

Grant rolled his eyes, but his exasperation was a veil, and a thin one at that. He was worried. "Shut your mouth and come along."

THIRTY-SEVEN

An Uncommon Remedy

MARY

My cell lay in an appropriately sinister region of the Ess Noti headquarters, complete with iron-banded doors—all locked—and the muted glow of under-populated dragonfly lanterns. Hae conferred with two guards in a side room, holding my arm all the while like one might an unruly toddler, then accepted a key and led me to the end of the corridor.

He unlocked a door and prodded me through into a startlingly large, clean room, which I saw from the floor as I promptly tripped on the carpet and went sprawling. The pain was obscene, and when my vision cleared, Hae watched me from the doorway.

Or rather, he looked through me, his gaze suddenly so intense, so vicious, gooseflesh prickled up my arms.

I knew that look, though on Samuel it was gentler. He was in the Dark Water. What did he see?

Not me.

I lunged towards him, intent on knocking him to the floor and—well, I hadn't thought further than that, but any form of violence seemed good.

His hand shot out and closed around my throat with preternatural speed.

"Hush," he breathed, still staring through me. "I must focus."

I made a sound between a squeak and a growl, both choked off as he squeezed.

I seized his forearm for support and dug my nails into his flesh. After a handful of heartbeats, loud and trapped in my swelling face, he dropped me. I staggered back into a table, which in turn clattered into the plastered wall.

"Try to leave and I will know." Hae held up the hand he'd just had around my throat and stretched his fingers meaningfully. His eyes were focused on this world again. "Your talisman is gone, I have your scent, and there is nowhere you can go where I will not see."

The slam of the door cut off any response I might have made.

I had been a fool. More than a fool—I had been the highest kind of idiot to think Ben and I could go near the Ess Noti, let alone find Samuel's cure.

Frustration lit in my chest, overriding lingering fear and pain and a plentiful dose of self-pity. I entertained those feelings for a few frustrated breaths before thoughts of Samuel and Charles overtook me.

I had to escape before they learned where I was and came after me, endangering themselves. But my leg quavered, my stomach was sour with pain, and the whole of me maddeningly weak.

First, assess my surroundings. Second, rest. Third, escape. Whether the instructions came from my subconscious or Tane, I didn't know. But I clung to them.

The room had a comfortable bed, a chest of drawers, and a bookshelf, both of which were empty except for a washbasin and pitcher of water. There were no windows save for half a dozen round, fist-sized inlets, which let in the very last daylight. Most of the light came from a dragonfly lantern, all golden males, and heat came from the walls themselves, accompanied by the hiss of unseen water.

Despite the weight of my situation, resting on a clean bed was not something I would waste. I hauled myself into the soft sheets and heavy blankets, and buried my face in a lavender-scented pillow.

See what you can learn? Watch over me? I asked of Tane as my burning eyes closed of their own accord.

Always.

Some time later, a knock came at the door. I'd just cracked open my eyes when a guard entered, holding her musket ready. A second guard followed with a chair, then a man in an apron.

The talisman maker. He looked haggard but nodded in thanks as the guard set down the chair.

I gingerly sat up.

"You can both go," the talisman maker said, unshouldering a structured bag, more like a small chest with a strap.

The guards looked from him to me.

"That is unwise, sir," one said in Mereish.

The man let out a sigh so exhausted that it trembled. "Fine, but do not bother me." He gestured for me to sit on the edge of the bed and dragged his chair to face me.

I did not move, looking from him to the guards, one of whom had closed the door. My nerves hummed. Why was he here?

"My name is Maren," the man said in Aeadine, setting his bag beside the chair. He appeared unrushed, even grateful for the chance to sit.

I recognized the name, though in my current state and the uncertainty of the moment, our connection eluded me.

"Speak in Mereish," one of the guards snapped.

Maren turned to look at him, somehow managing to look down his nose despite being seated. "She does not understand Mereish."

I eyed the guard, wondering how much they had been told about me. Would they believe Maren?

"Usti, then," the guard insisted.

"Usti from me shit," I replied helpfully in that tongue, looking appropriately chagrined and uncertain.

Maren gestured to me to prove his point, then turned away from the guards and resumed speaking in Aeadine. "Mary Firth. I met your captain in Hesten some time ago and made him a talisman."

This was *Sam's* talisman maker? I fought the urge to stare and tried to express fear for the benefit of the guards.

"We thought you were dead," I whispered.

"Hold your arm out," Maren instructed. "I must take your blood. It is the only way I could arrange to see you."

I had little choice but to comply. My desire to trust this man was strong, unexpectedly so. There was no sorcery around that feeling, though, in a place like this, I could never be certain of that.

"They burned your shop and abducted you?" I clarified. "*Them?*"

Maren set the back of my hand on his knee and fished a vial and a pin out of his bag. "Yes. Do you understand who these people are? The organization? I dare not speak the name, the guards will understand that. The Sheltering Hand. Once servants of a saint."

I nodded. "You're the one making the shot and the talismans, the ones that suppress sorcery?"

"I am not the only one, but I am the best." There was more regret than pride in his voice. He held up the pin. "This will hurt."

I held still as he stabbed my skin. Droplets of blood began to well and he squeezed my finger over the mouth of the vial. Not the most efficient method of blood-letting, I observed, but he seemed more concerned with buying time. In him, I might just have an ally within the Ess Noti.

But what would this blood be used for? Making talismans and shot to be used against *ghiseau* and Stormsingers?

"After the events beyond the Stormwall came to light, many of *them* came to Hesten," Maren explained, his tone empty and measured. "They asked questions, hunted down anyone with suspicious connections. Your captain's visit to my shop came to light, and I was... uncovered."

My stomach turned. This man's predicament was our fault. Had some of our companions from beyond the Stormwall ended up here too? Within these walls?

The brief and no doubt hopeless urge to search the other cells arose in me, though I tried to push it aside. If I made it out of here alone and alive, that would be a miracle. I had no time for daring rescues.

Still, the thought lingered, shifting towards *Hart* and the Uknaras.

"What are you talking about?" a guard demanded in Mereish.

"Her power, its limits, and so forth," Maren bit back. "Do not interrupt me again."

The guard spat on the floor—I frowned at him in disgust—but he fell silent.

I risked asking, "Were there others taken? Other *ghiseau*? Perhaps some recently, from my ship?"

Maren nodded. "A handful of *ghiseau* were brought in at the same time as I. If there have been more, I have not seen them."

"Do you know who they are?"

"No. They have since been… dispersed elsewhere."

"That sounds ominous."

"It is. Mages and *ghiseau*, particularly foreign ones, any who cannot be trusted to use their powers, are instead used for blood and bone and experimentation. And that is very much as dark as it sounds, Ms. Firth."

Crimson droplets trailed down the side of the vial and gathered slowly at the bottom, emphasizing his words.

"So you have not heard of any new *ghiseau*? An Usti couple?"

Maren shook his head and silence stretched.

"I'm sorry this happened to you, because of us," I said quietly, though the weight on my shoulders was not just for him. It was for the nameless *ghiseau*, whether comrades or enemies, who had come with us back over the Stormwall and been snatched away from the lives they tried to reclaim. It was for the Uknaras, wherever they might be.

Maren's smile was stilted and dry. "It was only a matter of time. I knew I walked a blade in Hesten. I spoke too freely, sold too many talismans. But until recently, *these* people, they were mostly just spies and meddlers." He dropped his voice. "Then Faucher took control, bringing his research and his wealth and the support of the king. Now, their advances are world-changing. I went from a loose thread to an asset to be reclaimed."

I lowered my voice, trying to obscure the name from the guard's listening ears. "Is he related to Jessin Faucher?"

Maren emitted a barely perceptible sigh. "He is his father. Which is the only reason why the son is still alive and free, considering his allegiances. He is a Separatist, those who believe the Usti should not hold the power that they do."

My mind flipped back to when we had encountered Jessin, the words he and Sam had exchanged and the papers he had given us. Could Jessin be working against his own father? Outright undermining the Mereish's relationship with Usti?

Too many connections and questions, not enough energy to unravel them.

"Jessin Faucher and the entirety of the Mereish Fleet are gathering in Ostchen," Maren admitted, raising grave eyes to mine.

"This is the Navy's main anchorage... Isn't it normal for them to gather here?"

"I speak of the *fleet* entire, Ms. Firth. Nearly every seaworthy vessel has been launched or recalled, all that can be without raising suspicion. They are preparing to invade Aeadine on next month's Black Tide. Surely you have seen the floodwaters? Next month it will be even greater, and the fleet will sail over the Aeadine Anchorage and straight up the swollen River Whall into Jurry. They will land their army, and Aeadine will be Mereish by the end of the year."

I felt myself pale, my cheeks going cold. I had never seen the Anchorage but knew it to be a long crescent of islets and hidden reefs that acted as a bulwark between Aeadine and Mereish waters. "Aeadine doesn't know about the tides. They won't be prepared for any of this."

"Precisely." Maren corked his vial. "We may see an end to war upon the Winter Sea, Ms. Firth. Only two powers will remain: the Usti, and the Mereish. The Capesh already follow the Mereish lead. Otherwise, they would have no source of ghistings, do you know this?"

I nodded distantly. An end to the war. Those words should have been full of hope, peace and brightness and the cessation of strife. It meant mothers and fathers and children and lovers finally being able to return home.

But not this way. Not with my people downtrodden, our Wolds harvested and our mages reaped.

"We need to warn Aeadine," I said, echoing the sentiments that had driven us down the road to Ostchen with our pockets full of stolen talismans and magecrafted shot.

His gaze flicked up. It was an unguarded moment, round-eyed, shocked, and more than a little uncertain. "We?"

I paused. I'd meant myself and Samuel and Benedict and Charles, *Hart* and the Uknaras, but why not include Maren? He was as much a prisoner as I. Removing him would certainly be a blow to the Ess Noti, and perhaps he could be persuaded to share his knowledge of magecraft with the Aeadine.

"I'm going to escape," I told the Mereish man, infusing my words with confidence. "I can try to take you with me. This manacle they put on me, what does it do?"

Maren blinked rapidly and made a show of cleaning his instruments. "It suppresses your sorcery."

"Does it inhibit connection to the Other?"

"It suppresses your sorcery, so yes?" His brows furrowed, though he did not look up. "That is the same thing."

"I mean in… other ways. Nevermind. Can you take it off?"

"Maybe." He shot me a tight look, still confused by my initial question. It occurred to me, not for the first time, that even the Mereish truly might not know the full extent of a Mother Ghisting *ghiseau's* powers. Or was Otherwalking simply a secret so guarded, even Maren had never learned of it?

Either way, it seemed I still had an advantage.

"Where do you sleep?" I asked.

"In my cell." Maren watched me with guarded eyes, his face angled away from the guards. "Two doors down, on the left."

"Do you know a discreet way out of here?"

He looked momentarily uncertain, then said, "Leave that with me."

I found a jagged smile. "Then I will come for you tonight. Be ready."

THIRTY-EIGHT

The Midwife

SAMUEL

I did not die of blood loss in the hour that Grant and I spent staggering out of the hills, though the impling's claws had turned my forearm to ribbons. Grant, demonstrating an admiral resourcefulness, charmed a wide-eyed midwife into stitching me back together in a little house set high on stilts outside one of the villages that clung to the bay.

"Ostchen is the safest city in the north, they say," the woman said once Grant had finished his dramatic recitation of how he and I, visitors from the Mereish South Isles, had encountered the ravening impling while searching for a view of the sea. "But so many creatures come here. They say that is because of *us*, that we are not careful enough to mark our lintels and ward our gardens."

At this, she gestured flippantly to a symbol carved into the wood of her fireplace. The same one stood over the windows and the door, along with pinned sprigs of what looked like holly.

"But we do. Still, the creatures come. I say..." She tugged the thread still embedded in my flesh, making me wince. Grant, sitting next to me on a narrow settle, leaned forward to meet her, conspiratorially. She happened to be rather pretty and only a few years our senior. "It is because of the ships. So many ghistings and mages. Things from the Other—they seek what is like them, do they not?"

"Is this a new occurrence?" I asked, grateful for the distraction. The sight of her curved needle approaching my splayed flesh again did not help. I looked pointedly past her shoulder to a hanging on the white-painted wall embroidered with Mereish words and a fawn in a meadow.

Around the edges of my vision, the Other still blurred like tears.

The woman nodded. "Yes, this season, since the ships began to return. They say tonight will be the worst for the beasts, as it is the first Black Tide. Not to mention the flooding."

Her words were delivered lightly, but I was deeply affected. Somewhere on the road, I had lost track of the day. Hastily, I ran back the nights in my head and reached inevitable agreement.

Tonight was the first Black Tide, second only to its successor, next month, when all four moons of the Other and the human world united in darkness.

Perhaps, then, the vestiges of the Other lingering around my vision were not wholly due to my corruption or Hae's summoning.

Perhaps.

"Which ships returned?" Grant asked. "The fleet?"

Another nod, though this one was more uncertain. "I have never seen such a thing. Over one hundred warships, the whores say. They row out, every night." She gave a wry smile. "I will have much work this winter."

The entirety of the Mereish Fleet was suspected to be some three hundred warships, spread between the North Isles, the Mereish mainland and the Southern Isles. But there should have been no more than two dozen active vessels in the vicinity of Ostchen at one time, a small percentage stationed while the rest came and went.

If there were a hundred warships near Ostchen, in addition to the other vessels in the harbor, no wonder the lights in the Other were so blinding.

"Done," the midwife said, clipping her last stitch and winding a clean bandage around my arm. She tied it off and patted my knee maternally, then sat back and held out a hand. "Three dettes."

Grant paid her and we left. As the scent of the sea and the prickle of fog replaced the woodsmoke and herb aroma of the house, I nodded Grant back towards the bridge that led to the mainland, though I was too slow to take the lead, lightheaded and still feeling drained.

The tide had swept back to reveal acres of tidal mud, piles of refuse and boulders and posts clung about with sea fauna and mussels.

"We may not have time to find *Hart*," I said. Our boots echoed too loudly on the bridge, wide enough for a cart but with more than a few rotting boards and a rail white with gull droppings. The responsible birds spun overhead, shrieking as the sun neared the western horizon and the sky began to blossom with pink and orange. "Our escaping with word of that fleet is now paramount. The Mereish must be on the cusp of invasion, and with their new magecrafts? We are helpless."

Grant paused to let a man and his clutch of children pass. A trail of day laborers came behind them, grimy and chatting away in a dialect so thick I hardly understood.

"What do we do, then?" Grant asked. "If we cannot find *Hart*… We need a ship."

"We take one." I rubbed the back of my neck with my good hand. "Damn, circumstances could not be worse. Though the darkness of the first Black Tide will certainly be an advantage, if we time our escape properly. Otherwise, we may be stranded longer."

We joined the main road heading back into Ostchen, going against the flow of workers and shoppers returning home. A few curious glances came our way, but the closer we came to the jumbled rise of buildings, docks and little islands, the more ignored we were. I began to note figures in the dark everywhere I looked, down beneath stilt houses and docks. Scavengers, recovering what they could and tapping mussels off the supports of their homes.

"It could get better," Grant pointed out with a wry grin. "There are so many ways it could get better."

A chittering snapped my gaze to the shadows between two barrels, where an impling crouched. Not the one with the collar, but the juvenile I had sent to look for *Hart*.

Hastily I beckoned Grant off the road and behind the barrels. The impling vanished and reappeared, thin talons clacking, and looked up at me with a disturbingly earnest face.

"I have found the stag." The creature's voice was high and frail, somehow both branches scraping in a high wind and the hiss of water through a cracked hull.

Grant made an undignified, choking sound. "It *speaks*?"

I spared him a glance. "Apparently so." I crouched slowly in front of the diminutive monster. "Where is the ship?"

The creature blinked its small, burnt-orange eyes and pointed north. "With the ships."

"Can it be more specific?" Grant asked.

The impling's tiny gaze moved to him and narrowed even further.

Hope ignited in me like oil-soaked tinder. "Please lead us there, but discreetly. Can you do that?"

It nodded eagerly and flickered half out of sight. When it spoke again, its voice was the hushed rasp of sand, falling through open fingers.

"This way."

THIRTY-NINE

The Serpent and the Stars

MARY

By midnight, the halls were quiet. Tane and I waited, poised at my door as the last footsteps of a guard on their rounds faded and silence reigned.

Are you ready? I asked Tane in the quiet of our mind.

In response, a wash of traitorous indigo light rushed down my hands and into the door, which promptly swung open and almost struck me in the face.

Two figures peered inside. Halfway through grabbing a chair to brandish—tottering dubiously as I did—I froze.

"Olsa?" I croaked. My eyes darted between the two. "Illya?"

"Hello, Mary." Olsa gave the room a practical sweep, naked sword in hand. They both looked whole, if tired, Olsa with her blond hair raked into a practical tuft and Illya... well, Illya frequently looked as if he'd just walked out of a storm, so today was no different.

"You are alone?" Olsa asked.

"Yes," I said, perplexed. "What—How did you know I'm here? I asked about you, but..."

Illya lifted the chair from my hands and looked me over. "What happened to you?"

I was reminded I was still in my infirmary shift and a bandage, and, though I was by no means prudish, I was without even stays.

"I was shot in the leg, and they took my clothes."

Illya *tsk*ed and put an arm around me. He doubtless intended only to hold me up, but my frayed nerves sensed an embrace. Before I knew what I was doing, I'd wrapped my arms tightly around his neck. A sob stuck in my throat.

Illya hugged me back, firm and warm, and patted my back with the ease of a veteran father. He, at least, was unbothered by my state of undress.

"Olsa saw you arrive," he explained, putting a more practical arm around my shoulders. "So we decided it was time to make our escape."

"That's fortunate." I squinted between the two of them, still in denial of my tears. "I was just about to leave too."

Olsa smiled, warm but distracted. "I know. But other Sooths may too. We must hurry."

I nodded but held up a hand. "The High Cleric said they could heal Samuel. Can we risk speaking to them? Searching their library?"

"I did try." Olsa gave me a tight, apologetic look. "I knew of Samuel's hope for a cure. We have discussed it many times. I found a book on the topic last week while attempting to recover the papers Jessin Faucher gave us. They were seized when the ship was taken."

"The papers?" I repeated, momentarily at a loss for what she was talking about and why they mattered. "Did you recover them? Where is the book?"

"Not the time for this," Illya broke in.

"The papers were in locked in an office—a very well-guarded one. We nearly escaped with the book on corrupted mages, though. That I found in the library."

"Now the book is gone, you are here, and time is running away," Illya cut in. "Let us *go*."

I grasped at one last hope. "Can we take the Cleric then?"

"That is too great a risk," Olsa said firmly.

The need to protest assailed me, but I knew she was right. Just because the Cleric had been relatively kind did not mean they would come easily, and they seemed to be involved with Enisca.

That left me feeling ill and disheartened, and my strength abandoned me. The importance of Faucher's papers was still vague to me, and our lives, I thought, simpler without them—however much Samuel might disagree.

But Samuel's cure was another matter entirely.

"Then there's no hope for him," I summarized, overwhelmed.

"Only if we are dead," Olsa said.

"Fine," I managed, walling off my fears. "But there's a man two doors down, he *must* come with us. He has a way out."

Olsa hesitated—evidently, she had not foreseen that—but only for a moment. She nodded and we set off, I limping but determined.

A stolen key in the lock of Maren's door and there he was, dressed in coat and hat with a heavy-laden satchel over one shoulder. His eyes went round when he saw my companions, but he joined us without a word.

I held up my wrist and its manacle meaningfully. Maren produced a key and clicked it in, pulling the manacle away from my reddened skin with gentle maneuvering.

My power rushed back in, and I sighed in relief.

"Also, you must take this." Maren held out two talismans on a single fine, golden chain.

"Against Sooth and Magni," the Mereish man explained and reached under his own collar to tug out its mirror image. He glanced at the Uknaras. "I did not expect company, but I will secure you talismans before we leave. Many of the guards are Magni—we must be prepared."

We set off. I was exhilarated, nervous and determined—a heady concoction that only faltered a little as we passed more and more locked doors. Every one of them marked another possible prisoner, another mage like us locked away and awaiting Saint knew what.

If we try to save them all, none of us will escape, Tane reminded me, giving voice to my own pragmatic side.

Samuel would probably try, I remarked, the thought of him compounding my guilt. Furthermore, if our roles were reversed, would he leave without a cure for me in hand?

How fortunate he is not here.

Maren took the lead, guiding us past a spattering of unconscious guards and through a concealed side door.

Two flights of stairs and a circular passage later, Olsa murmured, "There is someone up ahead. A ghisting?"

Maren nodded tightly. "I know, but I must fetch something from that room, including more talismans. Hurry."

Illya made a discontented noise, but Maren was already pushing open one side of a huge set of double doors.

I slowed as we passed inside, gaping at the enormous space. It was hexagonal like the other chambers, but larger and, I sensed, more central. The hub of the wheel.

Raised platforms stood here and there at various heights. Starlight filtered through hundreds of glass panes in the domed ceiling, illuminating our path as we circled the room. It glinted on metal instruments, perched atop the platforms—great spyglasses like the one I had glimpsed at the Oruse. Captured light glinted in the myriad glass scales of a great globe formed of thousands of pieces in an artful cage of wire.

"This is a Dark Observatory," Maren explained, already halfway across the room. I trailed behind, hobbling as he descended on a desk and fumbled a key into a lock. "Where the Ess Noti look into the Other. Those spyglasses are made with ghisten wood, though only the central one has a living ghisting. He is old and slow, but cruel. We must be wary of him."

Olsa and I looked to the spyglass in question. It was enormous, wood braced with brass and silver and perched on a tall tripod. Its body was longer than I was tall, and another small platform stood under one end, for an observer to peer through its narrow sight.

Maren clattered a drawer open and began to grab stacks of sealed documents and loose papers and shoved them into his satchel. Illya, meanwhile, patrolled the periphery of the observatory, passing through patches of milky starlight and murky shadows.

"These are records, calculations and predictions." Maren nudged the drawer closed and opened another.

"And why are we risking our lives for that?" Olsa said.

"Because otherwise the Mereish will become the singular power upon the Winter Sea." Maren pulled the entire drawer out, popped a false bottom, and drew out a collection of talismans, one of which he handed to Illya before he pocketed the rest.

"You do not want that?" Olsa asked. "Your people's supremacy?"

Maren gave a short huff of a laugh. "I left for good reason. Knowledge should not be used to subjugate, so I must share it. Let us go?"

We fell into step again.

"How is a Dark Observatory possible?" I asked, eyeing the great looking glasses again. "Can they truly look into the Other?"

"They can, by way of Sooth's blood and ghisten magic," Maren explained lowly. "Adamus Faucher was considered mad for many years, working in seclusion with remote monasteries, disrespected by the broader world. It only made him more determined. When he took control of the Ess Noti and their resources, he changed Mere overnight."

Maren's voice died in a thin breath. I cast a hasty look over my shoulder as ghisten light swelled, and there, between the great looking glasses, a ghisting materialized.

He watched us with sea-glass eyes in a broad, serpentine face. His body was coiled and scaled and three times taller than Illya, by far the largest manifestation of a ghisting I had ever seen. He sat heaped in the center of the chamber, spectral blue in the filtered light of the stars.

Brother, Tane greeted.

Trespassers, the serpent hissed. Its angular head tilted to one side, matte eyes following our path. *You should not be here.*

"Go." Olsa prodded Maren. "Now."

Maren didn't question her. He preceded us into an alcove and reached for the handle of a door. We hastened after him, crowding in.

A frustrated clatter echoed around the chamber. Maren fumbled with his cache of keys, then dropped them entirely. He crouched, fumbling to locate them in the shadows and glancing fearfully at the serpent ghisting.

Trespassers.

Tane nudged me, taking partial control of my limbs and prompting me to turn.

The serpent had begun to uncoil, his movements utterly silent, but I somehow felt them—through the floor, through the air, like ripples in water. No, there *were* ripples in water, black water that lapped around my ankles and hid the keys from Maren's searching hands. The sound of splashing was muted, distant and distorted, but I heard it as clearly as I heard Olsa's sudden intake of breath and Illya's low curse.

"What is happening?" I whispered. The serpent weaved through the instruments on the platform, delicate despite its massive size, and the eerie pallor of its light filled the room.

Maren cursed and Olsa dropped down to help him search.

The first Black Tide is coming in, Tane replied, her ghisten form beginning to shift across my skin as she prepared to manifest.

The serpent's head dropped down towards the floor—the Dark Water, somehow transposed—and its coils began to follow, lengthening and bunching as it lifted high out of the water and prepared to strike.

Tane stood manifested between us and the looming serpent. A
large feline shape joined her, Olsa's Ris, along with a disembodied
mist—Illya's Noek—which eddied around their feet.

"Can that… can it hurt us?" I hissed to Illya, resisting the urge
to step behind his larger bulk. My inability to run tormented me, and
I eased the weight on my bad leg. "Directly? Physically?"

In response, Illya stepped in front of me.

"Ah!" Maren's victorious gasp snapped my eyes back to the door.

The chamber exploded into sound. Cracks and splintering filled
the air, followed by shrieking whistles shards of wood—shattered
chairs, broken shelves—which sang towards us like canister shot.

Tane flicked one wrist. The first wave of shards went wide, but
another was already shattering, tearing through the air, splintering
desks and tables in the time it took me to inhale.

Ris vanished, joining Noek in a chaotic barrier of swirling ghisten
smoke. Shards fell like rain but more than one broke through,
peppering the stone around us and embedding in flesh.

Illya recoiled, twisting as a shard opened up the side of his face,
slicing through beard and ear. Olsa turned to take the assault from
the side, earning hand-length spears of wood to the hip and thigh.
Maren and I, largely hidden by the pair of them, were less exposed,
but I still nearly took a shard in the calf.

I turned away like Olsa and, out of the corner of my eye, saw
Maren slide a key into the lock on the door. It turned, and the Mereish
man threw his shoulder into the barrier.

It did not move. Ghisten light began to spill from its wood at
the same time as the serpent vanished. Shadows surged, leaving
us in a bubble of light from our own ghistings and the unyielding,
possessed door.

"Mar Oke!" a voice shouted.

We looked back as one to see a small figure stride into the room,
her challenge directed at the place the ghisting had been. The door
glowed more brightly, and other lights began to appear, every shard

of wood, every remaining wooden object in the room taking on an ominous illumination beneath the Dark Water.

I felt the movement of the serpent again, though he remained hidden in the wood.

The newcomer continued speaking, this time in Mereish. With Tane manifest and distracted, I had no translation.

Every glowing piece of wood in the room shuddered, casting rivulets of trembling light and shadow through the ankle-deep water, across us, the walls, even up to the ceiling. The Dark Water vanished and hundreds of fragments of light surged together, re-forming into the serpent in coiled, haughty repose on cool, bare stone. Other than itself only the door remained ignited, locked in place as the four of us faced the ghisting.

Enisca Alamay strode towards us, but spoke to the serpent. "Now," she said in Mereish, finally a word my mind could interpret.

The light faded from the door. Maren immediately darted through and held it open for us.

"Who are you?" Olsa demanded of Enisca.

"Go, quickly," the newcomer urged, ignoring the query. "Through the door."

That was all I needed. I limped painfully through, self-preservation driving me, and Olsa and Illya followed. Enisca, to my surprise, trailed us with one last word to the ghisting, then shut the door at our backs.

Tane, Ris and Noek came last, slipping through the now-abandoned wood of the door and back into our bones. With Tane's return, my thoughts tangled, assaulted with a chorus of new images and thoughts and implications, but my relief outweighed them all. The pain in my leg eased.

"What are you doing?" I asked Enisca in Mereish. When she did not look at me, instead starting up the dark passageway, I grabbed her arm. "Are you *helping* us?"

"I just saved you from the Mar Oke ghisting," the other woman returned, glancing from me to my companions. "I would think that is obvious." With that, her voice changed. She slipped into flawless Usti, her vowels rounding and her posture shifting. She met Olsa's eyes, then Illya's. "I am Enisca Alamay, and I am an Usti spy. If you want to escape, follow me."

I stared from the Uknaras to Maren, who hovered the farthest up the passage, looking as though he were about to abandon us if we didn't move soon.

"An *Usti* spy?" I repeated. Connections began to weave in the back of my mind, threaded memories of Jessin Faucher and his notions about the Usti, along with the thought of the papers he had entrusted to Samuel. Where were those papers now? Had they been seized along with the Uknaras?

"Or do not escape with me," Enisca snapped, brushing past Maren. "Either way, I need to leave Mere. I was hoping to do that with you, but I can find another way without your ship and crew."

Olsa stepped forward. "Do you know where they are?"

The other Usti woman nodded, holding her gaze. "I have even arranged for your crew to be kept in one place, ready to leave. Should they be rescued."

"Good enough for me," Illya grunted, shooing us on and glancing back at the door. I strained my ears and picked up shouting from the other side, distant but growing louder. "Time to run."

FORTY

The Four Faces

SAMUEL

Hart lay at the end of a long, broad dock on the west side of Ostchen. It was inaccessible from the main city, and not just because by the time we arrived, the tide had already begun to swallow large parts of the docks in calf-deep, icy water.

The area was guarded by a high wall and a strong gate, beyond which lay a private shipyard. As Grant and I watched from the shelter of an awning, guards moved into sight on the decks of the ships—all of them fastened to a nearly submerged dock. There was *Hart*, whole and well and facing out to sea, along with a nondescript galley with her rigging completely disassembled.

The question of whether or not my crew remained aboard *Hart* was quickly answered. A chorus of singing drifted up from the gratings in emphatic Aeadine. The guards, roused, stormed over to the grating and hammered. The crew sang louder.

I felt a hand on my shoulder and looked over to see Grant watching me with a broad grin.

"See, so many things can go well," he said.

"Since when are you the company optimist?" I replied, glancing at the sky. The sun had long since vanished over the western mountain now, and darkness was nearly complete. The tide would soon be at its highest.

Grant blew out his cheeks and gave a half shrug. "The post was vacant, I suppose. Should we make for the cathedral?"

"I will," I decided. "Please remain here and keep watch, mark if and when the guards change, and if anyone is allowed through that gate."

Grant saluted with a dandy's flick of the fingers. "Aye, aye, sir."

∞

The open square before the Cathedral of the Four Faces was packed despite the late hour. A small army of monks, priests and priestesses from various orders moved through a crowd thick with wagons, children, and livestock—refugees, fleeing the Black Tides. Families slept under their wagons or rough awnings, several dozen braziers burned and soldiers lingered on the periphery, watching the crowd with equal parts pity and wariness.

I wandered the edge of the crush as the bells clanged a merry midnight chorus, then a half hour passed. Faces were nearly impossible to discern, mottled with light and shadow. But the Other still lingered at the corners of my vision, pocked with magelights. If Mary was here and had taken off her talisman, there was a chance I would be close enough to see her without stepping fully into the Other.

"Samuel," a female voice called.

I turned to see not Mary, but Olsa Uknara. She left the brazier where she had been warming her hands and disappeared down a flight of stairs, into an alleyway.

Startled and in need of answers, I followed her down a stair and two streets into the flooding region of the city. Olsa did not speak the entire time, leading me in silence through rising, frigid water. Unidentifiable objects drifted past us, and the chill of the night failed to curb the stink of brine and stewing human refuse. But the floodwater meant we were relatively alone—an old man passed with a child on his shoulders and a raft on a rope, two lanky youths carried crates on their shoulders, and that was all.

Finally, Olsa climbed a set of stairs clinging to a warehouse near the central docks. I splashed up after her, my anticipation rising.

Four figures waited inside, in the light of an oil lamp. My eyes were inexorably drawn to Mary, her face pale in the warm light. She looked haggard, her hair falling in tangles from her braid and her body wrapped in a boat cloak.

Before I was fully through the door, she reached for me. I crossed the intervening space in two strides and folded her into my arms, loosening only when she made a soft sound of pain.

I pulled back and looked down at her, discovering she wore only a shift underneath the cloak. She held her thigh, visibly thick with bandages, and offered me a tense smile.

"Not your fault," she soothed. "I was shot. Do not stop hugging me."

I obeyed but asked over her head, looking at the others for explanation. "What happened?"

"Very little." Illya offered me a distracted wave and a crooked but not altogether humorous smile as he fell into conference with his wife.

"A great deal, rather." Closer to the back of the room, a face I thought I would never see again smiled and half-bowed in greeting.

"Mr. Maren," I said, stunned into incredulity. Questions of how he was here stalled on my tongue as I recognized the last person in the room.

I stepped away from Mary to reach for my pistol. "Why is she here?"

Enisca Alamay stood by the window, positioned to watch both the street and the door. Her expression was wary but she made no move towards the long musket leaning against the casement.

"She saved our lives," Mary said hastily. "She's an Usti spy, Sam. Inside the Ess Noti. She knows where *Hart* is and arranged for the crew to be held there together. In exchange for taking her with us when we leave."

Mr. Maren nodded, putting out an earnest hand between us. "She has been helping me for months, and she ensured we had a clear path to escape tonight."

"Escape?" I repeated, reeling. "From the Ess Noti? Where is Ben?"

"I was captured by the Ess Noti," Mary explained. "But Ben escaped earlier."

"Then where is he?"

Mary shook her head. "I don't know. He said he would try to meet up with me at *Hart*, but we never had a chance to look."

"Fuck," I muttered.

Illya gestured at me emphatically. "This is also what I said."

"Perhaps he has already found your ship," Alamay interrupted us. "You can join him after you give me a moment of your attention, Captain Rosser. I *was* an Usti spy inside the Ess Noti. Now, I am an Usti spy in need of a way out of Ostchen. I know you will not be inclined to trust me, but I have saved the lives of your companions, taken care of your crew, and I have something else for you as payment for my passage. Mr. Maren informed me of your quest."

I grew very, very still. I felt Mary's eyes on the side of my face, glimpsed the hope in her expression, but could not take my eyes from Alamay.

"What is that?" I prompted.

"I know how to cure you and your brother." Alamay's words were low and level, but seemed to reach every corner of the room. "I do not possess all the skills to execute the cure, but Mr. Maren does, and I have shared what I know with him."

"How?" The word cracked, a lifetime of dread and anxiety cresting around me. The blurred edges of the Other crept a little deeper into my vision, and my head began to ache.

I reached for Mary's hand. She fastened both her hands around mine, anchoring me without a word.

"How can it be done?"

Mr. Maren began to explain earnestly. "At the height of the second Black Tide, the barrier between the human world and the Other will be at its thinnest."

"The first Black Tide is tonight," Mary leapt in, her hope as fierce and sudden as my own. "Can we not use it?"

"It will not suffice." Mr. Maren shook his head, shattering the pair of us in four words. "The barrier is thinner, yes, but not enough for—"

He cut himself off as Alamay cast him a reprimanding look.

"At the right time, with the help of various… items, which I must make," he went on, somewhat more cagily, "both you and your twin can physically traverse the barrier between worlds. There, your bond to the Other—that which supplies your power—can be healed. It will take moments, I believe."

There was more than one way of Otherwalking, it seemed.

"Mr. Maren does not know what those items are yet, precisely," Enisca cut in. "So do not think to abandon me in favor of him. I come, or you go mad and your brother becomes a monster."

"Where did you find this information?" I demanded. A part of me was already rampant with elation, hope fizzling through my veins like sparks up long matches. "How do you know it is true?"

Alamay's patience with me was clearly wearing thin. She forced another of her small, tight smiles. "I am—was—close with the Ess Noti's High Cleric."

"Very close," Mr. Maren added. Alamay glared at him again and this time he looked away, his eyebrows high and a hint of a sad smile on his lips.

"The Ess Noti are a blight upon the world, and Cleric Ines is as much a victim as any of you. Only they fight from within, while we turn tail and run." Alamay exhaled a long, steadying breath. "Now, if you are satisfied, we do not have much time."

Mary's eyes flicked behind me, brows drawing together. "Where's Charles?"

I scrutinized Alamay a moment longer, weighing her words. "Mr. Grant is keeping watch on *Hart*. We located him earlier this evening."

Speaking the words aloud reset something inside of me, and I began to move past the last moments and their revelations, on to what needed to happen next.

Return to Grant. Reclaim *Hart*.

Find Ben.

In these clean-cut objectives, I found relief.

"Then Charles and Benedict may already have reunited," Mary said. "If Ben never came to the cathedral."

"Right," I said, gathering myself. "We make for *Hart*. Our priority is releasing him and the crew—if Ben has not arrived by then, I will go into the Other to search for him."

I expected a protest at the last, but my assertion was met only with silence and weighty looks.

At length, Alamay said, "There is a possibility that my betrayal has been revealed by now, though I believe my credentials will still get us onto the ship. Sailing out of the harbor will be another matter, even if the tide is with us. The entire fleet is in that fog."

"It will be treacherous," I affirmed.

"I can manage the fog," Mary said, to which Olsa nodded in agreement. "A distraction would be useful, though."

My mind drifted to the implings on the hill and the words of the midwife.

I straightened, feeling steadier and more confident than I had in weeks. "Leave that to me."

Enisca Alamay approached the gates to the small, private shipyard where *Hart* was moored. We watched from the shadows of an alleyway—Grant, Mary, the Uknaras, Mr. Maren, and I, all silent and still with weapons at the ready.

Alamay looked small before the closed gates, knee-deep in floodwaters with her hands shoved into her pockets. She removed one hand to tug a bell rope, then waited, growing visibly impatient.

"We could swim around," Mary whispered to me.

"It may soon come to that," I replied, though burdened by sodden clothes, damp powder and frozen muscles was not the way I wanted to enter any fight. "But Benedict has still not arrived. Let us wait a little longer."

Even as I spoke, my gaze traveled inexorably down the docks, searching for a tall, dark figure.

Instead, I saw a lantern swing into sight and a group of figures turn our way from another street. I had the coin pressed back to my skin, sacrificing presentience to a few more moments without Hae's watchful eyes, but I recognized the way they moved—urgent but contained, coordinated and watchful.

"Soldiers," I warned, motioning everyone back. They complied but I waited another moment, watching to ensure Alamay had marked the soldiers too.

Sure enough the Usti spy turned, glanced at the light, and promptly left the gate. She exited my line of sight, heading up another road with water sloshing behind her.

By the time she reappeared, materializing next to Grant farther down our alley—to his shock and a fumbled, whispered, "Well, hello,"—the soldiers were paces away. They moved more cautiously now, eyes scanning the night. I pressed myself back into a damp wall as the ripples of their passage invaded our alleyway.

The soldiers arrived at the gates that, after a breath, groaned open. Two more soldiers waited on the other side, and they began a hurried exchange.

"Now we move," Illya said, crouching next to me.

The soldiers, however, were no fools—the gate was already closing, barring a now-swelled number of enemies inside the shipyard,

while half a dozen broke off at a sloshing sprint in the direction
Alamay had gone.

That was when Benedict separated from the night. He walked
directly down the quayside towards the gate, black seawater tugging
back the hem of his long coat. He strode directly past us, casting us
not a glance.

"Ben," I started to hiss.

My twin either did not hear or ignored me. His focus was on the
gate and the soldiers who had just departed.

Bloody, bruised red slipped into the corners of my vision.
Screams and gunshots erupted from somewhere nearby, then silence
blossomed.

In that tense, horrified hush, one side of the gate creaked
open again. A single guard stumbled out, clutching at her chest.
She collapsed into the floodwaters—a wash of colorless ripples
swallowed her and she did not rise again.

"The Black Tide," Alamay's voice murmured, replying to a
question from Grant that I had not heard. "All mages are stronger
tonight."

Ben turned to look back at us, his black-rimmed eyes white in
the shadows. "Are you coming?"

By the time we followed my twin into the shipyard, the remainder
of the guards were either dead or in hiding. Ben preceded us, striding
to the end of a long, partially submerged dock where *Hart* lay.

I strode after him, Mary's low whistling haunting my steps. A fog
had already begun to roll in, shrouding us from sight.

"Your timing is impeccable," Ben said, waiting for me beside
Hart's placid bulk. Half the buttons on his coat had torn off and
he was soaked, his eyes reddened with sweat and seawater and
their dark rim of sailor's kohl bleeding down his cheeks. The
blade of the saber in his left hand was clean, pebbled with droplets
of water, but there was blood on his knuckles and caked around
his nails.

Whatever qualms I harbored towards my brother's actions and sinister appearance, they silenced as I climbed aboard *Hart*. The ship's namesake ghisting swirled through the wood beneath our feet in restrained welcome, and, as my officers began to climb through newly unlocked hatches, a grin split my face.

"Mr. Penn," I greeted, grasping the man's forearm. Fog swirled past us, and Mary's whistling transitioned into a low, humming song.

His grin was equally as broad, and there was a gleam in his eyes. "Captain Rosser, knew I'd be seein' you about some time soon."

I clasped his forearm a little tighter, then released him. "Ms. Skarrow and Mr. Keo?"

"All worse for wear, but present and accounted for," Ms. Skarrow herself replied, joining us and tugging her fringe. "Shall we make him ready, Captain?"

"Yes, very good. We will leave the harbor as soon as possible and make for the Aeadine Anchorage," I replied, easing back into my role like muscles in warm water. I leaned over the hatchway and saw the remainder of the crew arrayed below, peering up and beset by ripples of barely contained cheers. I saw Willoughby among them, his arm around a weary-looking Poverly. But they were all well.

"You will all be up and free very soon," I promised, raising my voice just enough to carry.

A few ragged cheers broke forth, to which I saluted and withdrew. Ms. Skarrow and Mr. Penn had already scattered, joining a dozen of the best hands in preparing the vessel for departure.

Mr. Keo remained, watching me with his chin raised and eyes expectant.

"Mr. Keo. Ms. Firth shall see to our cover and Ms. Uknara our course out of the harbor. I shall need to step into the Other. You have the deck until I return."

"Yessir." Keo saluted. His wide-set, hooded eyes were subdued, and his smile less wild than Mr. Penn's had been. "It is good to have you back, Captain. I see you have what we came for?"

Benedict strode by just then, heading through the companionway and calling, "Sam, you need to hire a surgeon."

"Yes," I said, my own smile tightening. "I suppose we do."

Getting the ship underway was no easy feat, but it was conducted with haste and discretion in record time. Mary and Olsa took position by the wheel as the former began to truly sing, drawing the perpetual fog down the bay to meet her existing, subtler miasma. Another wind stirred our sails alone, propelling us away from the docks with a care and delicacy Mary had rarely exhibited before.

With *Hart*'s ghisten light rippling through the deck beneath our feet, we passed ships of every size and stoically bore the occasional curious watchman. We passed sleeping outer villages with their stilts and bridges, some completely flooded, others barely above the high waters, and entered an open stretch between the last settlements and the lofty outlook of the fort.

I joined Mary and Olsa, whereupon I finally pried the coin from my flesh and dropped wholly into the Other.

Olsa was there in that second realm, inhabiting the edge between worlds—guiding our ship through the fog with careful commands to the helmsman. I noted her glow, then passed deeper into that realm.

As the midwife had said, the Otherborn creatures around Ostchen were countless. Their glows swelled from dim reflections in the corners of my vision to a chaos of clashing, blinding lights. They shone off the Dark Water, through the water, turning it everything *but* dark. The Other was color that night, vivid and assaulting. Even the lines of ghisten ships faded in the force of their illumination, and, for a moment, I was forced to close my eyes.

When I opened them again the lights were no less overwhelming, but my focus was steadier.

And so I began to call. I called the white lights and the orange ones, the bruised purple and the muddy yellow, the gold and the rarest, most subtle pulses of dusty, dark rose. Some were indifferent to my summons. Others were aggressive, outwardly resisting me.

The rest came in droves.

Thus it was that we left Ostchen in an unearthly cacophony of muffled screams, bells, gunshots and crashing water. Here and there as the fog eddied, I saw my beasts at their tasks. A familiar dittama dove beneath the waves and remerged beside an anchored ship, shrieking. An enormous octopus with the head of a budding flower clamped onto one of the fort's cannon batteries, its legs a whirl of water and sickly orange light. A huden charged across waves lit by the blinding white of a morgory swarm, swirling around a clutch of ships whose ghistings stood manifest, warding the creatures away from their hulls. A sleek creature between a shark and a serpent with shuddering, thundering wings reared up to the height of a foremast before it crashed back down in a scattering of smaller, lesser creatures.

The Otherborn were not the only lights to be seen, however—either in the Dark Water or the waking world or the mire between where I existed. The lights of Sooths, Magni, and Stormsingers were cast throughout, defending their vessels, turning the winds, clearing the fog. Each and every one was brighter than I had ever seen before.

These became stronger as we passed the mouth of the bay and the full Mereish Fleet came into sight. They were a forest of masts to all sides, every one of them lit with ghisten glow. Just when I thought I could discern the edge of the fleet, I saw another mast, the bulk of another hull, the glint of more magelight. Ghistings manifested throughout, driving back creatures as Sooths—many of them Summoners—worked from the decks of their ships.

A hand closed on my wrist and, distantly, I felt the press of the coin into my flesh. Mary's voice came to me, joining my will to draw me back to myself. The clash of lights faded, though not entirely—so many creatures had come through the boundary between worlds, and my sense of the Other could not be wholly stifled, not tonight. It was disorienting, more than a little nauseating—but, more than that, it was exhilarating. My blood surged hot through my veins, and I felt my power everywhere around us, swirling and billowing like the cool damp of the fog across my cheeks.

"We're nearly through," Mary murmured. She stood close, her hands still cupping mine, holding the coin to my palm. She nodded out to the fog-wrapped fleet, but my eyes, I found, refused to leave her face.

When my gaze was full of her, the heady rush of my power relented, the lights faded that much more, and I felt a little more at rest in my bones. She anchored me with the cool touch of her hands, her nearness, and the sound of her voice.

She returned my stare quizzically. I folded my other hand over hers, and we held one another there, suspended, as the fog billowed and the fleet and all its monsters faded back into obscurity.

The open sea was before us and we changed course, heading for home.

Heading for war.

FORTY-ONE

Truth

MARY

I had never been more grateful to step into the close confines of my cabin. I leaned against the closed door, letting the feeling of watching eyes slip away, and shedding weeks of anxiety with each breath.

The scent of the room came to me—a mix of stuffy shipboard odors mixed with beeswax from my candle lantern and the lavender I hung from the beams. My small table remained pushed against the wall as a desk, while my chair was hooked to the bulkhead to keep it from overturning in heavy swells.

I went over to one of my trunks and opened it. It had clearly been rifled through in my absence, but much of my clothing remained intact, and my hammock still lay bundled to one side.

I busied myself stringing my bed from the beams, then dug out a change of clothes. But I had not counted days' worth of stress sweat and grime on my body, and the idea of subjecting a clean shift to my skin was untenable.

I went to the galley and requested a bucket of hot water, then wandered to Sam's cabin door while I waited for it to heat.

"Come in."

I opened the door slowly, expecting to find Ben there too, but to my surprise Sam was alone. He sat next to the stove in his breeches, shirtless and barefoot. He looked clean, and his damp hair was combed back from his forehead.

"What is it?" he asked, catching my gaze. "It makes me nervous when you smile like that. I feel as though I am about to be mocked."

"You look like a country boy," I said, closing the door and crossing the room. We hadn't been alone together since the hallway in the river town—I left two paces between us.

"Ah." He looked down at himself, unabashed. He was less tense than I expected him to be, though I could see the weight of the last few weeks in his posture. "Mary?"

"Yes?"

"What am I to do?"

The rawness of his question made my heart flip. I snagged a chair and pulled it in front of him. "I'm afraid we are beset on every side, Sam. You must be more specific."

"Regarding Ben."

"Ah." I sat, waiting for him to go on.

He took my hand and rested it on his thigh. His thumb began a distracted sweep over the back of my fingers, and I shifted a little closer.

"We have escaped, yes, but Benedict's future is ruined. The Admiralty, if not all polite society, knows Ben was Ms. Irving's lover, not me. Now that we are bound for the Anchorage... I am forced to consider what the ramifications of that might be. Within a week Ben and I will be forced to present ourselves to the Admiral of the South Fleet. Given the news we bring, of the fleet and Mereish magecrafts, she will likely offer me—*Hart*—a commission. Perhaps temporary. Perhaps not."

"We are under contract to the Usti," I pointed out warily. The thought of Samuel returning to the Navy filled me with dread and raised questions about my future I was too tired to wrestle with.

"The need for ships to face the Mereish will be overwhelming," he went on. "They will not let *Hart* sail away in such times. And could we truly leave? Knowing how great a threat the Mereish Fleet is?"

"I might."

He gave a grudging half-smile. We both knew his principles would not permit him to leave, even if I did not feel so bound.

"I will be pressured, regardless," Sam said.

"What if they offer you a permanent commission?"

The stroking of his thumb slowed. A tightness crept around his eyes, and his gaze passed through me, through the deck.

I laid my free hand atop his. "Sam."

He seemed to come back to himself. "I am tempted."

He looked at me then, wholly looked at me, and the world shrank around us. Gone was the rush of waves against the hull, the creak of timber, and the grate and clack and rumble of the vessel's constant maintenance. All yielded to this singular moment—Sam and I and the uncertainty of what he would say next.

"But your contract remains with the Usti. They are your protection."

For a moment I couldn't find anything to say, then I managed, "If you decide to retake your commission, I would go south and join my mother and Demery."

"You would not find a new ship?" He seemed wary. I wondered precisely what had provoked him—the idea of me not wanting any other captain, or the reality that the small progress he and I had made for the good of my kind would quickly fade from memory.

I shrugged, forcing more nonchalance than I felt. "Who would I trust? But please, Sam, feel no obligation towards me. I have other prospects."

"There is no obligation. Though I intend to stay by you, if you will allow me to." A small smile touched the corner of his mouth, though sadness tugged about his eyes. "Aside from my affection for you, there are other complications. Ben, for one. I took the fall for his crime because I knew his discharge from the Navy would destroy him. That remains true."

He kept speaking but my attention had come to a sudden, jarring halt. *I intend stay by you.* How could he say that and continue speaking of other things?

I frowned at him.

"Ben is a villain, his reputation destroyed. He will be pushed even farther into the darkness. Yet we now have a cure—or so Ms. Alamay claims. And he will not use it," Sam continued, oblivious to my irritation. "Do I force him, then, to be healed? Must I trick him? If I do not, I am as good as abandoning him, and all the sacrifices I have made will be for nothing."

I do intend to keep you.

I forced my mind forward. "Yes, we trick him, lie to him, force him if need be. You have given everything for him, including nearly all our lives."

Guilt cluttered his expression.

"He lost the ability to make the right choice a long time ago," I stated, holding his fingers tighter than necessary, though Samuel seemed unbothered. "So make the choice for him. That is not so uncommon for the pair of you, is it?"

"No," he affirmed. "It is not."

"Then it's settled," I summarized, slipping farther forward on my chair. Our knees touched. "You will stop worrying, and I will help you trap Ben for his own good. And for your own good, I will now distract you."

Sam abruptly met my gaze. Emotions flickered through his eyes—a ghost of promised happiness. Then they were chased away by a familiar hesitation.

My stomach sank.

"Don't do that," I warned. "Don't close yourself off now."

All of a sudden both his hands cupped my head, pulling me in for a long, slow kiss. His wind-dry lips were rough against mine, but warm and needy. My head felt light and I leaned forward, but that was not close enough.

I jerked up my skirts carelessly, straddling him with a clatter of my chair and deepening the kiss. He let me grasp his face in turn and tilt his head back.

His hands fell lower, flexing on the curve of my waist and slipping their way under my skirts. Distantly, I felt Tane's presence leave, slipping away through the wood of the ship to keep watch outside the cabin door.

"I did not hesitate… about this. About you." He fumbled for words. I'd freed his mouth, using my own to plant a row of kisses and nibbles down the side of his throat. His fingers skimmed across the bare flesh of my thighs. "I was only thinking of… Saint, you are not wearing trousers. Mary. Why are you not wearing trousers?"

"I intended to bathe, but you distracted me."

"It is still quite cold."

"I'm quite warm."

His hands paused, and he cracked his eyes open. "Would you marry me, if I asked? We have had over a year in one another's company. We have seen one another at our worst and our best, and my affection for you has only grown, even against my own will."

I sat back, scowling. "Repeat that, slowly."

He grimaced. "What I mean is… what I feel for you is not something I can turn away from, even if I wanted to, which I wholeheartedly do not. Many marriages are built upon much less. I would give you security, and our relationship—as Captain and Stormsinger—legitimacy."

His hands slipped and settled higher, nails grazing my backside.

I suppressed a shiver. "Must we discuss this now? Or can I simply lock the cabin door and make love to you?"

He visibly fought himself, and gravity gradually replaced the want in his eyes. His hands moved again, gentling, and he rested them on the outside of my knees. I took a deep breath, waiting for the bough to break.

"There is nothing on these seas I would not do for you, Mary Firth," he said at length. "And so I will not risk you. Aside from our stations—"

"Our stations should not matter."

"*Aside* from them," he emphasized, "I will not risk taking more of you, getting a child on you, when I have given you no assurances. When I *can* give you no assurances—neither of myself, of my sanity and wholeness, nor of our future."

He faltered as I ran my thumbs over his bottom lip. "I would happily risk that," I murmured, not carelessly, not laughingly, but as solemnly as he looked at me now. "But I also will not ask you for more than you are willing to give."

Silently, he rested his head on my chest, and I my chin atop his head, and we simply... breathed. After an indefinable length of time I lifted his head away and sat back, dropping my hands to his chest to feel his heart, now slowed.

"Give me a little more time," he murmured into my hair, and kissed my head softly.

"All right. Just a little."

Tane slipped a warning through our connection just before a knock sounded at the door. Reluctantly I got up and rearranged my skirts as Samuel raked back his hair and, standing, reached for his shirt.

"Yes?" he called as he stuffed the shirt into his breeches.

"We need to speak." Olsa's voice came through the wood. "If you two are finished."

"Sooths," I muttered, brushing at my swollen lips, and opened the door.

Olsa entered with a coffee service, arranged with Willoughby's usual care, and placed it on the table. She poured us each a cup and ensured we had taken them and sat before she spoke again.

Tane wandered back into the cabin and rejoined with me.

"The papers Jessin Faucher gave us were seized when *Hart* was captured," she said without preamble. I had forgotten this in the wake of our escape, and I sipped my coffee slowly as I waited for Samuel to react.

Samuel loosely held his own cup on the table before him, the liquid gently sloshing with the movement of the ship. "You are sure?"

Olsa nodded. "I believe the Ess Noti were seeking them in particular. It was not our presence in Mere that resulted in *Hart*'s capture, nor the prison break—they occurred simultaneously, and. at first, our captors believed Illya to be captain and I his Sooth. They believed *Hart* to be its false name, *Macholka*, until they realized Illya and I are *ghiseau* and Benedict's escape came to light."

"The Ess Noti must have learned that Captain Faucher gave the documents to us," Samuel concluded. "And came to reclaim them."

"Jessin Faucher is the son of Adamus Faucher, head of the Ess Noti, and his father has been trying to protect his son from himself," I put in. "I doubt Jessin is unwatched. Spies among his crew?"

They both looked at me, Samuel clearly intrigued by this information and Olsa deep in thought.

"Mr. Maren may know more," I suggested.

"Enisca certainly would," Olsa added. "However, she has hardly left her cabin and will not speak to me. I doubt we will find any answers with her."

"But," I cut in quickly, "given the tide, the invasion, what we've learned about Mereish magecraft… Does any of it truly matter to us?"

"It matters if we are serving a nation that covertly perpetuates war on the Winter Sea," Samuel said. All remnants of our earlier encounter had faded from his expression and posture, and he was wholly captain now, Samuel Rosser, honor-bound and detached. "The same war that stole your mother from you and that is currently driving the Mereish Fleet to our shores. I will not be party to that."

Conviction and embarrassment collided inside me. "My mother is no longer involved, and neither must we be. The papers are gone. Whatever Jessin tried to pull us into is no longer our problem."

"Ms. Alamay—" Samuel began.

"Is an Usti *spy*," I returned. "Why would she tell us anything? Or do you plan to interrogate her? Unleash Ben on her?"

"I would not do that."

"Then you will get nothing from her," Olsa concluded. She blew calmly across the surface of her coffee, sending a swirl of steam over the table between Sam and I.

It occurred to me to wonder precisely how she and Illya felt about all this as Usti themselves, but she did not seem inclined to share.

Samuel looked as though he wanted to counter us, but took a deep breath instead and dropped his chin in something not quite a nod. "For the moment, I will concede. There is little we can do but speculate without the documents themselves, and more immediate concerns beset us. So, for now, we must put this aside. Ms. Alamay intends to remain with us for the time being?"

Olsa nodded. "Or so she says."

"Then an opportunity remains. However," Samuel went on, "I do not consider the matter closed. If our resident spy has information and decides to share, or Jessin Faucher and *The Red Tempest* cross our paths again, I will not let the opportunity to learn the truth pass me by."

FORTY-TWO

Admiral Rosser

SAMUEL

*H*art drifted into the channel south of Renown, the foremost settlement of the Aeadine Anchorage. A long arc of islands directly between Aeadine and Mere, the Anchorage had been contested since before clans became nations and the advent of gunpowder. The islands were scattered with ruined castles and fortifications from every era, and not a few visible shipwrecks on the treacherous outer reefs—left as warning to Mereish aggressors.

Three fortresses, however, stood whole. Fort Renown dominated its namesake town with seven-pointed walls, each bastion armed with a battery of long guns. Identical fortresses could be glimpsed to the north and south extremes of the chain, irregular blocks on the horizon.

Walls laced strategic points in between, and two smaller batteries guarded the only ingress to Renown Harbor from the west. A great chain was suspended between these pentagonal bastions, the sullied glisten of barnacle-crusted steel glinting between the waves.

"A salute, Ms. Skarrow," I instructed as we made our approach. The shadows of the sails shifted, letting a beam of sunlight into my eyes. "And see our colors run up."

"Aye, sir."

As she strode away I removed my hat, just for a moment, to catch more of the sun. Warmth seeped into my wind-chilled skin, and shadows of sailors flitted across the smooth planks of the deck.

Mary situated herself beside me, and, for a moment, we stood quietly. I closed my eyes again, half to retrieve the peace of the sunlight and half to better consider the memory of her long legs cinched around my hips.

"We are doing the right thing," she told me, and my imaginings tempered as I recognized her anxiety. "I have my papers—the Navy cannot press me. I have Tane."

"And you have me," I reminded her.

She smiled and surveyed the towers ahead, but the smile was not as wholehearted as I wished.

Clearing my throat, I fit my tricorn back in place. With it my responsibilities washed back over me, but they were ballast instead of a burden.

Ms. Skarrow topped the forecastle stairs. "At your pleasure, Cap'n."

I gave a nod.

Skarrow turned and called calmly amidships, "Touch match!"

A single gun boomed out, a sound that reverberated down the quiet line of the islands.

I expected to meet with a challenge, to be left at anchor and signaled to send a longboat ashore. But mere minutes after our salute, a bone-deep rumble filled the air. The chain at the mouth of the harbor began to sink, and the eastern tower raised a welcoming flag.

Hart manifested as the ship crept across the chain. The massive spectral beast strode across the waves ahead of the vessel, guiding him into the calm, sheltered waters of Renown. The watchtowers fell away, a grating moan signaled the chain was being raised back into position, and Fort Renown filled our sight.

Four flags flew high from the central keep. One was the Aeadine flag with its bloody crown, the second the golden pennant of the South Fleet and another the flag of the Anchorage itself: a castle on an island, nestled between two uncradled cannons.

It was the last flag, however, that demanded my attention: a pennant of deep indigo. I turned sharply, surveying the ships in the harbor.

The massive first-rater *Triumph* lay at anchor among half a dozen other vessels, sails furled to leave only her colors to the wind: the war-pennant of the Aeadine North Fleet. The colors of Admiral John Rosser Howe, my uncle and the man who had rescued Ben and I from the Black Tide, twenty years ago.

Triumph had still been ashore last time I saw her, at the naval docks in Ismoathe. Her wooden ribs were now clad and painted a pristine white with bold blue gunports and rails. Her name was painted in equally regal blue across her stern, just facing us, and outlined with golden gilt. The glass of her stern windows was so fine and clear that I could see movement within. I could almost imagine my uncle at his desk, cool sunlight pouring across his ledgers and charts. But he would likely be at the fort.

"What ill fortune." Ben drew up to my other side and blew out his cheeks with childish displeasure.

"Is that Captain Irving's ship?" Mary asked, voice low with concern.

"No," Ben answered before I could. "Our uncle's, Admiral Rosser." His eyes slid to me. "When was the last time you spoke?"

"When I forfeited my commission." I could not pry my gaze from the massive vessel. Insecurities flickered through me, not least shame at the state of *Hart*. We had retitled him and begun to repaint his hull during the voyage, eager not to be blown apart by our own ships, but the task was not complete.

The admiral knows now. He knows it was not you with Ms. Irving, a voice whispered in the back of my mind—a calloused, selfish version of myself. It was Ben who would receive the full force of our uncle's censure, not I.

And from the shadows in my brother's eyes, he knew it too.

∞

Admiral Rosser had aged little in the years since I had last seen him. The bloodline that had given Ben and I our strong jawlines had perhaps overextended with him, giving his clean-shaven profile the look of a spade. His head, I knew, was bald beneath a fine chestnut wig, scented with citrus, and his gold-buttoned, deep-indigo frock with its thick black collar and glistening pips carried the perpetual musk of cologne and cigars. His eyes were broad-set and dark-lashed, tempering the overall strength of his features and hinting at a subtle insight.

He surveyed us for a long moment as we entered the small, oak-paneled study, evidently making up his mind about something. Finally, once the door was closed, he shook his head. "My instinct is still to call you boys and offer you toffee. Sit, Captains Rosser."

For an opening salvo, that was much kinder than I had anticipated.

Ben gestured for me to take the only chair on the other side of the admiral's desk and pulled up a second, heavily upholstered with flourishes and waves for himself. It clattered a little too much, and Admiral Rosser's eyebrow crooked.

"Uncle," Ben said, sitting.

"Admiral," I intoned, giving a small bow before seating myself.

"Let me make several observations." Admiral Rosser laced his fingers together on the desk. "Last I heard, you, Benedict, had been drowned off the coast of Mere. And you, Samuel, had sailed south into Mereish waters in pursuit of a pirate on behalf of the Usti Crown. Am I to now understand that you… happened across one another, during that unsanctioned and entirely foolhardy venture?"

"Matters are a great deal more complex," I admitted. I had planned this conversation a dozen times since I saw the admiral's flag over the fort, but my chosen words suddenly felt inane. I had expected to begin with Ben and his downfall, not less personal matters. "The Usti remain a neutral party, Admiral, as I know you are well aware, and so my venture into Mereish waters is no concern of the Aeadine."

"Ah, yet *you* know how these matters are perceived," the admiral parried. "You are Aeadine, a former officer. Papers. Politics. Perception. Your ties to me. You have antagonized our greatest enemies in a time of active war, not to mention one of chaos—I speak of the high tides, which have been ravaging our coastlines. Many of the outer islands are submerged, did you note that? And four moons have been seen in the sky. Not only by Sooths, either."

"Yes, sir." I forged ahead, keeping my voice and expression relaxed. "And I have much to say on the matter. But as to how Ben and I came together, during my pursuit of the pirate I sensed my brother's presence and was able to rescue him. In the course of that venture, we uncovered many things, all of the utmost importance."

Ben picked up the narrative, briefly outlining the Mereish's advances in magecraft and the suppressive efforts of the Ess Noti. Then I spoke up again, revealing the reality of the Mereish Fleet's invasion and the upcoming Black Tides.

I did not, however, speak of Maren or Ms. Alamay. Ms. Alamay I had decided not to reveal of my own accord—another step, I hoped, towards earning her trust. But the Mereish man had come to me the night before we reached Renown and beseeched me not to reveal his presence aboard my ship, nor his skills for the time being.

"I would be prisoner again, this time of your people rather than mine," Mr. Maren had pointed out, and I could not contradict him.

He had, however, sent me with a stack of notes regarding his trade.

"Here is all we learned," I said, withdrawing the packet and sliding them across the desk. "However, I still have more to tell you."

My uncle raised his brows. "You have just informed me that we are on the brink of invasion and half the coastal villages will be swept away within a month. How can there be more?"

"Mereish Separatists claim that the Usti have been manipulating both the Mere and the Aeadine into continued conflict, thwarting attempts at peace, fabricating inciting incidents, and so forth. I cannot say whether I believe their claims. But they must be aired, regardless."

My uncle let out a long sigh and opened a desk drawer. He pulled out a cigar case and tossed it, open, on the desk with uncharacteristic carelessness.

"There have always been such claims," he said as he clipped the end off one, then two, then three, and passed them to each of us before he retrieved a candle and set it between us. "Conspiracies and hidden hands, knives in the dark and false colors. Why should I pay these rumors any mind?"

He lit his cigar, puffing slowly. Ben and I followed suit, and I took a deep inhale before I spoke again. "I do not know enough to make claims. I simply wanted to bring the information to your attention and leave it with your better judgement. These are matters that you, I presume, are more educated on than I."

A hint of amusement crinkled the admiral's eyes. "Your tact has always been admirable, Samuel, but that was heavy-handed. I can tell you little of what I know or suspect, even if I should know or suspect it. In fact, I must dissuade you from this topic entirely and encourage you to look to your own good in these troubled times."

I watched my uncle, trying to read between his words. "I see."

For a moment we sat in smoky, weighty silence. At length, I took the opportunity to broach another topic.

"I realize now that the truth of Ben's affair with Alice Irving is known." I did not look at Ben as I spoke, though out of the corner of my eye I saw him tilt his head back. Resigned, he exhaled a stream of smoke. "I am also aware that I misled the Admiralty in claiming his actions as my own, and that not all will be pleased with my foray into Mere. But I hope that, in light of our findings, the Admiralty will see our value. I intend to sail with the fleet against Mere. Benedict, despite his moral failings and the loss of his ship—I realize of course that under less pressing circumstances, an inquest may be warranted, however… He remains an officer of Her Majesty's Royal Navy and an invaluable asset."

I sensed my twin's focus snap to me, prying like needles under my skin.

Admiral Rosser huffed, seemingly uninterested in pursuing that particular conversation. "Noted. Now, tell me more of these Mereish observatories and their beliefs about these unprecedented tides."

I obliged and the interview began in earnest. My uncle queried and pried, testing the borders of our story and edging out concessions, new information, observations and facts. I spoke of the actions of the Ess Noti and the potency of their talismans, which I handed over at this time. My uncle took them in with narrowed eyes and a draconian exhale of smoke. I sensed a lack of surprise in his reaction, but any queries of my own were brushed aside.

At length, the admiral swept the pouch of talismans and magecrafted shot into his pocket. He tapped ash into a bowl in the center of the table and said, "I can make no promises as how any of this will be received, but I must urge the pair of you—and your crew, Samuel—to secrecy. Keep your heads low and your conduct clean."

"I always do," Benedict said, calm and guileless.

Our uncle gave him a quelling look. "Benedict. There will be an inquisition into the loss of your ship, though I doubt you will be barred from temporary action. So again, I repeat—keep your head low and your conduct clean. Remain with Samuel and wait for your summons to court. Though I dare say it will not be for some time, given we, apparently, face invasion."

"Of course." Ben leaned on one arm of his chair, casually brushing his lips with the end of his cigar. But I saw the fingers of his other hand shudder on the arm of his chair. A vision of our childhood came back to me in a flash—him holding freshly caned hands in his lap as we waited, together, on the bench outside our uncle's study. The weight of responsibility had haunted me then, and it did so again.

"I would invite you to my table this evening, but I need time to evaluate the reception of your arrival and your news," the admiral finished with the beginnings of a dismissal. "Irving is not here—in that we have found some grace. But again, I urge you. Keep your heads low and stay out of naval affairs."

I nodded and ashed my cigar, leaving the stub in the bowl. "Very good, sir."

"I am sorry I did it," Ben said unexpectedly.

The admiral's eyes fixed on my twin. I considered him too, searching him for a lie. Instead I found an intense defensiveness to his posture, a forced disregard. Ash from his cigar drifted onto the thick Ismani carpet.

"I should not have associated with Ms. Irving," Benedict added. "It was unsatisfying, and the complications far beyond what I anticipated."

"That is not the breed of regret that will sway those in power," our uncle stated. "You regret the repercussions, as always, not the wrongness of the act, nor letting your brother take the fall for your immorality."

"I have never failed at my duty," Ben returned stolidly. "And I will not. Give me a new ship, a ghisting and a Stormsinger, and I will prove my value tenfold."

"I do not doubt that," the admiral said. There was something about his eyes, perhaps regret or remembered gentleness, a recollection of our boyhood and his unexpected mantle of father. "But martial merit cannot redeem you from moral failings."

Redeem. With that word, I truly realized that the shame of the incident with Alice Irving had shifted from my shoulders. I was no longer the one in shadow, desperate to attach some good to my sullied name. Ben was the villain now, as he should have been all along.

But there was danger in that shift.

"Uncle," I said, eager to end the interview. "Thank you for interceding for us. We await your pleasure."

The admiral nodded. "I am glad to see the pair of you again, whole and well. You are… well?"

No one needed to clarify what he truly inquired about. I had an impulse to tell him of my continued degradation, of our looming cure. But mentioning a cure would open a door with Benedict I was not sure I had the ability to close.

"We are," I said, and Ben nodded, adding a surprisingly genuine curl of the lips.

"Good." The admiral cleared his throat. "I will send for you soon. Good day, my boys."

FORTY-THREE

Toffee

MARY

With the Rossers at the fort, the Uknaras holed up in their cabin and Enisca refusing visitors, Charles and I busied ourselves with practical matters in Renown. I found a seamstress, purchasing various necessities and ordering others to replace items stolen or destroyed in *Hart*'s capture. Charles, after being all too easily charmed by the shop owner, ordered an entirely impractical ensemble of dusty rose pink, trimmed with cream.

"And where will you wear that?" I inquired as we stepped back out into the slush and melt of the street. It was warm that day, the breeze mild and the only true cold wafting from alleyways still burdened by packed snow.

"Wooing," was his response.

"You'll hardly be wooing anyone if we die in the battle," I pointed out, speaking with forced lightness. The possibility of imminent death was something I held distant. "You may have wasted your money."

"I cannot take my money to the grave, Mary."

"Fair enough," I conceded.

Next I acquired a pair of boots, used but of fine quality, and replaced my sodden shoes against the slush and melt of the streets. I also purchased a cache of toffee and sweets, which I felt wholly justified considering the strain of the current situation—not least because I could not stop looking over my shoulder.

Our flight through Mere had been harrowing, nerve-shattering. But even though I now stood on Aeadine cobblestones with Charles at my side, I felt only marginally less vulnerable. How long would it take for a naval Sooth to notice a free Stormsinger on the streets? Would they snatch me without question?

I preferred not to find out. Sweets in my pocket, we returned to the docks near *Hart*'s longboat and lingered close by, waiting for Mr. Keo and our oarsmen to return from their own errands.

Time stretched. Charles shifted, sniffing the breeze, and cast his eye at a nearby tavern. "What if we went for a drink? And a good meal. I appreciate Willoughby's efforts, but a simple steak and potato would be a relief right about now."

I shook my head. "I'd prefer to return to the ship. Go on, *Hart* can see me from here." I indicated the ship, out across the water.

Charles considered a moment longer, then nodded. "Scream if someone tries to carry you off. Ah, and try not to kill them?"

He issued the request lightly, with a grin and a tap to the brim of his hat before sauntering away. But his words sat heavy in my stomach.

I popped a toffee into my mouth to distract myself. The minutes crawled by and I shifted on my feet, beginning to grow cold. I consumed half the toffees, all the while trying not to think of the coming invasion or the lungs I had stilled in Mere.

I was staring into the box regretfully when I sensed someone approach.

"You are the Stormsinger from *Hart*." The man, in his early forties and wearing the double-breasted, black-collared coat of a naval officer, faced me on the dock. I couldn't immediately read his rank, but my stomach hit the dock beneath my feet.

"Sir," I greeted him, and, on impulse, offered the sweets. "Would you like a toffee? I'm afraid I've already eaten half the box. If I don't start sharing, I'll certainly eat them all."

The offer had the exact effect I'd hoped for. Off-footed, he blinked at me. "You *are* the Stormsinger from Samuel Rosser's *Hart*," he clarified, this time more forcefully.

"Please have a toffee," I insisted. Internally, I scrambled. This man wouldn't try to conscript me in broad daylight, would he? How far away was Charles? He was nowhere in sight, and the tavern shutters were closed.

The stranger looked further disgruntled, but after a moment reached out and plucked one of the sweets. He popped it in his mouth and chewed, eyes widening. "Do these have chocolate inside them?"

I nodded. "They do."

The man chewed for a minute longer, working the tough sweet between his teeth, and by the end of it was clearly more relaxed.

"My apologies," he said, offering his hand. "I forgot myself. I'm Lieutenant Adler of Her Majesty's *Recompense*, and our Stormsinger was gravely injured last month. If you will permit me, I would greatly appreciate the opportunity to speak to you regarding your skills."

I paused, about to pop another toffee into my mouth. "You would like the opportunity to tempt me away from my ship?"

He had the grace to look abashed. "I should like to speak to you about taking a position aboard *Recompense*, yes."

"You wouldn't prefer to throw me over your shoulder and carry me off?" My instinctual fear expressed as an unexpected brazenness, and I fixed upon it. "Or do you intend to do that once we're somewhere more private and not being watched by my crew across the water?"

Lieutenant Adler glanced over my shoulder. At that very moment, light glinted off a spyglass pointed in our direction from *Hart*'s anchorage.

"If I implored you to consider joining me for the good of your country, would that sway you?" he asked, speaking more lowly.

I put the toffee in my mouth and began to chew. I had no idea how much of the situation with the Mereish had filtered down through the rankings, but if Adler was coming to me on behalf of his captain and ship, he seemed like the type to keep himself informed.

Adler smiled thinly. "Is silence your response?"

"I am contracted to the Usti Crown and the *Hart*," I informed him, though only after taking the time to swallow. "Not only am I loyal to my captain, but I am bound by that contract. I appreciate you not simply abducting me, Lieutenant Adler. But I cannot be convinced to leave *Hart*."

He inclined his head. "I see. Thank you for your time, madam."

I inclined my head in return, and he left me. I was no Sooth, but, as I watched him fade into the crowd, I could not shake the feeling I would see him again.

AEADINE HERESIES—*To speak on the many heresies of the Aeadine peoples and their singular saint would be to detract from the purpose of this study. However, the Aeadine Cult of the Moon certainly bears mentioning. In sympathy with lost traditions of their land, including the worship of ghistings and the veneration of the dark of the moon, they have taken what little is known to them of Mereish magics and beliefs and formed their own, repressed cultus among the Aeadine peoples. During past peacetimes, Mereish missionaries have sought to understand and monitor this cult, and even to aid them upon occasion, but these efforts were not condoned by the Mereish Crown.*

—FROM A DEFINITIVE STUDY OF THE BLESSED: MAGES
AND MAGECRAFT OF THE MEREISH ISLES, *TRANSLATED
FROM THE MEREISH BY SAMUEL I. ROSSER*

FORTY-FOUR

The Black Tide Gathers

SAMUEL

The following day, Benedict was summoned to the fort. Uninvited and taut with nerves, I occupied myself with practical matters, perusing requests from quartermaster, gunner, carpenter, purser, and so forth for resupply while in port. I put the final details into a written report to the Admiralty of all we had seen in Mere and knew of the Black Tides, the Ess Noti, and Faucher's magics. Then I laboriously made two copies, adding them to my personal copies of Maren's notes. One bundle I stowed in my sea-chest and the other I quietly posted to my parents' largely forgotten house east of the Lesterwold. No matter what transpired next, no matter how the powers that be reacted to the revelations, there would be record.

I sent several other letters besides, requesting an update on the Rosser household and reaching out to old friends. I had not done the latter in years and had to swallow a great deal of pride to do so now, but I felt in want of allies, and hoped the truth of Alice Irving's affair with Ben might have begun to soften their opinion of me.

The cabin door slammed open. Ben strode in, throwing his hat onto the floor and pulling at his cravat like a man fighting with a noose. Mary appeared in the doorway behind him, slipped inside, and shut the door cautiously.

"I am barred until an official inquisition," my brother raged. He threw a hand out, the strangled cravat clutched in his fingers. What little control he had left faded with each word until he was screaming. "The fucking Mereish Fleet is coming and they will not give me a ship!"

Magni power billowed out through the room, wave upon wave of hateful, intense magic.

Mary came to stand with me, shoulder to shoulder, as Tane flickered across her skin. "He has been raging at the crew," she whispered.

"What are you saying?" Ben snapped.

Mary flinched, and I glared at him. "Calm yourself."

Ben's rage peaked. "Do not look at me like that! Not the two of you. Do you think I would hurt you? My only allies in this shit-smeared world? The only people who I do not have to *bewitch* into enduring me?"

"That may be the kindest thing you've said to me," Mary commented.

He glowered at her.

"Ben." I did not approach him. "Your ship was lost with all hands, and only you survived. An inquisition is not uncalled for."

"This is not about the wreck! It's about *Alice*!" Ben threw the cravat at me, but it only fluttered placidly to the deck. Unsatisfied, he advanced on us, breaths ragged, half a dozen aborted ravings on his lips. He stopped at the warning expression on my face, with visible strain.

"I am disgraced. They will not let me fight. Before the week is out they will be pressing drunken wastrels from the gutters, but they will not have *me*."

I felt no pity, which, upon reflection, surprised me. He was experiencing what I had endured for the past four years.

"*Hart* will not sit in harbor," I said steadily. "And anyone aboard my ship when we engage is required to do their part. Have you been ordered to stay on shore?"

"What? Ordered? No." Ben stared at me for a long moment, then seized his own forehead and pressed his temples so hard his thumbs turned white. "Sam, I earned my rankings. I will not be degraded to fucking privateer."

"Then don't," Mary suggested, her patience clearly at an end. "Find a tavern, get drunk and pity yourself. If we survive, we'll peel you off the floor. And if we die because you were not there to help us? You can always bewitch yourself a few new allies."

Ben jerked out a chair at the table and sat. Every line of him quivered, fraught with tension, then the life drained out of him. He opened his mouth to speak, and my mind raced ahead, hoping for an apology, a confession, gratitude. None came.

"Fine," he said at last. He looked around the cabin, bleary-eyed. "I can stay aboard? Fight with you?"

I nodded.

"Good. I need a drink."

Mary came to stand over Ben. "No, you need company. And if we happen to drink and play dice and pillage the pockets of every fool in Renown, that will be an aside."

Ben looked at her warily. "Where is the highwayman? Is he not your usual accomplice?"

"He'll come too."

Ben seemed to calculate for a moment, then leaned around her to look at me. "Well, are you coming?"

I had watched Mary and Grant play cards before, but that night, as I watched them win and lose and win again, I realized two things. The first was that they played more than cards—the two of them were working in concert, tactfully fleecing specific targets while the locals, sailors, and petty officers all around were none the wiser. The second was that they communicated through subtleties of movement and phrase that I only started to catch after my second drink, when I lost the will not to openly admire Mary.

I saw their hands lingering on the wood of the table at the same time, and knew without a doubt that Tane was in on their little scheme, whispering cues only *ghiseau* could hear. It was admirable and deplorable, but for once in my life I could not care. Mary was happy, and I could not help but share that, warmth growing between us. My veins hummed with a pleasant lightness, Ben was relaxed, if subdued at my side, and so far no one seemed to have recognized us.

Illya joined us at some point during the night, depositing a bottle of vaguely red cinnamon liquor on the table and initiating a drinking game that, while absolutely nonsensical, succeeded in getting half the tavern roiling with laughter. After that he had command of the establishment, and, somewhere between my second and third knuckle of the liquor, the tables were pushed back and dancing began. Someone produced a fiddle, someone else a drum.

I sat deeper into my chair, side-by-side with Ben, and watched as five women—three sailors and two locals, one of whom passed off her baby as she rose—took to the empty space and began a southern Aeadine dance, with plenty of heel-swinging, skirt-tossing, and coordinated shouts. After a moment two more women joined them, the cheers of the tavern-goers grew and, attracted by the sounds, more people crowded in from the street.

"It's the Shepherdess!" Mary shouted, too loud in my ear. She shoved her drink into my hand and tugged her skirts up through her belt, grinning at me. "I know this one!"

All I could do was laugh—truly laugh, deep and relieved and freeing—as she launched into the fray. The other women greeted her with whoops and laughter and reaching hands, the fiddle flew, and the steps of the dance became even more rapid.

"How profoundly rural," Ben commented. When I did not reply, he tipped his head to the side to consider me. "You look like an imbecile."

I met his gaze, fully aware of the wideness of my grin. Thoughts and worries crowded the back of my mind as they always did, and the Dark Water lingered in the edges of my vision. But I had no headache, and, between the drink and the music, I could ignore the wider world.

For now.

"Now that you cannot be healed, what will you do with her?" Ben asked.

That made my grin falter. The women's dance ended with a roar of laughter and cheers. The dancers sagged, breathless, Mary in their midst with her fraying braid flung over her shoulder. Then the music struck up again, and the women reorganized into a new dance. Mary did not seem to know this one as well, but that did not dissuade her, and the others swept her along.

"I haven't the faintest idea," I replied to Ben.

"What does she want?" he prompted.

I sipped at Mary's drink instead of replying.

"How long do you think you have? Before the Other takes you?"

His questions were starting to grate, and my peace to fray. The Dark Water swelled, leaving the corners of my vision and broadening to veil the room. Mary's form became a whirl of teal and grey, reflecting off the obsidian waves around my ankles. The moody red pulse of Ben's magic washed over half my face.

"I would give myself a year," I replied. The words came with a surprising lack of emotion—it was a thing I simply knew now, even if I had not examined the knowledge beforehand. I blinked the Dark Water back to the edges of my vision. "This matter with Hae has shortened my time significantly."

Ben stared at me, as inscrutable as always.

I emptied the glass. Cinnamon burned up into my nose and tugged me fully back into the human world.

"I would have done it. The… healing."

It took me a remarkable length of time to realize Ben had truly spoken those words. I turned to find him watching Mary dance, and I saw not sadness in his eyes, not truly, but something close to it.

"You are sure?" I asked, the secret of what Mary and I intended to do rattling about in my skull.

"Yes," he replied. "After the Mereish Fleet was turned back. We will both need our powers at their fullest until then. I understand that, short of a miracle, my career is over. My life as it is, is over. I must change too."

I could not contest that. In fact, I could hardly speak. I wanted to blame the alcohol in my veins for the sudden rush of emotion and the hot, damp blur in my eyes. How could Ben be speaking like this? Was he lying? Did he suspect I was hiding the cure from him and intended to use it whether he agreed or not?

The temptation to tell him was strong. Fortunately, Ben looked away as the song ended and more dancers flooded the floor, the women partnering up with one another and random men.

Mary glanced at us, mouth open, perhaps to call for me to join. But when she saw the seriousness of our expressions, a little of the mirth faded from her eyes.

A stranger stepped up and offered his hand. Mary curtsied and joined the dance with him.

I felt a shadow touch my brow. "Does she know that man?"

Grant sank down in the chair on my other side, flushed and holding his hat in his lap, brimming with coins and cheap jewelry. "No idea," he said absently, putting his feet up on another empty chair and beginning to sort through his winnings, tucking them into his pockets. "But no need to get ruffled, he looks a decent fellow."

I watched Mary and her partner swirl around the floor in yet another rural dance. His hand was easy on her waist, hers across his shoulders, and they executed the steps with a fluidity and unity that told me they had both known this dance since childhood.

I felt a flush of possessiveness, brief and visceral. Then I recalled the way Mary had looked at me only moments before and extinguished the feeling with a long, steadying breath.

"Thank you for being willing," I said to Ben, my eyes still on Mary. "Truly."

Ben waved the words away. He looked less than pleased at Mary's choice of partner. "Are you going to do something about that?"

"No." I smirked. "I am grateful you have found a place in… well not your heart, but that you have some acceptance of Mary."

"You care for her," Ben scoffed, his countenance one of droll incredulity. "Therefore, she is you, and you are my blood. Besides, she is useful. So are you going to dance with her, or let that bumpkin grope her all night?"

"There is no groping," I calmed him. "Have another drink."

When the song ended Mary brought her dancing companion over, and introductions were made. One August Wade, a soldier stationed at the fort, took in Ben's and my nearly identical faces with a predictable degree of startlement, then gave me a salute. His smile was a genuine thing, full-cheeked and boyish, though he could not have been much younger than me.

"Captains Rosser, yours is a name I've heard many a time," he said to the pair of us, revealing the same accent as Mary's in a deeper, masculine rumble. "For good and ill, I'll admit, but I'll not judge a man 'til I've laid eyes on him, and you both seem a fine sort."

"We do?" Ben asked sardonically, and I resisted the urge to kick him.

"They can be," Mary hedged, glancing at me with a depth of pride that made my heart swell. "August is from the Wold too, from Round-the-hill."

"Is that the name of a town?" Ben smirked.

"Nay, not a town." August laughed, grinning in a way that said he both saw Ben's scorn and had borne it before. He glanced at Mary. "A hamlet?"

"A hut, a mill, and some cows." She shrugged.

"There about," August agreed. "Now, I promised the next dance to a friend. If you'll excuse me? Innkeep's daughter, was a pleasure to see you again."

"Cowherd's boy," she returned, touching the brim of a nonexistent hat.

As if on cue, another woman edged from the crowd, plump and pretty and wearing her soldier's uniform with the collar unbuttoned and cravat undone. She swept us an acknowledging look, offered Mary a small, peaceable smile, and held out her hand to August. Together, they moved off.

Another song began, this one with Illya in the middle of the fray.

"So you *do* know him?" I clarified.

"We met once or twice." Mary situated herself in my lap, smiled at my startlement, and took her drink back.

I recovered enough to slip my arms around her waist, breathing in her scent of sea and lavender and fresh, sweet sweat. Ben sat beside us, drinking restfully, as the tavern burst with music and dance and raucous singing.

Conversation became impossible, but I did not care. I ignored the voice at the back of my mind, the one that sounded much like my uncle, encouraging decorum. I resisted memories of another tavern, another night, and the disagreement that had divided us for so long and still whispered cautions.

Instead, I rested my head on Mary's chest as she draped her arms around my neck and kissed my temple. We were hardly the only couple in the tavern in such a state.

"Sir." I twisted to look in the direction of the speaker and saw a middle-aged man, leaning through the crowd towards me. He looked like a landsman, with a long coat and tall boots, better for trudging across snowy countryside than working aboard ship. His skin was weatherworn and his body wiry, with the hint of a paunch.

His expression was friendly, but there was an odd eagerness in his eyes that made my arms stiffen around Mary.

Mary turned, following my gaze, and Ben looked up from his drink.

"Sirs," the man corrected himself, smiling nervously and tugging off his cap. "You may not remember me, beyond some twenty years ago it were, last we met. My name is Pitten, Mr. Jeremy Pitten, and I was a friend of your mum, Saint keep the kind lady's soul."

Memory rushed at me like a rogue wave. I remembered this man, younger, holding his cap the same way as he did now, in the entryway of Rosser House as Black Tide elders greeted my mother. He had smiled at Ben and I, lingering in the door of the study with chalk on our fingers from our lessons. Our governess had called us back, but not before I had seen my mother lead this man, and those elders, into the sitting room and close the door.

Mary stood sharply, inserting herself between Pitten and I in the cramped space. I stood just a breath behind her and, dimly, was aware of Ben stepping around to flank the man.

Pitten forced another smile. The jolly, rapid music and the laughter and chatter of the patrons took on an ominous quality now, unsettling and discordant with the deadly drum of my blood.

"I—Ah—I came to give you this, is all." Pitten held out a letter with one hand, leaning around Mary to try and give it directly to me.

Mary snatched it. "Leave. Now."

"Of course, of course," Pitten said, taking as much of a step back as he could in the press, wringing his worn cap in his hands.

Ben materialized behind the man, separated by only a handful of raucous tavern-goers. For once, the murder in his eyes was reflected in my own.

Pitten retreated another step, then seemed beset by impulse. "You and your brother are Black Tide Sons, Mr. Rosser." His gaze flitted about for Ben, not realizing he was behind him. "And this is a sacred time. You should join us to pay respect to the Midden Ghist. Your mother would have wanted it so."

The Midden Ghist. The creature who inhabited the abandoned chapel in the forest, the only ghisting in the Lesterwold.

Mary, crushing the unopened letter in one hand, advanced. "Leave before I lose my temper and do something I will regret."

Pitten turned twitchily, nervous to take his eyes off my face, and froze at the sight of Ben watching him over the heads of the crowd.

Mary added, "Or he does something he will not."

Esteemed Captains Samuel and Benedict Rosser,

On this the 7th Day of the Second Turning of the Black Moons,

It was with great reverence that I learned of the events north of the Stormwall this past year. Through the rumor and speculation, it is clear to me your mother's faith has come to fruition, and, as her spirit has already preceded us into the Infinite, it would be my greatest honor to offer you guidance and council as you reach the height of your power. The Black Tides approach and the Faithful gather in holy places across Aeadine, as I am sure you recall from those gentler days when your mother worshipped with us.

I offer my council to you freely and with great concern. I am not unaware of the scorn with which our people regard the Black Tide's teachings, and how they have turned you against us. They do this from ignorance and fear, denying our clear and evident achievements. But you are men of the world, and you know the depths of your own power, brought about through our intervention. You, I learned upon my arrival here in Renown, have been to Mere. No doubt you have seen their reverence for mages and magecraft, and perhaps you felt just indignation that your own people do not hold you in such regard.

We see you for what you are. You are Black Tide Sons, most powerful and honored under the Moonless Sky, and, as the Second Turning of this season draws close, I have no doubt you will feel the same pull as we—to the Other, to the power within, to the sanctity of the shadows between the stars.

I have more to tell you, revelations that should not be rendered to text, particularly in light of what is to come. I implore you, seek me out at The Silver Serpent.

Yours in reverence,

J. Pitten

FORTY-FIVE

Nomad

SAMUEL

The following day dawned snowy, somber, and hushed. A note arrived from my uncle inviting Ben and I to take the noon meal with him at one of Renown's many inns. A dinner invitation would have been more likely to include other powerful men and women—no dinner table was to be wasted, especially in times of conflict. It would have been a chance to share more of what we had learned and to impress upon those in power the need for quick action.

A private luncheon did not bode well for how our news had been received.

I left the invitation on the table next to Mr. Pitten's crumpled, unopened letter, staring out the window past a mug of cold coffee. The ship was quiet, the crew at rest or on shore, with only the usual creaks and distant footfalls to disturb the ringing quiet. The warm weather had turned as it so often did in spring, and thick, fat snowflakes fell beyond the gallery windows, muffling the sounds of the port and immediately melting on the waves. The flat-fronted buildings on the docks looked like a painting, with snow-dusted ships in the foreground, the specks of townsfolk going about their days, and layer upon layer of white-patched roofs and chimney smoke fading into the overcast gloom of Fort Renown.

My gaze inevitably returned to Mr. Pitten's letter. Moving with disconnected precision, I popped the seal and unfolded the many creases in the parchment. Inside I found a square of words in a serviceable, unadorned hand. I dropped my eyes to the signature first. *J. Pitten.*

The author of this letter had been one of those who manipulated my mother into funding them, who had convinced her to poison and torture her own sons. They were the reason she had been locked away for her own good and had, eventually, died.

Fury made my neck flush and my ears roar. I jerked at my cravat to loosen it and read the letter twice. An offer of aid. Reverence. I gave a bitter huff and imagined Ben stepping into a meeting of worshipful Black Tide devotees. The scenario played out like a fox in a henhouse, and, in my imagining, I did not intervene.

Soon though, my visceral reaction to the letter cooled into something more calculating. I scanned it a third time, pulling out individual points and turning them over more slowly in my mind.

If the Black Tide knew there was more to this spring's tide than usual, *how* did they know it? They were not the Ess Noti, with their Dark Observatories and ghisten saints. They were peasants dancing naked in the moss, and they had no way to communicate with the Midden Ghist, even if he was inclined to share.

Yet they, and the Midden Ghist, were here.

I have more to tell you, revelations that should not be rendered to text. That line stayed with me the longest, and, through my lingering rage and resentment, I forced myself to consider just what Pitten might have to say. For all their manipulations and crimes, the Black Tide had succeeded in amplifying Ben and I, even if they corrupted us in the process. They were the only ones in Aeadine—let alone the Anchorage—who might know more about the Black Tides than us.

I picked up my cold cup of coffee and drained it, then went to find Mary.

"What does he mean, 'in light of what is to come'?" Mary asked, seated on a rickety chair next to the stove in her cabin. She leaned back against the bulkhead, her arm precariously close to the stove, her ankles stacked beneath her skirts and a thick quilt I vaguely remembered her sewing. Several patches of fabric—mustard-yellow with pale-green motifs—looked suspiciously like one of my cravats, which had gone missing several months ago.

Mary waved the letter, pointing at the words in question. "Does he know about the Mereish Fleet? Or is this all about the Black Tide and their rituals? Perhaps they've concluded there is more power in the spring tides than usual."

"That troubled me too," I admitted, thinking of all the harm the cult could do to the mages of the Anchorage if given the chance. "Would you and Tane accompany me to meet with Mr. Pitten? I must learn more but I cannot… should not, do so alone."

Her expression remained serious. "Of course."

"We must alert the Uknaras," I went on. "They can intervene if anything goes awry. Perhaps Mr. Grant can keep watch on Ben. He should not be anywhere near the cultists. Where is Ms. Alamay?"

"She went ashore," Mary replied, scanning the letter again. "Mr. Penn told me."

"Oh?" I prompted, but Mary only shrugged.

"She's not a prisoner."

"She is a spy."

"A spy who grows hungry and perhaps needs to buy a change of clothing, perhaps a book to read while sitting in her cabin until we drop her in Hesten or whatever she intends to do." Mary waved the matter aside. "Sam, what should I expect? I have no experience with the Black Tide Cult. They were not welcome in my village, though I do remember them gathering in the Ghistwold in spring for their ceremonies until the Foresters chased them out. They would camp in the woods, and sometimes I would hear them singing. The village boys said they saw them dancing naked, in the cold. Even in the snow. Spring is *not* warm in the Ghistwold, even if the trees think it's already high summer."

She sounded far more concerned about the cold than the nudity of the dancers, and, against all odds, a smile tugged the corner of my lips. Then I recalled my mother had often been one of those celebrants and the smile faded.

Mary studied me, obviously trying to parse my thoughts. "I can go with Charles," she suggested. "On your behalf."

"That will not be necessary." I took the letter back from her and folded it, then stowed it in my pocket. "I must do this. We will find out what they are doing and deliver any pertinent information to the Admiralty."

"They do believe us, right?" she asked, her eyes distant and her thoughts deep. "About Mereish magecraft? I know matters with the Usti are more complex, but…"

"Hopefully I can gain some sense of that when I speak to my uncle," I promised. "Ben and I will meet him at noon today. Would you come with us?"

Her brows furrowed. "Why?"

I came closer and leaned over her chair, planting my hands on its back, to either side of her head. "Because I want him to see you for the person that you are and not a weather witch unjustly stolen from the fleet."

"Are you concerned?" she asked, meeting my eyes. "That the Navy will try to take me?"

"I always am," I replied somberly. "But he is the head of my family. I would like my intentions with you to be clear and known."

She cocked her head, sparse inches from mine, and laced her arms over her chest.

"Your rumored intentions," she said tartly. "I've heard of these but still rarely experience them."

I kissed her, light and soft, more breath than touch, and enjoyed a flush of satisfaction as she stilled, head tilted back, waiting for more.

As I retreated, she made a discontented sound.

"Noon," I said.

∞

As the church bells of Renown tolled half past eleven, I heard a shout off the larboard bow.

"Samuel Rosser!"

I squinted into the sun to see a familiar, black-hulled ship dropping anchor.

For a moment, I saw the predatory, three-masted vessel as he had once been—*Nameless*—with a faceless figurehead and a captain who had tormented the Winter Sea for decades. Now he was called *Nomad*—bearing a striking figurehead of a cloaked monk with all but his wide, shouting mouth hidden beneath a grey cowl—and a figure in a bicorn hat stood at the forecastle.

"Captain Fisher!" I called back, a grin in my voice. I leaned over the rail. "What brings you to Renown?"

"Yes, I accept your kind invitation to table!" she shouted back, making a show of cupping her hands around her ears. "Send a boat for me seven o'clock!"

I laughed. "Yes, Captain!"

"Very good, Captain!" Fisher waved her hat, then strolled away across the deck of her ship.

I turned, catching the attention of Poverly as the girl crossed the deck, pink-cheeked in the cold. "Ms. Poverly, be so good as to go inform Mr. Willoughby we will have a guest at table this evening, and use the good wine."

"Yessir." Poverly touched the curls bursting from her cap and darted away across the deck.

Mary glanced at the girl as she passed, then looked from me to *Nomad*. Her eyebrows rose. "Helena?"

Mary had clearly put a great deal of thought into her appearance today—her hair swept up and her cheeks rouged. I could not see what she was wearing beneath her thick, cloak-like coat, but the garment itself was fine, blue with a fringe of white fur around an expansive hood. She looked older than her years, the powerful Stormsinger I knew her to be. My uncle, I was sure, would see the same.

"I was unaware that tents were considered formal attire," Ben commented, joining us with the collar of his overcoat popped and his eyes slightly shadowed. "Shall we?"

Admiral Rosser surveyed the three of us as the staff of the well-appointed inn The Gilded Peacock finished depositing shallow bowls of soup before us and filed out of the room. The chamber was large, clearly meant for a larger company, but it was warm and had an unparalleled view of the sea west of Renown.

My dreamer's senses overlaid the blurry line of the blue-and-grey horizon with a fleet, specks growing to towers of sails, the sparks of cannon muzzles and the whistle of shot.

I blinked the imagining away.

"I do not remember inviting your weather witch," the admiral stated, addressing Ben and I and ignoring Mary. My guard immediately rose—Admiral Rosser was in one of his darker moods. His movements were abrupt, his words sharp-edged, and there was tension in his eyes that bordered on resentment. "This is highly irregular."

Mary smiled politely and sipped at a cup of wine.

"I believed it prudent for you to become acquainted," I said, my spine stiff. "Mary Firth is a member of my crew."

I almost added that she was more than that, but my uncle's demeanor told me that would not go over well today. I had rarely seen him in such a state—the most recent being when I resigned my commission in disgrace.

"Then why did you not bring your carpenter? Where is your bosun?" Admiral Rosser gestured to the rest of the table. "By all means, send for them!"

"I take it our news was not well received," Ben cut in, fishing grains of fine black rice from his amber onion soup.

The older man pried his gaze from Mary and surveyed Ben with frayed patience. "The approach of the Mereish Fleet was taken quite seriously, I assure you. We were, you understand, already on alert—the growing tides have not precisely been subtle, nor certain unnatural appearances of the Other and its moons and the increasing power of mages. The return of various ships to Mere was certainly marked."

"Why did we come here at all, then?" Ben asked coldly.

"You gave us clarity and direction, knowing when and where the Mereish Fleet will strike." The admiral somehow made the words sound utterly devoid of praise. "Regarding the new Mereish magics, that is not something I am at liberty to discuss. Nor is the matter of Jessin Faucher's assertions about the Usti—though again, I advise you to cast them from your minds."

Mary had yet to touch her soup, but she held her spoon on the table with pointed care.

"But the Admiralty *is* taking action?" she asked. I noticed she made an effort to smooth her rural accent. That she felt the need to do so, that my uncle had already treated her with such disregard, irked me more than my ignorance of the Admiralty's decisions. "The matter is being brought to the queen? I know we've little time to arm ourselves against ensorcelled shot and the like, but surely some defenses can be—"

"The queen? Woman, do you have even a base understanding of how this nation is run?" Admiral Rosser's eyelids fluttered in disbelief. He gestured to the door. "You are excused."

Ben's head swiveled to watch me. He sat back slightly, a spectator preparing for the curtain to rise.

"Admiral Rosser," I cut in. "I brought Ms. Firth for a reason—"

"To insult me? To disregard my wishes?" the admiral returned. "Samuel, this woman is hardly housebroken. Questioning me? She is an asset, that is all, and unfit company." His gaze hardened at the last, making it very clear what kind of company he assumed Mary and I were keeping. "I intended to speak with my nephews in privacy."

I rose and offered Mary my hand, my mind already storming out the door.

Mary, however, did not move. Instead, Tane manifested. She left Mary's skin like river mist and took form, standing directly behind Mary with her hands resting on the chair back. As she did, the entire room trembled, just enough to make the soup and the contents of our cups quiver.

The hair on the back of my neck rose.

"Admiral Rosser." Tane's deeper tones laced Mary's voice, slipping from the Stormsinger's lips with calm precision and—I noted with satisfaction—Mary's own accent. "A man of your station can't be ignorant of the Mereish's beliefs about their High Captains, even if the extent of their true abilities is cloaked in rumor. So I tell you now, I am the same as them. And if you expect any aid from me or my kind in the coming battle, you will speak to me with respect."

Ben, picking up his soup bowl with both hands, leaned back in his chair and began to sip.

Admiral Rosser rose. Looking from Mary to me in astonishment and not a little unease, he leaned to brace his hands on the table. "What is this?"

"We are *ghiseau*," Tane replied through Mary. "I am a Mother Ghisting, but I am Mary, and Mary is me."

Admiral Rosser stared at Mary and Tane for another long, long moment. Then he gave a slow incline of his head and sat back down. One thing was clear—either my uncle had become considerably more open-minded in recent years, or the existence of *ghiseau* was no great shock.

"I beg your forgiveness, Ms. Firth," he said, and cleared his throat. "Perhaps I should speak more candidly. Samuel, sit. Let us begin again."

By the time the main course was served, the reason for my uncle's anxiety was clear.

"We have suspected a change in the winds for some time," he said as our food grew cold—all save Ben's, which had long vanished. "First, you must understand, strange accounts of conflict with the Mereish have always abounded, but High Captains and their High Ships are not common, and none have ever been captured and held alive. One was taken in the last season of the war—the one in which your mother served, Ms. Firth—but they killed themselves within hours.

"More recently, I have heard the accounts of Aeadine Magni who claim their powers did not affect certain Mereish enemies. So too did I hear of a Sooth who claimed her sight had been cut off during an engagement with the Mereish, in which she was shot. However, when she awoke after surgery, she was restored and the matter explained by blood fugue and injury. No one suspected the musket ball might be the culprit."

"Thus, nothing has been done yet," Ben observed.

"The items you retrieved and your notes will go a long way to convincing the world to both believe and act, though it will take more time than we now have, with the Great Tide approaching." The admiral inclined his head to Mary again. Tane had retreated and she appeared herself once more. "As will Ms. Firth's and Mother Tane's bond. That is, if you are willing to make yourself known beyond the confines of this room."

While I relished the notion of the world acknowledging Mary and all that she was, I feared it too. Mary would not simply be a powerful Stormsinger. She would be a singular anomaly. That could either protect her or put her at greater risk than ever before.

"I'm not," Mary said, to my selfish relief. "I won't be bought or threatened or puppeted, and I know that will be my fate if I come forward publicly. I'll sing against the Mereish from *Hart*, do what I can, and I'll go my own way when I'm done. Let my actions speak for themselves in my absence."

"Very well," my uncle said, looking to his meal. "Now, eat, and I will tell you all I can."

FORTY-SIX

Revelations

MARY

Six hours later, Helena Fisher sank into a chair at another table beside Sam, letting her unbuttoned jacket fall open with a long sigh. Charles, Ben and the Uknaras had yet to join us, but the table was immaculate, plates and cutlery laid out on a crisp white tablecloth, rounds of toasted bread topped with savory preserves and cheeses set between two bottles of wine and steaming oysters. Willoughby had held nothing back.

I bit back a smile as, under the table, I heard the clatter of the other privateer captain kicking off her boots. I didn't know her well, but she was Sam's closest friend, and I enjoyed watching the two of them.

"Are you in your socks at my table?" Samuel inquired.

"Captain Rosser," Fisher said, gesturing to her open coat and finely embroidered waistcoat, complete with lace cravat. "I am in the company of trusted friends. And I am as near to a pirate as a Letter of Marque will permit. Thus, I have decided to embrace the life."

Sam looked like he was trying very hard not to beam. The expression was painfully endearing.

"Well," he said, snagging a bottle of wine from her hand before she could pour. He filled her cup himself. "At least let me be a proper host."

Fisher relented. Sam filled all our cups and sat back down.

"I want to know all that's befallen you and *Hart*." Fisher sobered slightly, the events of the past years leaking through her ease. *Hart* used to be her ship too, I recalled, back when she and Sam had been first and second officer, and they'd shared the cabin that was now mine. I'd heard several members of the crew greeting her earlier with enthusiasm.

"But before that, and before the rest of our company arrives," Fisher nodded to the table, "let me say—I am in Renown because a Mereish man-o'-war harried us out of the Free Channel. We were cruising rather near Mereish waters, I admit, but that ship tailed us far over the line. I've already reported to the Admiralty. But what did I see when we sailed in? The flag of the Admiral of the *North*? Samuel, why is your uncle here?"

"Admiral Rosser's presence is not of particular note," Sam began. "His ship was undergoing repairs, and he intended to head north next week to rejoin the North Fleet in preparation for the Tide— that is, general preparations for the expected tide and the usual vulnerabilities that arise with it. But there is more to the situation, I am afraid."

Sam began to recount recent events. Over the course of the tale the Uknaras joined us, along with Charles and Ben, Ms. Skarrow, and Mr. Keo. Enisca and Maren had elected to keep to themselves, Maren ensconced in research and Enisca doing Saint knew what with her time. She might be ashore again for all I knew, and had gently rebutted my overtures of coffee and sweets earlier in the day.

Sam held nothing back and concluded, as the plates were cleared and cakes and coffee put out, "By our calculations, we have sixteen remaining days to prepare for the second Black Tide and the arrival of the Mereish Fleet. If I might offer a suggestion, Helena—stay here. Offer yourself to the Admiralty before you are pressed into service. Secure a written contract. You will receive better compensation and share of the prizes than if they are forced to press you. I will send you with a letter for my uncle."

"I see... and I appreciate that."

"There is not enough time to recall the North Fleet, or even the entirety of the South," Ben put in over the delicate layered cake on his plate and a mug of steaming, spiked cardamom coffee. "Once these buffoons get their wigs on straight, there will be an uproar. How did they take word of your pursuit in the channel?"

"Evasively," Fisher replied. She added cream to her own coffee and stirred. "I suppose I could flee before we are conscripted, but that seems rather cowardly, and I do appreciate prize money."

"There will only be prize money if we survive," Charles, who had taken the meal as an opportunity to don his new rose-and-cream ensemble, said from next to me. He'd been quiet so far, and I noted a fresh weariness in his eyes. I'd been so focused on Sam in recent days, I had thought little of my friend and how the pressure of recent events might affect him, along with the ever-increasing activity of his ghisting. "I've half a mind to head for the South Isles and impose myself on Demery again."

"That is..." Sam had one hand on the table, small fork forgotten between his fingers. "That is not unwise. I begrudge no one who wants to evade this fight. I will also be offering my crew the choice to stay or go their own way."

He looked at Olsa and Illya and added, with a touch of regret, "There is no need to involve yourselves in our conflicts."

"We know," Illya said, scraping the last smears of chocolate from his plate.

"We will remain on board but not fight," Olsa said. She glanced at Skarrow and Keo and stopped there, but I caught her meaning— she would remain to see Ben and Sam through the healing ritual. "We are Usti, and the involvement in the battle would not reflect well, given the current rumors."

Sam nodded and the conversation went on, but my mind lingered on the Uknaras. For the first time, I had time to truly contemplate what Faucher's accusations and their position in this conflict meant for the Usti couple. I rarely thought of them purely in terms of their heritage—they were simply friends, allies with whom we had faced great challenges, and who had proven their loyalty many times.

Despite that loyalty, a thread of unease worked its way up my spine. Yes, Olsa staying aboard was practical; she wished to be involved in Sam's and Ben's healing, and her advice would be invaluable. But what would she, an Usti, do with all she had learned? Was it not the Usti's hunger for Mereish knowledge, their hunt for Monna, that had initiated recent events?

Across the table, I recognized the flicker of premonition in Olsa's Sooth eyes. Her bare hand rested on the tabletop and I—Tane—felt a thrum through our ghisten connection. It was wordless, quizzical, and reassuring.

I offered a small tug of a smile. I was being foolish. I trusted Olsa nearly as much as I trusted my own mother.

Within me, Tane shifted.

But can we trust Enisca?

FORTY-SEVEN

The Drowning Wood

SAMUEL

Mary and I approached The Silver Serpent as sunset wrapped Renown in muffled orange light. Whistles piped in the distance, and somewhere to the north the boom of cannons sounded out in near flawless synchronicity.

I was dressed as a landsman today, with no hint of the captain in my practical, dark-green coat, open over a common waistcoat, shirt and neckerchief. Mary had dressed with equal modesty—a knitted shawl wound around her upper body, and she wore her hair under a felted hat with a broad yellow ribbon.

"They are only drills," I told her, and rapped on the door of the inn. It was three-storied and broad, but in some state of disrepair. Its pale-blue paint was peeling and sun-bleached closer to grey.

"That lot? I've got a good two dozen of them here—though believe me, if times weren't so hard, I wouldn't have a single one," the innwife said a few moments later in response to our inquiring after Mr. Pitten. "But they've gone out some time ago. Off to another isle for some heresy or another. Don't tell me a fine pair such as yourselves pay them mind?"

"We most assuredly do not," I replied. "Can you direct us to this island?"

After gleaning directions from the innwife, Mary and I set off once more. Thankfully the way took us directly out of town, across several bridges in the shadow of the east-facing sea wall and over patches of land, some more worthy than others to be called an island.

Finally, the wall ended at a large, antique watchtower, and we were afforded an unobstructed view of the western sea across a sweep of rock, winter-dulled scrub and plumes of spray.

One final bridge, this one wooden and creaky underfoot, took us to our destination. This was one of the few islands in the chain to support a tract of forest, all conifers rooted in soft sand, interspersed with rock and moss and beds of pungent needles. Ridges of snow still latticed the wood, but the breeze was warm.

"Fitting that the cult should come here," I commented as Mary and I stopped at the edge of the forest. A clear path roamed ahead, girded with moss and shifted stones.

Mary reached out to squeeze my fingers, just for a moment. Then she approached the nearest tree and laid her palm on the bark.

"They're at the western edge," she said, her eyes searching my face. "I can go without you, Sam."

I shook my head firmly and set off. After a step she caught up, and we proceeded side by side around the periphery of the forest. We moved quietly, not speaking, though there was little need for stealth. The island was full of the sound of waves, the dwindling cries of gulls, and the moan of the windblown trees.

When the latter yielded to the sound of singing, we slowed and continued more discreetly through the trees. The wash of the waves grew closer, and, ahead in the fading daylight, I saw the glint of water among the trees.

I slowed, sure I had wandered into the Other. But though it still inhabited the periphery of my vision, the forest was whole and real, and Mary's form was unchanged. This side of the island had simply flooded with the rising tides.

Harmonies drifted among the trees, interspersed with laughter and clapping.

"Eerie," Mary murmured as she tugged her skirts up through her belt and pulled off her shoes, which she began to shove into one pocket.

I watched the second shoe disappear, momentarily distracted. "Just how much can you fit in there?"

"A bottle of wine. An infant."

"You tried?"

"The wine, yes."

The sound of the Black Tide cultists' singing rose with the waves and the wind, and my eyes strayed back towards them. Lights pricked in the glowing gloom, a dance of flame amid shades of grey and lavender twilight.

By unspoken agreement, we set off again. The water grew deeper the closer we came, thick with drifting pine needles and twigs, and the occasional brush of what I hoped were fish. When it soaked even the hem of Mary's hiked skirts, we paused behind a large, stocky tree and peered through the gloaming.

Some thirty figures occupied a clearing at the edge of the forest, facing the west and the last vestiges of violet-orange sunlight. The tide was so high in places that some figures were submerged to their waists, while the body of the group moved about through knee-deep water. Some were fully clothed. Some had their trousers or skirts tucked up, while one man, his eyes dulled with drug, wandered nude through the shadowed trees, singing in a baritone so deep I felt its rumble in my skull. He bore a torch, and every so often a bit of oiled reed peeled away. Flaming, it drifted down onto the waves and extinguished.

By far the eeriest sight, however, was the ghisting. The cowled figure of the Midden Ghist was thinly manifest, spectral flesh cladding his harvested wooden statue in the center of the clearing. Evidently it had been placed on an unseen pedestal to keep it from the salty waves, and it presided over its worshippers with luminescent, sea-glass eyes. It had its familiar crown about its throat like a noose, and its arms clasped over its chest in a cadaver's repose.

Mary's fingers dug into my arm. "I know that ghisting," she hissed. Her voice shifted, drifting into Tane's lower register. "We saw its likeness in the halls of the Ess Noti."

"The Black Tide have been worshipping that ghisting for generations," I murmured. "It does not seem far-fetched to imagine the Ess Noti informed themselves about the creature and the cult."

"Informing themselves is one thing, carving a stone statue is another," Mary returned. "Tane could speak with it, but not every ghisting respects a Mother Ghisting as they should. Particularly the worshipped ones."

I made a sound of agreement, recalling Adalia Day's roots harrying us out of the Oruse.

I pulled her after me into the shadow of my tree, farther into concealment. "This connection sits ill with me. I need to speak with my uncle… the loyalties of all Black Tide cultists are suspect."

Mary began to nod, but froze. Leaning back out around the tree, she peered through the darkness. "That's Lieutenant Adler! The one who attempted to recruit me."

Following her gaze, I found the offending man dressed in common garb and leaning against one of the trees and staring out at the ocean with drug-hazed eyes.

"He shames himself," I muttered, neglecting to mention how the sight of him made rage coil in my chest. "Himself and the entire service."

The lieutenant's presence was more than shameful, however. It meant the Black Tide had devotees among the Navy, and, where an officer went, many common sailors and soldiers would follow. The Black Tide had never been outwardly violent—save towards the mages submitted to their ministrations—but any connection to military power sat ill in my mind.

I said as much to Mary, my voice so low that I had to repeat myself.

"I dislike that Adler is the one who approached you," I added, the words far too mild. "Perhaps it is no coincidence to find him here."

"Or perhaps he is simply more unorthodox than his peers," Mary pointed out. "Regardless, I refuse to be afraid of the Black Tide."

The image of Mary, held down and blinded by chanting cultists, momentarily assaulted me. It was no vision, but it was still clear enough to make my mouth dry. "Do you see anyone else you recognize?"

"Enisca."

"Pardon me?"

I twisted to follow Mary's gaze. There, in the shadow of another tree, Enisca Alamay watched us. She raised a hand, gesturing for quiet with the Usti's three-fingered tap to the lips, then she approached.

"What are you doing here?" Mary asked the spy in a whisper.

Ms. Alamay wore trousers and a long coat, loose about the waist. Her hair was hidden under a kerchief, and I caught the scent of pine sap and salt.

"How long have you been watching them?" I added.

"Since I saw the first group leave town with the ghisting. I have counted over one hundred devotees coming and going, and have heard them speak of others joining them in the next weeks."

"Why are you watching them?" Mary pressed.

"The Ess Noti naturally have a particular interest in the Black Tide Cult," Alamay explained. "Surely you understand why."

Mary and I exchanged a glance.

"What of their ghisting?" I asked. I was still disinclined to trust Alamay with anything beyond the necessities, and the connections between the cult and the Ess Noti did little to settle me. "Do the Ess Noti know of him?"

Alamay stood straighter in the shelter of our tree, her eyes lingering on the cultists. "Yes, though I know nothing myself. A cultist tried to recruit me in Renown and it seemed prudent to investigate. You recognized someone? I saw you pointing."

Mary identified Adler, though the night was growing closer and the figures harder to distinguish. The water too continued to rise and the forest to flood, inching towards its full depth. Waves crept up around the carved robes of the Midden Ghist.

We fell silent as several torchbearers began to leave, wading out of the ever-deepening water. Firelight flickered on rivulets behind them, and the trunks of the trees cast long, eerie shadows through the drowning wood.

Mary shifted back, Alamay retreated into the shelter of another tree and I crouched as they came closer.

Voices came, soft and conspiratorial, but amplified by the water.

"...such honors," a young male voice insisted, his tone one of admiration. "I shall of course play my part."

A woman replied, her voice deep, mature and calm. Her words did not carry as the young man's did, but his response came to us again.

"If it must be so," he said, sounding less enthusiastic now. "A matter of course."

A vision swam towards me from the shadows, tapping against my defenses like sea snakes against a hull. I inched onto the divide between the human world and the Other.

The vision rushed forward, filling my senses. I saw the young man full of shards, bleeding to death in the shattered gun deck of a ship. I saw him spend a night of awkward but sincere passion with a young woman, and the pride in her eyes as he left her on the docks. I saw him mere moments ago, trailing his fingers through the waters of the rising tide in the Midden Ghist's glow.

I also foresaw the rest of the cult dispersing and passing this very tree moments from now. They would bring the ghisting with them, and he would certainly sense Tane.

"We need to go." I beckoned, and, in wordless agreement, we departed.

We did not stop until we reached drier, more elevated regions of the forest. The little wold was quiet around us, once again full of the simple, constant sounds of washing water and wind through bent pines.

I found the forest night distinctly unsettling, surrounded by such layers of shadow. Alamay seemed to share my sentiment, keeping close watch on the trees, but Mary was at ease.

"What did you see?" Alamay asked me. "In the Other?"

"That young man is going to die." I delivered the truth with solemnity. "Aboard ship, in the coming battle. Little else of consequence."

Alamay shrugged. "He is a sailor. Many will die."

"Unfortunately so. In any case, I must speak with my uncle. Even if the Midden Ghist's connection to the Ess Noti is irrelevant, the cult should not be allowed to gather in such numbers."

"What are they harming?" Alamay asked, her question sounding genuine.

"It is a matter of principle," I replied and shoved my hands into the pockets of my coat. Despite its warmth, the water had chilled me to the bone. "Now, let us retire. Perhaps there will be clarity with the new day."

FORTY-EIGHT

Preparations

SAMUEL

Spring rains began to fall on the Aeadine Anchorage. For ten days they continued unabated, dispelling the last vestiges of snow from the alleyways and raising a stifling fog. The temperature rose but remained rather cool, the kind of damp chill that made bones ache and the wood of the ship creak all the louder, even in the quiet waters of the harbor.

I met with my uncle twice during this time. They were largely impersonal affairs in which I strove to impress upon him my concerns about the Black Tide and reacquaint myself with the current state of the Navy and the government.

I found my questions rebutted at nearly every turn. Even though *Hart* would be sailing with the fleet, I was no longer one of Her Majesty's officers, and my uncle could not speak freely.

Being shut out by my own uncle and former admiral was not only painful, but endlessly frustrating. Even when I broached topics not directly related to the fleet and the coming conflict, such as restricting the arrival of Black Tide devotees, I was disregarded.

"I say this with full awareness of the past, but the Black Tide poses no real threat to Renown. Why ever would they? They are a nuisance, to be sure, and fools, but there is no law against idiocy," my uncle told me at our first meeting. "This port is not simply a naval base. It is a

settlement, with citizenry who may do as they wish, within the law.
I advise you to ignore them, Samuel."

"What of their ghisting?" I pressed. "The Ess Noti know of it, sir.
What if there is a connection?"

"Then that is a matter for more appropriate parties to concern
themselves with," was the admiral's reply. "Not an Usti privateer."

"Of greater concern is the mere twenty armed vessels in
Renown," Alamay said that evening as I hosted a dinner in *Hart's*
great cabin, a company that included Maren, the Uknaras, Grant
and Mary, and even Fisher, who had been brought fully into our
confidences. She sat beside Maren, who nursed a cup of mildly
alcoholic tea. "How many more ships can be brought in before the
Mereish Fleet arrives?"

"Fifty," Ben replied. He had taken to smoking a pipe since our
arrival, and a cloud of blue-tinted smoke clung to the ceiling above
his head. The habit seemed to calm him, however, and no one
complained.

"If we are fortunate," I hedged. Outside the open gallery windows
to the rear of the room, rain pattered on the quiet harbor waters and
fog obscured the town.

Fisher raised her own mug of rum-laced tea. "I shall be among them.
I've accepted a temporary commission, and I was not alone. Three
armed merchants have been pressed, captain through cabin boy."

"Still, I do not believe your people understand the threat to be as
great as it is," Alamay said. "They do not believe the Tide will reach
the heights the Ess Noti predict. They still believe their fortifications
will mean something."

I watched the small woman, considering, not for the first time,
what an asset she would be not only to the Aeadine but to my concerns
about the Black Tide. She was already investigating. Perhaps I
should encourage her efforts. Equip her, even. Perhaps she could
not be wholly trusted, and I would need to be careful, but I was in
want of allies.

And she had far more skills in espionage than I.

"How do you know what they believe?" Grant asked her from where he hunched over a spread of cards, playing a distracted game with himself. "Have you been spying on them?"

Alamay's level look was enough of an answer. She said, "Missives have been sent to Tithe to enlist the Usti's aid, but I doubt we have enough time."

"Tithe rarely has more than four Usti warships in the area," I said. "Even if they could render us aid, they must remain neutral."

"Outwardly, in any case," Olsa said.

"What will you do?" Benedict asked Alamay.

"I cannot say. It may be some time before I receive new orders."

"That is not what I asked," he pressed. "What will *you* do in the coming conflict? With your skills?"

The company was quiet, waiting for her response.

"I will remain aboard ship until after the Black Tide," the Usti spy said, though she did not add why—Ben remained in the dark about our plan to heal him. "But I will not fight, that is not my way. Then I will return to Hesten. Your brother has promised to deliver me there."

Ben did not look convinced. "You should tell us what you know of the Usti's meddling. Whatever documents Jessin Faucher gave Sam may be gone, but I cannot believe you are ignorant of what was in them."

Ben's words must have come with Otherworldly force, because Alamay's expression tightened in the barest, unwilling betrayal. She did know more than she chose to share. But that in itself was no great shock.

Ben caught my eye meaningfully.

"Why do you care?" Mary challenged Ben.

Ben only shrugged.

Alamay rallied, her expression growing opaque once more. "Even if Jessin's claims are true, and the powers of Mere and Aeadine could be convinced that my people are propagating their conflict, will they care? Do your divisions not already run too deep? Or will it cause a greater war—one where Usti is no longer neutral?"

"That would be catastrophic for everyone on the Winter Sea," Olsa pointed out.

Ben hid a smile in the corner of his lips. "What a shame that would be," he commented, placing his pipe back between his teeth and unleashing a fresh stream of smoke. "What chaos."

More ships began to arrive. Less than half of them had more than twenty guns, much to my uncle's displeasure, or were so new their paint glistened as they were drawn into Renown Harbor.

"Those ships are barely out of their cradles, and their crews might as well be," my uncle commented at our next meeting. We stood on the wall to the east of town, watching the newcomers drop anchor in organized formation. "Would that I could reinstate Benedict myself. His influence would go a very long way aboard one of those."

I slipped my hands into my pockets. "Can you not make an exception?"

My uncle's lips pressed into a thin line. At length he said, "No. However," his gaze swiveled to me, "if he were to prove himself during the battle, that would go a very long way. Unless, Samuel, you would advise me to abandon all hope for the boy and see him imprisoned for his own good. If you believe him too far gone—you must tell me."

I was grateful my hands were out of sight, concealing their sudden clench. "That did not end well for our mother."

Admiral Rosser's regret was clear but stiffened by practicality and years of acceptance. "No, it did not."

I gave myself a moment to breathe, pushing thoughts of my mother aside. "Ben is not lost yet, Uncle. He will prove himself."

Admiral Rosser nodded, and we returned to surveying the harbor.

I avoided the Black Tide Cult during this time, but Alamay, her efforts now quietly endorsed—in the privacy of my cabin by a pouch of gold and my own insight into the cult—brought me multiple reports of their movements.

"There are many more cultists than I saw in the forest, and I do not just mean that more have arrived—though some certainly have," Alamay told me one evening as we stood on deck, watching the new ships from Ismoathe run gun drills. Their crews scurried into the bellows, whistles and occasional lashes of their officers. "How prevalent is the cult, in general?"

I shook my head. "They've perhaps five thousand affiliates in all of Aeadine."

Alamay considered this, thoughts passing behind her blue eyes. "Perhaps a tenth of them are here now."

My skin crawled. "To worship the tides? Or have you uncovered any other purpose?"

The Usti woman shrugged. "I found nothing untoward in Mr. Pitten's personal correspondences, nor Lieutenant Adler's—he seems the most influential of the lot, thus far."

"Then we must bear with them and hope they do not shirk their duties in religious fervor," I said.

"Indeed."

On the thirteenth day, the rain broke and the sun washed Renown in a wave of unseasonable heat. The winds, too, shifted, coming up from the south in a steady stream. In the mornings the rock of the islands steamed in the sun, and the tides continued to rise. Two days on the waters also ceased any retreat, until the outer islands became perpetually submerged.

On the morning of our fifteenth day in Renown, as the rising sun cast *Hart*'s shadow across the waves and glinted in every east-facing window of the town, the warning bells began to ring.

I climbed to the maintop to find Mary already there, clustered with two crewfolk and a spyglass, conferring in low voices.

We could just see the western horizon around the shoulder of the fort and the stretch of the town. And there, where the line of the sea met the clear, brightening sky, I saw specks—towers of sails, white with a scattering of red and deep, lavish purple.

The Mereish Fleet had cleared the horizon. A mere thirty Aeadine vessels had arrived in Renown, and the outer islands were already submerged.

"A count, Ms. Echings?" I quietly asked one of the watch.

"Three dozen was my first count, sir," the wiry Ms. Echings, a dark-skinned northern Aeadine woman, replied. Her wide-set, round eyes were grim and humorless, well aware of all this meant. "But there are more."

"The proper tide is not until tomorrow morning," Mary whispered. Her hand slipped into mine, her other braced on the rail as *Hart* rocked in the gentle harbor waters. "Why are they here early? Shouldn't they wait for the water to be at its highest?"

"They know we have no hope of rallying aid in time," I replied, low enough for the wind to keep my words from Ms. Echings and her fellow watchman. "But we are not completely unprepared. Our orders will come soon."

"If they attack before the height of the tide…" Mary spoke equally quietly, her lips close enough to send gooseflesh prickling down my neck. "How long can the action last? If the highest tide comes and we're under attack… Your healing, Sam. How can we do that in the middle of battle?"

"We need to speak to Mr. Maren," I concluded.

We descended together. I dropped to the deck first and offered Mary a hand again, which she accepted. On our way across the deck

I caught Olsa's eye, prying her from where she and a portion of the crew conferred over a spyglass and a narrow view of the Mereish lines, and nodded for her to follow.

"Ms. Poverly!" I called to the girl, who had been in Olsa's company. I nodded towards the fort. "Mind the signal flags and alert me as soon as there are any changes."

The girl bobbed her head. I brushed aside questioning glances from the rest of the crew, keeping my expression calm as we disappeared below.

Moments later, Mary, myself, and Olsa held council with Mr. Maren and Alamay in my cabin.

"The ritual must be done during the height of the Tide itself," Alamay said with a note of irritation. "Regardless of any ongoing battle."

"The Mereish may not wait until then to engage," I said, my mind a churning diagram of timings and tactics. "They likely intend to reduce Renown to rubble before then and head for the mainland before the waters retreat."

"Meaning we may all be dead or captured," Mary pointed out.

Alamay nodded stiffly. "Yes, but we cannot know that now unless a Sooth foresees it, and even then there may be leeway. Regardless. We have a day before the healing can be done, and, by my calculations, the best time will be soon after third morning bell. Too early, or too late, and the risk to all of us grows. If we are not finished by dawn, you will need to wait until next year, and our task will be much harder without the aid of the Other's moons."

"And if the time comes in the middle of battle?" Mary asked. She flicked her gaze to me. "Would you leave your post?"

"He must," Alamay returned flatly.

"The ritual will take no more than a few minutes," Mr. Maren added. "Though I cannot speak to your condition when we are through."

"Our plan remains unchanged, then," I summarized. "At third bell during the Second Turning of the Black Tides, we will convene here, perform the ritual with all haste, and return to duty. I will prepare my officers. And I will ensure Ben accompanies me below. Olsa, you and Illya should have your talismans ready—you must be prepared to subdue him."

FORTY-NINE

Possession

MARY

Benedict leaned against the ramparts next to Charles and I, watching the Mereish Fleet with an ever-shifting regiment of curious townsfolk.

Hours had passed since the fleet filled the horizon, and Samuel, along with the captain of nearly every other ship in Renown, had been summoned to the fort. The remainder were either already cruising or had departed to reinforce key points along the anchorage, and message flags flew continuously from the fort's heights.

"The Anchorage is soon to fall," Benedict said without preamble. "And my career is over."

"Your career should have been over a long time ago," I reminded him.

Charles was silent, either lost in his own thoughts or determined not to involve himself in another of Benedict's self-pitying moments.

"I have been a good officer," Ben countered. "I have obeyed orders. Protected my country and my crew. I helped bring down Lirr and escaped Mere, and brought back word of the Mereish Fleet and other threats besides. Why, then, am I punished for a private action in the dark? 'Conduct unbecoming'—who are they to dictate who I bed?"

I met his heated gaze. I knew the brunt of his resentment wasn't meant for me, but my heart still gave a primal, terrified twist. I kept it from my face, responding with dignity and coldness to rival his ire.

"Ben, for once, think of someone other than yourself."

"I am," he growled. "I need a ship. I need the opportunity to do my duty and prove myself once again."

Charles cleared his throat and straightened. "I'll take a turn down the wall," he said, shoved his hands into his pockets and meandered away through the sober, chattering townsfolk.

"Still, selfishness," I said to Ben. "You will never feel true compassion or sincerity or regret unless you're healed."

Ben watched me a moment, a cat deciding whether to torture a trapped mouse, then looked back out to sea. "Do you truly believe it would work?"

"I do." I gestured to the fleet, deflecting from the truth. "There must be a High Cleric out there we can capture. You did tell Samuel you would have done it, if we had found a cure in Mere."

Ben grunted. "I meant it at the time. But I enjoy what I am. My existence is not a crime."

I suppressed a wave of frustration. "Ben. What did you feel when Lady Alice took you to bed?"

His mouth started to twist in a leering grin but stopped as I continued, "What did you feel when she smiled at you, and looked at you with love?"

"She thought I was Samuel."

"Yes, and?"

He seemed perplexed by the question. There was a lull in the sound of the townsfolk around us too, and for a time the wash of waves and the distant toll of a bell rose to prominence.

At the fort, the flags changed again, and spyglasses glinted.

"Jealous," Ben said finally. "Surprised. I did not have to use my power on her. She was… still happy."

"And knowing *you* caused that happiness, even accidentally? Is that a feeling you'd want again—but truer?"

He turned his head, and suddenly his eyes, his breath, were very close. He asked in a soft, power-laced rumble, "Are you asking to go to bed with me, Mary?"

A passing man shot us a disapproving look and hurried on, propelling his staring daughter ahead of him.

For an instant I couldn't think, wrapped in power and want and a blooming heat, then Tane nudged me. I breathed again, swallowing my temper.

"I am trying to help you," I replied, dropping my voice equally low. "Your career might be over, but your life is not. And—as useless as it might be for me to point this out—Samuel needs you to be healed. One day he will become trapped in the Other and no one will be able to save him."

"He manages." Ben tossed aside the notion, but there was something raw, half-buried, in his expression. "I know he will not bed you or marry you unless he is healed. But Mary." He smiled, slow and seductive, and leaned closer to whisper, "I can be him."

His power brushed over my skin again, but less potent.

"Let yourself be healed, if the opportunity arises," I returned coldly, though we were nearly nose-to-nose. North of the Stormwall, Samuel had ensured Benedict's co-operation with promises of glory and power. I could do the same. "Promise me you will. And I'll do everything in my power to make you the hero of this battle."

"How?"

"The Mereish ships with the red sails, they're important, right? Jessin Faucher's is one, and he's son of the head of the Ess Noti."

His smirk told me I sounded ignorant. "Yes," he said with exaggerated patience. "Purple sails are flagships. Red are squadron heads."

"We'll take one, and I'll ensure you get the credit. Saint, we'll capture their admiral and her flagship and cause chaos. And I, under *your* command, will shatter that fleet."

Ben's mouth quirked. There was fascination in his eyes, as if he couldn't believe what I was saying, but was delighted by it. "That is madness."

"I can sink their ship with a word. I cannot die. You can bring the crew to heel without speaking."

"We sound deadly."

"Will you do it?"

"I cannot control a thousand men at once," Ben warned. "They will have Sooths and Stormsingers of their own, if not Adjacents and talismans. And Samuel will want to participate in our little game. They will give him the credit if they can."

"He will do anything for you," I reminded him, bitter though the words felt. "Come now, Benedict. Let's do it. We've faced worse odds."

"Fine." Abruptly, Ben straightened and looked over the crowd. The sound of their chatter had changed, and, following his gaze, I saw soldiers making their way along the wall.

"No loitering about!" one soldier called. "These ramparts must be cleared for military action!"

"Time to go back to the ship," Ben observed. His breath curled as he shoved his hands into his pockets and strode away.

I paused, but a quick glance through the now-thinning crowd turned up no sign of Charles. Deciding he would likely meet us back at the ship and unwilling to face the soldiers, I joined the flow of townsfolk down the stairs and into Renown proper.

Mary, Tane's voice sifted up through the back of my thoughts. *There is a disturbance in the Other. Take a breath.*

I left the flow of the crowd and stepped into a quiet street, tucking myself into an alcove between the cluttered old buildings.

With a long, slow exhale, I relinquished control, and Tane pulled us into the Other. The houses faded, and water began to lap around my ankles, colder than I remembered.

There.

I followed the push of Tane's will and looked not north or south, but directly up.

I see nothing, I said, disquieted. Nothing but the fleeting passage of a few distant creatures, glowing soft oranges and yellows. The glows of ghisten ships and Stormsingers occupied the harbor, and a gathering of other mages lingered at the fort.

Look at the moons, Tane urged.

My lungs began to ache. I released my first breath and stole my second as I searched the Other's sky.

Four moons presided, all of them precisely the same—the barest of sickles, nearly invisible.

A chill crept up my spine. *Our moon is visible in the Other too? Is this what you wanted me to see?*

Look more carefully. A purple glow.

I did, filtering all the other clashing lights of the port away and focusing on the four darkening moons. Gradually, I registered a deep purple glow, the color of overripe plums and old bruises. There was a shape to it too, winged and bony.

To be discernable at this distance, it must be massive.

What is that? I whispered to Tane.

Her response was more chilling than the sight of the strange, skeletal creature against the moons.

I do not know. A pause, then an urgent, *Someone comes.*

I exhaled my last breath and slipped back into the human world to the rhythm of boots on the cobblestones. They were quiet, not creeping but contained, and by the time my eyes found their owners, my exit into the street was already blocked.

The foremost figure, a middle-aged woman with narrow shoulders and broad hips, held out a sheaf of papers. She spoke in a hard, bracing voice that made my blood run cold. "Mary Firth. I am Lieutenant Isolde Barlowe. You have been reclaimed by Her Majesty's Royal Navy. Come willingly for the sake of your country and your captain. The tide is rising, and Aeadine's hour of need has come. Resist, and you will be taken by force."

There was a pace and a half between the woman and I. She had a sword at her hip, one gloved hand resting on its hilt. The six burgundy-coated marines behind her had bayonets fixed to their muskets, their eyes shadowed beneath cocked hats.

"Reclaimed?" I repeated. "I have never belonged to them. I am protected by the Usti Crown."

"Then your captain is free to bring your contract to the Admiralty and speak your case, but for now, you must come with me," Barlowe said.

"I will not go." The words left me of their own accord, but I meant them. Rage burned up my throat, indignation and injustice that made the air feel taut around us, like water on the brink of freezing.

Barlowe noted this with a long, unimpressed blink. "If you do not, your captain will be arrested and tried for withholding property of the Aeadine Crown." She raised a hand, two fingers up, as if to gesture her soldiers forward.

My stare turned into a glare fueled by a lifetime of warnings, fear and injustice. "You're bluffing. You've a Mereish fleet on your doorsteps, and the Black Tide is rising. My ship needs me, and you need him."

"If you fear the Tide, lend your voice where it matters most." Barlowe's voice was iron. She waved her soldiers forward, and rough hands seized my arms. "Come. Now."

"I won't be used!" I felt Tane in my glare, not in spectral shadow but in essence—her long years, our power. My winds came too, swirling and ready to act, ready to assault and disorient. Another song lingered on the back of my tongue, prepared to pull the breath from the soldiers' lungs.

But I faced a dozen enemies in an open space, and my chances of winning this battle were low. Ben was long gone by now, and there was no sign of Charles. Samuel was still up at the fort. I hated how vulnerable their absences made me feel, how abandoned.

I steeled myself, though a trembling had set into my hands. I knew from experience that if I fought back, I would only earn myself pain and a tighter leash. But if I went willingly, I might find a chance to escape.

So I allowed myself to be hustled from the alleyway and into the clutches of the Aeadine Royal Navy.

Admiral Evane Solace was a broad woman with a trim black wig, contained by a dark-blue ribbon at the nape of her neck. Her bicorn hat threatened to jostle the brims of the dozen other captains crammed in the grand cabin aboard *Recompense*, flagship of the Aeadine South Fleet.

I was damp and cold from the journey through the towering forest of masts west of the Aeadine Anchorage. Anger smoldered in my chest, but my hands had stopped shaking by the time Solace met my gaze.

I hoped she would see my righteous indignation, that it would at least give her pause. But Solace's eyes barely lingered before she returned to the conversation. She gestured absently to one side, and Barlowe pointed me into a line of four other women against the bulkhead.

One wore a Stormsinger's mask. She was young, barely into womanhood, her cheeks tear-stained and plump. Two others were grey-haired, one with a distant gaze and the other with a steady, confident air. The last was a spindly, middle-aged woman with a narrow face and eyes that reminded me of my mother—harrowed, resigned. Hollow.

"Who are you?" the spindly woman asked. The words were barely out of her mouth when she cut off into a pained grunt.

One of the grey-haired women reclasped her hands in front of her skirts. The spindly woman tucked her arm protectively into her side and fell silent, staring straight ahead.

I followed her gaze across the cabin, looking through the company as my mind churned. Clearly, just because these other women were Stormsingers did not mean they were allies.

"Attention," a male voice snapped. A lieutenant situated himself in front of us, marked by the broad black cuffs on his dark navy coat and the three points of his hat instead of two.

Lieutenant Adler. Of course. This was his ship, *Recompense*.

The girl in the mask started to cry. The urge to go to her, to put an arm around her, made me waver on my feet.

In my bones, Tane stirred. *We free the girl first.*

Agreed.

"Ms. Slorach and Ms. Elsher have seen fleet action before and are experienced working in concert with other Stormsingers," Adler stated. "They will direct you. You will obey all orders. One step out of line, one note of deviance, and it will be marked." At this, his eyes swung to the wiry woman, then to me. His gaze narrowed, then returned to Slorach and Elsher—the older women with grey hair. I wasn't sure which was which.

"This," he pointed at me, "is Anne Firth's daughter. She is untrained, but I am sure you can make good use of her."

I watched him, my expression flat. "Let me loose and I will sink the fleet alone," I baited.

The lieutenant advanced to stare directly into my eyes. The man from the docks was nowhere to be seen, startled by an offer of toffee. Here, he was in his power, and his superiors were watching us.

Perhaps he'd hoped to loom, but we were of a height, and I'd faced down Benedict Rosser at the height of his rage.

I stared right back.

"Ten lashes for Ms. Firth," the lieutenant said without taking his eyes from me. "On the legs. We do not want her struggling to fill her lungs."

I Quelled the air around him with a single inhale—and didn't even realize I'd done it until he started to gasp and weaken at the knees.

A hand seized the back of my neck. I cried out and twisted to find one of the grey-haired Stormsingers hauling me backwards, spinning me around and pinning me to the bulkhead. More hands came, crushing me. I struggled until I felt the familiar straps of a mask around my head, then I lost control.

These men and women were not my people, not the only defense of my homeland and kin and the village between the Ghistwold and the slate hills. They were my enemies.

Fresh air hit my face above the mask. I blinked streams of rage-filled tears from my eyes as I was hustled onto the forecastle of *Recompense*, into the wind. I was divested of my coat and outer garments, stripped to shirt and trousers. My arms were forced above my head. I jerked and struggled, trying to turn, only to glimpse a grim-faced man with a whip taking position behind me. Around him, sailors stared from the rigging, gunners faltered at their work and the other Stormsingers were lined up to watch. The young girl was crying again, near the point of smothering herself with tears and snot.

I wanted to scream, to demand the wind tear across this deck and prove I couldn't be subjugated and controlled. But I had no voice.

The wind gentled, as if it watched. The rocking of the ship was light, and across the deck, crewfolk continued to stare even as the bosun's whistle shrilled and an officer shouted for them to return to work.

I wondered if those on the other ships watched too—Stormsingers and Sooths, officers and common sailors, marines and soldiers.

I twisted, searching uselessly for *Hart*. I saw only the other Stormsingers again—the girl, the older women, and the spindly one—holding my gaze with something that might have been compassion, had it not been so cold.

Courage, that look demanded.

Tane, help me, I whispered. Tears began to freeze on my cheeks and lashes. I wanted to step into the Other, to slip from my bonds and leap into the sea. Tane knew that, as readily as I knew that if I did, I'd just be fished out of the water again and Sam and *Hart* would be punished.

My plea shifted. *Help me endure this.*

I felt her slip to the front of my mind, taking control. My panic ebbed as if I wandered on the edge of sleep, as did the pain of my strained arms and a dozen new bruises.

We will endure, I murmured in the quiet of my thoughts as I leaned my forehead into the damp wood of the mast and heard a whistle pipe. *We will endure. And we will break fleets upon the water.*

Sleep, Mary, Tane whispered.

I closed my eyes as the first lash struck.

FIFTY

My Boys

SAMUEL

"How could you let this happen?"

The door slammed behind me, rattling the glass in the window and causing the wood in the fireplace to crumble in a plume of sparks. Sparks wafted over the ornate black screen and into the candlelight that illuminated my uncle at his desk.

Admiral Rosser set his quill aside and rose. I knew that look—the guardedness and calculation. He was trying to figure out which twin I was, and I supposed that, wild-haired and enraged as I was, I must have looked more like Ben than ever.

"Control yourself," Admiral Rosser commanded. "This was out of my hands."

"'Out of your hands'?" I repeated, advancing. "Admiral Solace overruled you?"

"Sit down, Samuel."

"Are you not equals?" I demanded, planting my palms on the desk and leaning forward. "Do you have no voice? Did you even *try* to defend her?"

"Sit down!" The command came so sharp and so firm, my knees bent—just a fraction. I shoved the chair away, and it toppled with a satisfying clatter.

Admiral Rosser stepped back from the desk, thumb to his temple, fingers digging into his forehead as he took a deep, calming breath.

"*Hart* is a fine ship, Samuel. But we cannot waste a Fleetbreaker on him. Mary must sail with Solace. With any luck, they will fracture the Mereish before they are in range of our guns. This matter is larger than you or I or one witch, and duty demands sacrifice—you are the last person I should need to explain that to."

His words drilled home, angling towards the supposedly selfless, stoic convictions I had once based my life upon—and still longed to, in a withering corner of my heart. But the idea of Mary carried off without her consent, stolen into the hands of the very same people who had used her mother and lost her to pirates... that could not be borne. Least of all not when my own uncle, whom I had trusted and whom Mary had revealed Tane to, stood complicit.

"I give you my word, she will be returned to you after the action." The admiral began to round the desk, abandoning the shelter of its divide to face me. Encouraged by my silence, he continued in a lower voice, "There is no more natural feeling than the desire to protect and keep those you care for. But this is war, Sam. Your Mary could save us all, given the opportunity. So we shall give it to her."

"If she is killed—" I started but could not finish.

My uncle stepped no closer, but the hard edges of his face softened a fraction. "I can make no guarantees. But I *will* ensure she is freed after the battle. You have my word."

I resisted the urge to scoff. My head was aching—a warning of Hae's searching or simply a physical response, I could not tell. The Dark Water waxed and waned with every beat of my heart and the natural lights of the port outside the windows transformed into the illuminations of every ghisting, mage, and lurking monster in range.

I felt for Mary instinctively, merged with the blur of other Stormsingers' lights aboard *Recompense*.

Visions came, assaulting me in quick succession. I foresaw a ship with red sails, looming over me. I saw a serpentine, Otherborn beast burst from the fabric of the sky and cannon embossed with scenes from myth drifting downwards, past the trees of a submerged forest.

I glimpsed death and destruction in a hundred ways, and Mary's singing voice threaded through it all.

Cool metal pressed into my hand, and I blinked, swaying. My uncle stood before me, clasping my hand around my coin. His eyes were round, the pomp and practicality of his station abandoned.

"Samuel?" he asked, patting the side of my face as a father might. For an instant he *was* my father, visions twisting with memory.

My father with one hand cupping my cheek, one Ben's.

Take care of one another, my boys.

My uncle released me, and the Dark Water, along with the visions, retreated.

For once, Admiral Rosser was nearly speechless. "Samuel... you need a physician."

"I *need* Mary," I replied, my coldness undercut by the fact that I had to steady myself on the desk. "And I must return to my ship."

"I will do all in my power to free her, after the Black Tide has waned and the threat passed," the admiral vowed, yet again. "It will be mere months, Samuel."

"Months?" I tossed back. I pushed myself upright and stepped towards the door, propelled by the need to be alone, to separate myself from the admiral and the confusion of emotions he elicited. "I will reclaim her after this battle. The Tides be damned."

I did not linger to hear my uncle's counter.

To my shock, Ben stood in the darkness of the hallway. Dark Water lapped around the heels of his boots, and his head was cocked to one side.

"You heard?" I asked as he turned on his heel and fell into step with me. I spoke low so as not to alert my uncle, the lush carpet muffling our footfalls and, distantly, at the edge of my perception, a slosh of water.

"I did," my brother returned. "Though I am surprised you are laying the blame so thoroughly on Uncle, instead of raging at Charlie and I for not being there."

"Do not tempt me," I warned. "She should have been safe, regardless."

"Then you are truly going to let this go?"

"No," I growled. "But *Hart* will take his place in the lines. If *Recompense*'s Stormsingers can stop the Mereish Fleet without a gun fired? So be it. But I doubt it will be so."

We did not speak again until we were in the cool damp of the street. The weather was shifting, though whether it was natural or not was impossible to know. Snow fell for the first time in a week, heavy and thick with moisture, already turning to sleet.

"I was promised glory when this is over, Sam," Ben prompted, evidently moved on from our previous discussion. "And a new chance at life."

"Will you settle for notoriety and a chance at life?"

Ben eyed me askance. "What would I be notorious for?"

"Hopefully valor. Possibly treason. Because I will not leave the Anchorage without Mary back aboard my ship."

Ben considered this, then shrugged and pulled off his hat, turning his face into the sleet as if it were a summer breeze. "So be it."

Bitter rain sheeted from the sky as *Hart* took his position in a small flotilla of privateers and pressed merchants at the far south of the Aeadine lines.

Damp clung to my clothing, hair and beard, and my oiled coat did little to stop its pervasive chill. Despite the applications of various Stormsingers, it had yet to disperse—solidifying the conclusion that it was Mereish in design. I listened to the threads of their voices on the wind, but none belonged to Mary.

The rain not only shortened our line of sight and ensured every sailor in the fleet was miserably wet, but it threatened to spoil powder—even moisture-resistant Usti gunpowder, sealed in its red wood barrels. The deck was slick. Around me, hands threw down buckets of sand, and Ms. Skarrow oversaw the preparations of the long guns, while Mr. Penn instructed our sharpshooters and Mr. Keo strode the deck. At the stern, Poverly reported to Ms. Echings, and together they ran a series of colored flags up the mizzen. We were ready.

Similar flags went up from the other ships in our company, all bright and new and yet hardly visible in the downpour. *Nomad* lurked nearby, black hull blurred against the rain-mottled waves. The former pirate vessel's ghisting was partially manifest, slipping over the wood of its cloaked figurehead like luminescent, indigo oil. Hart himself was in full manifest, lingering on the waves before his figurehead, just as I lingered behind it at the fore. His tines spread wide as the branches of a winter oak, impervious to the rain, and his sea-glass eyes were fixed west as he pawed the waves.

Drake, our leader, was a two-masted naval brigantine of red and gold. His namesake ghisting—a great serpent with multiple sets of shuddering wings, just like the beast I had summoned upon our escape from Ostchen—coiled around the mainmast in the same manner as his figurehead entwined the fore of the ship from keel to rails to bowsprit, which was capped with a wild-eyed draconian head full of teeth and frothed with rage. As I watched, a boy ran the length of the bowsprit and hung over the beast's gilded head. A second later, flames sparked—bright one moment, then dimmed in a plume of smoke. The boy retreated, leaving thick, dark-grey smoke to eddy from the figurehead's jaws despite the rain.

"How dramatic," Grant muttered at my side, admiration leaking through his scorn. He was fully armed with sword, pistols and musket, but hardly looked himself with his usually fine clothing abandoned in favor of a dour oil coat and neckerchief.

Across the fleet, more ghistings awoke. This was not uncommon in the face of battle, but the degree of manifestation was beyond anything I had seen. Every ship-bound ghisting was in some stage of exhibition, their shifting, spectral lights joining the illumination of ships' lanterns in the human world. A handful of Otherborn creatures, too, lurked in the sea, a scattering of blood-red huden and a distant swirl of white morgories, flocking through the deep like sparrows across a stormy sky. An impling crested the top of a great man-o'-war's mizzenmast, chased by a vaguely ursine ghisting. At will, it fizzled from the human world and back to the Other.

Other than that impling, I could hardly say which world the creatures truly resided in. I lingered perpetually on the edge now, suspended both by my curse and by the inexorable, blurring pressure of the true Black Tide. Even my talisman, resting passively against my sweaty skin, could not keep me rooted.

The Black Tide had come, and the fabric of the worlds was paper-thin, as was my grip upon the waking world.

"Ben," I said lowly.

He did not acknowledge me, though he had drawn up behind Grant and I. His power lingered around him in a perpetual cloud, crimson as bloodmist and visibly agitated, swirling in an unseen wind.

"If I should become trapped in the Other, see me to my cabin and take command," I said because, for all else that my brother was, he was a competent strategist and commander.

"Of course," Ben said, unflinching.

"And ensure Mary does not remain in the hands of the Navy."

Rain pounded on the deck and dripped off the brim of his hat. "That is no small request."

I nodded. "I am aware. Still, after all I have done for you, do this for me."

"You speak as if you are dying, Samuel. You will come back."

Grant looked at me too, unspeaking and subdued.

My voice did not waver, though my admission should have panicked me. "Perhaps."

Before the conversation could go further, a cannon fired in the distance. The Mereish, testing their range. I flicked my gaze along the front line of Aeadine ships, all massive warships with a hundred or more guns, but was much too distant to see the splash.

Another gun cracked in response, this time from the Aeadine Fleet. I saw its muzzle flash and even fancied I heard the whistle of the shot, audible over the creaks and rustles of nearly one hundred ships.

Then the singing began.

FIFTY-ONE

Tempest Sisters

MARY

My world became song and chaos and wind. My voice merged with my fellow Stormsingers', led by hard-eyed Slorach and the occasional orders of Admiral Solace. Our voices bled into numerous harmonies that urged the rain back towards the Mereish Fleet and an ever-thickening crown of slate cloud and churning wind.

As fierce as my indignation towards the Navy was, I felt a certain kind of freedom as I lilted and roared and sent my voice to the sky. A release. A revelry that made my blood surge through my veins and my lungs savor every breath of salty, livid air.

The rising of the Black Tide was intoxicating. I felt as though I were drawing close to a hearth on a cold winter's night, though rain still lashed my scalp and my damp hair clung to my throat. Power saturated me like heat seeping through frozen flesh, leaving room for one, singular goal.

To let that power free.

My voice began to slip out of concert. I closed my eyes, pulling new threads of wind to me. I tasted each one, sensing their possibilities.

Aboard the ships all around us, other Stormsingers sang their own occasionally discordant chants to the sea and sky. Many fought contrary winds and swaths of rain from the Mereish Stormsingers— first a wave of tearing squalls then familiar banks of fog, creeping across the waves before the enemy fleet. Their every sail was full of unnatural wind—and that wind, I decided, to steal from them.

The other Aeadine Stormsingers pulled a new, fresh easterly, and the Aeadine Fleet began a gentle, arcing advance towards the Mereish.

"*Come as the winds come,*" the women around me sang. "*When forests are rended.*"

"*Mother, mother, oh mother of mine,*" I sang in harmony, my voice softening as I drew into myself. Tane flickered across my skin like a winter chill. "*Deep in forest and woodland shrine…*"

Guns began to boom, but I did not flinch. My eyes were closed, but I could still see the wind and a mist of fine, twisting rain. I saw, too, the clouds boiling across the sky—the sky above both fleets now brimmed with coming wrath.

"*Come as the waves come, when Navies are stranded,*" my companions sang.

I felt someone take my arm. I ignored them, continuing my own song. "*Our bows will hide you, our roots grow deep…*"

Someone pried the hand from my arm and I heard a heated exchange. Then the space around me broadened—full of wind now, instead of bodies and voices.

I opened my eyes. The other Stormsingers had moved away, leaving me in a semi-circle with my back to the stern railing. Their eyes were on me, and, slowly, they began to echo my song.

Wind swirled between us, its strength growing with each passing moment.

"*In our shelter, find your sleep,*" I sang.

Behind the Stormsingers I saw the grim faces of Admiral Solace and Lieutenant Barlowe—Adler was nowhere to be seen. Beyond them stood a line of red-coated backs and primed muskets, separating us from the rest of the ship.

Beyond all of them, the space between the fleets—the black, choppy waves full of Otherworldly lights—grew ever shorter. Swaths of fog eddied, thickening with gunsmoke and muting flashes of cannons into pulses of orange and red.

"*Leaf and branch and root and vine,*" I fixed my gaze and will across the water, on the Mereish ships. The other Stormsingers' voices twisted with mine—amplifying my power and carrying my words far farther than they could have ever traveled alone.

"*Bend no knee to the march of time...*"

The rainstorm began to cede to me—to us, to our choir of power and influence. I felt its last resistance give way in a rush and swirl, and the air on my face grew suddenly warm.

Distantly, I was aware of Admiral Solace bellowing orders. The songs of my fellow Stormsingers faltered, as did the movement of our ship.

I carried on as the first cyclone touched down on the waves. Water exploded upwards in stuttering plumes as the whirlwind skimmed the surface—one plume, two, then a waterspout shot from sea to sky in a terrifying, marrow-curdling roar of water and wind. It crashed through a Mereish ship with steady indifference and plunged deeper into the fleet, drowning the sound of cracking wood and screaming sailors.

The youngest Stormsinger shrieked in horror and clapped her hands over her mouth.

Something inside me faltered then. I saw my mother's harrowed eyes as she recounted her time with the Navy, of breaking fleets upon the water and sending thousands to a watery grave. This was the future she had tried to protect me from.

Tane felt it too. She rippled under my skin and her light hazed my eyes—I knew that light was visible now. My eyes shone in the human world, just like the Otherborn creatures that combed the sea between the fleets.

Another Stormsinger gave a startled cry. Some of the soldiers turned, and Admiral Solace stared at me with an uncertain intensity that, strangely, filled me with satisfaction.

"*Pay no heed to winter's chill,*" I sang, though my voice was immediately swept away by the wind. I met the gazes of my fellow weather mages, urging them to maintain their song, to lend me their power. Half continued, their voices stronger than ever. "*The axes of men or the blood they spill.*"

Another cyclone surged up into the sky at my beckoning, then another and another. The thunder of cannons joined with the roar of wind and water, the hum of taut lines, the crash of hulls through water and the snap of sails. Across the ship, sailors whooped and cheers drifted to us from other vessels, even through the chaos.

Then we entered cannon range. Marines closed more tightly around the Stormsingers, a physical wall of flesh protecting us from marksmen, while still allowing us full view of the fleets.

I gave a breathless, hitching laugh as a fifth and sixth cyclone surged towards the sky, water chasing wind and bearing a moaning deluge of hail. The sky was my cathedral and the cyclones its pillars, surrounded by fog blooming with muzzle flashes and fire, and a bruised backdrop of indolent daylight.

Our voices began to split, harmonies twisting in a near-discordance so unsettling, so lovely, every hair on my arms stood on end.

A great warship cut between us and the Mereish Fleet—one of the Aeadine's massive first-raters, with her towering masts and a figurehead of a female warrior, her six great wings clothing the fore of the ship as Hart's tines enclosed his. The warship loosed a full broadside, and, through the billow of gunsmoke, I saw the mast of a not-so-distant Mereish frigate sway in a tangle of rigging and sail.

I pinched my eyes closed, focusing on my song alone. Tane's light still shone, though, and her awareness continued, filling me with a rush of more inhuman observations: the Otherborn beasts in the water beneath us, the mind of the *Recompense*'s ghisting, whispering to Tane through the wood beneath my feet. I glimpsed a purple beast with skeletal wings, sweeping over the dim reflections of ghisten ships in the Dark Water, and a dittama landing on our bowsprit.

Mary!

Tane forced my eyes open as three of the marines, their wall of red coats still barring me from the rest of the ship, turned. The first one—pretty and round-cheeked—raised her musket.

Directly at me.

I saw the conflict in her eyes for the briefest instant. But when her finger closed on the trigger, marked by a ring with an obsidian rendering of the new moon, there was nothing conflicted about it.

I threw up my arms and turned aside. The musket ball, bound for my head, tore through one hand before searing across my bicep and the side of my neck. As it passed I felt the muting power of a Mereish talisman—then it was gone, and Lieutenant Barlowe bundled me onto the deck. All I could see was her blue jacket and clamor of bodies, and all I felt was the burning, blinding pain in my open wounds.

When I could see again, horizontal and still cluttered with boots, I saw two other Stormsingers dead upon the deck. The thin woman who had tried to greet me was missing the back of her head. The other, Slorach, clutched uselessly at her back, choking through a lung full of blood. It gushed from her open lips and dripped to the deck in viscous threads.

"Get below!" Lieutenant Barlowe said in my ear. She jerked me sideways, still keeping me in the shelter of her body. "Move!"

But we were trapped at the stern. The quarterdeck had broken into melee, swords flashing and bodies roiling.

I found my feet and backed against the rail. Tane was already at work, dulling my pain enough for me to begin to navigate my thoughts.

"Ess Noti," I breathed to Barlowe, who had situated herself directly in front of me. I had no doubt of it, though the logistics, the fine details escaped me just then. Distantly, I felt my cyclones still tearing through the Mereish Fleet—extensions of myself, hounds on leads as thin as silk threads. They were straining, and I needed to regain control. "That woman, that soldier, she was wearing a ring with a new moon. The Black Tide Cult? But the musket ball was Ess Noti."

Whether Barlowe had been informed of either the Ess Noti or the Black Tide Cult's threats was unclear. She repeated, "We must get you below. As soon as I tell you to move, follow me and keep low."

"No," I replied. Fear was a distant and irrelevant thing, now separate from my body. No part of me could countenance leaving the wind, not when I had felt so much power, so much potential. Even if the Ess Noti were at work, that was not my task. "I can do more above. The Black Tide and the Ess Noti, Barlowe. What are you going to do about them?"

Barlowe signaled to two marines. They broke the line and advanced.

"Take all of the mages below," she added, gesturing more marines towards the remaining Stormsingers—Elsher and the perpetually crying girl.

The ship rocked with an explosion, and the world seemed to pause, caught on a startled breath. An Aeadine brigantine to our right, just visible through the rain and fog, shattered from the belly out. Fire burst in a blaze of orange and red, searing itself into my staring eyes. Debris shrilled in every direction—audible, if rendered ineffectual by the distance.

Barlowe's voice was slow to pry through my ears, despite the fact that she was shouting not a pace away. "Escort her below! You! Fetch me the Fourth Lieutenant. Where is the admiral?"

The marines took my arms as, out in the Mereish Fleet, one of my cyclones collapsed in a deluge of water. It crashed over a small ship and sent it rocking so fiercely sailors toppled into the sea like dolls from an overturned trunk.

We remaining Stormsingers were led away—only three of us now. We were halfway down the quarterdeck stairs when a second explosion shook the ship, this one so close everyone ducked—save me. Shards sang through the air, one skimming so close to my head that I felt the rush of wind.

Distantly, I knew I'd lost control of all my cyclones, but I was too shocked to grasp them again. Past my blood-soaked sleeve, I saw fragments of sail flutter to the waves next to another Aeadine ship—this one with almost the entirety of her forecastle blown away and bleeding fire. Frantic sailors ran up her masts as the ship yielded to the sea, her hatches spewing as much water and flotsam as men and women.

I barely had time to assess my companions—one guard scrambling to help another, who clutched a long shard in his thigh—before shots cracked across *Recompense*'s deck. Screams rekindled, and a nearby soldier with the red collar of a Magni collapsed in a spray of blood. A shriller shriek accompanied the stumbling form of the young girl. I'd no time to see her injuries before she was swept below decks with Elsher.

For an instant, a feeling of solitude struck me—every eye was somewhere else. I could jump ship now. Surely, I had no real loyalty to the other Stormsingers, no hope of freeing them in any lasting way. I could still fight the Mereish from *Hart*.

Then I remembered the power of the cyclones, the churn of all our voices in concert. How much had been Tane and I, and how much had been them?

I felt another shot strike the rail beside me and plunged below after the other Stormsingers.

BEASTS, OTHER—*Sooth Mages have long spoken of beasts who reside within the Other that defy established classifications and titles. The majority of these, unlike implings and their ilk, cannot pass at will between realms, or emerge so rarely as to remain in folklore alone. However, recent attempts to classify these creatures have been made, and new categories proposed: the squid-like ishalk, the winged argreth, and the ursine andowt. See also:* ANDOWT, ARGRETH, ISHALK, OTHERBORN.

—*FROM* THE WORDBOOK ALPHABETICA: A NEW
WORDBOOK OF THE AEADINES

FIFTY-TWO

The Summoners

SAMUEL

I saw Her Majesty's *Drake*'s demise moments before he shuddered with an unseen explosion.

"Brace!" I bellowed across *Hart*. Everywhere, my crew dropped to the deck, and Olsa, at my side, stepped behind the mizzenmast.

Blasts rippled through *Drake*, spewing fire from gunports and shaking marksmen from the rigging. His ghisting circled the ship in distress as fire raced from stern to bow. When it reached the figurehead, the ghisting Drake reared in silent, terrified pain, and I saw Hart's light ripple through the deck at my feet in agitated response.

"That was no accident," Olsa said beside me, her posture still crooked with tension. She cast her gaze out across the fleet at another explosion, then another.

The third explosion, however, could hardly be heard over the roar of a whirlwind. I shouted another warning as one of the Aeadine Stormsingers'—now, apparently wayward—cyclones touched down three ships away. The sea erupted towards the sky, taking with it a glistening, churning stream of morgories from the water below.

For a breath, I could only gape at the sight, then orders cut from my lips. *Hart*'s crew scrambled to respond, and I clutched the shrouds as wind and spray battered us. Slowly, *Hart* eased away from the cyclone. The other ships in our squadron scrambled to do the same, and *Nomad* nosed out into the sparse stretch of empty sea between us and the Mereish. He loosed a broadside, cannons firing in a synchronous ripple I had no time to laud.

"Samuel!"

Benedict advanced up the quarterdeck stairs, prodding a sailor ahead of him at cutlass point. Despite the man's obvious ensorcellment, Benedict was careless with his blade, and several bloody puncture marks marred the back of the man's jacket by the time he fell to his knees before me.

Benedict grabbed his prisoner by the hair and tipped his head back. "Recognize this bastard?"

Mr. Pitten stared up at me with Magni-dulled eyes.

"What were you doing aboard my ship?" I asked, though my Sooth's senses—so sharp I felt as though I knew each sound before heard it—had already delivered me an answer. "Sabotage and murder."

Mr. Pitten contorted, fighting not to react.

Benedict nodded to his pocket. "I found an Ess Noti talisman on him, a Magni one." He shook Pitten's head pointedly, and the man's face creased in pain. "Pity I am a Black Tide Son, Mr. Pitten, and that thing was a fucking trinket."

Pitten gasped in sudden, unmitigated terror, and Benedict's power billowed around him in my doubled vision.

"You came to sabotage my ship," I repeated. "And kill, but who? All of us, Mr. Pitten? Can you bear to have so much blood on your hands?"

"I was to disable the ship, that is all, I swear!" the cultist protested.

"Why? Under whose orders? The cult's?" I gestured to the charred wreckage of *Drake*.

Pitten tried to scream in frustration but choked off as Benedict's power rushed into his nose and mouth. He spasmed.

"Answer, now," Ben demanded.

"They sent after the man, the Mereish man!" Tears streamed down the landsman's face, but hints of accusation battered their way into his gaze. "I have no choice. I have to kill him. He told me to! The Midden Ghist! He—"

"Maren! Secure Mr. Maren!" I snapped to Olsa. She was already running across the deck and vanished through a hatch. Illya raced to join her as I added, "And look in on Alamay!"

Beyond the lattice of lines and sails and the wreckage of *Drake*, a massive, dark-purple light bubbled between the ships of the Mereish Fleet.

Dread assailed me. Something large was trying to break through from the Other, and, with the veil as thin as it was, I doubted it would be long before it succeeded. Whether it yielded to a Mereish Summoner or came of its own accord, I had little doubt it would be dangerous.

"See Mr. Pitten secured below," I said to Benedict, then made my way to the rail looking midships. "Hear me! We will take no one aboard from *Drake*, we can risk no saboteurs. Mr. Penn! Organize a search of the hold, we may have more stowaways aboard. Mr. Keo, take us south."

My orders were being executed before I finished issuing them. As we slipped carefully through the battle, navigating the other ships and entering more open waters, I drew my spyglass and trained it back on that roiling, purple light. I glimpsed two Sooths on the deck of a Mereish ship next to the anomaly, a brownish hedge to the forest green of their lights.

Sooths, but Adjacent. Summoners.

"Ms. Poverly." The girl had frozen at my side, transfixed by one sight or another. I placed my coin in her palm. "I must go into the Other. Give this back to me in three minutes and ensure I hold on to it, do you understand? Do you have a pocket watch?"

Poverly nodded fervently. She looked less frightened than I anticipated, more overwhelmed and grateful for a task. She held the coin in one hand and took her watch in the other, then hovered close as I took the quarterdeck rail in both hands and lowered my head.

The Other leapt up to swallow me. The fleets thinned, becoming little more than reflections of ghisting-inhabited wood and magelights. The lights of Otherborn beasts between—and occasionally on—the vessels doubled.

I focused on the bruised purple light. I saw the creature here, whole and manifest as it hovered, shuddering through the paper-thin wall between the worlds.

The beast was like none I had ever seen. It swept into the water and rose again on broad, avian wings—though its feathers had the texture of seaweed, rippling with water and slung from a thin frame of raw bone. Its head was capped by an eyeless skull and a long, vicious beak, and its legs ended in talons longer than boarding pikes.

I watched it strain at the barrier for a breath, debating my course of action. The Mereish Summoners clearly intended to use the beast against the Aeadine—but should I try to stop them, or allow the beast through and turn it back on the Mereish? If I pitted my strength against the Mereish mages, could I win?

Something skimmed past my cheek. I turned as it passed and, in my mind's eye, saw a musket ball. Shock, then a spike of fear stabbed through me.

Someone had shot at me, but not in the human world.

In the Other.

I dropped into a crouch behind the rail just as another shot slammed into it. The ghisten wood, present in both realms, swallowed the ball like living flesh. No crack, no shatter. No splinters.

There, across the water, I saw one of the Mereish Summoners had turned to me. A long rifle rested against her shoulder as she lined up for a third shot.

I barely registered the faint glow of her weapon—radiant as ghisten wood—before the great winged beast finally tore fully into the human world. It faded to a glow, a reflection like the hundreds of other beasts and mages scattered across the fleet. I saw that glow descend on an Aeadine ship, its brightness vibrating as claws raked the deck and shredded rigging.

Another shot struck the rail behind me and my mind stuttered, threatening to blank. Only one thought took root in that thunder of heartbeats and roar of blood in my ears. More lights were converging on me, and I had no idea how many of them answered the will of a Mereish Summoner. My chances of stopping the beasts—particularly the winged one now terrorizing the fleet—were slim.

I needed a weapon of my own.

FIFTY-THREE

Fates Worse Than Death

MARY

The remaining two Stormsingers were gathered in Solace's grand cabin, one of the few compartments whose walls had not been taken down for action. Now that it was not packed with figures, I could see that the room was lavish, with cases of books and drapes of velvet, rugs on the floor and ornate lanterns fixed to the beams, though none were now lit.

The door to the stern balcony stood open between the gallery windows, filling the cabin with damp, smoke-thick air. We clustered before it, watched by half a dozen, hopefully trustworthy, marines, led by a midshipman barely older than sixteen. Evidentially we were expected to continue our tasks, despite the threat of assassination, sabotaged ships, limited line of sight and no new instructions.

The midshipman, for his part, turned away to drink from a flask and avoided the prompting looks of everyone in the room. His hands shook, and there was blood on his face. I might have felt pity for him, had all our lives not been in jeopardy.

"What are we to do?" I finally demanded, interrupting the boy's poor attempt at discreetly intoxicating himself.

"We will remain here until the threat has passed," he rattled out, dropping the flask to his side. His cheeks flushed in shame as he heard the quaver in his own voice. "Carry on."

"With what? We can hardly see," Elsher snapped.

"They're trying to kill us!" the young Stormsinger said. Her terror was a baffled thing, all wide eyes and shaking hands. She had a bandaged arm and numerous cuts, including one on her face that sluiced crimson down her throat and soaked her shirt.

Elsher and the midshipman descended into a short, heated confrontation, he delivering vague instruction and she countering. It was growing rapidly clear that the boy had little concept of the situation or what to do about it.

From the expressions on their faces, the marines agreed with me.

Tane's and my thoughts ran seamlessly together. The Black Tide had Ess Noti provisions, worshipped a ghisting known to the Ess Noti, and had no reason to attack their own people other than under Mereish pressure. Just how that pressure had come and how willing the Black Tide were was unclear and, to some extent, didn't matter. They, it seemed, would kill us if given the chance.

The young Stormsinger met my eyes, and through the melee of my emotions—elation, horror, confusion, determination—I suddenly, fiercely, wished I had jumped overboard and swam for *Hart* when I had the chance. But at the same time, I was relieved I had not.

I raised my voice over the conflict. "I have a plan. And, I believe, some insight into the situation."

"Then speak." Elsher turned on me, giving up on the midshipman.

"The Black Tide Cult is killing Aeadine mages and, I suspect, sabotaging our ships," I said, including everyone in the room. "The weapons they are using are tied to Mereish spies. They can resist sorcery, if they have the right talismans, and their musket balls can stifle our power if we are shot."

"How?" the midshipman asked, sounding lost. His flask hung from his fingers now.

Anger flared through me, though I was not wholly surprised. "Your superiors should have told you this. You should have been warned."

The midshipman's face burned an even darker shade of crimson. He took a swig from his flask and wiped his mouth. "Why would the Black Tide betray us? They are… they are Aeadine."

"But they worship Mereish sorceries," Elsher stated.

I nodded. "They've a bastard kinship. Whatever their reasoning, this is the situation we are in. Now." I glanced at the open balcony door and caught Elsher's eye. "We need to regain control of the cyclones."

The pair of us moved out onto the balcony, followed a breath later by the girl. We crowded against the rail as the winds came to us, laden with the stink of gunsmoke and fire and blood and burning tar and hemp. The thunder of cannons was constant, and flotsam thudded against the hull. I watched a body eddy past, face-down, and forced my gaze upwards.

Our view of the battle was stunted, choked with fog and comprised almost solely of the middle and rear lines of Aeadine ships—or what had been, and was now a scattering of a dozen burning hulks and desperately maneuvering vessels. I could not see my cyclones, and I felt only two remaining, far to the west.

"We are useless from here," Elsher stated, craning around the stern of the ship. "We are as like to destroy our own vessels as theirs."

"Then we hide!" the girl said. "That's what they want, isn't it? Maybe they'll leave us alone."

I glanced at her with growing irritation, but, before I could speak again, I heard the door to the cabin open and a male voice.

"Oh, thank the Saint," Elsher muttered, and she and the girl hastened back into the cabin.

I froze, framed in the doorway.

"There is a Mereish vessel making to board us. Marines, above, now." Lieutenant Adler was efficient and brusque, at ease in his command. His sword was sheathed, no pistols in sight. He did not look like a man who had come to assassinate three trapped mages, but…

Damn it all. How could I have forgotten Adler was here? Even in the chaos, I should have remembered, should have—

The soldiers started to leave. The midshipman fiddled with his hat in the doorway, asking some hushed and nervous question, clearly reluctant to leave the safety of the cabin.

"He's Black Tide!" I shouted. The midshipman looked back at me, perplexed, but Adler shoved him into the hall, shut the door and flipped the latch.

Elsher shot me a startled look.

The corners of Adler's mouth pulled up in what I supposed was a bracing smile. Somehow the contrast between his reluctant expression and the hand he laid on the hilt of his sword was all the more terrifying.

His hand was smeared with blood.

Behind him, someone started pounding on the door.

"I am to kill only those who threaten the Mereish Fleet," he said, his voice low and calm. His eyes fixed on me, and, with his free hand, he fished a glass bottle from his coat. "So decide, witches. Are you a threat? Drink this, and your power will be suppressed for the remainder of the battle. Solace will not be able to use you, and you may live. Otherwise…" He drew his cutlass and tilted it, letting light flow down the blade.

The girl flinched forward, eyes fixed on the bottle, but Elsher shoved her forcefully back.

"We are the queen's." The older woman glared. As she did, the air in the cabin shifted, stirring our hair and clothing. "We live and die at her pleasure."

"Speak for yourself," I muttered. I threw out an open palm, hummed one low note, and closed my fingers.

The Quelling affected Adler instantly. He staggered, trying to gasp. He won a thread of breath, only for me to stifle it again, holding his breath captive.

His stare became a lance, spearing through me as he found his feet, cutlass still clutched, and stalked across the cabin. As he passed the table, he set the bottle out with stiff, pointed movements, then, in a sudden change, unfolded like a whip towards me.

I darted to the side. He missed my arm by a hair, and, as his face swelled red and his eyes bulged with near-manic determination, he seized Elsher instead and ran her through.

"Run!" I shouted to the girl. I seized a chair and threw it at Adler but missed, hitting the bulkhead with a resounding crack.

My control faltered. I heard the lieutenant rake a shallow breath and he grabbed for the girl.

"I'll drink it!" she shrieked, snatching desperately for the bottle. "I'll drink it!"

He pinned her to the windows. Somewhere in the struggle, the bottle slipped from the girl's hands and shattered on the floor. Light cut around the young mage, igniting stray, glossy dark hair in a halo. Her already bloody face became a mask of shock, her hands limp at her sides.

Adler's muscles twitched to strike, delivering me one last, warning look.

I let my power fall. He gasped like a drowning man, still holding the girl in place. Never once did his eyes leave me.

Elsher was dying not far away, leaking blood and more pungent fluids onto the deck as she sobbed in disbelief.

"What did you do to me?" Adler growled.

An impact shook the deck. Shouts arose and feet pounded—not just above our heads, but in the passage outside the cabin. Fists pounded on the door with renewed urgency, and voices clamored. Wood began to splinter.

Any second, they would break through. Elsher and the girl—they could still be saved.

Then why did Adler look so calm?

He seemed to read my thoughts. "We *were* about to be boarded, that was no lie." I saw a flicker of something new in his eyes, not threat, but avarice. "I also meant what I said—I will kill only those who are a threat. Come with me alive, or I will kill you like the rest. You have no loyalty to Solace, Ms. Firth, I know that."

Perhaps it should shame me to admit it, but I was sorely tempted to give in, to buy even a few more minutes of life.

Still, I had one more card to play.

Against the window, the girl shuddered. Fearing her legs might give out, I spoke faster.

"You realize what they think of you, don't you?" I asked. "The Ess Noti?"

He was unsurprised by the name. "They are our brethren."

"They despise you," I threw back. More pieces were clicking into place now, nudged in the right direction by Adler's actions and expressions. "Ignorant savages dancing in the moonlight. They are using you."

Adler, to my dismay, laughed. The sound was jarring and genuine and made my blood run cold.

"Of course they use us," he tossed back. "As we use them. That is the way of humanity, Ms. Firth. Of all nature."

The door buckled. Figures poured through the doorway, led by a Mereish officer with a pistol raised.

Adler momentarily looked down the barrel of that pistol before the deafening report filled the cabin.

I grabbed the girl, the last of my sisters, and dragged her out onto the balcony. She let me, her body loose and her eyes blank with shock.

I slammed the balcony door. Just before it closed, I summoned every scrap of air in the room and pulled it in a blood-scented, smoky gust.

Beyond the glass, the Mereish staggered. The room wasn't sealed well enough for the Quelling to last, but I'd bought us precious seconds.

"We have to swim!" I grabbed the sides of the girl's head. My heart hammered, all too aware of the Mereish still pouring into the cabin. Their officer was mere paces away, wheezing but intent.

"I can't swim," the girl whispered, her voice thready and toneless. Her eyes were listless, struggling to meet mine.

I have to leave her, I said to Tane. *I have to, but I can't.*

Then push her.

I shoved the girl into the railing.

"No!" She panicked, suddenly coming to life. "We'll drown! We'll die!"

"There are fates worse than death!"

"No!" She tore away and lunged for the balcony door just as it opened and Mereish poured through.

I leapt for the rail. My hip went over—I felt the pain of it, the jar of wood on flesh, then the shift of balance as I fell off the balcony, down into the miasma of smoke and fog and the churn of the swollen sea.

FIFTY-FOUR

Black Tide Sons

SAMUEL

Wood moaned and rigging rattled as *Hart* came alongside a Mereish brigantine. I knelt on the quarterdeck, sighted down the length of a long Usti rifle, and picked a marksman from the enemy's deck.

Muzzles flashed, gun crews hastened to take up small arms, and boarding nets clotted the sloshing, jarring divide between ships. Benedict and his boarding party pressed at the rails, buoyed by my brother's magic into a courageous, stolid line.

I reloaded with thoughtless movements, my focus on my brother and the haze of Magni magic that wafted from him like smoke. To me, the Dark Water was fully overlaid with the human world now, hardly a gossamer veil between the two. The effect was nauseating, but the intoxication of my heightened power overrode it—along with any qualms I might have had at my brother ensorcelling my crew.

I heard Mereish commands amid the furore. The voice was obscured by the melee, but my dreamer's senses knew precisely where she was, who she was, *what* she was. She stood on the foredeck, a woman of forty-five years—an artist in her childhood, duelist in her youth, and today she would die of a shot to the chest.

I sighted down the barrel of my rifle, though I knew I would not be the one to kill her.

My mind began to divide. I saw a dittama snatch a mage from our prize's deck six heartbeats before the creature wriggled from the Other. I felt the thud of another ship's fallen, listless spar collide with our hull at the same moment as Mereish bar shot shattered it from its mast.

I existed outside of time. And for the first time, my mind bore it.

"With me!" Benedict roared, leaping up onto the rail.

His boarding party, drunk on Magni valor, surged aboard our prize. I landed one more shot, taking a marksman down with a ball to the shoulder, then the melee was too thick.

The clash was brief, as Ben's power swept the ship and Mereish weapons clattered to the deck. The dittama dove, dragging a screaming Stormsinger with it. The captured ship's ghisting, manifest as a robed saint near the bowsprit, yielded back into their figurehead in a slow pulse of ghisten light. The captain took her shot to the chest and proceeded to die.

After that, enemy sailors and marines dropped to their knees and allowed themselves to be bound. Ben and select members of his party stripped them of their clothing and donned it themselves, transforming boarders to crew in moments. The prisoners were hustled below, and Ben saluted me with the Mereish's commander's ceded sidesword.

I raised a hand in return.

"Cast us off, Mr. Keo!" I shouted down the length of *Hart*.

"Sir!" Keo acknowledged, and under his direction we began to disentangle from the prize.

"Are you sure we have time for such… deceptions?" Grant asked, his hat gone, his sandy hair pulled into a hasty tuft and his skin darkened by powdersmoke. He cradled a musket in the crook of his arm. "Do not mistake me, I admire a good disguise, but should you separate so close to the ritual?"

"We have time," I said. I reached for my former intoxication, seeking to pull it over myself like a blanket, but, as Ben and his new ship began to cast off, my expression must have betrayed my concern.

Grant slung his musket over his back and adjusted the strap across his chest. "I shall see him back in time."

"I would be grateful," I conceded. "He seems to have some respect for you."

Grant grinned broadly. "Pestering a soulless Magni into friendship is among the grandest of my achievements."

"I would not claim friendship so soon," I warned. "Be careful."

"Aye, aye, Captain." The former highwayman saluted and made for the rail. I watched as he leapt the growing gap between ships, landing with moderate grace. Sweeping up a fallen Mereish officer's hat, he planted it on his head and sauntered off to join Ben on the quarterdeck.

My Sooth's senses reached after the pair, searching the constant influx of premonitions for their faces, their new ship, for a glimpse at whether our plan would succeed. All I saw was a chaos of conflict.

I retreated to stand beside the helmsman and clasped my hands behind my back. I leaned into my power, shirking my concerns to focus on *Hart*'s impending route through the fog—and the eerie, shifting green light that was Inis Hae.

"Nor-nor east, Mr. Kennedy," I said.

We began a circuitous route through the battle, trailed closely by *Nomad*. I remained beside the helmsman, giving frequent corrections to our course and occasionally calling orders down the deck. When a swarm of morgories surged our way, I diverted them to a Mereish frigate, whose own Sooth—if they were still alive— was no Summoner. The creatures battered the hull as we passed from sight. When a sudden, unsettling doldrum overtook us and a Stormsinger's voice drifted across the wind—singing a Mereish hymn to the sea—I knew where to train the mouth of my rifle to silence but not kill. When her song cut off, the wind returned and we continued forward.

At last, we came into sight of a familiar Mereish frigate with towering red sails. Ben's smaller vessel emerged from the fog a moment later, to all appearances adrift—her deck scattered with limp figures and swaths of blood, and her sails drooping.

Ben's commandeered ship rammed Jessin Faucher's *The Red Tempest* in a moan of wood, clatter of spars and slosh of water. A ship's bell clanged and the frigate rocked dangerously towards us—her deck bared, crew screaming and grabbing onto anything they could. Half a dozen slid down into the water with splashes and suddenly extinguished cries.

"Fire!" Ms. Skarrow roared.

The deck shuddered beneath my boots as our guns sounded. Canister shot harried *The Red Tempest*'s deck before she could rock level once more, and, in the belly of the ship, I saw Hae's light flare. My head immediately began to ache, and I took a moment to clutch the coin in my pocket and grit my teeth.

"Make ready to board, Mr. Penn!" I shouted to midships, where the bald man and his armsmen waited. Through the fog, I saw *Nomad* begin to drop his boats, brimming with Fisher's boarders.

Minutes contracted into seconds as we came alongside our prize. Grappling hooks clattered and boarding pikes stretched across the gap like emaciated fingers under a barrage of musket fire. Swivel guns on the rails of both ships barked in a deadly contention, but, facing threats on three sides, the frigate was overwrought.

Hae was not passive, however. His unseen assault continued, a holystone wearing through my skull and into my mind. I saw his signature light move, heading for the companionway midships.

My time had come. "You have the deck, Mr. Keo!"

I seized a tattered rope and swung the gap between ships to land solidly on the hull, both feet planted between two gunports.

I veritably ran up the remaining distance to the ship's rail. Just as I was about to reach the top a figure appeared, hatless and dishevelled, his edges obscured by the boiling, slate-dark sky. He raised a hatchet and hacked.

The rope gave way. I swung at the last moment and landed on an open gunport, which rattled under my sudden weight. I crouched, seized the edge of the port, and swung under it just as musket fire peppered the wood where I had been standing.

Tired muscles howling with the strain, I latched my legs over the lip of the port and sat up.

The muzzle of a cannon yawned at my chest, so close I could feel its heat.

A ramrod stabbed towards my face. I twisted to the side and tumbled through the hatch.

I hit the deck in a roll and made to stagger upright, only to be bowled back over by Hae. We fell together. I sensed a nearby bucket of sand, ready to soak up blood and water, and threw a handful in Hae's face.

The other man reared back. I grabbed the whole bucket this time and swung it at his head.

He surged to his feet and retreated, drawing his sword as gunners scattered. I let the bucket go and drew my cutlass in the same movement. There were no useless words or threats, no dancing about and wasting breath. He lunged. I caught his blade and twisted into a thrust. He sidestepped and disengaged, his attention dividing as a fresh thunder of feet battered the deck above and the shouting above took on a fevered pitch. Somewhere nearby, an officer shouted close quarters, and the cannons were abandoned.

I gave Hae no reprieve. I attacked in a series of sharp, tight cuts and thrusts, parrying and deflecting his recourses in seamless, timeless action. He met each one with the same ease, the impossible swiftness of premonition.

The exchange lasted seconds. Then, with only the slightest drop, I tucked my sword around his, took control of his blade and thrust.

The tip of my sword slit his wrist like butter. Hae cursed, dropped his weapon, and vanished into the melee.

I made it two steps before a snap and rumble brought me up short. The deck tilted. A badly fastened gun broke loose and began to slide, scattering a cradle of shot as it went. Cannonballs tumbled to the deck as the gun crashed into one of its fellows, crushing a hapless sailor and toppling yet another rack of shot. More cannon balls began to thunder across the deck, smashing ankles and scattering everyone in their path.

I darted out of the way and searched the chaos for Hae—his face or his light.

Above. I fought my way to the stairs and emerged on deck. There Ben and Grant fought their way up the quarterdeck stairs to where Jessin Faucher was surrounded by a guard of twenty armsmen. Fisher was nowhere to be seen, but I recognized her first officer organizing the flow of boarders midships.

"Samuel!" Ben roared. Half the armsmen faltered under an onslaught of Ben's power, but the rest, evidentially guarded by talismans, resisted. "If you please!"

Hae was gone again—below. Hiding? Cowering? My headache eased.

What happened from my feet meeting the quarterdeck to the moment I laid my sword at Jessin Faucher's, I could not recount. My memory is a blur of action and movement, the swift responses of instinct and a cacophony of violent images, one cutting in the next. But soon after, he relinquished his blade, and the ship surrendered.

"So this is your response?" Faucher demanded. His expression was one of betrayal, of all things. "To all I have told you?"

"Not at all. You and I need to speak of many things, but later." I pointed my sword at him before I turned on Mr. Penn, Benedict, and Grant. "Run up our colors and secure the ship."

Penn saluted, and Grant sketched a bow in response.

"Captain," Ben returned, planting Faucher's hat on his head as the man and his loyalists were led below. The rest were already either being corralled into the hold, accompanied by flying fists and last bouts of resistance, or sent over the side to the tenuous mercy of dumped longboats.

"If you will pardon me," I said, cleaning off my cutlass with a handkerchief. "I must seek out Mr. Hae."

FIFTY-FIVE

Flotsam

MARY

I sank at a leisurely pace, dragged down by the weight of my clothes and bracketed by increasing pressure. The drum of my heart and the rush of bubbles was all I could hear, and, though fear lanced through me, I forced myself to calm. I would not drown. My life came from another world, just like the roots of a ghisten tree.

I flexed my jaw to pop my ears and began to methodically work at the buttons of my coat, all the while blocking out my memories of the other Stormsingers, dead or alive, and the reality that Admiral Solace's flagship had fallen with the aid of her own people.

I had to get to *Hart*, to Sam. But first I needed to be able to move freely.

I tore off my coat, neckerchief, boots and stockings. Once the coat was free the water ceased to drag so forcefully, and I began to kick upwards in my trousers and shirt. My braid drifted around my shoulders and loose locks tickled at my face. They reminded me distantly of tentacles, and the last time I had leapt from a ship—out of the clutches of Silvanus Lirr and into the company of the kindly ghisting, Juliette.

I could see *Recompense*'s hull from this depth, side-by-side with the Mereish vessel who had boarded her. Debris and bodies floated everywhere in between, already bumping together in islands of grim flotsam.

Dancing orange firelight ignited the waves. And below them... I spied islands. Not just shoals hidden by the waves, but islands of the Anchorage, complete with drowning trees whose branches brushed the bellies of the ships. I saw a cottage with waving garden plants, the thatch of its roof beginning to fray and lift with the currents.

A piece of cloth drifted past—a woman's lace cap.

The Black Tide had taken the Aeadine Anchorage, and the battle had already drifted from the western sea into the eastern.

A swarm of white lights surged towards me out of the deep.

Tane!

Hold fast.

Tane manifested just as the morgories arrived. The ghisting erupted from my frame as cat-sized, vaguely equine creatures of feathered ruffs and endless teeth surrounded me in a chattering, boiling rush. I felt their cries in my bones, in my frozen lungs— jittering, rattling, a horrible combination of teeth and hunting, hungry moans.

But Tane, too, encircled me. She enveloped me in a spectral body much larger than my own, a goddess of the deep with skin like eddying smoke. She moved with me as I spun, trailing ethereal flesh, and most of the morgories retreated.

One lunged in, snapping for my face. Tane's massive head descended with equal speed. She bit at the morgory like a wolf, and in that moment her aspect *was* lupine, a vague suggestion of elongated head and pointed ears and snarling teeth.

The morgory twisted, but too late. Tane's ghisten teeth plunged into the other creature's flesh and it seized, then flickered out of existence. I heard—I *felt*—a muffled rush and the water contorted, as if suddenly being pulled through a punctured hull. Into the Other.

Then Tane retreated. The rupture between worlds closed once more, and the water stilled.

The remaining morgories vanished off through the fleet in panicked ribbons of light. I was still gaping at the place where that single, attacking morgory had been a moment before.

I didn't know you could do that.

Nor did I. But this is the Black Tide, was Tane's simple reply. She began to shrink, retreating until she outlined my body in a shallow, nearly invisible layer of pale indigo-grey light.

I thought of Sam and Ben and the pending ritual, and the apprehension that crackled through me was too strong to bear. How much time did we have? Was *Hart* still afloat?

I turned in the water, scanning for more murderous Otherborn creatures. Aside from a few manifest ghistings around their ships, every other had fled.

Well then, I steeled myself. *Let's find* Hart.

I surfaced some distance from *Recompense*. But sighting *Hart* was no easier above than below. I was in a maze of battling and burning ships. Smoke stung my eyes, and the air was full of the crack of cannons and the roar of fire and the screams of combatants, the ringing of bells and the moan of wood.

"Tane," I said aloud, itself a testament to how shaken I was. "Can you sense *Hart* at all?"

No, best to start swimming.

So, we swam. I passed other survivors in the water, swimming for wreckage or milling longboats. An Aeadine sailor spied me and beckoned from a boat, but to their confusion I waved them off and kept my own course.

Once, in the distance, I saw morgories swarm again. This time there was no ghisting to intercede for their intended victim, and a floundering woman shrieked as she was encircled by white light and boiling waves. To my relief—and, perhaps, hers—she was quickly consumed and vanished beneath the water.

An indistinct roar turned into the crackle of flames, the moan and whine of overheated timbers and the hiss of steam. A burning

Mereish frigate emerged from the miasma, too close, too fast. Heat came with it, waves and waves of it, and I barely ducked under the water before flaming debris peppered the place where I'd been.

"Shit, shit, shit," I panted as I resurfaced, still so close my flesh threatened to sear. I was losing control of my fear, despite Tane's near indomitable ability to keep me alive. I was lost. No part of me *wanted* to be in this water, wanted to be swimming frantically away from burning ships and watching morgories eat people alive. "Shit!"

Cannons boomed. My teeth jarred. A length of bar shot whirled over my head and impacted with the burning frigate, taking a spar and a tangle of rigging and sail to the deck. Sparks plumed. The finer shriek of canister shot followed on its heels, and, though I could not see the carnage it wrought on the deck of the ship, I heard the pain it brought.

Then, through the chaos, I saw Hart. He charged across the waves, away from a vessel whose bowsprit was all I could see, given the jumble of ships and monsters between us. Ghisten light flared as he met the charge of another ghisting, a great bull, and the two locked in battle.

Another ship drifted between us, blocking the sparring ghistings from sight, but I knew where to go now.

I started swimming.

FIFTY-SIX

Stormlight, Shadow, and the Veil Between Worlds

SAMUEL

I ducked under a low beam and peered through the shadows. I was in what might have been the wardroom, with a long table, toppled chairs and a scattering of hammocks illuminated by several fae dragonflies. Their shattered lantern rolled across the deck as I lingered just inside the doorframe, blocking my quarry's escape.

"Mr. Hae," I called. "Shall we continue to chase one another like children, or face one another like men?"

Hae shifted on the other side of the cabin. His signature in the Other was particularly murky now, more brown than green, and it cast little illumination.

I slipped more deeply into the Other. He must have done the same, for his form solidified—masculine and clad, like me, in billows of Tide-amplified power. The walls of the ship thinned around us, retaining only a vague ghisten glow, and the lights of other mages and creatures beyond took on greater strength.

"Where is Enisca Alamay?" Hae asked. His voice was still foreign, though I had seen his face many times in my memories and visions. "She fled with you. I sensed it."

"She is well. She proved to be a valuable ally."

Hae's expression turned stormier, and I knew I had struck a chord. But precisely why eluded me, chased by vague visions of a partnership and travel, side-by-side. I sensed nothing romantic

404 H. M. LONG

between them, but there was a loyalty, an expectation now thwarted and worthy of the worst of punishments.

"She is still aboard your ship with the documents," Hae concluded, straightening slightly. "No matter. I will see to her once I am through with you."

I kept my expression composed. *The* documents? Alamay had stolen back Faucher's documents, and they had been aboard my ship the entire time?

Whether or not he sensed my line of thought, Hae's lips twisted smugly. "It has been a fine chase, Mr. Rosser. But the Tide will not last, and I have much to accomplish."

A pistol cracked—not now, but in the moments to come. In the present I dodged, seeking the protective shadows outside the cabin and farther up the passage, but Hae was a breath ahead of me. He surged across the space with preternatural speed and filled the passageway behind me.

I had the briefest of moments to register a new glow, outlining the shape of a pistol in Hae's hand—its ghisten wood the palest indigo and its metals infused with a Sooth's faded green.

Then Hae's finger closed on the trigger. There was no visible muzzle flash, not on this side of the worlds. But there was pain.

And a spreading stain across my shirt.

FIFTY-SEVEN

Otherwalker

MARY

H art paced about his ship as I closed, his head low, chest heaving and hooves pawing. There was no sign of his former foe, but a nearby Mereish vessel with the figurehead of a lean, monstrous bull drifted listlessly. *Nomad* was here too, along with Jessin Faucher's *The Red Tempest* and a smaller Mereish vessel who appeared to be under Aeadine control.

Someone must have recognized me in the water, for a line slapped down into the waves. I seized it and held on as I was drawn up to *Hart*'s rail and used the last of my strength to clamber aboard.

"Ms. Firth!" Mr. Penn met me as I fumbled my sodden way over the rail. He helped me upright, but the anxiety in his face was not for me. "Hurry to the main cabin, miss. It's the captain."

Fear clamped over me. Moments later I lunged, breathless, into Samuel's cabin. Sam was splayed across the table on his back, his chest covered with blood. Olsa and Enisca braced over him, the Usti spy holding a compress to the source of the blood while Illya stood guard next to the door with Charles. Poverly patted her captain's face with a damp cloth while Maren laid a series of talismans on his bare, bloody chest.

"Hold him still if he rouses," the Mereish man said to Olsa, and caught sight of me. Relief flooded his expression before his eyes flicked to Illya and Charles. "We need to act now. Find Benedict."

The pair hastened past me, Charles catching my eye as he did. His worried eyes only compounded my fear.

"What is happening?" I panted, clutching the doorframe. My head was light and my breathing too fast, too shallow.

"He is dying and his spirit is trapped in the Other," Maren replied. Below him, Samuel's chest hardly rose, and his stomach was still over the high buttons of his breeches. Enisca did not lessen the pressure on his compress, which was already soaked with blood. "He was shot with an ensorcelled pistol. The ball was made for a Sooth, but not to cut them off from the Other. To imprison them there. I have removed it, but he was too weakened to come back. He is still trapped."

"It is too early to do the ritual," Enisca said, half to me, half to the others in the cabin. "But if we do not try, we may never have the chance. Should we proceed without the brother?" She directed the last at Maren.

"Try what?" Benedict stopped just inside the doorway, staring at his twin. His expression was impassive, locked in stone, but I saw the way his fingers twitched at his sides.

"Your brother's spirit is trapped in the Other," Enisca said, her words blunt and clipped. "Hae shot him, and no talisman can bring him back. Either we heal your corruption, the both of you, or your twin will die. His body cannot fight with his spirit absent."

"Our chances of succeeding are already low with Mr. Rosser unconscious," Maren admitted.

Benedict crossed to stand at the foot of the table, looking down the length of Samuel's body. "Remove the shot."

"We already did. That is not the problem," Olsa snapped. "He is too far gone."

"Ben." I drew up to the other side of the table, bracing my hands on the wood to stop their shaking. The urge to touch Samuel was nearly overpowering, to clutch him and speak to him and beg him to wake.

Ben and I were close, closer than my instincts considered safe. "Please. You have to do this. Please."

He did not reply.

"This," I said, holding his gaze, "is the right thing to do."

"Is it?" he asked hollowly. "To risk my power for a chance at…"

"At saving his life," I finished, speaking the words he seemed unable to. "He took the fall for you. He fought for you. He came for you in Mere. We did."

At the last he seemed to truly look at *me*, for an instant.

"Please, Benedict," I said, infusing my words with every ounce of sincerity and compulsion I could muster. "Please."

Illya stepped forward, backing up my words with more explicit force.

"No need for that, Usti," Ben muttered and turned his attention to Maren. "Tell me what to do."

"Ms. Poverly," Maren prompted.

Poverly approached Benedict and held out a bottle of vaguely bloody-looking liquid, coppery and thick.

"Drink that. It will help you shift physically into the Other. Samuel will be there too, but he may be disoriented, even unconscious."

"I'll go with Ben," I offered.

Enisca released the compress to Poverly's smaller but no less capable hands and took up a second bottle in blood-pinked fingers. She tipped it towards Benedict in a mock salute.

Benedict stiffened—my months in the man's presence told me that the tic in his jaw was more alarm than anger. He held up his own bottle. "This will send me into the Other? How this different than what *they* did to Sam?"

Enisca's reply was unflinching. "We know what we are doing."

Benedict's fingers contracted around the bottle, and for a moment I feared he might crush it.

Olsa took one of Samuel's limp hands, clasping it between both of her own and settling her shoulders in preparation. "I will not cross over physically, but I will in spirit."

I longed to be in Olsa's place, her hands wrapped around Sam's, but knew the other Sooth was far more capable than I of managing Samuel's disoriented, injured body.

I could see Benedict's anger and growing frustration, making his chest rise in tight, short movements. He hung his head briefly, eyes closed, simply breathing.

I forced myself to offer him an open palm.

"What do you want?" Ben asked.

"Hold my hand." I still did not look at him, focusing on Sam's closed eyes instead. "I'll be with you. I'll Otherwalk and anchor you as long as I can."

"You must move more quickly," Maren interjected. "Do not speak. You will all have four breaths before the danger of corruption— further corruption, for the twins—becomes too great, so hold each breath as long as you can."

Ben ignored my proffered hand but downed the bottle in one long swill.

At the top of the table, Maren gently hefted Samuel's shoulders and tilted back his head. "Mr. Grant."

Charles carefully poured the liquid between Samuel's lips, and, under Maren's direction, massaged his throat to help him swallow. Sam did not stir.

"Do not let him breathe more than four times on the Other side," Enisca instructed Ben, Olsa and I. "Cover his nose and mouth between breaths."

I couldn't bear it—the sight of Samuel's limpness, the slosh of strange liquid or the suggestion that we would need to smother Samuel to keep his physical form in the Other.

I left Benedict at the foot of the table and took up position next to Maren. Then I drew a deep, level breath. As I let it out again,

Tane's presence surged, and indigo-grey light filtered around my vision.

The human world dropped away with ease. The walls, the table, every object in the room faded, until only the lights that were our companions remained. The distant boom of cannons and clashing storms vanished. Olsa's brightness became stronger as her spirit followed us over the divide and began to pace the cabin, surveying the Dark Water beyond with vigilant eyes.

Samuel's body lingered, suspended in the air before us and wrapped in his dark, forest-green glow. Still limp. Still unresponsive.

I heard the sharp intake of Ben's breath—a gasp, shuddering on the way out. His first breath.

Samuel's physical form suddenly crumpled to the deck of the ethereal cabin. I bit my lips closed and dropped down next to him, pulling his head into my lap and covering his nose and mouth with careful hands.

A heartbeat later, the red-hazed body of Enisca joined us. Her eyes were wide, her lips pinched, and her hands pressed to her stomach in apparent nausea. Still, her movements were quick as she reached into the pocket of her coat. She pulled out a wooden knife, the blade glowing like ghisten wood.

"Help me lift him. We head to the water now," she said—her first breath. Her voice was low but clean and natural, and I fully comprehended that, along with Samuel, she and Benedict were wholly in the Other with me. Olsa's form was still ethereal, half-present and watchful, ready to warn us of approaching danger. But Samuel, Benedict and Enisca were Otherwalking.

I had known this was coming, conceptually, but hadn't anticipated the rush of emotion it brought. I was not alone in the Dark Water, with the lights of a thousand monsters beyond tenuous walls.

I reached to heft Samuel's shoulders, but Ben pushed me aside. He heaved Samuel up on his own despite his barely healed shoulder, expression straining, nostrils flaring as he battled not to breathe, and looked at Olsa promptingly. A breath slipped through Samuel's lips, then I covered his nose and mouth once more.

The Sooth woman led the way to the bulwark. She passed through without hesitation and stepped, bizarrely, directly into the water paces below—ankle-deep water for her, though the draft of the ship ran far beyond that.

One breath later, we were with her. The Dark Water lapped as Enisca motioned—hastily now, all of us nearing our final breaths— for Ben to put Samuel down. I crouched with him, and Ben arranged his brother's head in my lap above the slosh of the black waves.

Fae dragonflies converged in languorous gold and purple swirls as Enisca took one of Samuel's hands and slit his palm open, her lips pinched, her movements fast. She set his hand back under the waves, dark blood merging with darker water.

She took Benedict's hand next, opening it shallowly from thumb to little finger in one clean swipe. He watched her without expression, though I saw the strain in his jaw and the way he fought not to speak.

He held out his hand and watched his blood drip into the Dark Water. As it fell, spectral tendrils of light surged into existence, lacing Samuel and Benedict to the world all around them and one another. The ties between them were strong, a clean and unyielding black that Tane sensed as healthy. But another cord wound around it, a muddied mingling of forest green and burned red that pulsed and strained. That same cord passed through each of the twins and trailed off into the water—Ben's more sickly pink than red or green, and Sam's tinted with orange.

Then, just as my lungs began to scream and Ben tipped his head back, chest spasming for want of air, a pure, blood-red color trailed up from the water. It wrapped around the men's bleeding hands and seemed to pry *into* them, into their veins.

The muddied mingling of colors clarified, each color separating into individual strands, still entwined but whole in their own right.

The fae dragonflies around us surged and brighter lights began to close—morgories, I knew, among other monstrosities.

We had to leave, and not just because of the creatures closing in. Enisca put a hand to her chest, clearly straining, and caught my eye. She nodded once, her expression ill for want of air, and gasped.

The solidity of her form vanished, transitioning into a red haze. But I hardly saw.

Samuel, Ben and I all shuddered back between worlds. Water clapped over my head. I struck out, flailing—not to save myself, but to find Samuel. Limp, unconscious Samuel.

I surfaced and raked in a frantic breath. For an instant all I could do was fill my lungs—they were bottomless, ravenous, and burning. I tried to claw the hair from my face but my eyes stung with saltwater and I couldn't see, couldn't find—

A strong hand seized me by the collar. It jerked me forward until I bumped into a piece of wood—wreckage. I clung to it, instinctive as a newborn babe.

Benedict did not let go, holding me on one side of a drifting spar while, on the other, he held Samuel's shoulders above the water. Samuel, whose eyes were slowly opening beneath a hedge of sodden hair.

"Thank you," I tried to splutter, but ended up coughing instead. I fumbled to wrap my arms around the spar.

"Do not drown," Ben rasped. His power came with it, lending strength to my limbs and clarity to my mind I hadn't had before. It felt different—clearer, truer—and his voice was not entirely devoid of emotion. If anything, he sounded overcome.

"Saint." Samuel coughed. He fumbled weakly for the spar too, and Ben pulled him closer, bracing him against the wood.

I reached across to grab his hand, and he grabbed mine in return. His face was deathly pale and creased with pain, and I tried not to think of his wound bleeding into the water.

"What happened? Where is *Hart*?" he asked.

I twisted, blinking stinging eyes as a bank of smoke blew across us. We were alone between unfamiliar ships, save for the spar, trails of rope and patch of tattered sail. *Hart* was out of sight, Samuel was bleeding into the sea. And Enisca was gone.

"We need to get you to a surgeon," I said to Samuel, eyes flicking between the nearby ships. The smoke was thickened with fog, forming a dense miasma. Two vessels in sight were disabled, one burning. Another appeared to be Aeadine and mostly intact, but was swarming with Otherborn beasts. The screaming of her crew was muffled, not only by the fog but by the roaring of the fire and wash of the waves, as if a boundary had been set between us and her horrors.

"I can search for *Hart*," Benedict said. "I can still swim."

"No." Samuel seized his wrist. His expression was thick with bewilderment, disconnected, but, as he looked down at himself, memory must have slowly returned. He paled even further—as impossible as that seemed—and he grasped the spar more tightly. "Something is coming. Stay together, at all costs."

A horrific screech chased his words. A heartbeat later a spindly, bone-limbed monstrosity of Otherborn flesh plummeted out of the sky—straight down upon us.

FIFTY-EIGHT

The Fog of War

SAMUEL

Tane manifested, standing atop the waves with her arms thrown out in defense. Mary dropped beneath the water just as claws tore the waves where she had been into frothing furrows. The winged beast shrieked in frustration and swatted at our spar, sending it spinning before the creature swooped back into the sky.

Only Ben's iron grip kept me above the water as our tenuous raft bobbed and jarred. I felt immeasurably weak, beset by a pain so all-encompassing that I hardly felt the sting of salt in my wound and my eyes. My memory was fragmented, but my Sooth's Knowing was there to fill in the gaps.

Hae's shot. Struggling back on deck and collapsing in sight of Penn and Fisher, who must have seen me safely delivered to my cabin. Then... blood and binding threads in the Dark Water.

How I had come to be in the water was beyond me, but that hardly mattered now.

"Mary?" I rasped, attempting to twist and survey the waves around us, but I was thwarted by a shock of pain.

Mary resurfaced between Ben and I, and I nearly let go of the spar in relief.

"That *thing* is wearing a collar. Did you see it? Sam?" She panted. "Where did it go?"

"Hae," I concluded, dread assailing me. A thin hope that I had killed the man and simply forgotten was extinguished.

Ben pointed straight up to where the beast circled, preparing for another pass. "Can you stop it?"

Not with my voice, that I knew. The edges of the world had blurred again, but this time with fatigue instead of the Dark Water.

So I spoke to the beast in silence, a wordless stretch of will near Magni in its function. That will reverberated through the fabric of the worlds and directly into the mind of Hae's beast. I sent it one instruction, clear and simple.

Go back.

"Get under the water!" I rasped, reaching for Mary, who wrapped an arm around my shoulders and drew a hasty breath.

Light burst across the sky as the waves closed over our heads. It came with a bone-deep boom that sent ripples in all directions, stirring our hair and clothes and turning back the very waves of the sea.

I stared through a veil of salt-blurred water as the purple light vanished. Relief coursed through me, then faltered. The creature, temporarily pushed back over the divide between worlds, re-emerged in a struggling, raging clamor of bone wings and shuddering seaweed.

More lights joined it, rushing towards us in the human world, from sky and ships and the depths below. Creatures converging on the presence of a Summoner—or perhaps, at another Summoner's command.

Fucking Hae. I cursed him and myself, but regret was useless now.

Huden. Morgories. Dittama. More beasts I had read of but never seen converged, with streams of fae dragonflies swirling throughout. Some were already in the human world. More crackled through the barrier between realms, bursting through the Tide-thinned veil with ravenous speed.

"Mary," I panted, pulling her into me and bracing us both against the spar. Ben clung beside us now. "Can you clear the fog? I need to see."

She nodded and began to sing, one of her arms still around me in turn, anchoring us.

The fog began to move, clearing the area around us with alacrity. No other Stormsingers contradicted her, though I heard distant voices join in. Bells rang in rhythm and songs spread—both Mereish and Aeadine, even Capesh and Usti and Ismani and Sunjani—as captive Stormsingers across the fleet joined in chorus.

Ships came into view: whole ships, battered ships, great drifts of wreckage and bobbing boats, overloaded with survivors. All was lit by lanterns and Otherborn beasts, and more than one burning ship.

I glimpsed *Hart* in the distance, then *Nomad*. The urge to swim towards them was strong, but there was no way my body could comply.

My fatigue shifted towards resignation as more beasts emerged from the Other, one by one. My pain yielded to the awesome horror of it, and, from the cries drifting across the water, I was not alone in that feeling. But still, the Stormsingers sang.

There was a moment of assessment, in which I could imagine every captain in the fleet staring, conferring, beginning to disseminate orders. I could imagine the other Sooths, staring as I did, with the burden of responsibility heavy on their shoulders.

Then the beasts began to attack. I heard the crack of a mast as Hae's winged monster latched onto it. The vessel rocked and sailors toppled, shrieking into the sea. A loose cannon went with them, striking the waves with a muffled gong, a crack of cooling metal and a plume of steam.

For one more heartbeat, I prepared. I relished the feeling of Mary, bracketed between my arms, the sound of her voice and the movement of her legs, brushing mine. I looked to Benedict, clutching my arm in urgent prompt, his eyes more open and honest than I had seen in twenty years. I cherished the pain, the sting of saltwater in my wounds.

Tilting my head back and pressing Mary into my chest, I filled my eyes with a hundred Otherborn beasts. I spoke again, in that second world. I commanded them to go, and shrieking, sucking cracks began to reverberate across the fleet.

Lesser beasts vanished back into the Other. Some returned, fighting me, while others continued to ravage the fleets without care for which ships they attacked. Ghistings manifested everywhere, including Tane, who still guarded us. Hart was there too in the distance, stamping the waves and swinging his massive antlers as morgories swirled around his drifting ship.

New voices joined me, springing up one after another. Men and women, young and old, Mereish and Capesh—all Summoners. Fainter voices called too, Sooths whose unaltered, natural abilities were amplified by the rise of the tides and the darkening of the moons.

Beasts began to depart, one by one. Soon only the strongest of them remained, interspersed with clouds of harmless dragonflies. The latter swirled up masts and raced over the glistening surface of the water while the former, including Hae's avian monstrosity, continued to ravage the fleets.

"Cap'n!" a voice shouted from a longboat. Mr. Penn, along with two other sailors. "Best we get back aboard, sir!"

Mary prodded me, opening my arms and hauling on one of my hands as she started for the boat. Ben joined in, holding the boat steady as she clambered aboard, then forcing me to go after her. Pain made my world skew briefly, what little wit I had focused on the beasts, but when I came back to myself Ben was in the boat with us, raking hair back from his face.

"Did you find Enisca?" I heard Mary ask Penn. "She should have come out of the Other with us, but—"

"We'll keep searching, Ms. Firth," Penn replied, casting a glance over the water. "Soon as you're safe aboard *Hart*."

Safety, however, proved an evasive thing that night. Otherborn beasts demanded my attention at every moment, and I was forced to situate myself on *Hart*'s foredeck while Mr. Keo continued his capable command and the fleets' Stormsingers, including Mary at my side, labored to dispel the fog. Willoughby and Poverly tended my wounds, and I felt marginally better with a numbing poultice on my chest and a heavy dose of rum in my belly.

Would, though, that I could give a thorough account of that final hour. Swarms of Otherborn creatures, banished once more from our world. Mereish and Aeadine vessels, turning on one another once again. The half-drowned town of Renown in the center of the battle as we drifted east, its docks and buildings submerged, its people fled to the fort and higher ground. A flaming brigantine, sailing past a northern bastion, where cannons steamed and tattered Aeadine colors spasmed in an ever-changing witch wind.

I recall Mary, standing at my side, her voice joined with a dozen other Aeadine Stormsingers across the fleet as cyclones erupted and the waves themselves turned on the Mereish. I do question, however, if she retained any awareness of me. She was lost in her magic, in the strength of her voice and the ghisten light that prickled from her skin.

Benedict stood with us. His presence was unfailing, his power dulling my pain and strengthening *Hart*'s crew. His expression was distant, as opaque as it had ever been.

Some small part of me, freed by the instinctiveness of my actions, feared that we had failed. That my brother remained as he had been.

Then lanternlight passed across his face, and I saw the brightness of tears in the corners of his eyes.

FIFTY-NINE

Her Majesty's Commission

SAMUEL

"Victory is not what we have achieved." Admiral Solace spoke to a table adorned by ornate silver coffee services, platters of victuals and more than one bottle of rum, which the company poured liberally into their coffee despite the early hour. The sun barely touched the swirled-glass windows of Fort Renown's admiral's chambers, and there was not a face in the room unmarred by wounds or sleeplessness.

It had been two days since the battle and the height of the Black Tide. My wounds ached and my body was still riddled with fatigue, not to mention the weight of the battle's aftermath—hundreds of bodies pulled from the water, survivors rescued from wrecks only to succumb to wounds, the haunted eyes of the residents of the Anchorage, and the reality that so, so many good men and women would simply never be found.

Enisca Alamay was among them.

There were some forty men and women present—nearly every high-ranking officer left in the Anchorage, aside from those overseeing the continued recovery efforts, those warding against the remainder of the Mereish Fleet in the west, and those too wounded to leave their beds.

Nearly everyone had noted my twin and I entering the room.

"Our losses were unconscionable. Obscene. And it means little that the Mereish took equal losses before their retreat—they have more to spare." Solace looked back to the company. "The most we can say is that we have not yet surrendered. If the Other had not spewed such quantities of beasts into our laps and distracted the Mereish, or our Stormsingers had not rallied… We would not be sitting here today."

Pride settled across my shoulders, though not at my own involvement. Mary had been a critical force among the Stormsingers, and it was her cyclones that had done the greatest damage to the enemy.

"And the wolves yet stalk the horizon," a grey-haired man added, his captain's hat cast boldly on the table.

Admiral Rosser surveyed his peers. "How many Mereish remain in our waters?"

"Eight, of those that broke through," a woman I did not know replied. She was stocky and looked too young for the captain's cuffs on her high-buttoned coat. Many other faces at the table did too, officers elevated in battle or in the wake of it as their superiors succumbed to injuries. "Two have already been captured. Just this morning I received word that another was stranded off Barrowman's Cay when the tide receded."

Mention of the Black Tide's waning made me glance towards the window, though little was visible of the Anchorage's sodden, debris-scattered islands. Beside me, Benedict stared at a bottle of rum, then picked up a pitcher of coffee instead and filled it, black, to the brim.

He took a long sip and met my gaze out of the corner of his eye, eyebrow cocked.

I held out my cup.

Admiral Rosser spoke up. "Mr. Poleye, Mr. Dusset, your vessels are fit for action?"

"Yes, sir," Mr. Poleye replied, nodding his dark-haired head.

Mr. Dusset, another young and unexpected promotion, murmured his affirmative.

"Reinforce *Indomitable* up north. No Mereish who broke into Aeadine waters will reach Tithe to claim safe harbor, do you understand?" Admiral Rosser said. "At all costs. We may not have won a resounding victory, but we are not defeated. The Anchorage is still ours. These waters are still ours. And we will show our strength."

Fists pounded on the table, and a few heartfelt mutters of "Hear, hear," rippled down the table.

"Yes, hear, hear," said a familiar voice. "However, there is another pressing matter that must be addressed."

Down the table, Captain Irving rose to his feet and surveyed Benedict and I with a hatred so direct I felt myself flag. His hair was grey as steel, fastened into a short braid. His narrow jaw was clean-shaven and his form trim, barely touched by age.

"Keep your tempers," Admiral Rosser said quietly to Ben and I. "He is unlikely to, and that will serve you well."

"While it is expected that uncommon allowances must be made in times of need," Captain Irving went on, "I see no reason why men of such ignoble character are present at this table. One is not even commissioned, the other awaiting trial for gross neglect of his former captaincy and the deaths of innumerable souls under his command."

"They are here because I invited them," Admiral Rosser replied, tossing down his napkin and leaning back in his chair, wrists clasped over his stomach. "Because, as you said, in times of great need uncommon allowances must be made. As you all know, Samuel Rosser proved himself invaluable during the battle. Benedict, though undoubtedly marked by his past, is still one of Her Majesty's officers and acquitted himself more than admirably. Together, these two men oversaw the taking or disabling of no less than five enemy ships."

Murmurs rippled down the table, though whether in surprise, disapproval or support, it was unclear.

I leveled my chin and waited.

"Mere actions—subject to myriad and no doubt venal motivations—cannot cleanse a sullied soul," Captain Irving countered. His voice was a fraction sharper now, his posture a little less composed. "Benedict Rosser is a man without honor. Samuel, whatever part he played in past events, was still complicit, whether in the orchestration of events or their concealment."

Several of the younger occupants of the table looked confused, and whispers began—explanations of and speculation upon the past Irving now referenced.

"Samuel had no part in what I did." Benedict's voice was as calm and cool as an autumn breeze.

"Your wife, Captain Irving, sent my brother dozens of solicitations," Ben continued. "He did not open them. *I* stole those letters. *I* stole his name and the affection your wife had for him—earned, I might add, through the common goodness and respect he extends to all. Yes, he did conceal the truth. Because my magecraft, my soul, was corrupted by the Black Tide Cult, and his silence ensured I was protected from the world. I had the opportunity to use my power to protect this nation, and I acquitted myself well, you must agree. Until the wreck, which my Sooth foresaw, and I took every action to prevent."

"For your own benefit," Irving snapped back.

Benedict shrugged. "Show me one person seated at this table who acts solely for the good of others. Even my brother cannot qualify, try as he might."

I nearly spoke up, but this was Benedict's moment. Benedict's reckoning.

Silence enshrouded the company. Solace was looking at Admiral Rosser with unspoken questions, and Captain Irving's face had begun to blotch with rage.

"For those still confused, I slept with Captain Irving's wife," Benedict informed the table. The silence fractured into murmurs and cries of indignation, which Solace shushed with a hand. Her eyes were curious now, but tight with warning.

Ben went on, "A young woman lonely and driven to seek comfort in me—in my brother—because of her husband's braggartly ways, his disregard for her and others, his gross and obvious favoritism, and his frequent, casual cruelty towards her inability to bear him a child. An inability, I might point out, that was rectified by a single night with me—"

"You bastard!" Captain Irving roared. "Silence yourself or I will have—"

Benedict continued, unruffled. "So perhaps, Captain, you might begin reconciliation with your wife by admitting your own faults in that matter. I understand that my daughter is healthy and whole, and I should think that you would consider her a gift."

Captain Irving's chair hit the floor with a clatter. Benedict and I both stood, facing our former mentor as the room looked on.

Irving stopped two paces away, his face scarlet with rage. "I have and will have nothing to do with your *spawn*. And you, the pair of you? I demand your blood."

"No." Admiral Solace also rose to her feet at the far end of the table. "Captain, your conduct is unbecoming. This incident, though unpleasant, is well in the past and, clearly, personal. If you cannot control yourself considering the threat our people face, I fear my confidence in you has been misplaced."

Captain Irving struggled to restrain himself. His feet still jerked compulsively forward, and I thought he might throw himself at Benedict and I. Instead, he stormed out of the room.

The door slammed with such ferocity, one of the youngest officers squeaked.

"Please, Rossers, sit," Solace said into the ensuing hush. "I intended to deal with you once the threat had passed, however… it seems this particular wound must be cauterized. Admiral Rosser, proceed."

Benedict and I slowly returned to our seats as our uncle presided.

"In light of recent revelations, Samuel Rosser, I am pleased to offer you a new commission in Her Majesty's Royal Navy," Admiral Rosser said. "And before accusations of favoritism arise, this was put forward by Admiral Solace and numerous others following the battle. Mr. Samuel Rosser, your ship and your crew are all welcome under Her Majesty's flag, if you so choose. Otherwise, another vessel will be appointed to you."

My ears began to ring. I stared at my uncle, then down the length of the table to Solace. Not every face between the Admiral of the South Fleet and I was friendly, but more than I anticipated.

Solace met my gaze. I saw no apology, but no hostility, either.

This woman had stolen Mary from me, and yet now she sat down the table with, to all appearances, no remorse. She spoke benevolently, calmly, with no regard for the violation she had orchestrated.

She offered me the boon I had desired for long, torturous years, and, by her expression, she expected my gratitude.

A new commission.

"Captain Benedict Rosser, your hearing will proceed as anticipated," Solace said. "But other concerns have been raised. Reports have been brought forward concerning other… questionable incidents during your career, all of which must be fairly investigated before your status can be decided."

I could well imagine what kind of incidents those might be.

"Your admission that your magecraft was corrupted by the Black Tide Cult will join these matters… though perhaps it also explains many of them," Admiral Solace added. Her gaze swept to me, knowledge there. "A corrupted Sooth or a Stormsinger is one matter, but a Magni, as we all well know, is another. None of us have forgotten Silvanus Lirr."

Benedict stiffened. I seized his hand under the table. He tried to pull away, but I squeezed.

"We have been healed," I stated, speaking before he could. "During the height of the Black Tide, the cult's actions were rectified through methods we were able to learn during our time in Mere."

"Why was this not shared with your report? Upon your return?" Admiral Rosser asked.

"It was unfounded and undertested," I replied. "Little more than speculation."

"How was it accomplished?" someone else asked. "Such healing is impossible."

"It is not impossible with Mereish magics," Benedict said. "Surely no one at this table can deny their advances now."

"Mereish magecraft and practices are topics for another day." Solace raised her voice to override all others. "What remains is this: Samuel Rosser, you are officially welcomed back into Her Majesty's Royal Navy. Please give us your decision by the end of the day. Benedict Rosser, until such a time as a determination can be struck, you will have no ship."

In my grasp, Benedict's hand began to shake. I recognized the point he was reaching, the threshold where he would be unable to stop himself from acting, from breaking, from tearing.

But he did not topple over the edge.

"I understand," he said, his voice devoid of emotion once more. He pried his hand from mine. "Admiral."

Other voices spoke up, but my ears filled with a ringing, ominous hiss. The stiff back of the chair dug into my flesh as I sat, pinned to it.

"I cannot accept." My voice was drowned by the chatter down the table, but it was loud enough for those nearest me to hear. My uncle's sharp look and Benedict's inscrutable stare followed me as I rose and, giving the table a shallow bow, repeated myself into a recaptured silence, "I cannot accept the commission, not from an Admiralty who violated my Stormsinger's freedom and will continue to do so to her kind. I will not continue to fight a war with questionable roots. I will labor for what is good and right in this world, but I cannot do it with you."

Every word was a revelation. And as they left my lips, so did a weight lift from my back.

"I remain Aeadine and an ally, no matter whose colors I sail under," I added, locking my eyes on Solace's. "But if anyone comes after my Stormsinger again, they will discover what it means to be my enemy."

I turned to my uncle. "I trust that *Hart*'s prize money will be forthcoming? My crew will have their due."

Admiral Rosser sat frozen, coffee abandoned between limp fingers. He subtly cleared his throat, but he could not disguise the tightness in his voice as he grated out, "You will have your lawful share. Though it may take some time."

"Have it put in trust, accounts for each of my crew at Gawell's in Jurry. I have already submitted my assessment and statement of shares." I refastened the top button of my coat and nodded to Benedict, then strode out of the room.

"What did you just do?" my brother hissed as we reconvened in the hallway. Our footsteps echoed on the stone, barely dampened by thick carpets and row upon row of captured flags and complex tapestries.

"I made a choice," I said. I grinned thinly. "They took Mary. I cannot serve them."

"What of my situation? You do not protest that."

I shook my head. "Ben, you are capable and intelligent, and dangerous. You have done terrible things—as have many of them."

"So you agree with them?" He paused a breath, visibly trying to rein in his anger. "They will never give me a ship again, Samuel. I am no Sooth, but a fool could see that. I am being put off."

We descended a staircase, at the bottom of which we waited while a stream of soldiers passed by. I considered my brother from the corner of my eye, weighing how honest I could be. In many ways, his moods felt more unpredictable since his healing, and I had yet to assess his new boundaries.

"Your corruption was healed, but your actions remain," I said as we crossed the corridor and left the keep, circumnavigating a courtyard and heading for the main gate—down to the town, the docks, and *Hart*. "You may regret what you did, now that you can. But feelings mean little to the world. It requires action. Restitution."

Benedict stopped and faced me just outside of the gate, staring with such injury that I nearly regretted my words, though I held to the truth of them.

The sea wind buffeted us and, far out on the western horizon, the sails of lingering Mereish watchers stood out against a pale lavender sky.

"You believe I am incapable of doing that," Benedict accused.

I shook my head. "No. But you need time to heal first."

Benedict snorted. "So what do you propose I do? Take the airs in Caffith Sound?"

"Stay with me." I started walking, but he grabbed my arm and pulled me back. I elaborated: "Not as crew, just as yourself. Take time to reflect. Learn to make better choices, now that you can."

Disgust flooded his eyes. "Oh, and you will teach me to do that, will you? Saint, you are still a self-righteous ass. What will *you* do? Bless the world with your pomposity?"

"I do not know," I admitted, looking down towards the harbor and the distant shape of *Hart*. "But we cannot stay here, not with Irving on a warpath and the Navy's eyes on Mary. Not to mention the Ess Noti's shadow at our backs—I doubt they will relent so easily, and the Black Tide Cult is everywhere, as we have well seen."

Benedict let me go, and, slowly, his emotion retreated behind a cool mask. He started walking, hands shoved deep into his pockets.

And though we walked the same road down to the harbor, I sensed
he had another direction in mind.

"Ben?" I called, starting after him.

He made no reply.

SIXTY

The Red Tempest

MARY

A knock came at the door. I sat up in my hammock, muscles aching in protest, and dropped my bare feet to the deck. My lantern was lit, but the candle inside burned low and the cabin was riddled with shadows.

"Who is it?" I called, pulling my blanket more tightly around my shoulders and making no move towards the door.

"Me, Mary," Samuel's voice replied, just loud enough to be heard. He sounded tired and overburdened, and my caution slipped into concern.

I briefly considered my state of undress, then let the blanket slip farther down from my shoulders and lifted the latch.

Samuel paused, his gaze dragging to my exposed collarbones and the curve of one shoulder. Then he rallied and looked back to my face. "Would… would you prefer a moment to dress?"

I considered myself, adjusting my arms to give my breasts a more satisfying plump. "No. What's wrong? You should sit."

"Mary…" He closed the door and took up station beside it, watching as I moved to the table and sat on the bench. "I came on a rather important matter."

I patted the bench beside me. "Then please sit, Captain. You're pale and hardly recovered."

He perched on the other end of the bench, his focus somewhere else. "I was offered a new commission today. Not just for myself, but for *Hart*. I turned it down."

All my coyness fled. I jerked the blanket up. "You what? Sam. Samuel. This is what you wanted."

For a stretch, he wouldn't meet my eyes. But when he finally did, the determination in his expression sent a curl of heat through my belly.

"They took you. They ignored our warnings. They *took you*." The repetition seemed to cut out of him, compulsive and jagged. "I cannot... Mary."

His voice broke, and my composure with it. I closed the space between us and wrapped my arms around him, careful of his wound but caring nothing for the awkwardness of the moment—one knee on the bench, one bare foot on the deck. His arms locked around me in return and we hovered there, his breath warm on my skin, I stroking his hair.

When some of his tension eased, I sat back on the bench, hands still lingering on his arm and thigh.

"So, what do we do?" I asked, trying to sound factual, even as my heart hammered in my chest. "Are we willing to go back to the Usti?"

"I must speak to Jessin Faucher, first. These allegations... I must put them to rest before I return to Hesten." Sam took one of my hands between his and anchored it there, on his thigh. "With Enisca Alamay missing, I am not bound to return any time soon."

Missing, not dead. I wasn't sure I shared his hope for the Usti spy, but that was a matter for another time.

I slowly nodded, searching my own conscience and gradually giving voice to my thoughts. "If the Usti are responsible for rekindling the war, my mother might never have had to leave the Wold. So many years of conflict could have been avoided. So many people would still be alive. We can't even know how many, or how long this has been going on."

"I agree." He let out a long breath and turned to face me more directly. "I feel as though... I know what I should want to do. I should want to investigate this thoroughly and reveal the truth to the world." He laughed. "Saint, that would have been easier as an officer."

I gave a wry smile and waited for him to go on. If anything, his choice made my affection for him all the stronger. It was an ache in my chest, a tightness in my throat, and a smoldering coal in my belly that refused to cool.

"You should want that, but you don't?" I eventually prompted.

He considered me. "What do *you* want?"

"I don't want anything to do with Faucher or uncovering truths. It would be... it would be right, the proper thing to do, I'm sure. But I'm tired. I'm tired of running and being afraid. Until we're out of this harbor, I feel that at any moment they'll come to take me away. Or some Black Tide zealot will murder us and sink *Hart*."

His grip tightened on my hand, and, for another long moment, he sat sequestered in his thoughts.

"Shall we visit your mother?" He asked the question so suddenly, it took me a moment to register his words. "I will still speak to Jessin Faucher, but, regardless of what I learn, we can go to Demery in the Mereish South Isles. We heal. We rest. Decide what to do, safe from the world."

"Safe from the world in a lawless kingdom of pirates? Well, Charles has still been threatening to return to Demery. What about Benedict?"

"I have asked him to come with us."

"To the Isles?"

"Not specifically. But I offered him a place with us. Are you comfortable with that?"

I huffed a laugh. "Well, I've grown accustomed to him. And I do want to see... what he becomes now. What of his commission?"

Even as I asked the question, I suspected the answer. It was written in the lines of Samuel's shoulders.

"The Navy will not give him his commission back, and any court he faces will condemn him."

"Then he stays with us," I decided. I spoke lightly, but the weight of what I needed to say sat heavy in my chest. "Now, can we discuss another important matter?"

"What would that be?"

"Us," I said. The word sounded far more casual than it felt, forced out between a teasing grin and an overpowering urge to back away. But I didn't. "We care for one another. Want one another. But despite your clear intent to keep me about, I have received no proposal, a grand sum of four kisses and one interrupted tryst."

Samuel pulled back slightly, and even in the low light I saw the flush creeping up his neck. "I…"

I crossed my arms over my chest and stared at him, awaiting an answer.

"Then marry me." He looked startled as the words left his mouth, as if he was taken aback at the simplicity of the request. "We have discussed it before."

"That's it?"

"Please."

"You must do better than that."

"Better than… Mary. Should I kneel? Is that what—" He faltered as my face split into a wide smile, and cursed. "Saint, Mary, I beg you. Answer me."

I began to unbutton his coat. He watched me, breathless, as I pried one button after another and pushed it gently from his shoulders.

"Yes," I said, and covered his mouth with mine.

∽

Some time later, we sought the cool of the deck. Samuel's hand trailed across my back as he spoke quietly to Mr. Keo, ordering the crew rallied and the ship prepared for departure. We did not risk taking the time to restock—the battered town had little enough to offer, anyway.

"Ready, sir," Mr. Penn murmured soon after as the crew was assembled on the gun deck.

Sam pulled his hat from his head and addressed the crew. Men and women crowded the deck or perched on the cannons, many sporting bandages and bruises or the startling lack of vanished limbs.

"We are departing Renown tonight. I realize this comes suddenly, and I do not wish to press any of you to a premature decision, but we are not safe here. The Navy violated our contract with the Usti. They stole our Stormsinger. And I will not hide the truth—the Ess Noti and the Black Tide Cult remain our enemies. *My* enemies. Anyone who does not wish to share that burden may leave the ship with no guilt, no shame, and my wholehearted gratitude for your service."

A murmur rippled down the deck, startlement and agreement from some, a few mutters of displeasure from others.

Samuel was unruffled. "However, those of you who wish to remain aboard *Hart* are more than welcome. I cannot yet say what our destination will be, but you will not go without work or pay. All of you, your prize moneys will be put in trust once they become available—please see Mr. Willoughby if you have any concerns about claiming them; he will instruct you. Those of you who have not yet been compensated for injuries, do so immediately."

Samuel fell silent for a few heartbeats, then spoke again. "Thank you all for staying by me during our time in Mere and this last, hardest of battles. It is more loyalty than any captain can rightly expect. Each one of you has proved yourself invaluable, and if you choose to go, know you will be missed. But I truly wish you all the very best."

The crew's response was subdued. There were nods and salutes, and even the grumblers quietened.

Samuel surveyed them for a moment longer, then tapped his hat to his chest and retreated up the companionway. I followed, joining him midships.

"I will head immediately to *The Red Tempest* and speak to Faucher. There are too many prisoners, and he was never brought ashore." His words slowed, and his brow furrowed. "Mary… Where is Benedict?"

We searched the ship, then I remained behind while Samuel and a small party searched the docks. I watched them from the deck, spying—or fancying that I spied—their forms move from tavern to tavern, business to business, searching for Samuel's elusive brother.

Weary and uncertain, I finally went to Samuel's cabin. Benedict was not there, not that I had expected him to be, but the solitude was welcome. I lingered near the gallery windows, watching as a captured Mereish vessel, bedecked with red sails, slipped from the harbor mouth.

I can't say how long it was until I noticed the letter on the floor, fallen beneath the table. It was unsealed, but securely folded, and marked with a simple "S."

I fetched it to the window and angled it towards the fading light. I should have waited for Samuel to open it, but I had a suspicion as to what I would find inside. And time might be very short.

I unfolded the heavy linen paper and scanned Benedict's quick, but surprisingly artful, hand.

Sam,

I have taken your advice to heart, though as you will undoubtedly question my methods,

I leave you this note. I have gone to seek calmer waters, and perhaps a little sun. I have met several others with a similar mind, and together we have claimed the prize that I fairly earned, yet the Admiralty would deny me.

I have taken a Sooth's talisman with me, so feel no compulsion to follow me. I will be, at last, hidden from your sight, and I believe that division is for the best. I will not be dissuaded from my choices, and I do not wish to sully the peace we have struck between us.

I am not ungrateful for what you have done. Rather, it is because of your actions that I assure you: I am no longer your burden to bear.

Ben

P.S. I have taken Mr. Grant with me, so do not trouble your soft heart over his disappearance.

I looked from the letter towards the tower of red sails just as guns began to boom and warning bells rang out. Other ships began to move to intercept, but they were too slow. Soon the Mereish prize was out of Renown Harbor and broke into open sea. Its sails billowed full as I threw open the gallery door and trained Samuel's spyglass upon the vessel. Before I caught the fine Mereish letters painted across her stern, I heard a Stormsinger's song. To my surprise it was deep, not feminine in the slightest. A male Stormsinger.

My last glimpse of the vessel was the name painted across her bow in scrolling, scarlet letters.

The Red Tempest.

BENEDICT

I propelled Grant from the mouth of the alleyway and began to stalk after him, hands deep in the pockets of my worn Capesh coat. Behind us, a dozen of my crew fell into step, quiet and hard-eyed. Even the Stormsinger, Alfwin, showed none of his stolid good humor today.

In any other city the crowds might have parted for a company such as ours—a clutch of armed men and women, strung about with weapons and clearly intent on violence. But in Port Sen, we barely earned a pause. A few side steps, wary or assessing gazes, but even the grandmothers sported knives, and the children underfoot knew how to use them.

"I did not come along to be a walking shield. In fact, I've no clue why I came along—ah, yes, *I was carried off against my will*," Grant muttered over his shoulder, though his countenance remained suspended between his usual charming smile and vigilance. High roofs leaned above us, wooden buildings of slap-dash, irregular construction united in their battle to claim a scrap of daylight.

"I did not have enough time to convince you," I replied, keeping my eyes on the crowd.

"You cannot abduct people and call it friendship." The blond man began to fume.

"Did I call it friendship?"

Grant ground his teeth, beginning to lose his composure. "Listen. She knows we are following her. If you would hire another Sooth, we might have some sense of what we're walking into."

"Hush."

Grant turned a corner, and we approached a door tucked into an haphazard courtyard. There was no one in sight, though sound drifted from the windows all around and the door was cracked open. A cat peered out, assessed us, then leapt off into the shadows.

"Go on," I prompted Grant.

He muttered something under his breath as he approached the door and rapped. A voice shouted from inside in a language I did not know, then Grant went in.

At the same time, a figure moved across the rooftops. I might have missed her for the chimneys and random flags and the glare of the summer sun, but I *felt* her in a way I had come to recognize since that night in the Other, when Samuel's and my ties to that world had healed.

Another mage. Another Magni.

Enisca Alamay vanished over the peak of a roof, but not before I caught sight of the satchel at her side. A satchel filled with incendiary documents, proof of the Usti's treachery. Paper and ink with the potential to upend the balance of power on the Winter Sea. To end a war.

Or start a new one.

"There," I said to my company, pointing one long finger up to the roof. "Now go catch her."

APPENDICES

A Calendar of the Winter Sea

Sweet Moons (June–August)
–First Turning
–Second Turning
–Third Turning

Bountiful Moons (September–November)
–First Turning
–Second Turning
–Third Turning

The Year's Turning (December)

Bitter/Wanting Moons (January–March)
–First Turning
–Second Turning
–Third Turning

Black Moons/Black Tides (April–May)
–First Turning
–Second Turning

SONGS REFERENCED

"Pibroch of Donald Dhu" by Sir Walter Scott

"The Bard's Incantation" by Sir Walter Scott

"The Dance of Death" by Sir Walter Scott

"The Ash Grove," a traditional Welsh folk song

"The Fox is in the Bushes," a traditional song

ABOUT THE AUTHOR

H.M. Long is a Canadian author who inhabits a ramshackle cabin in Ontario, Canada, with her husband and dog. However, she can often be spotted snooping about museums or wandering the Alps. She is the author of *Hall of Smoke, Temple of No God, Barrow of Winter,* and *Pillar of Ash*, along with *Dark Water Daughter* and *Black Tide Son*.

HALL OF SMOKE

BY H.M LONG

Hessa is an Eangi: a warrior priestess of the Goddess of War, with the power to turn an enemy's bones to dust with a scream. Banished for disobeying her goddess's command to murder a traveller, she prays for forgiveness alone on a mountainside.

While she is gone, raiders raze her village and obliterate the Eangi priesthood. Grieving and alone, Hessa—the last Eangi—must find the traveller and atone for her weakness and secure her place with her loved ones in the High Halls. As clans from the north and legionaries from the south tear through her homeland, slaughtering everyone in their path, Hessa strives to win back her goddess' favour.

Beset by zealot soldiers, deceitful gods, and newly-awakened demons at every turn, Hessa burns her path towards redemption and revenge. But her journey reveals a harrowing truth: the gods are dying and the High Halls of the afterlife are fading. Soon Hessa's trust in her goddess weakens with every unheeded prayer.

Thrust into a battle between the gods of the Old World and the New, Hessa realizes there is far more on the line than securing a life beyond her own death. Bigger, older powers slumber beneath the surface of her world. And they're about to wake up.

For more fantastic fiction, author events,
exclusive excerpts, competitions, limited editions and more

VISIT OUR WEBSITE
titanbooks.com

LIKE US ON FACEBOOK
facebook.com/titanbooks

FOLLOW US ON TWITTER AND INSTAGRAM
@TitanBooks

EMAIL US
readerfeedback@titanemail.com